"The Shadow" and "The Broken Napoleons"

TWO CLASSIC ADVENTURES OF

THE Shadow ™

by Walter B. Gibson
writing as Maxwell Grant

with New Historical Essays by
Anthony Tollin and Will Murray

Published by Sanctum Productions for
NOSTALGIA VENTURES, INC.
P.O. Box 231183; Encinitas, CA 92023-1183

This Nostalgia Ventures edition is an unabridged republication of the text and
illustrations of two stories from *The Shadow Magazine,* as originally published
by Street & Smith Publications, Inc., N.Y.: *The Shadow's Justice* from the April
15, 1933 issue, and *The Broken Napoleons* from the July 15, 1936 issue.
Typographical errors have been tacitly corrected in this edition.

International Standard Book Numbers:
ISBN 1-932806-58-X   13 DIGIT 978-1-932806-58-8

First printing: April 2007

Series editor: Anthony Tollin
P.O. Box 761474
San Antonio, TX 78245-1474
sanctumotr@earthlink.net

Consulting editor: Will Murray

Copy editor: Joseph Wrzos

Cover restoration: Michael Piper

The editor gratefully acknowledges the assistance of Robert W. Gibson, Ed
Hulse, Geoffrey Wynkoop, Neil Mechem and Joel Frieman.

Nostalgia Ventures, Inc.
P.O. Box 231183; Encinitas, CA 92023-1183

Visit The Shadow at www.nostalgiatown.com

Volume 6

CONTENTS

Two Complete Novels From The Shadow's Private Annals As told to Maxwell Grant

Thrilling Tales and Features

THE SHADOW'S JUSTICE by Walter B. Gibson (writing as "Maxwell Grant") 4

INTERLUDE by Will Murray 63

THE BROKEN NAPOLEONS by Walter B. Gibson (writing as "Maxwell Grant") 66

SPOTLIGHT ON THE SHADOW:
TOM LOVELL—STUDIES IN LIGHT AND DARKNESS
by Anthony Tollin and Tom Roberts 123

THE MAN WHO CAST THE SHADOW 127

**Cover art by George Rozen
Interior illustrations by Tom Lovell**

The Shadow's Justice

A thrilling exploit of The Shadow, from his private annals, as told to

Maxwell Grant

CHAPTER I
SHADOWS OF NIGHT

"TURN left, Holland."

"Yes, sir."

The uniformed chauffeur thrust a warning arm from the window of the sedan. He swung the big car across the slippery road. The glaring headlights showed a driveway between two lion-topped stone posts. Gravel crunched beneath the tires as the automobile rolled through the entrance of the Long Island estate.

The man in the rear seat was leaning forward, watching the driveway reveal itself through the drizzling mist. Rain-soaked shrubs and dripping trees bounded both sides of the roadway. The chauffeur drove carefully as he settled back behind the wheel, relieved now that he was free of the heavy traffic on the highway.

The headlights, swinging along the curving drive, invoked moving shadows of the night.

Broad streaks of blackness wavered and swung away. Heavy blotches faded as the car passed. They seemed like living things, these shadows. The passenger watched them as he stared over the chauffeur's shoulder.

A bright light gleamed like a beacon through the night. The car swerved and pulled up before a flight of steps that led to the doorway of a large mansion. The beckoning light was under the sheltering roof that extended from above that door. Compared to it, the glimmers from the windows of the house seemed faint and obscure.

The passenger stepped from the sedan and spoke to the chauffeur:

"You may call for me in one hour, Holland."

"Yes, Mr. Tracy," replied the uniformed man.

The sedan rolled away and left the passenger standing under the sheltering roof. While he waited for an answer to his ring at the door, Tracy turned toward the steps, and his face was clearly discernible in the night.

A MAN of medium height, his face firm and aristocratic, this individual made an impressive appearance as he waited before the closed door. His eyes, keen and perceptive, were staring out into the night, toward those spots where the sedan's headlights had so recently invoked strange, moving shadows.

All was blackness now. Tracy's eyes saw only mist; his ears heard nothing but the sounds of dripping water.

The door opened behind his shoulder. Turning, the man entered with the assurance of an expected guest.

Farland Tracy, attorney at law, now stood within the confines of a gloomy hall. The man who admitted him was standing a few feet away, bowing in courteous greeting.

"Ah, Headley," said the lawyer. "Mr. Boswick is expecting me?"

"He is upstairs, sir," responded the attendant, in a quiet monotone. "I shall inform him that you are here."

Tracy watched Headley walk across the hall and up the stairs. The man's tread was soft and catlike, quite in contrast to his heavy appearance. The lawyer rubbed his hands thoughtfully and turned his gaze toward the floor, until the sound of approaching footsteps caused him to glance up.

A young man had entered the hall from a side room. Slight of form, sallow of complexion, and drooping in appearance, he made an excellent picture of dissipated youth. He was attired in a tuxedo, and in his loose left hand he held a long holder which contained a lighted cigarette.

"Drew Westling!" exclaimed Farland Tracy. "How are you, boy? I haven't seen you for a month!"

"Perhaps it's as well you haven't," drawled Westling, with a sickly grin. "I haven't forgotten the last time. I hope you don't intend to mention it to the old gentleman."

"To your Uncle Houston?" quizzed Tracy. Then, in an amiable tone: "No, Drew. Lawyers usually keep their clients' affairs to themselves. I am here to discuss business affairs with your uncle. Your name will not be mentioned—that is, in reference to the matter of which you have just spoken."

"Thanks," responded Westling, in a relieved tone. "The old gentleman has been quizzy enough about my affairs without him learning anything that won't do any good. I've kept out of jams since that last one—"

"And you don't intend to get into any more," smiled Farland Tracy. "All right, Drew. I'm glad to hear it."

Drew Westling turned away and strolled back across the hall.

FARLAND TRACY noticed that Headley was returning down the stairs. The lawyer smiled. He fancied that Drew Westling would not want the attendant to hear the discussion that had just taken place.

THE SHADOW!

In London, in Berlin, in Madrid—in all corners of the world—crooks lower their voices when they discuss The Shadow. In Paris, skulking creatures of the underworld still mumble tales of The Shadow's prowess—of that eerie night when an unknown being in black had battled, single-handed, against a horde of apaches. In Moscow, there are men who talk about the time when The Shadow had fought himself free from the midst of a regiment of troops.

When crime becomes rampant, then does The Shadow strike!

A living being of the darkness, he comes and goes unseen. Always his objective is the stamping out of supercrime.

Dying gangsters expire with the name of The Shadow upon their blood-flecked lips. Hordes of mobsmen have felt The Shadow's wrath.

A man garbed in black, his face unseen beneath the turned-down brim of a slouch hat—that is the spectral form that all evil men fear; that is

THE SHADOW!

Houston Boswick, owner of this mansion, was, as Tracy had mentioned, Westling's uncle. The old man had been away for several months, and hence knew nothing of Westling's activities during his absence.

It was Farland Tracy who had twice gained Westling's release, without scandal, after raids on gambling houses where the young man had been. Such information, coming to Houston Boswick, would prove most embarrassing to Drew Westling. The young man depended entirely upon his uncle for support.

"Mr. Boswick will see you, sir," announced Headley. "He is in the upstairs study."

Farland Tracy walked up the steps. Drew Westling, slowly puffing through his long cigarette holder, stood in a corner of the hall. With shrewd gaze, he watched Headley depart toward the kitchen. Then, turning his eyes upward, he waited until Farland Tracy had passed the head of the stairs.

Hastily ejecting his cigarette into an ash stand, Drew Westling pocketed the holder and followed the direction that the lawyer had taken. He tiptoed rapidly up the steps, turned into a narrow hallway, and softly approached a door near a turn in the corridor. He stopped beside the closed portal, turned about, and crouched with his ear to the door.

Watching toward the steps, Westling knew that he would be instantly aware of Headley's approach, should the butler come upstairs. Listening intently, he could hear the greetings being exchanged between Farland Tracy and Houston Boswick.

Ready to glide along the hall at the slightest alarm, Drew Westling was in an ideal position to learn what might be said within the study.

STRANGE purposes were at work within this gloomy old mansion. Standing secluded from the highway, it was invisible to the passing world. But while one man listened within, there were others who were watching without.

Across from the lighted porch, amid the blackness of a clump of shrubbery, low voices were discussing the arrival of Farland Tracy. Those voices came from a spot where the lawyer had looked, but had seen nothing in the misty night.

"Just lay low, Scully," came a smooth command. "We've got an hour to wait, at least."

"An' maybe nothin' to wait for" was the growled reply.

"Probably nothing," rejoined the smooth voice. "But we're not going in while the old man has a visitor. We're not going in blindly, either. That sort of stuff is through. We'll wait until we have a reason."

"All right, Stacks. You're the boss. But it's too blamed wet out here—"

"Come along," interrupted "Stacks" impatiently. "We'll slide under the cover of the side porch."

Two figures emerged from the bushes. They were no more than huddled shapes, but they cast long shadows as they moved toward the shelter of the side portico. Both Stacks and "Scully" were cautious in this maneuver, keeping just on the fringe of light that came from above the front door.

Confident that they were not being watched as they crept through the blurry drizzle, the men did not bother to look behind them. Hence they failed to notice a peculiar phenomenon which accompanied them.

From a spot not ten feet away from the bush where they had hidden came a third shadow, longer and more pronounced than their own. A sinister shape of unreality, this strange silhouette accompanied the men. A black vagueness in the mist—so obscure as to be almost unseen—was the only living token of this weird streak of blackness.

Yet, had Stacks or his companion stared back toward the bushes, they would have seen a more potent sign of a being in the darkness. Two burning eyes, their brightness reflecting the glimmer of the light above the door, were following the sneaking men. Phantom eyes that seemed to float through the mist, they watched the progress of these stealthy spies.

"We'll be all right here?" came Scully's question, as the porch was reached.

"Sure" was the whisper that came from Stacks. "Old Boswick will be up in his study—the little room that opens on the backyard—"

As he broke off his statement, Stacks chanced to glance back toward the driveway. He caught a momentary glimpse of a gliding shape along the ground; then attributed it to his imagination.

THE owner of that shadow was invisible. The tall form of a living being was skirting the edge of the porch even as Stacks spoke. Sharp ears had heard the reference to the little upstairs room. The phantom shape moved onward, unseen in the darkness.

A dim light glimmered from a small window on the second floor, at the back of the house. Beneath that window, a tall form emerged from the dampening darkness. Gloved hands pressed against the rough stone wall of the building.

A figure moved upward. The folds of a rain-soaked cloak flapped gently against the stones. A creature of the night was making its way to the window. Shortly afterward, a blackened hand appeared against the dim light, and noiselessly pushed the window sash upward.

The shadowy shape of a slouch hat was

momentarily revealed by the vague illumination. A few seconds later, the head beneath the hat had moved to the side, and was no longer visible. The weird phantom of the night clung batlike to the side of the house.

While Drew Westling, listening by the door of the study, overheard the conversation within the room, this eerie visitant of darkness was also learning what passed between Houston Boswick and Farland Tracy.

Silent, sinister, and unseen, The Shadow, man of darkness, had come to this secluded spot. The Shadow, mysterious personage who thwarted crime, was interested in the same discussion that had intrigued Drew Westling.

What was the purpose of The Shadow's visit? Did danger lurk about this place? Did the presence of huddled watchers in the shrubbery mean that crime was brewing?

Shadows of the night had moved amidst the drizzling mist. One was a living shadow. Where plans and cross-purposes unfolded; where men of evil design maintained a secret vigil; there did The Shadow venture!

CHAPTER II
TALK OF WEALTH

WITHIN a small, but finely furnished study, Houston Boswick and Farland Tracy faced each other across a mahogany desk, totally unaware that listeners were stationed at both door and window.

The two men formed an interesting contrast in the glow of the desk lamp. Farland Tracy, still in his forties, showed virility in every action. Firm-faced, square-jawed, and stalwart, he had a dynamic air combined with self-assurance. With it, his eyes expressed understanding and sympathetic feeling.

Houston Boswick, in opposition, was aged and weary. He was a man past sixty, and his thin face marked him as one who had lost all former initiative.

His eyes, alone, revealed his intellect. At times they were colorless; but at intervals they sparkled with quick purpose. Occasionally, they showed a distinct trace of innate shrewdness.

Those eyes were Tracy's key. The lawyer watched them steadily and calmly, knowing that they alone could serve as an index to Houston Boswick's true emotions.

"Tracy"—Boswick's voice was pitifully thin— "I am an old man who has nothing left to live for."

"Hardly old," rejoined Tracy, in a quiet tone. "You have not yet reached the dividing line of threescore and ten."

"I am nearing it," asserted Boswick, with a slight shrug of his narrow shoulders, "and my life

has been one of ceaseless labor. The accumulation of wealth is no sinecure, Tracy. I have made my share—more than my share, to be exact. I began almost in childhood. That is why I am nearing the end of life."

"You have retired from business," Tracy reminded him. "That should give you the opportunity to recuperate."

"I retired," interrupted Boswick, "purely because I could no longer continue. When an old horse can no longer stand in harness, his days are numbered."

Farland Tracy had no reply. Houston Boswick could see the sympathy in his expression. The old man smiled wanly.

"Do not attempt to delude me, Tracy," declared Boswick. "This last trip to Florida was for my health. Its purpose failed. The writing is on the wall. My physicians have told me that I may not have long to live. I am ready to die."

"Why?" questioned Tracy incredulously.

"Because," explained Boswick, "life holds nothing in store for me. What is wealth when one can no longer work? That has been my creed, Tracy. I shall always adhere to it.

"All my business associates were older than myself. One by one they have dropped from sight. Death has accounted for most of them. Senility has seized the rest. For the past year, I have lived with only one hope."

"Your son's return."

"Yes. Now, Tracy, that hope is assured."

"You have heard from Carter?"

Houston Boswick nodded.

REAL elation appeared upon Farland Tracy's countenance. The lawyer had often heard Houston Boswick speak of his absent son, Carter.

Years before, the younger Boswick had gone out to seek his own fortune. He had traveled in many parts of the world. Indirect reports had reached Houston Boswick that Carter was doing well. But not until now had the old man received direct news from Carter Boswick himself.

"Let me become reminiscent," remarked Houston Boswick. "Tragedy entered my life some twenty-odd years ago. Directly following the death of my wife, my sister Stella—my only living relation—perished in a train wreck with her husband, Hugh Westling.

"I raised their boy with mine. My son, Carter, and my nephew, Drew Westling, were like brothers. The same age—but Carter was the stronger, and Drew the weaker. Realizing it, I favored Drew."

"That was considerate," observed Tracy.

"Too considerate," corrected Houston Boswick. "Carter became obsessed with independence.

CARTER BOSWICK, adventurous son of Houston Boswick, returning after years of absence to claim the heritage left him by his father—a heritage that resolves itself into a dangerous adventure.

Drew became a weakling, with no initiative. The result was that Carter went away, and Drew remained.

"Only a week ago, I received a letter from Montevideo. It was from Carter. A friend of mine had met him there, and had given him my Florida address. In that letter, Carter announced that he was coming home."

"How soon?"

"He has already sailed. He is aboard the steamship *Southern Star*. He is coming by way of Havana, and will be here within two weeks."

"Wonderful news!" exclaimed Tracy. "He will be glad to see you—and I know that he will receive a glorious welcome."

"Hardly," responded Boswick, in a wistful tone. "I shall not be here to greet him."

"You will be—"

"Dead. Yes, Tracy, I shall be dead."

The lawyer slapped his hand upon the table. He could not believe his ears. This statement seemed incredible—the absurd fancy of a failing mind.

"Dead," repeated Houston Boswick quietly. "I feel the end of life approaching. It will be for the best, Tracy. I should not like Carter to see me as I am now. He should always remember me as I was when he went away—close to ten years ago."

The lawyer settled back in resignation. He saw that it was no use to dispute the matter with the old man.

"That is why I have summoned you, Tracy," resumed Houston Boswick. "You have been my lawyer since my old friend, Glade Rupert, passed away. Our friendship has been a matter of but a few years, but I feel that you have been most competent and kindly. Therefore, I am relying upon you now."

Farland Tracy bowed quietly.

"First of all," resumed Boswick, "my son Carter must not know of my death until after his arrival in New York. You understand?"

Tracy nodded. The lawyer, to humor the old man, was accepting Houston Boswick's death as a forgone matter of the immediate future.

"Then," added Boswick, "you will arrange full discharge of my estate, according to the terms. The bulk to Carter, with the provision of a comfortable life income for Drew Westling."

The old man paused speculatively. Then, with a sad air, he continued on a new theme.

"My nephew Drew," he started, "is a waster. I have provided for him because he is my sister's son. I have lost all confidence in Drew. I have not told him that I have heard from Carter. Drew knows that my health is failing. He will expect the full estate for himself. Indeed, it would be his, but for Carter.

"That is the reason, Tracy, why I have always minimized the amount of my possessions. People will be surprised, after my death, to learn that my estate is scarcely more than a round million. Only the heir—whether it be Carter or Drew—will learn, sometime after my death, that ten times that sum is available!"

"You have made a great mistake," declared Tracy seriously. "This secret of yours—the strange hiding of a vast sum of money—might lead to serious consequences. Some schemer might seek to learn the place of its deposit."

"How can anyone learn?" questioned Boswick, with a shrewd smile. "I, alone, have knowledge of the hiding place. My old lawyer, Rupert, told me that he thought the scheme was safe."

"Even though he, like myself, was never informed of the spot where you had placed the money?"

"Rupert never knew," smiled Boswick. "But he knew me when I was younger—at the time when I first evolved the plan of hidden wealth. He had more confidence in me than you have, Tracy. You have known me only since I became old."

The lawyer nodded. He realized that Houston Boswick spoke the truth. Nevertheless, his expression still betrayed doubt, and old Boswick was aware of it.

"Secrets," remarked Tracy, "have a way of leaking out. Your constant effort to minimize the size of your estate could certainly excite suspicion."

"I believe it has," declared Boswick quietly.

"You do?" questioned Tracy, in momentary alarm. "What cause have you to think so?"

DREW WESTLING, cousin of Carter Boswick, and possible heir—if Carter does not arrive. But the younger Boswick reaches home, despite attempts to end his life, and begins the quest for wealth.

"This house," explained Houston Boswick, "was closed while I was away. Drew Westling was living at his club. Headley paid occasional visits here to see that all was well. Upon my return, today, I noticed that certain things had been disturbed. I questioned both Drew and Headley."

"What did they say?"

"Drew claimed to know nothing about it. Nor did Headley, until I pointed out certain traces which he had not noticed. He became alarmed then, Tracy. He believed, with me, that this house had been entered and searched from top to bottom."

"Hm-m-m," mused Tracy. "Was anything missing?"

"Nothing," responded Houston Boswick. "That shows that a definite purpose was at work. Someone was looking for something that could not be found."

"You are sure that the marauders were not successful?"

"Positive. They would never discover my secret, Tracy, although it lies within this house. Only my heir—whether he be Carter or Drew—can gain the clew to my hidden wealth."

FARLAND TRACY was thoughtful. Houston Boswick's discovery surprised the lawyer; now, he was trying to find a plausible explanation for this mysterious occurrence. The old man divined the attorney's thoughts.

"Do not worry, Tracy," he said dryly. "I do not care to know the identity of the instigator. It could be Drew Westling; it could be Headley; it could be someone entirely unknown to me. As you say, I have been almost over-emphatic in my efforts to make it appear that my supply of worldly possessions has shrunk to exceedingly small proportions.

"But what do I care now? Carter is returning. He will receive my visible wealth. Let him find the unknown treasure, if he has the initiative. Should anything happen to prevent Carter's return, the task will belong to Drew Westling."

Farland Tracy shook his head in stern disapproval. This strange method of handling vast resources seemed atrocious to the lawyer.

"Suppose," he presumed, "that Carter—or Drew, for that matter—lacks the initiative. Then what will become of the wealth?"

"It will remain where it is," smiled Houston Boswick weakly. "Why not? I shall have no use for it. My heir will not deserve it. But do not fear that consequence, Tracy. Simply proceed with the simple duties governing the affairs of my estate. The rest will take care of itself."

The old man's gaze became prophetic. Farland Tracy was amazed at the change which filled those sad gray eyes. He listened while Houston Boswick spoke in a faraway voice.

"Carter will return," presaged the old man. "I am sure of it now. He will find the wealth that is rightfully his. Drew Westling will subsist upon the income that I have provided for him.

"I know this, Tracy. I know it as positively as I know that I shall be dead when Carter reaches New York. I have made my plans. They will succeed, no matter what may oppose them."

The old man was leaning weakly on his desk. With one hand, he made a feeble motion to indicate that the interview was ended. Farland Tracy arose and grasped the hand. Concern showed in the lawyer's face.

NEITHER Tracy nor Boswick heard the slight motion that occurred outside the study door. Drew Westling, hearing footsteps on the stairs, had moved quickly along the hall.

Now came a rap at the door, followed by the even voice of Headley, Boswick's serving man. The old man pointed to the door; Farland Tracy gave the order to enter. In came Headley.

"Mr. Tracy's car is here, sir," announced the servant.

"Good night," said Houston Boswick. "Remember, Tracy. Remember. I rely upon you."

"I shall remember," replied the lawyer.

Farland Tracy's last view of Houston Boswick showed the old man collapsed upon the desk, with Headley bending over him in apprehension. Going downstairs alone, the lawyer began to believe the old man's statement that his death was near.

There was no sign of Drew Westling on the gloomy first floor. Farland Tracy donned coat and hat, and left the house. He found Holland standing by the door of the sedan. Tracy hurried into the car to escape the drizzle. He ordered the chauffeur to drive him home.

Lurking figures came from the side portico after the automobile had gone. They reached the shrubbery and lingered there for several minutes. Then came a low voice in the darkness:

"All right, Scully. It's all off for tonight. Slide along. I'll take care of myself."

"O.K., Stacks. I thought this waiting would be a lot of hooey."

The figure of Scully moved along the shrub-fringed drive, and was swallowed by the darkened mist. Stacks still remained, as though expecting some signal from the house. Finally, he followed in his companion's course.

A dim shape emerged from the shelter of the side portico. It was the same vague figure that had clung to the wall outside of Houston Boswick's study window. Weird and phantom-like, it took up the trail of "Stacks."

The Shadow was following the chief of the two watchers. Into the darkness he had gone, trailing a man whose purpose here had been one of evil. Silently, mysteriously, a being of darkness was hounding a minion of crime.

The light went out above the front porch of Houston Boswick's home. The old mansion loomed dull and forlorn amid the swirling drizzle. Its inmates no longer concerned The Shadow this night. Hidden watchers had remained unsummoned. Their work still belonged to the future. Representatives of a plotter who had sent them here, they had retired.

Out of the night had The Shadow come; into the night had he returned.

An unwitting spy was leading this master of darkness to an evil lair where a man higher up awaited!

CHAPTER III
THE BIG SHOT

"STACKS LODI is outside, chief."

"Bring him in, Twister."

The man who uttered the order was seated in a deep-cushioned chair, in the corner of a sumptuous apartment. His words were spoken in a harsh monotone that befitted his importance.

For the speaker was none other than "Hub" Rowley, big-time gambler and racketeer, a man whose disdain for the law had gained him fortune, and whose smooth and devious cunning had kept him aloof from the toils of the police.

Here, in his apartment on the twentieth floor of the Hotel Castillian, Hub Rowley dwelt in royal state. The portals of his abode were under the juris-diction of "Twister" Edmonds, Hub's bodyguard. The magnificent suite occupied half the floor.

Attired in garish dressing gown, cigarette in hand, and a half-emptied glass upon the table beside him, Hub Rowley appeared to be a gentleman of leisure.

His hardened face, with pudgy lips and thick black eyebrows, marked him otherwise. Yet Hub preferred to keep up the pretense. He considered himself an aristocrat, even though he bore the stamp of the underworld.

The door opened, and Twister, a wiry, leering fellow, ushered in the visitor. Stacks Lodi, wearing a rain-soaked overcoat and carrying a dripping hat, came into the presence of his chief.

Stacks was a suitable underling for such a master as Hub Rowley. Stocky, swarthy, and shrewd of eye, he was schemer rather than mobster, yet his deportment showed him to be a hardened product of the school of crime.

"Hello, Stacks," greeted Rowley, in a methodical tone.

"Hello, Hub" was the rejoinder. "Nothing doing tonight."

"So I supposed," remarked the big shot. "Call Twister. He'll get you a drink. I guess you can use it from the way you look."

Twister, stepping out through the door, heard the order and promptly reappeared. Stacks Lodi threw his hat and coat on a table, and took a chair near Hub Rowley. Both men watched Twister Edmonds while the man uncorked a bottle and poured out a supply of liquor for the visitor.

IT was one of those minor incidents that happened to attract the attention of all concerned. Hence it was not surprising that none of the three observed what was happening at the half-opened door while their interest was centered on the bottles.

There, from the gloom of the dim outer room, came a tall, gliding shape that stopped when only partially in view. Gleaming eyes detected that the men in the room were looking elsewhere. Those same eyes spied a pair of curtains that led to another part of the apartment.

There was not an instant's delay. A tall form clad in black moved boldly into Hub Rowley's reception room. The Shadow stood in full view; then, with swift, silent stride, the black-garbed visitant glided toward the curtains beyond which lay darkness.

It was a cool, daring venture; and one that succeeded only by the fraction of a second. Hub Rowley, glancing up, noted that the door was ajar. He grunted his disapproval as his eyes swept about the room, stopping at the curtains just after The Shadow had vanished behind them.

"Close that door, Twister," ordered the big shot. "Stay outside. I'll let you know when I need you."

Twister handed the drink to Stacks, and obsequiously obeyed Hub Rowley's order. A few moments later, the big shot and his caller were alone in the room, neither one suspecting that a hidden listener was there to hear the conversation.

"Nothing to report, eh?" growled Hub.

"Only that some fellow called to see the old man," declared Stacks. "That was about nine o'clock. The guy went away at ten. You told me that some fellow was coming there, and to lay low until after he had gone. That was the time for the tip-off; but it didn't come."

"I doubted that it would," said Rowley, in a calm tone. "In fact, I felt rather sure that I would not need you tonight. Just the same, I wanted you there—in case—"

Stacks nodded.

"O.K. by me, Hub," he affirmed. "Scully acted grouchy because he was getting soaked in the drizzle. I told him it was all in the night's work. Sent him away when I figured all was off. Say, Hub"—Stacks paused to consider his words—"who was that bird that came to see the old man tonight? I wouldn't be asking you to tell me if he hadn't looked like someone I've seen before—"

"There's no harm in your knowing," interposed Hub Rowley. "That was Farland Tracy, the lawyer. He represents old Houston Boswick."

"Now I remember him!" exclaimed Stacks. "He was the guy who came to see you about young Westling, Boswick's nephew—the time the kid dropped ten grand in your uptown joint when—"

"Say Louie Gurtz's joint," corrected Hub in a cold tone.

"Well—Louie Gurtz's joint," repeated Stacks, with a sheepish grin. "I always call it that, Hub, except when I'm talking to you. Anyway, I remember Tracy now. He came to see you about getting back Westling's I O U, didn't he?"

"Yes," admitted Hub Rowley, "but I still have it. Just holding it—that's all. Westling knew he was in a jam, so he went to his uncle's lawyer. When Tracy came to me, he asked me to go easy on the boy. I figured that if I didn't, the old man would throw the nephew out, so I talked it over with Westling himself.

"That's the way it looked to the kid. A throwout—no dough for me. So I'm holding Westling until I want him, that's all. I've worked the same way before."

"What did the lawyer think about it?"

"Well, he'd like to have that I O U, all right. I've got a few more of Westling's, besides. Just about twenty grand in the hole—that's where the kid stands."

"He'll never have the dough to pay it."

"That's what Tracy told me. But I talked with Westling. His uncle's estate is coming through one of these days. Twenty grand—with plenty of interest."

"I guess you're sitting pretty, Hub," said Stacks admiringly. "But listen—if the dough's sure, what's the good of going through the place while the old man is away?"

"Stacks," remarked Hub reprovingly, "sometimes it is not wise to know too much. That applies to you. Understand? However, just to ease your mind, I'll ask you to recall my policy concerning every I O U that I hold. What do I do when one isn't paid?"

"You collect it."

"Right. Do I stop with the face amount?"

"No. You take plenty over."

"How much over?"

"No limit. Whatever you can get."

"All right," concluded Hub. "Westling didn't pay. His uncle's lawyer told me that the old man wouldn't pay. The old man's got some dough that I know about. It's likely to be Westling's later on. If I can get it now, I will. If I can't get it now, I'll get it after Westling has it. The sooner the better—that's all."

THERE was silence. Stacks Lodi sensed the keenness of Hub Rowley's words. Stacks, with Scully and others, had invaded Houston Boswick's home not long ago. Their search for a treasure vault had brought no results.

But Stacks could see the probabilities. Somewhere, Hub Rowley must suspect, the old man had hidden wealth. Hub Rowley intended to get it.

Stacks shrugged his shoulders as he thought of Drew Westling. The young man was a weakling, and a spendthrift. What could he do to oppose Hub Rowley? In fact, it would be easy for Hub to force Drew Westling to do his bidding.

Stacks recalled measures that the big shot had adopted in the past. He had made his victims squeal; double-cross their friends; stoop to any foul measures to meet their gaming debts.

The telephone bell rang while Stacks Lodi was engaged in this soliloquy. With an easy sweep of his hand, Hub Rowley plucked the double-ended instrument from its hook and quietly spoke into the mouthpiece. Stacks listened intently.

"Hello... Yes..." Rowley's voice was unperturbed. "Yes, I thought so... Nothing developed tonight, eh?...The old man looks bad, you say... His son is coming back?...When?...Where is..."

Consternation suddenly came upon Hub Rowley's thick brow. The big shot did not like this news concerning Carter Boswick's return. Stacks

Lodi had assumed—logically and correctly—that the term "old man" referred to Houston Boswick.

"All right..." Rowley was speaking again. "Don't worry...You just play the game...I'm holding those I O Us until the pudding's baked, that's all... Sure, I understand. If the son gets the tip-off the old man talked about, it leaves you in a hole... Well—there's ways of handling that... Left Montevideo, eh? What boat? Yes... Steamship *Southern Star*... Havana... Say, just keep mum. Leave it to me..."

Hub Rowley finished his conversation and laid the phone in the cradle. He studied Stacks Lodi thoughtfully; then asked a pointed question.

"How would you like to play the boats again, Stacks?"

"I wouldn't care for it," said Stacks suavely.

"That's where you got your name, wasn't it?" purred Hub. "Stacks Lodi—the smoothest card sharper in the business. You can stack a full house, deal bottoms and seconds—"

"But on the boats no more, Hub."

The big shot smiled.

"They made it pretty hot for you, didn't they, Stacks?" he questioned. "Got to know you too well. Faro dealing in a gambling joint became a healthier job."

"They knew me on every first-class ship between here and Europe. They've got nothing on me, you understand; but the name "Stacks" has stuck. They called me that because of the way I handled the pasteboards, and it's suicide for me to try that racket any longer—"

"How about the South American boats?" interposed Hub.

"No gravy on them" was Stacks Lodi's verdict.

"But do they know you?" questioned Hub.

"No," responded Stacks. "I'd be as safe as a person aboard one of those packets. But there'd be nobody to trim unless a Paraguayan ambassador or some such bird showed up to be plucked."

"I think a boat trip would do you good," nodded Hub Rowley, with a quiet smile. "Just a little tester—that's all. Suppose, Stacks, that you hop down to Havana by air. Spend a few days around the casino. Pick a few friends there and invite them to travel up to New York with you by steamship."

"On any boat?" Stacks was wondering at Hub's purpose.

"No," responded the big shot. "Not any boat, Stacks. A particular boat—the *Southern Star* of the Panorama Line."

Hub Rowley continued to smile as a sudden light appeared on Stacks Lodi's face. The suave henchman was connecting this suggestion with the big shot's telephone conversation.

THE smile faded, and Hub Rowley became suddenly grim and emphatic.

"Listen, Stacks," he said, in a firm tone, "I've got an important job for you. I'm counting on you to do it—and I'm giving you enough reason for it. Keep mum about what I'm telling you.

"Big rackets are my business. I don't go in for small stuff. Whatever I do, I do right. Savvy? That's enough to let you know that I'm not playing old Houston Boswick for lunch money. I'm after plenty, and I don't mind you knowing it.

"I had things the way I wanted them. The old man away at first—ready to kick in now that he's back—young Westling sewed up so he can't move. But I haven't been able to locate what I'm after. I wanted to grab the gravy right away, and let the howl follow, if there is one. I've seen too many good lays spoiled by a bad break.

"Right now, the bad break is coming. It just shows that my hunch was right. I've got dope that Carter Boswick—the old man's son—is coming back to America. He'd been gone so long, it looked like he might be dead. If he gets here, Westling will be out. No money—no pay—no chance for me to pick up the dough without a fight on my hands.

"Carter Boswick. That's his name. Coming north on the steamship *Southern Star*. It's due in New York on the twentieth, and it comes by way of Havana, with a layover. You're coming in on that boat"—Hub Rowley's voice became low and deliberate—"and Carter Boswick is not. Do you get me now?"

"Sure thing," nodded Stacks slowly. "But you know my limit, Hub. I'm all right at the card table."

"But not with the rod, eh?"

"I'm O.K. there, too," asserted Stacks, now hasty in his tone, "but I may not be one hundred percent—and, besides, on board a boat—"

Hub Rowley was leaning forward in his chair, eyes agleam.

"You heard what I told you, Stacks," he insisted. "Find yourselves some friends. Invite them aboard. Play your own part—the lone gambler. Even if you get watched, it will be all the better. It leaves you out of what may happen."

"You mean the others—"

"Certainly. But I want you there to make sure. You can handle Scully and other gorillas like him, can't you? Well—this is the same thing in a different way."

"Sure enough, Hub," agreed Stacks, in a relieved tone. "Say—this won't be hard at all. I'll need dough—"

"I'm giving you twenty grand—"

"And I'll have to hustle for Havana so—"

"By air, tomorrow morning. Pick your gorillas

down there. The town is full of them. They're getting ideas from Chicago, those people. Bumped off a big political friend of the president with machine guns."

"Leave it to me, Hub."

The big shot smiled, broadly this time. The smirk showed his glittering gold teeth. Hub pulled a thick wallet from his pocket and counted off a mass of bills which he handed to Stacks Lodi.

The former card shark knew that the interview was ended. He rose, donned his hat and coat; then departed toward the anteroom, followed by Hub Rowley's shrewd gaze.

MINUTES drifted by. The big shot finished his drink and arose from his chair. He walked across the room to a door opposite the hanging curtains. He went into a next room; then called loudly for Twister Edmonds.

The bodyguard appeared from the outside room and came to join his chief.

The way to the outer door was clear. The blackness below the hanging curtains seemed to move. As if by wizardry, it transformed itself into an upright shape—the tall figure of a weird being clad in black.

As silently as he had entered, The Shadow made his departure, crossing the reception room, and entering the outer chamber that gave him access to the outside door. Stacks Lodi had gone; again, The Shadow had followed.

The aftermath to this strange scene occurred an hour later at an agency where air travelers made their reservations. The man who was going off duty made a chance comment to the one who relieved him.

"Funny how they come in at the last minute sometimes," he observed. "Take that Havana plane, for instance. Here we figured she would run light on this trip. Now, within a half hour of each other, two men book transportation."

The new man looked at the list. He saw the names inscribed there. One was Antonio Lodi; the other was Lamont Cranston. Those names meant nothing to the agent. He shrugged his shoulders and went about his duty.

Yet those names actually held a peculiar significance. The first was the genuine name of a man of crime; the second, the assumed identity of one who warred against the denizens of crookdom, from small to large.

Stacks Lodi was Havana bound; tomorrow, his plane was sailing. Aboard the same ship— unknown and unrecognized by Hub Rowley's agent—would be the one personage whom all the underworld feared.

The Shadow, like Stacks Lodi, was traveling to Havana!

CHAPTER IV
IN HAVANA

STACKS LODI, versatile minion of Hub Rowley, was a man of chameleon qualities. His ability to change his physical appearance was remarkable, despite its limitations; but his great aptitude was the facility with which he fitted himself into any environment.

During the period that he had gained a profitable living through his gambling activities aboard transatlantic liners, Stacks had frequently resorted to methods of semidisguise which had served him well until all of his various artifices had become known.

After that, he had settled down to the routine existence of a faro dealer in gambling joints secretly controlled by Hub Rowley. The big shot had finally promoted Stacks to the role of lieutenant in charge of mobsmen. Stacks had served as such when he had been conducting activities at the home of Houston Boswick.

Now, as ambassador of hidden crime, Stacks had been dispatched on a new mission which had begun with the airplane flight from New York to Havana. At the time of his departure, Stacks had boasted a short, flat mustache across his upper lip. From the hour that he had left Hub's apartment, Stacks had paid particular attention to that adornment.

Perhaps the effect of tropical climate had helped the quick growth of hair upon the gambler's upper lip. Perhaps the judicious use of dark dye and wax were chiefly responsible; whatever the case might have been, Stacks Lodi, by the time he had been three days in Havana, was possessed of a conspicuous mustache with pointed ends.

Now, as he stood within the portals of the magnificent Gran Casino Nacional, Stacks had the appearance of a suave, sophisticated habitué of palatial gambling halls.

His keen, intuitive eye was watching the brilliant throng which crowded about the whirling roulette wheels. There, Stacks was observing people, not the game; although any who noticed him would have fancied that he was most interested in the way the croupiers deftly raked in the stacks of coins that lay upon the gaming tables.

Stacks Lodi had spent most of his time in the casino. He had come there because the place was the natural gathering point of all adventurous persons who visited Havana.

With the cool, practiced eye of the professional gambler, Stacks had been looking for men whose faces were no more than masks that hid the cunning brains of criminals. He had not only discovered three such individuals; he had made the acquaintance of the trio.

Those three were in the Gran Casino Nacional tonight. But they were not under Stacks Lodi's surveillance for the present. The shrewd, mustached observer had found a new interest.

He was watching a small group of Americans who were enjoying their roulette. These were passengers who had come ashore from the steamship *Southern Star,* which had docked in Havana that afternoon.

Bound from Montevideo to New York, the *Southern Star,* delayed by a heavy equatorial storm, was slated to remain in Havana for only twenty-four hours. The ship would sail tomorrow afternoon. Between now and then, Stacks Lodi planned nefarious action.

ONE man among the Americans from the *Southern Star* was the individual whom Stacks Lodi sought. This man, tall, vigorous, and youthful, possessed the qualities of a powerful athlete.

His face was well molded, and showed a carefree disposition, backed by self-control. His dark-blue eyes and light-brown hair rendered him conspicuous among his companions. Stacks had heard the young man's name spoken by two of those who were with him. He knew that this was Carter Boswick.

"Hey, Carter"—one of the crowd was addressing the young man now—"we're going to skid out of here. We're running down to Sloppy Joe's bar. Coming along?"

Carter Boswick smiled and shook his head as he placed a stack of money upon the roulette table.

"I'll be here a while," he remarked. "I'm staking three hundred and fifty dollars just to see how I make out. It's half gone now; if I get it back or lose it, I quit. I'll see you fellows on the boat."

Three minutes later, Carter Boswick was deserted by his friends.

Completely engaged by the play at the roulette table, the young man was due to remain there for some time at least. This was the very opportunity that Stacks had awaited.

Strolling through the room, the gambler stopped three times. On each occasion, he dropped a chance remark in the ear of a different man. Then, continuing his stroll, Stacks reached the outside garden, and followed the promenade that circled about the beautiful pond, with its central fountain of dancing bacchantes.

Here, at an appointed spot, Stacks found three men awaiting him. All were garbed in evening clothes—the same attire which Stacks Lodi wore.

Although they had no more than a speaking acquaintance with each other, these men possessed much in common. They were adventurers all, and Stacks Lodi had made no hazardous guess when he had judged them as men to whom crime was not foreign.

"Buenos noches," purred Stacks Lodi, speaking in smooth Spanish. "I have something to engage your attention, *senores.* It will bring money more swiftly than a good turn of the roulette wheel."

Sparkling eyes and crafty glances assured Stacks that his listeners were interested.

"Tomorrow," resumed the gambler, "the steamship *Southern Star* sails for New York. I shall be aboard that vessel. I am quite willing to engage first-class passage for three gentlemen such as yourselves. It will be a delightful trip—"

Stacks paused to light a cigarette. His cunning face showed above the flame of the match. The listening men detected the knowing smile that curled the lips below the black, pointed mustache.

"There will be another person aboard," continued Stacks, as though changing the subject. *"Señor* Carter Boswick is his name. An *Americano* booked through from Montevideo.

"I do not care to make his acquaintance, senores, but I have no objection to my friends doing so. Much comes from chance acquaintance. I do not object to seeing *Señor* Boswick go aboard the *Southern Star* tomorrow afternoon but I would feel a keen regret should I see him leaving the same boat at New York."

The innuendo was plain. The hearers knew it. They exchanged cunning glances. Then one spoke in a low tone.

"What is your offer, *Señor?"*

STACKS was thoughtful. His eyes suddenly wandered as he fancied that he saw a slight motion beside a hibiscus bush a dozen feet away. A second glance reassured him. He was positive that no one could be in the vicinity.

A long stretch of black shadow extended from the bush, and reached across the promenade to Stacks Lodi's feet. But the gambler thought nothing of that phenomenon. Other bushes in the luxuriant garden cast shadows also.

"Two thousand dollars to each of my friends," remarked Stacks quietly. "Two thousand dollars payable immediately after—"

The questioner nodded. Another man uttered a short ejaculation beneath his breath:

"Two thousand dollars! Four thousand pesos!"

This expression of the sum in terms of South American currency was gratifying to Stacks Lodi. He was sure that his offer would be accepted. The conjecture proved correct.

"I am ready, *señor,"* announced one of the trio.

The others followed the acceptance.

Stacks Lodi smiled. He knew now that these men were polished assassins—a fact that he had already discerned. Only the arrangements for passage remained. Stacks was about to explain this detail when one of his hirelings put forth a question.

"This man we are to meet," suggested the would-be assassin. *"Señor Carter Boswick—we shall see him aboard the Southern Star?"*

"You may see him now," responded Stacks.

"Where is he?" came the question.

"In the casino," answered Stacks. "At the roulette table."

"Alone?"

"Yes."

The man laughed in an even tone as he heard Stacks Lodi's reply. With a twisting smile upon his dark lips, he asked another question.

"Would it disappoint you, *señor,"* he quizzed, "to have this *Señor* Boswick stay always in Havana? Would you regret it if tonight—"

The man's eyes were flashing with a murderous intention. Stacks Lodi smiled. The others buzzed their approval. Stacks shrugged his shoulders.

"Would you be kind enough," continued the man who made the suggestion, "to point out to us this Senor Boswick? There are opportunities in this city of Havana. Perhaps we shall make use of one.

"Whether we succeed or fail, we shall board the *Southern Star.* Success will mean that New York would be preferable to Havana, despite the climate; failure would mean the necessity of a new opportunity aboard the steamship."

"Come," said Stacks.

He led his new hirelings along the promenade, past the hibiscus bush where the long stretch of blackness still manifested itself.

The brightly lighted door of the casino attracted the attention of the four walkers. None glanced back. They did not see the motion in the blackness beside the hibiscus. Nor did they see the strange, phantom-like shape that emerged from that patch of dark.

A being of the night was following the quartet along the paved promenade. The Shadow, strange shape of mystery, had overheard the negotiations. He, too, was interested in Stacks Lodi's plans.

At the door of the gambling room, Stacks Lodi, with a low tone and an almost imperceptible motion of his hand, signaled out Carter Boswick. The young American now sported a large stack of winnings. He was preparing to leave the gambling hall.

The three minions of Stacks Lodi took their separate courses. They spread out, each with no apparent purpose. Stacks Lodi, idling by the door, was watching them.

He knew that when Carter Boswick left, these three would follow. Stacks had given them final instructions: they were to call for their steamship tickets at the Hotel Seville.

Stacks had not introduced the men to each other; but he knew their individual names. None of them was Cuban; all were South Americans.

Stacks made a final note of them:

Cassalta—he was the one with the traces of pockmarks on his face. Bolano—that man had busy eyebrows and protruding jaw. Herrando—he had been the spokesman with the murderous grin.

Now, as Stacks Lodi calmly watched them, these men appeared to be persons of leisure, their veneer of gentlemanly deportment completely covering their actual evilness.

STACKS became suddenly conscious that another man was standing beside him. He turned to see a tall individual with calm, cold-chiseled face and hawklike nose.

He recognized Lamont Cranston—an American who had come down to Havana on the same plane with him.

Stacks smiled. He was sure that Cranston would not recognize Stacks Lodi.

The tall American was just beginning a chance conversation with a Cuban friend at the moment Stacks happened to turn. The gambler overheard them.

"You say that a boat sails for New York tomorrow?" Cranston was asking. "That surprises me. I did not see it on the sailing schedules."

"It is a ship from Montevideo, *señor,"* the Cuban replied. "The *Southern Star,* of the Panorama Line. If you wish to return to New York by sea, you can probably engage passage aboard that boat."

"Excellent," decided Cranston. "I believe I shall do that. Thank you, *señor,* for the suggestion."

Stacks Lodi gave no further consideration to the talk that he had overheard. He threw a final glance toward Lamont Cranston and turned away.

Had Stacks allowed his gaze to drop to the floor, he might have gained a momentary surprise. For the length of Lamont Cranston's shadow was very strangely like that splotch of darkness that had extended from the hibiscus bush in the garden.

That silhouette, alone, was the feature that marked Lamont Cranston as the hidden observer who had overheard the conversation between Stacks Lodi and the three South Americans. This man who called himself Lamont Cranston was actually The Shadow.

Keenly watching the roulette table where Carter Boswick had been playing, Stacks Lodi did not realize that he, himself, was under observation. All during his sojourns in the Gran Casino Nacional he had been under the surveillance of the eyes that were now watching him—the eyes of The Shadow!

Carter Boswick was leaving. His stakes had been changed to United States paper currency, and he was pleased because he had regained his original sum. He passed within two yards of Stacks Lodi, but did not even glance in the direction of the shrewd-faced gambler.

Stacks watched the trio of intended assassins follow. Cassalta, Bolano, and Herrando—these were the stalwarts who would work for him tonight. They disappeared in the same direction that Carter Boswick had taken. A triumphant smile curled upon the gambler's lips.

Stacks Lodi did not notice that Lamont Cranston, too, had left the gambling hall. In fact, he had forgotten all about the man. Hence Stacks had no reason to suspect that trouble was brewing for his minions.

He did not know that the evil trio who were trailing Carter Boswick were themselves being followed. Outside the Gran Casino Nacional, a strange, uncanny figure had materialized the moment that the three had passed.

In a spot of seclusion, the tall figure of Lamont Cranston had stepped unobserved. Now, when it emerged, it was the man no longer. The Shadow, master of darkness, was the being who had taken up the trail of Stacks Lodi's hired killers!

CHAPTER V
THE SHADOW'S MIGHT

HAD Carter Boswick been of a less adventurous temperament, he might have completely avoided danger on that evening in Havana.

His first impulse, upon leaving the Gran Casino Nacional was to return to the *Southern Star.* But as he hailed a waiting taxi, it suddenly occurred to him that this evening was yet young. He had no desire to join the other Americans in such a tourists' resort as Sloppy Joe's; but he did have a yearning to see the night life of old Havana.

Speaking in fluent Spanish, Carter quizzed the cab driver before entering the vehicle. The Cuban grinned and nodded.

The *Americano* would like to visit a place where tourists seldom went? Very well; he would be taken there. He would visit the old Barcelona Club—at one time the most exclusive private gambling place in Havana—now a spot where revolutionary plots were hatched.

Scarcely had the taxi drawn away before a man stepped into view and beckoned to two others who were a short distance away. Herrando was summoning Cassalta and Bolano.

In a few quick words, he explained what he had heard—the destination chosen by Carter Boswick. Gleaming smiles greeted the revelation. Calling another cab, the three South Americans entered

and gave instructions to be driven to the Barcelona Club, in the old city. No one was in sight when Herrando gave the order, but the words were loud enough to be heard in the darkness that lurked beyond the pavement where the cab had stopped.

Meanwhile, Carter Boswick, in the cab ahead, was finding his ride most intriguing. After rolling along broad boulevards, the taxi entered an area of crooked, winding streets, among picturesque buildings that had stood here for years—some, perhaps, for centuries.

Accustomed to life in South America, familiar with the cities of Buenos Aires and Montevideo, Carter Boswick, with his knowledge of Spanish, had no qualms whatever about visiting a district so little frequented by Americans. When his cab pulled up before an archway that was blocked by an iron-grilled gate, Carter Boswick felt the intriguing appeal of the unusual.

The cab driver spoke to a man who was standing by the gate. He was explaining that this *Americano* wished to enter. Carter followed with a few words of his own. The gate opened, and he walked through the archway into a patio with a little fountain in the center.

Passing beyond the fountain, Carter ascended a flight of steps and came to a large room that once must have been the chief gaming hall of the club. It was surrounded with small, uncurtained booths; and the center portion of the floor had scattered tables. The place had been changed into a restaurant.

Carter took his seat at one of these tables and surveyed the motley persons assembled there. Grimy, sordid faces showed members of Havana's underworld; but mingled with them were persons of a higher social plane.

Carter noted that the more respectable people seemed to segregate themselves in the little booths at the sides. He remembered what the cab driver had said about revolutionary activities.

EVIDENTLY this place was tolerated because it enabled the police to keep tabs on the meetings of persons who were under ban. Carter knew that Cuba was a republic which seethed with an undercurrent of repressed animosity toward the existing administration. He imagined that some of the persons here were government spies.

His own experience of intrigues and counterplots which he had found existing in Buenos Aires and Montevideo enabled him to identify this former club immediately.

Here, Carter felt, one sat just above the crater of a quieted volcano. One untoward incident—a cry of revolution—an accusation of a police spy—an unexpected brawl—such would suffice to create tumult.

Carter noted a huge stairway at the side of the room. It started at one corner, ran upward diagonally along the wall, and terminated in a balcony that made three sides of a square. He could see little doorways up there; and he sensed that they marked the entrances of private dining rooms or gambling apartments.

While Carter was watching, a Spaniard of dignified appearance entered and went up the stairs. A few moments later, a handful of ruffians came in and scattered themselves about at different tables.

Carter noticed that the gentleman entered one of the upstairs rooms. He caught a few words in Spanish uttered at another table. They gave him an inkling. This man was a former senator, no longer in political favor. His purpose here might be a secret meeting; these ruffians were, in all likelihood, a bodyguard.

Interested in the buzz that passed through the room, Carter did not observe the three men who entered and sidled over toward his table. They were the trio sent by Stacks Lodi.

With mutual design, they reached a table only a short distance from where Carter was sitting, but behind his back.

The room was quieting when one of these men arose. It was Herrando, the one who had appointed himself a leader. Leering as he stared at Carter's back, the man caught the attention of various persons in the place.

Carter, unaware of Herrando's presence, saw the scattered ruffians stare suspiciously in his direction. The next moment, he was seized roughly by the shoulder, and loud words of accusation were hissed in his ear.

"*Americano!* Bah!" Herrando's words came in a venomous voice. "You are a traitor! You have come here to spy—"

Like a flash, Carter was on his feet. He swung a swift punch in Herrando's direction, and sent the man sprawling. Cassalta and Bolano were leaping forward.

In the gloomy light of the big hall, Carter could not distinguish their faces—he knew only that they were enemies. Plucking up the light table beside him, he flung it against the pair, and saw the two men sprawl backward. Then, with a mad rush, he ran toward the door, seeking escape.

Escape was not so easy. Carter's quick response had done exactly what Herrando had hoped. It had excited wild alarm, and had apparently proven the truth of the accusation.

The scattered ruffians were on their feet, ready to block the flight of this false *Americano*. A spark of flame had been set to the powder barrel of lurking suspicion.

A machete gleamed as one of Havana's mobsmen leaped forward to end Carter Boswick's dash. The American sidestepped the ruffian's swing, and planted a swift blow upon the Cuban's cheek. The machete flew across the floor; the man sprawled and started to draw a revolver from his belt.

Seeing his intention, Carter fell upon him. The action was a wise one. Just as Carter yanked the gun from the downed man's grasp, other revolvers flashed. Loud cries sounded, and startled men came from the booths to join the attack in which Carter Boswick was the focal point.

Rising, Carter pointed the revolver and fired toward a ruffian who was aiming at him. The shot went wide. With a snarl, the man moved his finger against the trigger.

But the report which followed did not come from the Cuban's gun. Instead, it issued from the door that led to the patio. It was the terrific roar of an automatic.

The Cuban sprawled upon the floor, and all the others turned quickly to greet the source of the unexpected attack.

Just within the doorway stood a tall figure in black. A sinister form, garbed in flowing black cloak and broad-brimmed slouch hat, The Shadow had arrived in time to save the doomed American!

Each hand, covered with a thin black glove, held a powerful automatic. Sharp, burning eyes glowed beneath the brim of the slouch hat. The Shadow's perfect aim had crippled Carter Boswick's antagonist.

Realizing that aid had come, Carter dropped almost to the floor. Crouching, he headed for the nearest corner.

The Shadow had diverted the attack. Fiendish cries arose as the ruffians and others of their ilk turned toward the invader. Revolvers flashed and scattered shots broke forth.

The reports of The Shadow's automatics sounded above the din. Stabs of flame burst from the huge .45s. Hostile weapons seemed useless. Bullets struck the wall beside The Shadow, but his tall form seemed to weave back and forth with uncanny precision.

The hasty aimers had no luck; those who were more deliberate never gained the chance they sought. For The Shadow's unerring guns delivered their shots at the ruffians who were coolly seeking to slay him.

Gun arms dropped as The Shadow's bullets found them. Evil-faced killers staggered and dropped to the floor before the thunder of The Shadow's wrath.

The briefness of the fight was surprising. The Shadow was aiming to wound, not to kill; and that very policy brought quick results. The cries of the crippled men were appalling to their comrades.

There were doors in the wall away from the spot where The Shadow stood. Realizing the power that lurked in The Shadow's weapons, some of the fighters began a mad dash for safety.

The flight stimulated a general effort toward escape. Many of the denizens of this place were fearful of consequences, should they be discovered here.

Scurrying fugitives headed for the path that led away from this danger zone. The Shadow's guns spoke only at intervals, when some more daring ruffian would turn in an effort to shoot him down.

Suddenly, the black-gloved fingers opened. The automatics, their bullets spent, clattered to the floor. In a twinkling, those hands, reaching beneath the folds of the black cloak, produced another brace of guns.

The gesture was sufficient. With wild cries, the last of the fugitives hurried through the doorways, and did not return.

Three men, however, had avoided The Shadow's shots with fell design. Those three were Stacks Lodi's men. Balked in their first attack on Carter Boswick, the trio had left the American in the hands of the ruffians.

With The Shadow's intervention, Herrando had immediately feared the consequences of the riot that he had begun. With a quick gesture to Cassalta and Bolano, he had gained the long flight of stairs, and the other two had followed him.

Upon the balcony, the three were waiting. They were alone, for there was another exit from the second floor; and all upstairs had taken it. The trio remained, with revolvers in their grasp, awaiting a moment of opportunity.

Carter Boswick, back against the wall below, did not offer the suitable target that they wanted, but a strange freak of chance brought him into range.

As the last of the departing patrons were scurrying from the rear doors, whistles sounded from beyond the gate outside the patio. The shrill sounds signaled the arrival of the police.

Carter Boswick, acting upon impulse, sought a quick exit. He sprang to the stairs, and hurried upward, at the same time calling out a warning to the black-clad rescuer at the outer door.

THE SHADOW'S eyes gleamed as they turned upward. He saw Carter Boswick's intention, and realized that the American was trying to show him a way to safety. The Shadow's laugh resounded through the room, a burst of triumph that rang out in the face of danger.

To The Shadow, the invasion of the police was no more a menace than the flight of the panic-stricken cowards who were now scurrying through the doors beyond. But there was a note in The Shadow's mirth that betokened more.

His keen eyes saw that Carter Boswick, who thought himself safe, but feared for The Shadow, was actually the one who was about to encounter danger.

Three figures were rising to block the young man's path. Foremost was Herrando; behind him, ready to join in the assassination, were Cassalta and Bolano.

As he faced the top of the stairs, Carter Boswick stopped short. Almost before his eyes was the gleaming muzzle of a revolver. Herrando, leaning coolly upon the newel post of the balcony balustrade, was about to deliver a fatal shot.

Carter's gun was in his hand—the weapon that he had seized from the ruffian whom he had downed in combat. It was too late to use it now. He had run into certain death. The barrel of a threatening revolver scarcely a yard from his face; The Shadow, his rescuer, rods away, by the outer door!

Instinctively, Carter was sure that The Shadow could not aid him now, due to the distance of the range. The same thought had occurred to Herrando. It accounted for the South American's boldness.

But neither Carter nor Herrando had reckoned with The Shadow's might.

In that moment of tense suspense, when Herrando's finger wavered on the trigger, The Shadow's right hand acted. The same hand had raised its automatic in time with the lifting of the head above it. The automatic spoke. One single shot.

Herrando's body twisted. A cry came from the assassin's evil lips. His murderous form toppled against the balustrade. The ornamental parapet failed beneath his sagging weight. Decayed wood crackled; the rail broke, and Herrando shot forward with a wild shriek, plunging headlong to the floor below.

The Shadow's thrust shattered the morale of the other two villains. Cassalta and Bolano did not wait to learn of Herrando's fate. The unexpected stroke was proof of The Shadow's power, even at this distance.

Carter Boswick, raising his revolver as Herrando fell, was also a menace close at hand. Instead of raising their guns, the two South Americans plunged madly into the doorway of a room behind them. Carter Boswick fired futile shots at their retreating forms.

With the foiled assassins gone, Carter looked below to see what The Shadow was about to do. He saw one black arm raised; he noted the pointing finger that bade him to follow the route which the fleeing pair had taken. Carter hesitated a moment; then, as the stern finger continued to point, the young man obeyed.

He found that the room into which his enemies had run had an opening to an outside corridor. He followed this and came to a stairway. It led him to an outer doorway on a narrow, deserted street.

This was the way that all upstairs had taken. No one had remained in the vicinity. No police had arrived here as yet. Pocketing the revolver, Carter Boswick moved rapidly along, confident that he could find his way to the *Southern Star* unmolested.

BACK in the main room of the old Barcelona Club, The Shadow stood alone. The iron gate was clanging as police sought to break their way into the patio. Calmly sliding his two braces of automatics beneath the folds of his cloak, The Shadow moved among the tables until he reached the spot where Herrando lay.

The murderous villain was dead. The Shadow's timely shot had not killed, for it had been designed to prevent Herrando from using his own weapon, and The Shadow had picked the man's right shoulder as the most accessible spot. But the plunge from the balcony had finished The Shadow's work. Herrando's neck was broken.

A terrific clang came from the distance as the iron gate broke before the attacks of the enraged police. The Shadow's laugh seemed to join in the echoes of the clatter. There was a reason now why The Shadow did not want his presence known to these invaders.

With strident mirth still ringing from his lips, the black-garbed fighter stooped and picked up the body of Herrando as one would lift the form of a small child. With his burden slung across his shoulder, The Shadow strode through one of the farther doorways.

When the police arrived, a minute later, they found the hall deserted, save for a few wounded ruffians who still lay among the tables. These were attackers whom The Shadow had crippled so effectively that they had been unable to join the others in hasty flight.

The Shadow, himself, was gone, leaving no token of his departure. Somewhere amid the narrow streets of old Havana, he was carrying away the dead body of the final victim.

The Shadow had prevented assassination tonight. In so doing, he had defeated a horde of Cuban apaches, and had spread terror among the evildoers of the island's capital.

The Shadow's work was not yet ended. He had not prevented the danger that was due to come. How the intended murder of Carter Boswick could still be thwarted was the next problem that The Shadow must meet.

Carter Boswick might believe himself safe aboard the *Southern Star.* The Shadow knew that the menace still hung over the homeward-bound New Yorker. When danger ruled again, The Shadow would meet it, by craft as well as might.

CHAPTER VI
THE SHADOW'S STRATEGY

THE *Southern Star* was plowing northward. The first night out of Havana, new passengers were making friends, and old ones were renewing acquaintances. Only the more experienced seafarers were in the smoking room, however, as the weather was rough, and the rolling of the ship was none too pleasant.

Two men—apparently chance acquaintances—were seated in a corner of the smoking room. One was Cassalta; the other Bolano. Each had picked up his ticket without reporting to Stacks Lodi. This was their first meeting, and they had not yet interviewed their chief.

Bolano was raising a glass of liquor to his lips. Suddenly he stopped, and his hand trembled. Cassalta looked in the direction of his companion's eyes. There, approaching the table, was their fellow villain of the night before—Herrando.

Both the seated men repressed gasps of astonishment as Herrando joined them. They noted that their returned comrade was pale; that his right arm was held stiffly at his side. But he smiled in the villainous fashion of Herrando.

"You thought I was dead, eh?" he questioned, in Spanish. "Well, comrades, you were wrong!"

"But you were shot."

Herrando still smiled as he heard Bolano's muffled exclamation.

"In the shoulder," he said calmly. "A flesh wound—that was all."

"You fell through the rail?"

"Yes. A nasty tumble. It shook me terribly, but did not injure me."

"But the man at the door?"

"He fled. The police were coming. I, too, was able to escape. It was most fortunate."

A pause followed. Bolano and Cassalta gulped their drinks in silence, wondering at the miraculous escape which Herrando had made. Then their newly arrived comrade spoke again.

"I have seen *Señor* Lodi," he announced quietly. "I talked with him but an hour ago. He gave me a message. He does not wish to talk with any of us at present."

The others nodded. They knew that this policy was a wise one.

"The weather is rough tonight," continued Herrando. "It is lessening, so the captain has said.

Therefore, tonight would be best for the—let us say accident—that we propose. I am confident that the *Americano* will not recognize us, if we keep well away from him. I spoke to *Señor* Lodi about last night's mishap, and he agrees.

"*Señor* Boswick has an outside cabin. It is likely that he will come to the smoking room tonight. Afterward, he will probably go by the door over yonder. When he shows such signs of departure, I shall precede him. You, my comrades, will follow."

More nods of agreement. Herrando arose to go away, giving his last words of instruction.

"*Señor* Lodi will be here to give the signal for each of us. Keep apart, *señores.*"

With that, Herrando went across the smoking room. Cassalta and Bolano separated. The three were apart and obscurely situated, when Carter Boswick entered the smoking room. Stacks Lodi came later, and joined a group in a card game.

The gambler was wise. He did not care if he might be recognized as a card sharp. The offense would be passed over; and it would free him from connection with the other work.

IN Carter Boswick's mind, last night's events were a muddle. He knew nothing of what had caused the trouble at the Barcelona Club. He remembered very little concerning any of his assailants.

He thought the whole affair had been a matter of mistaken identity. Furthermore, he was elated by a letter that he had received on shipboard just before sailing.

He produced the letter now. It was from his father in New York, and it filled Carter Boswick with gladness, despite a tinge of apprehension that it had also created.

He looked at the message.

> Your return will be a welcome one, my son. I am overjoyed because you have been successful in foreign lands. I am nearing the end of life; whatever I have will be yours, save for a pension to your cousin, Drew Westling.
>
> Life is uncertain; although your return will be soon, I may not be here to welcome you. But I have confidence in you, and whatever test may arise, I know that you will meet it.
>
> Should I not be here, Carter, my lawyer, Farland Tracy will tell you of my wishes. From him you will learn much—but there will be more to learn, even though I may be dead. Be discreet, my son, beware of hidden danger and meet all hazards that may confront you.

The odd phraseology of the letter was startling to Carter Boswick. He read the message over and over; still, he wondered at its hidden meaning. He thrust the letter in his pocket, lighted a cigar, and lapsed into a reverie of the past.

Stacks Lodi, seated at the card table, was watching Carter Boswick from the corner of his eye.

There was another for whom Lodi was watching—Lamont Cranston. He did not know why; he simply wondered if Cranston were about. He had learned that the man had booked passage on this ship. Not seeing Cranston, Lodi decided that the man must be in his stateroom. Many of the passengers had kept to their cabins tonight.

Carter Boswick was finishing his cigar. Stacks Lodi sensed that he would soon leave the smoking room. The gambler was pleased when a timely lull occurred in the game. He got up from the table and walked to the bar. On the way, he flashed a quick signal to Herrando.

The South American arose and left the smoking room. But he did not stop when he reached the outside deck. He moved swiftly, despite the roll of the ship, and gained a nearby cabin. It was not the one that belonged to Herrando. It was the cabin engaged by Lamont Cranston.

A few moments later, a figure emerged from the cabin door. Tall, black, and spectral, it loomed like a ghost from the brine that swept the deck. Herrando, the man who had so strangely come back to life, was no longer Herrando. He was The Shadow!

Had Stacks Lodi been there, he might have understood. Lamont Cranston had come aboard, and had left the ship later. Then Herrando had come on board in his place. So far as anyone knew, both men were on the *Southern Star;* in reality, both men were one!

Within the smoking room, Stacks Lodi saw Carter Boswick arise and start for the door that made the shortest way to his cabin. Stacks was pleased to note that no one else seemed to observe Carter's departure.

From the bar, Stacks caught the eye of Cassalta, and made a slight sign. Then he spotted Bolano, and repeated the action. The two men, surreptitiously, followed the path that Carter Boswick had taken.

Stacks Lodi, his fingers gripping a revolver in his pocket, grimly resolved to follow also. He wanted to be sure that his assassins did not fail tonight.

CARTER Boswick, when he reached the deserted deck, did not go directly to his cabin. Instead, he stopped beside the rail and watched the surging sea that swirled and battered at the side of the plunging ship. In this action, he once again played into the hands of enemies.

The door opened behind him. Carter did not hear it. An instant later, Cassalta and Bolano, recognizing their intended victim, leaped forward with no thought of where Herrando might be. They caught Carter Boswick unaware.

The young man felt his body lifted upward by the rail—in another second, he would have been hurled out into the ocean, but for the intervention which occurred.

A mass of darkness swept upward from a spot beside the rail. A living creature conjured from nothingness, The Shadow flung himself into the fray. He sent both Cassalta and Bolano spinning. Carter Boswick plunged safely to the deck, and lay there, half stunned.

The South Americans, sprawling, did not know what had struck them, until they glanced up, terrorized, to see the strange being who had balked them in the fight of the night before.

These men were at The Shadow's mercy; but it was now their turn to gain by intervention. Stacks Lodi, stepping from the door with gun in hand, saw The Shadow. The gambler, versed in the lore of New York's underworld, recognized this terrible foe. He raised his revolver to fire.

But The Shadow, turning, saw the menace. The black-gloved hands shot forward. They caught Stacks Lodi with incredible swiftness. The gun went spinning across the deck. Stacks and The Shadow were locked in a furious tussle.

Cassalta and Bolano sprang to their feet, and rushed to aid their chief. As they arrived, Stacks shot headforemost along the slippery deck, skidding up against the rail.

The two South Americans hit The Shadow at once, from behind. The black-gloved hands caught Cassalta's wrists. The Shadow's body seemed to crumple to the deck; then snapped upward like a whipcord.

The mighty effort succeeded with amazing results. The Shadow had taken no direction in his aim. His purpose was merely to fling Cassalta away. But the twist of his body headed the assassin directly toward the rail.

As the ship rolled, Cassalta went spinning through the air like a huge missile flung from a catapult. Timed with the sidewise descent of the ship, The Shadow's terrific heave sent the assassin a dozen feet through the air, clear over the rail by a space of a full yard, and on out into the raging sea!

Bolano had no inkling of his comrade's fate. He and The Shadow were rolling across the deck. Bolano's hand fell upon Stacks Lodi's gun. With a savage cry, the second killer gripped the weapon and sought to press the trigger.

His effort was successful, but not with the result that he expected. The hand of The Shadow caught his wrist as he was about to fire. A twist occurred just as Bolano discharged the gun. Bolano groaned and crumpled away, the bullet in his own body. His fingers lost their grip, and the revolver bounced upon the deck.

Stacks Lodi, disarmed, had seen the amazing fight. He heard the shot, and saw The Shadow rolling free. With a gasp of terror, he ran along the deck, turned into a door that led to a corridor, and made his way back to the smoking room.

THE SHADOW arose. He saw the form of Bolano, dying on the deck. He reached the spot where Carter Boswick lay, and helped the groggy young man to his feet. When Carter Boswick fully regained his senses, he found himself lying on the berth in his own stateroom.

The aftermath of the strange fray began later that night, when a steward discovered the body of Bolano with the gun beside it. Stacks Lodi was still gambling in the smoking room when the news broke.

An investigation followed. It was learned that two men were missing—both South Americans—Cassalta and Herrando. Nothing else could be ascertained; but it was decided that all three—Bolano as well as the missing men—were of questionable character.

The report was that a quarrel must have occurred; that two had united to throw the third overboard. Then the two had battled: Bolano, shot by his antagonist, had managed to hurl him into the sea.

Carter Boswick wisely kept his peace. There was much that he did not understand about the attack which had been made upon him. He knew only that a mysterious stranger had once again appeared to beat off his antagonists.

It was Stacks Lodi who maintained a trembling silence. He, too, was perplexed. He wondered what had happened to Herrando. He believed that The Shadow must have dispatched that villain before he attended to the others. He never dreamed that The Shadow had assumed the guise of Herrando!

Stacks Lodi did not see Lamont Cranston on board the ship. The reason was that Stacks Lodi seldom left his stateroom. He lay in hiding, hoping only that his share in the strange events had not been known by the dread avenger.

For Stacks Lodi had recognized The Shadow. He had terrible news to bear to Hub Rowley. There would be a new menace to confront the big shot's schemes.

The Shadow, mastermind opposed to crime, had shown his hand. Now, hidden and mysterious, he was permitting Stacks Lodi to carry back the word. Contemptuous of the criminals whom he opposed, he had spared this skulking underling.

The *Southern Star* plowed on through lessening seas. Each day was indicative of approaching calmness on the ocean. But when the steamship landed, there would be no quietude ashore. Then forces of evil would be met by the hand of The Shadow!

During this strange lull, Carter Boswick, entirely unconscious of the cause, still wondered why he had been attacked by unknown enemies. Little did he know of the turmoil in store for him.

A mass of darkness swept upward ... sent both Cassalta and Bolano spinning ...

He had been saved by The Shadow. Would that same hand strike again to rescue him when hidden danger came?

Only The Shadow could answer!

CHAPTER VII
THE HOMECOMING

WHEN the *Southern Star* docked at its North River pier, Carter Boswick was one of the first persons ashore. All the way up the river, the young man had imbibed the breeze of New York Harbor with a sense of new elation.

The skyline of Manhattan, replenished with huge buildings which had been erected during his absence, the familiarity of old views which Carter had not seen for years—these conspired to give the returning man an unexpected yearning for home.

Carter's thoughts were of his father. All during the voyage from Havana he had read and reread the letter. His eagerness to greet his lone parent had reached the proportions of a mania. The details of customs examinations on the pier were an annoyance that Carter Boswick could scarcely undergo.

His luggage, each item labeled with a letter B, was subjected to an immediate examination, while Carter waited impatiently. Close beside him were passengers whose names began with C. One of those passengers—Lamont Cranston—was watching Boswick with careful gaze. Carter Boswick was not conscious of the surveillance.

While Carter Boswick waited, he felt a touch upon his shoulder. Turning, he faced a well-dressed man of medium height, whose features were firm and aristocratic. Carter had never seen this individual before. He was evidently someone who had come to meet the boat, for Carter did not recall him as a passenger.

"You are Carter Boswick?"

The man's question was calm, but solemn. Carter nodded, wondering who the man might be.

"I am Farland Tracy. I have come to meet you."

The name was momentarily unfamiliar. Then Carter recalled his father's letter. The young man thrust his right hand forward.

"My father's attorney," he said.

"Yes," responded Tracy, in an even tone. "I was your father's attorney."

As Carter blinked in slow understanding, Tracy's hand dropped gently upon the young man's shoulder. The lawyer's eyes were sympathetic.

"Your father is dead, Carter," he explained quietly. "He felt that the end was near the day he wrote his last letter to you. You received it? In Havana?"

Carter Boswick nodded.

"Your father lived scarcely more than twenty-four hours after he sent that letter," resumed Tracy. "He was weary of life—incurably ill—a shell of himself as you had known him. He chose that you should not know until you had reached New York."

It was with difficulty that Carter Boswick controlled his emotions. For years, his father had been scarcely more than a name to him. They had never quarreled, but there had never been a real understanding between them. Returning to America, Carter had sensed that his present maturity might enable him to meet his father on a basis of mutual friendship that had not existed in the past.

A surge of regret swept through the young man's mind. He realized that he, while not a prodigal, was scarcely a deserving son. Farland Tracy sensed the mingling of emotions. He seemed to understand, and his kindly sympathy came to the fore. He beckoned toward his chauffeur, who had followed him on the pier.

"Take charge of Mr. Boswick's luggage, Holland," the lawyer ordered. "He and I will take a taxi to the Law Club. We are having luncheon there. Call for us about three thirty."

HOLLAND was not the only person who heard the order. Lamont Cranston, apparently busy with a customs agent, had listened to Farland Tracy's words.

A few minutes after Tracy and Carter Boswick had left the pier, Lamont Cranston followed. He stopped in a telephone booth and made a brief call. After that, he hailed a taxi and ordered the driver to take him to the Law Club.

There was a thin smile on Cranston's lips as he alighted at the portals of the Law Club. He entered the building, and spoke to the attendant who inquired his business there.

"I am Mr. Cranston," he said in a quiet tone.

"Yes, Mr. Cranston," responded the attendant. "You may enter, sir. Judge Lamark just called, sir. He said that you were to he admitted."

Cranston still smiled as he walked through the lobby of the exclusive club. His phone call from the pier had brought quick results. Judge Vanniman Lamark was a friend of Lamont Cranston. He had been pleased to hear from him. He had promised to arrange Cranston's admittance to the club, and would try to meet his friend there at three o'clock.

In the grillroom of the club, Cranston discovered Farland Tracy and Carter Boswick ordering lunch in a booth at the side of the room. Unnoticed, Cranston slipped into the adjoining booth. He gave a quiet order to a waiter; then listened intently. His keen ears caught every word that passed between Farland Tracy and Carter Boswick.

"As I have stated," Tracy was saying, "your father made you his sole heir—except for a moderate but ample income that he left to your cousin, Drew Westling."

"Why wasn't Drew at the boat to meet me?" questioned Carter.

"I don't believe that he knew when you were coming in," answered Tracy. "Your father told him that you were on your way from Montevideo; but I don't think that Drew inquired the day of your arrival. Your father's death was a blow to Drew."

"Of course," agreed Carter. His tone, however, showed a tinge of disappointment. Drew Westling was his only relation, now that Houston Boswick was dead.

"You will probably find Drew at the house," declared Tracy. "He is living there; and Headley, your father's servant, has remained. There are other domestics—Headley is the only one of consequence. He is something of a supervisor, or caretaker."

Farland Tracy paused after this explanation. Then, in a new train of thought, he came to a matter that proved to be of special consequence.

"There is a certain factor regarding your father's estate," resumed the lawyer, "that I cannot mention just at present. I discussed it with your father shortly before his death. My instructions were to wait until you had reached the home, and had established a residence there.

"Technically, such residence will begin as soon as you have stepped across the threshold, providing you announce your intention of keeping the old house. You will assume your father's place as master there. So I shall come to visit you this evening. We can discuss affairs in the room that used to be your father's study."

There was a seriousness in the lawyer's tone that impressed Carter Boswick.

"TELL me," questioned the young man. "Was all well at the time of my father's death?"

"Yes and no," responded the lawyer thoughtfully. "Your father, Carter, had been living under certain apprehension. He had hoped for your return. If you had not come back, Drew Westling would have been his heir. Therefore, he took rather extraordinary methods to protect his estate.

"At the time he died, he believed that certain efforts were being made to interfere with his plans. He did not seem to fear that his life was in danger; but he did think that his property might be in jeopardy.

"He was positive that unknown persons had entered his home during his absence, in an effort to frustrate his plans. There was, however, no trace of an actual plot. He might have been mistaken—"

Carter Boswick interrupted. In a low, tense voice, he recounted his adventure in Havana, and the episode that had taken place aboard the *Southern Star*. Farland Tracy listened intently to the story. When Carter had concluded, the lawyer rubbed his chin in deep thought.

"Those events may be of a serious nature, Carter," he declared. "It seems amazing that two attempts should have been made upon your life, at a time when you were coming home to gain a heritage. On the contrary, they may have been chance episodes. They may have no bearing upon your present situation. That, I sincerely hope, is the case."

"Why?" questioned Carter, as the lawyer paused.

"Because," continued Tracy, in a regretful tone, "there is only one person who could profit by your death."

"Drew Westling?"

"Yes."

Carter Boswick chewed his lips. He knew that Farland Tracy had spoken an apparent truth.

Nevertheless, he was loath to believe that his cousin could be planning perfidy.

That, too, appeared to be Tracy's thought. The lawyer expressed it in definite terms.

"Drew Westling is a spendthrift," he declared. "Shortly before your father's death, Drew lost heavily at the gaming table. I did my utmost to disentangle him from the snare. I succeeded only partially—enough to protect Drew for the time.

"I said nothing to your father regarding the matter. Had I mentioned it, Drew would probably have lost his income, and all claim to the estate, had you failed to arrive home."

While Carter was still nodding his understanding, Tracy continued in a milder, more tolerant tone.

"Nevertheless," he resumed, "Drew is a likable young man, with all his faults. I would hesitate to class him as a plotter. I feel that he should be given the benefit of all doubt. At the same time, you should use discretion, Carter. My visit tonight will be important. It must be between ourselves. It concerns your affairs only.

"Drew Westling is entitled to his provision in the terms of the will. He is your cousin. He has a right to live with you at the old mansion. I know that you will treat him generously. Still, you must remember the existing facts. Give affairs a chance to adjust themselves. Be cordial to Drew, but make your renewed friendship one of slow culmination."

"I appreciate the advice," responded Carter. "It is well given, Mr. Tracy. Drew Westling's lack of interest in my arrival gives me an excellent starting point. I shall be cordial and glad to see my cousin. But my experiences in foreign lands have shown me the folly of becoming too friendly all at once—even when a relative and boyhood chum is concerned."

The men finished their lunch. Farland Tracy glanced at his watch and noticed that it was half past three.

"Holland must be here with the car," said the attorney. "He will drive you to your home, Carter. I shall call tonight shortly before nine. It will apparently be no more than a chance visit; actually it will be a matter of greatest consequence. You understand?"

"Absolutely," replied Carter Boswick. "You may rely upon me."

The two men left the grillroom. Lamont Cranston remained. A few minutes later, an entering man stopped at Cranston's table. It was Judge Vanniman Lamark, pleased to greet an old friend whom he had not seen for nine months.

As he chatted idly with the judge, Lamont Cranston still wore his thin smile. He was thinking of that appointment between Farland Tracy and Carter Boswick. He, too, would be there at nine o'clock.

But he would not visit the Boswick mansion as Lamont Cranston. Tonight, The Shadow would reappear to again play a hidden part in the destinies of Carter Boswick!

CHAPTER VIII
THE SECRET MESSAGE

IT was eight o'clock that evening. Carter Boswick, back in his father's old mansion, was pacing the floor of the gloomy hall. He spied Headley walking morosely toward the dining room. The servant turned as Carter spoke.

"Has Mr. Westling called?" inquired Carter.

"No, sir," answered Headley.

"Very well, then," said Carter, with a tone of impatience. "I shall go ahead with dinner."

"It is ready, sir. Mr. Westling is usually quite late—"

The front door opened by way of interruption. Carter Boswick turned. His keen eyes studied a man who was entering. He saw a young fellow of slight build, whose carriage and pale features marked him of the lounging type. The arrival was holding a long cigarette holder in one hand. This added to his listless appearance.

For a moment the two faced each other. Then a light crept over the features of the man who had just entered. His eyes showed an unexpected sparkle. He sprang forward with hand extended.

"Carter!" he cried. "Carter!"

The enthusiastic greeting seemed genuine. Carter Boswick caught Drew Westling's hand, and grinned at the cousin whom he had not seen for years.

They had been boys together—these two—and the physical superiority of Carter Boswick was even more marked than before. Drew Westling seemed pitifully frail beside the stalwart form of his newly returned cousin.

A few minutes later, the pair was seated at the dining-room table. The spontaneous meeting had brought a quick bond of unrestrained cordiality. They were talking over boyhood events with real enthusiasm. To Carter Boswick, this get-together had taken an unexpected turn.

"Do you remember that game we used to play so often"—Drew Westling's voice had assumed a reminiscent tone—"and how exact we were in every detail?"

"You mean the duel between D'Artagnan and De Guise?" smiled Carter.

"Yes," nodded Drew. "We used those short billiard cues for swords, and chalked the ends of them so we could count the thrusts."

"We must have played that battle a hundred times."

"Right out of the pages of *The Three Musketeers*. We used to read the old volume of Dumas for inspiration—then change them into action. We passed that stage of life, though. Funny thing, Carter"—Drew paused wistfully—"I never could think of reading a Dumas story again, after you went away."

Carter made no reply. His cousin was thoughtful then returned to his reminiscences.

"The old duel," he recalled. "The one game that Uncle Houston would tolerate about the house. Perhaps that's why we played it so often. Remember how he used to watch us, Carter? How he used to criticize each thrust?"

Carter Boswick nodded. Drew Westling had brought back the one boyhood memory that was indelibly impressed upon his mind. Only when he and Drew had fought their duel had Houston Boswick shown the real interest of a proud father and an indulgent uncle.

"Say, Carter"—Drew was on a more immediate subject—"it was pretty small of me not to meet you at the boat today. I knew you were coming in, and I should have called up Farland Tracy about it. But somehow, I've been pretty blue since my uncle—since your father—died. I was afraid you wouldn't know, and I didn't see just how—just how I could tell you. I thought if Tracy was there alone—"

"That's all right, Drew," interrupted Carter quietly. "I understand. I did feel mighty broken up. I'm glad I didn't see you until now."

DESPITE a resentful antagonism that he had held earlier in the evening, Carter Boswick now felt a warmth of kindliness toward Drew Westling. He recognized that his cousin was a weakling, but the sentiment in Drew's nature did much to excuse that fault.

Just as dinner was ending, the doorbell rang. Headley answered it, and returned a few minutes later to announce that Farland Tracy was calling to see Mr. Boswick.

"Finish your dinner, old top," Carter said to Drew. "I'll see what Tracy wants. Probably a friendly call. You can join us later."

Reaching the hall, Carter found Tracy standing with a warning hand uplifted. Carter nodded, and led the lawyer upstairs to the study. The room was lighted; the shade was drawn. Carter closed the door. Tracy motioned for him to turn the key. Carter complied, and the lawyer brought out a bundle of papers.

"We must go through these," he stated.

The inspection began. Most of the papers were

FARLAND TRACY, as legal adviser to the elder Boswick, carries out the requests of the will. How much does he know—and how well does he keep the provisions of the bequests under his care?

of purely legal nature. But at the bottom lay two envelopes. One was addressed to Carter Boswick; the other to Drew Westling; each envelope bore the statement that it was to be destroyed intact, should the other be the heir.

"These are letters which your father wrote," explained Tracy. "Their contents are practically identical. He showed them to me before he sealed them. One for you—one for Drew—whichever might inherit the estate."

Carter nodded and opened his envelope. He drew out the letter, and read it slowly, holding it so that the lawyer could also see the careful handwriting.

The letter read as follows:

My Dear Son Carter:

When you read this letter, I shall be dead. You will be my sole heir. You will be the recipient of a considerable estate. Nevertheless, if you are at all familiar with my reputed wealth, you may be somewhat disappointed.

During the past few years, I have made a constant effort to minimize the extent of my possessions. In this I have been fairly successful. I have had a definite purpose in such action. Men of great wealth are subject to preying enemies.

Their estates often are in jeopardy because the expectant heirs show jealousy or cross purposes.

In accordance with my policy, I have actually minimized my known estate. I have left it ample for your needs. You may be satisfied with its present size. At the same time, I must inform you that I have deposited, in a place of absolute safety, a sum nearly ten times as great as my announced estate.

If you wish that wealth, you may seek it. You can learn, if you will, where I have placed it. If you are a true son—as I feel sure you are—your thoughts of your dead father will prove a helpful guide.

It is my one regret, Carter, that we never understood each other as many fathers and sons have done. That lack of understanding was my fault—not yours.

When you and Drew Westling were boys together, I seldom showed interest in your activities. Only when you played your game of duel did I respond to your natural, boyish yearnings for the fatherly interest of an older man.

Perhaps you will be able to picture those exact scenes when we were together. I trust that you will go over them in detail, recalling all incidents, planning your game, and remembering me as I was then.

Perhaps the long-forgotten thrill of the battle between D'Artagnan and De Guise will enable you to understand your father as he really was— to help you know how much you mean to him today.

I possess wealth and I possess memories. To me, those memories are wealth itself. I trust that you will feel the same, Carter. This is the message that I give you. I feel sure that the future will hold in store the wealth that has been established for you by

Your father,

Houston Boswick.

Carter Boswick studied the written lines. He checked each paragraph as he reviewed it. Finally, he laid the letter on the table, and turned to Farland Tracy.

"Is this the only communication that my father left for me?"

"Yes."

"He speaks of a great sum of hidden wealth."

"Yes," declared Tracy. "Something in the neighborhood of ten million dollars, if his statement is correct. But the clue to its hiding place is one that you must find."

"Have you any inkling of it?" questioned Carter.

"None at all," admitted Tracy. "Your father was convinced that you would learn it after his death. How he arranged to lead you to it is beyond my comprehension. This letter is very vague; it turns from business to sentiment at a most unfortunate point. My only theory is that your father may have arranged for some communication to reach you from another source."

"Perhaps," agreed Carter.

"Should you learn more," stated Tracy, "I advise you to be very careful. This letter is a private one. Another communication, if received, should be guarded. I am speaking now as your father's attorney—also as your attorney *pro tem.*"

"You will continue to be my lawyer," said Carter.

HEADLEY, butler to the Boswicks, and caretaker of the family home. Headley first notices that strange things have occurred in the old homestead, but Headley does not say too much.

"I appreciate that," responded Tracy. "But now that my mission is completed, I shall leave you. It is most advisable that no one should know of any purpose in this visit."

"I understand."

Carter Boswick folded his letter, and placed it in his pocket. He took up the envelope addressed to Drew Westling, and tore it into four pieces, letter and all. He dropped the fragments in the wastebasket.

Farland Tracy was ready to leave. Carter Boswick accompanied him from the study. The door closed, and the room was empty.

That condition did not long exist.

THE window shade slowly arose, guided by a black-gloved hand from without. A tall form slid through the opening. The Shadow stood in the study. Softly, he lowered sash and shade. With quick stride, he moved toward the desk. Stooping, he plucked the torn letter from the wastebasket.

Listening outside the window, The Shadow had heard Farland Tracy's statement that the two letters—one to Carter, the other to Drew—were couched in similar phraseology. Hence, when The Shadow had quickly assembled the fragments of the torn letter, he possessed a practical replica of the epistle which Carter Boswick had so recently perused.

There, on the table, before the keen eyes of The Shadow, lay a note from uncle to nephew that carried the same theme—even to the dash of sentimental conclusion—that had appeared in the letter from father to son.

A soft laugh came from The Shadow's hidden lips. To the black-clad being, this letter had a definite meaning. Where Farland Tracy had seen nothing more than a mere statement of existing wealth that lay hidden, The Shadow was picking out a definite clue.

The subtlety of old Houston Boswick was manifested in this letter. The Shadow's black finger rested upon one vital phrase:

If you are a true nephew—as I feel sure you are —the thoughts of your dead uncle will prove a helpful guide.

That sentence was a key to the part of the letter that followed. With Drew Westling, as with Carter Boswick, the dead man had made a definite effort to guide the reader's thoughts!

Again, The Shadow laughed. Here, in this reclaimed letter that had never been delivered, he was finding the clue to Houston Boswick's secret!

CHAPTER IX
THE STOLEN CLUE

DOWNSTAIRS, Carter Boswick was bidding Farland Tracy good night. The lawyer was standing at the open door. Headley, the attendant, was holding his coat. In the driveway outside, Tracy's car was waiting with Holland, the chauffeur, beside it.

Beyond were bushes. Dark splotches above a blackened lawn, they seemed to shout out a warning of hidden eyes that watched the scene at the doorway. Men were lurking in that shrubbery, but there was no tangible evidence of their presence.

The door closed. The muffled purr of Tracy's car sounded from the drive. Headley walked across the hall toward the back of the house. Carter noticed Drew Westling standing by the door of the dining room. His cousin was smoking the inevitable cigarette, in its accustomed holder.

Without comment, Carter turned back toward the stairs, which were just beyond Drew Westling's range of vision. When he reached the bottom of the steps, he did not ascend; instead, he went through a short hallway that led to the library.

This was an old room lined with many shelves of books. It was at the middle of one side of the house. It had one doorway entering from this hall, and at either end were curtained openings that led into adjacent rooms.

Carter softly closed the door behind him. He turned out a single lamp that rested on a table. Satisfied that he was free from observation, he began a prompt examination of the bookshelves.

For Carter Boswick, the moment that he had finished the second reading of his father's letter, had gained a sudden knowledge that he had kept entirely to himself. Inspired by the thought of a possible clue, he had said nothing to Farland Tracy.

It was evident that Houston Boswick had wanted his heir alone to learn of the place where wealth was hidden. The tone of the letter had given that indication. In reading, Carter had wondered at first how the information would be gained. Then, the reference to boyhood days had dropped like a bolt from a clear sky.

The very subject that Carter and Drew had discussed—those days when the two boys had played at duel with the elderly man watching them. That was a reference which only two persons could have understood with surety. Carter or Drew—either one as Houston Boswick's heir—might quickly catch the meaning. Carter believed that he had done so.

To picture past events—to go over the details of long-remembered scenes—to follow his father's track of memory—that was the duty imposed upon Carter Boswick. In the letter, now reposing in Carter's pocket, was the statement that memories were as important as wealth.

Perhaps there was a connection between the two!

A PAIR of dusty volumes reposed high upon a neglected shelf. They were both portions of the same work—"The Three Musketeers," by Alexandre Dumas. Carter reached up and brought down one of the volumes. He ran through the yellowed pages, skimming them with his thumb, until there was a sudden stop. With a smile of elation, Carter drew forth a thin manila envelope from between the pages.

He shook the book to make sure that this was all. Satisfied, he laid the volume on the table where the lamp rested close beside a hanging curtain.

With eager fingers, Carter tore open the envelope and drew forth a slip of yellow paper. It bore a brief notation:

Lat. 46° 18' N.
Long. 88° 12' W.

Carter Boswick's mind was retentive. He read this location, in terms of latitude and longitude, and the exact position made a definite impression. Accustomed to long sea trips, Carter was used to speaking of places in such terms. He noted this as exactly as another person might have noted a telephone number.

Carter laid the paper and the envelope upon the closed book. He turned back to the shelf. Still running through his brain was the statement he had just noted:

Lat. 46° 18' N.
Long. 88° 12' W.

Carter repeated the words with silent lips as he drew down the other volume of "The Three Musketeers," and stepped back to whisk its pages.

The curtain moved beside the lamp. The slight, wavering tremble was not noticed by Carter Boswick, for the young man's mind was upon the second book which he held.

From the curtain came a slow, cautious hand. Its fingers spread beneath the soft glow of the light; they closed upon the paper and the envelope, and withdrew as quietly as they had come. Only the book remained. The direction sheet and its container werc gone!

Carter was shaking the second volume. Nothing between its leaves. The one message was all that his father had left. It was enough. It marked a definite location. There, in all probability, would lie the beginning of a trail—perhaps the wealth itself.

Carter's musing ended abruptly. He was staring at the table where he had placed the first volume of Dumas. To his amazement, he noted that the paper and the envelope were gone!

Quickly, the young man began a futile search. He looked through the pages of the first volume. He found nothing. He frantically looked beneath the table; he shook the curtain. It required only a few minutes to convince him that the message was gone!

HAD the whole discovery been a product of his imagination? For a moment, Carter fancied so; but the constant running of the tabulated location still persisted in his mind.

Methodically, Carter drew his father's letter from his pocket. With a pencil, he wrote down the exact latitude and longitude.

Impelled by a new idea, he hastily replaced the two books upon the shelf. He opened the little door, came out through the entry, and walked across the hall. He reached the door of the dining room. Drew Westling was seated at the table, still smoking. Cigarette stumps lay in the ashtray before him.

Drew looked up as he saw Carter enter, and smiled nervously. It seemed obvious that he was trying to keep his thoughts to himself. When he spoke, he adopted an affable tone that was a trifle forced.

"Thought I'd stay in here while you finished your meal," he explained to Carter. "Now that Tracy went away, I figured you would come back for dessert."

"Of course," said Carter calmly. "Very thoughtful of you, Drew."

Headley entered while Carter was eating. The attendant cleared away the remaining dishes and went stolidly about his duty. Very few words were exchanged between Carter and Drew. Each appeared quite engrossed in his own thoughts.

Carter's mind was still picturing the scene in the library. The young man wondered if Drew Westling chanced to be considering it also. Nothing could be gained by silence; moreover, it would be wise not to mention that particular subject. Finishing his dessert, Carter opened a quiet but friendly conversation into which Drew entered with increasing vivacity.

BACK in the quiet library, the curtain moved once again; this time in darkness, for Carter Boswick had extinguished the lamp. A tiny light glimmered, held by an unseen hand. It ran along the bookshelves and stopped at two volumes that were very slightly out of place.

A black-gloved hand removed the two volumes of *The Three Musketeers*. The books were placed upon the table there; the flashlight glowed while fingers went through their pages.

A low, laugh-like whisper came from lips in the dark. The Shadow, following a clue that he had gained, had arrived after Carter Boswick had inspected these very books. A slight yielding of one volume at a certain spot indicated the place from which Carter had removed a message.

The books closed. The hands replaced them upon the shelf. The Shadow's light went out. The whisper died away in the darkness as an unseen form passed from the library, reached the hall, and looked into the dining room, where Carter still chatted with his cousin.

The figure moved toward the rear of the house. Soon it was gone. It reappeared momentarily from the side porch, and crossed the driveway toward the bushes. There, The Shadow listened. There was no sound.

Vigilant watchers were no longer here. The Shadow had detected them upon their arrival; now he discovered that they had left.

Why?

The Shadow, even though he had arrived late in the library, sensed the explanation. The young Boswick, The Shadow knew, had found some message.

Had word of that finding been passed to those outside? Would an attack be made tonight?

Possibly; although the sudden departure of the watchers made it unlikely.

There was another explanation.

Someone within the house could have learned what Carter Boswick had found; or could even have taken whatever the young man had discovered. These watchers could have left with important information.

The Shadow had waited long in the upstairs study, believing that Carter Boswick had either failed to discover the meaning of his father's let-

ter, or would have waited to follow instructions later in the evening. It was Carter's prompt actions that had blocked The Shadow's careful plan of previous inspection.

Much might have happened during that unanticipated interim. But The Shadow, even when he encountered ill fortune, never faltered. This strange personage had a weird ability to turn all events to his advantage. Such would be his plan tonight.

The stealthy figure made no sound, nor did it show itself as it moved across the lawn. Darkness seemed to swallow The Shadow as he set forth.

It was not until later that another figure made its appearance within the confines of the Boswick estate. A young man, cautious, but by no means invisible, took up his vigil at a convenient spot some distance from the house.

Harry Vincent, agent of The Shadow, had been summoned to keep watch and to report on Carter Boswick's actions. That would be his duty for the present. The Shadow, himself, had other work to do.

Into the darkness he had gone; within darkness would he remain. From somewhere, unseen, he would plan his campaign of swift action. The Shadow, alone, could frustrate the designs of those who had gained the stolen clue!

CHAPTER X
CARTER TAKES A TRIP

CARTER Boswick possessed an amazing faculty for walking into trouble. In Havana, aboard the *Southern Star,* he had deliberately stepped into difficulties. That same oddity was due to manifest itself again.

Had Carter Boswick failed to remember the latitude and longitude mentioned in the message he had found, he would no longer have been a factor in the grim game which Hub Rowley was playing. The Shadow, shrouded in darkness, knew well who was seeking the information which Carter had discovered.

Hence the course of The Shadow's investigation lay toward Hub Rowley. But The Shadow, wise in all procedure, had not neglected Carter Boswick as a possibility.

Nor had Hub Rowley.

When morning was well under way, the Boswick mansion was under surveillance from two directions, watched by men of opposing sides, neither of whom knew the others were on the job.

Harry Vincent, agent of The Shadow, was lounging by the side of his coupé at a filling station across the highway from the Boswick home. Stacks Lodi, underling of Hub Rowley, was eating a belated breakfast in a little restaurant a few hundred yards farther down the road.

Meanwhile, within the big house, Carter Boswick was announcing plans. Those arrangements, from their very start, were destined to bring the young man back into the zone of action, making him a principal factor in the battle for wealth. For Carter, after a night of troubled sleep, had decided definitely to follow the lead that he had found in his father's message.

This meant that now, more than before, Carter Boswick would be slated for elimination by Hub Rowley. It also meant that he would be of vital importance to The Shadow—as a shortcut to the information which The Shadow now was seeking to obtain.

Without realizing it, Carter was making himself a pawn on the board that lay between two shrewd and relentless players.

Yet Carter felt that he was taking every precaution when he spoke to both Drew Westling and Headley, in the dining room where he and his cousin had just finished breakfast.

"I intend to establish my residence here," declared Carter. "Nevertheless it is essential that I follow business plans which I made before I left Montevideo. I represent a large South American importing house. My trip to New York was intended purely as a step toward a further business voyage to Europe.

"My original intention was to remain here a few weeks; then to go to Paris and Berlin. My father's death has caused me to change my plans. I must conclude the obligation which I owe to my associates in Montevideo; then I shall be free entirely. The sooner I discharge my duty, the better.

"Therefore, I shall book passage for Europe at once. I shall be back in New York within six weeks, and this will then become my permanent home. With Farland Tracy handling the affairs of the estate, there should be no obstacle in the arrangement. If you choose to remain here, Drew, you are welcome to do so—"

"Never mind about me," interrupted Drew Westling. "I'll stay here when you're here, Carter; but in the meantime, I'd as soon drop away for a while. I'll move into the club as soon as you leave."

"Which will be today," remarked Carter, in an offhand tone. "I plan to go by way of Montreal and the St. Lawrence waterway. So I should like to start for Canada this evening."

"Suits me," returned Drew.

"As for you, Headley," stated Carter, "you can resume your old duties of caretaker. The house will be closed; you can stay wherever you choose."

"Very well, sir," said the solemn attendant.

"That settles everything, then," concluded Carter. "I have packed sufficient luggage. I shall start for the city at once. Call a cab, Headley."

WHEN Carter Boswick's taxi rolled forth from the driveway, it became a target for watching eyes. Harry Vincent, nonchalantly stepping into his coupé, took up immediate pursuit. Stacks Lodi hurried from the restaurant and entered a sedan which had Scully at the wheel.

The flow of traffic along the highway, the fact that the road led directly into Manhattan—these were the factors that prevented either of the trailers from noticing the presence of the other.

When the course finally ended on an uptown street in New York, and Carter Boswick left the cab and entered a towering skyscraper, it was obvious that the young man intended to visit some office in the building.

Both of the pursuers worked similarly. Harry parked his coupé across the street, and watched the door of the building. Stacks dropped from the sedan and lounged at a convenient post, while Scully managed to find a stopping point for the sedan, about half a block away.

Carter Boswick's business was brief. He told Farland Tracy exactly the same story that he had given Drew Westling and Headley. The lawyer agreed that the European trip should best be handled at once, so as to assure a return at the earliest opportunity.

He expressed only one doubt; namely, the possibility of Carter receiving some communication from a source not known.

"Remember," he said sagely, "you may have an immense fortune almost within your grasp. It might be advisable to remain at the old home."

"I thought of that," returned Carter abruptly. "Nevertheless, I feel confident that my father planned well. No, Mr. Tracy, there is really no possibility of my failing to receive the information which belongs to me."

"You speak with assurance," said Tracy. "If you feel that way about it, I can see no objections to your voyage. Have a good trip, Carter, and do not worry. I shall attend to all affairs of the estate, and be ready with an exact report when you return."

Coming from the building, Carter Boswick took a cab and went directly to the Grand Central Station. There, at the information booth, he drew a large map from his pocket and, after partially unfolding it, consulted certain notations which he had made on the back of it.

Carter had found this map before leaving the house; it was one of many old guides and charts that had belonged to his father's library.

Pocketing the map, Carter made inquiries regarding Western railroad lines running northwest from Chicago. He did not ask a single question concerning trains to Montreal. He named certain towns in the State of Wisconsin. The man at the booth consulted a huge railroad guide.

WHILE this was going on, other persons began to form in line. Half a dozen men were behind the rotunda counter, but all were busy. Carter paid no attention to the people close by; hence he did not realize that two men were overhearing his plans.

One was Harry Vincent. The Shadow's agent, a young man of athletic appearance, might well have been a chance traveler seeking routine information for a trip.

The other was Stacks Lodi.

But Carter would not have recognized Hub Rowley's underling, even though the man had been a passenger aboard the *Southern Star*. Stacks had shaved away his darkened, waxed mustache. The smooth upper lip gave him an entirely different appearance.

When Carter Boswick had finished his questioning, he sauntered away from the information booth, his luggage in the custody of a porter. Harry Vincent stepped up and asked for a railroad timetable. Stacks Lodi did the same. Both, in walking away, followed the direction that Carter had taken.

Harry, consulting his timetable, passed the ticket window where Carter now stood, and overheard the young man making reservations. Harry kept on his way.

Stacks Lodi, arriving later, stood at the next window and heard the negotiations between Carter Boswick and the agent.

From then on, all paths diverged. Carter's Western Limited did not leave for a few hours. The young man checked his luggage and went from the station.

Harry Vincent sought a telephone booth. Calling a number, he stated what he had learned. He hung up the receiver and awaited a return call.

Stacks Lodi also used a telephone, in a different part of the station. His call was to Hub Rowley. He listened intently to the big-shot's response. His face gleamed as he heard Hub's words. He was smiling a wicked grin when he walked away from the booth.

The aftermath of this sequence of events came when the *Western Limited* pulled out of the Grand Central Station on its trip to Chicago.

Carter Boswick, deeply engrossed in a book that he had purchased, was seated in the club car. His mind was at ease. He had made it quite evident that he was going to Europe, via Montreal. Instead, he was off to visit the exact spot mentioned in his father's secret message—some unknown locality in the wilds of Wisconsin.

Across the way sat Harry Vincent—a quiet young man who was apparently unconcerned with those about him. At the card table, Stacks Lodi had already begun to amuse himself with a game of solitaire.

OPPOSING forces were at work. Carter Boswick, sure that he was free, with all knowledge of his secret trip a minus quantity, was already under the vigilant surveillance of two men—one who represented justice; the other, a tool of crime.

Once again, Carter Boswick was heading into trouble. Stacks Lodi, the troublemaker, was on his trail. But still, Carter was under the secret protection of The Shadow. Harry Vincent, The Shadow's agent, had been deputed to be close at hand, forewarned that danger might strike.

Action was in abeyance on this journey. These men—neither of whom suspected the other's presence—were the advance guards. They were but the instruments of greater minds, the nullifying influences put forth by Hub Rowley and The Shadow.

Conflict was brewing between the big shot and the dread avenger. The struggle would center about Carter Boswick, who had plunged himself into this fray for millions which rightfully belonged to him.

The impending battle was one that promised strange results—and into its fury would come others; men whose important parts in the drama of crime had not yet been revealed. Carter Boswick was totally unsuspecting of what lay ahead.

But The Shadow, hidden being of darkness, knew that unexpected consequences would soon manifest themselves. Plans long fostered were due to reach their startling climax when Carter Boswick gained the goal that he sought!

CHAPTER XI
THE SHADOW'S PLAN

TWO nights had passed since Carter Boswick had set out from New York City. The third evening had fallen. Along a lonely road in northwestern Michigan, a swift coupé was speeding at sixty miles an hour.

Harry Vincent was the man behind the wheel. His eyes were steadily focused upon the gravel road that stretched before him. His hands responded to every bump of the jolting highway.

Despite the ordeal of the rapid drive, Harry wore a smile. He was nearing the end of his journey.

Obedient to The Shadow's order, Harry had followed Carter Boswick to Chicago; and had again taken up the trail when the young man had boarded a train north. At Green Bay, Wisconsin, a long break had occurred. Carter Boswick had been forced to wait over several hours for a connection.

This had given Harry an excellent idea. He was confident that no harm would befall the man whom he was protecting while Carter was traveling by train. The real danger lay at the stopping points. Hence Harry had used the interval to obtain an automobile capable of high speed. His study of the road maps convinced him that he could beat the time of Carter Boswick's train.

Now, with only a few miles to go, Harry was half an hour ahead of his schedule. He had waited at Green Bay until Carter Boswick had left; then he had burned up the roads in his untiring effort to reach the final destination before Carter arrived. This place was Junction City, a Michigan town some miles north of the Wisconsin border.

What was to happen at Junction City?

Harry had no inkling. He had been instructed to stay close to Carter Boswick, particularly after the end of the journey had been reached. That was exactly what Harry intended to do now. His only qualms concerned the fact that he had let Carter get out of sight during the travel from Green Bay to Junction City.

Harry Vincent had long been an agent of The Shadow. He had encountered many adventures while working in behalf of his mysterious master. In every instance, Harry had been free to act upon his own judgment when occasions arose. This had proven to be one of those cases.

Harry had changed from train to automobile for two definite reasons. First, because he feared that Carter Boswick might become aware of his presence during the final stage of the trip; second, because he knew that a car might come in handy at Junction City. The opportunity to obtain one at Green Bay had been too good to miss.

In all his episodes in The Shadow's service, Harry had encountered mystery. He had never gained an inkling as to the identity of his unknown employer.

Instructions came through only two sources— Rutledge Mann, a chubby-faced insurance broker in the Badger Building in New York City; and over the telephone, from a hidden agent named Burbank.

Through contact with one or the other, Harry received all routine information; but in times of emergency, he frequently received mysterious orders from The Shadow himself. Harry anticipated some such occurrences during this new adventure; for he was now faraway from the usual base of operations.

THOUGHTS of the unfolding mission, coupled with anxiety for Carter Boswick's present safety,

spurred Harry unto a final burst of speed which ceased only when his headlights revealed a welcoming sign on the outskirts of Junction City. Here, Harry slackened the speed of the car and rolled easily through the lighted streets of a small town.

The sight of a signal light down a side street showed Harry that he was near the railroad, and he guided his car to a bumpy road that ran alongside the tracks. He finally came to a stop close beside a dilapidated railroad station.

Harry parked and waited. With lights extinguished, he could see the station platform beneath the dim glow of lamps from the overhanging roof. Leaning back in the seat, Harry took account of other surroundings. Down the street was an old building which bore the weather-beaten sign: "Junction House."

That, in all probability, would be Carter Boswick's stopping place.

A tenseness came over Harry Vincent as he began to review all that had happened since he had watched Carter Boswick at the information booth in the Grand Central Station in New York.

It was evident that Carter Boswick, although he had come directly to Junction City, had not made the best possible use of his time. Harry was already here ahead of him; and other persons could easily have achieved the same result. Therefore, trouble, if brewing, could begin tonight.

Harry glanced anxiously toward the station. His eyes became suddenly intent as he noted a peculiar phenomenon. One of the overhanging lights twinkled, as though something had passed between it and Harry. Then came a second twinkle from the next light; a third from the one farther on.

The whole effect was ghostly. Apparently, the solid form of a living being had moved along that platform; yet Harry had seen no more than an instantaneous blinking of each light.

It was happening again! This time from the opposite direction. Harry gripped the steering wheel. He knew that this could not be due to a peculiarity of the electric current that supplied the lights. No—someone had certainly passed along that platform!

In moments such as these, Harry Vincent regarded all signs as matters of consequence to himself. At first, his thought was one of hidden enemies. Then, puzzling the matter over, he gained a more hopeful thought.

Perhaps that curious manifestation signified the presence of The Shadow! Harry drew a breath of relief. It was possible that The Shadow, himself, might have come to Junction City. A fast hop by air—the slow progress of trains and attendant connections would be bettered by many hours.

While Harry still watched the lights, wondering if they would blink again, he heard the distant whistle of a locomotive. The sound was repeated with increasing loudness.

At last, the bright headlight of the engine bathed the station with brilliance. Harry still gazed at the platform. He saw no one lurking there.

The train came to a stop. Harry saw a young man alight, and recognized the figure of Carter Boswick. He saw Carter pick up a pair of heavy suitcases and start diagonally across the street. He was obviously going to the Junction House.

But Harry, yielding to a hunch, still waited. He saw another man get off the train, with a valise in hand. Harry stared in sudden recognition. He was sure that he had seen the man before—on the limited between New York and Chicago!

HARRY was correct. This man was Stacks Lodi, still on Carter Boswick's trail. Harry saw Stacks light a cigarette, then leisurely follow the course that Carter had taken.

As soon as the second man had entered the hotel, Harry started the motor of his coupé, drove a short way up the street, turned, and pulled up at the door of the Junction House.

Harry carried his own suitcase into the hotel. No bellboy came to receive it. Harry guessed the reason. The place would not have more than two attendants; both were at present employed in showing the previous guests to rooms.

Signing the register, Harry noted two names inscribed there. One was Carter Boswick, in Room 208; the other was Antonio Lodi, in Room 215.

The slouching clerk read Harry's name; then wrote 222 after it. He rang a bell, but nothing occurred for several minutes. Then an unkempt bellboy came shambling down the stairs. The clerk tossed him the key.

After establishing himself in Room 222, Harry donned a pair of soft-soled slippers, and went out into the hallway. He noted a light beneath the door of Room 215, which was near the head of the stairs. He went on to the front of the hall, and spied Room 208. No light showed there. Evidently Carter Boswick had retired.

Starting back, Harry heard a click. He slid to the stairway that led toward the third floor, just as Stacks Lodi came out of Room 215. The man was fully dressed. Harry saw him go downstairs.

Listening at the top, Harry could hear him talking with the clerk. The discussion seemed to concern a good brand of cigar for a discriminating smoker.

The clink of coins indicated that the purchase had been made. Harry heard a remark concerning the coolness of the night. Stacks was praising the fine air of the vicinity. The slam of the front door meant that someone had gone outside.

Harry stole to the front of the hall. He opened a window above a small porch that projected over the sidewalk. This portion of the hall was almost totally dark. Harry slipped noiselessly to the porch and lay flat, peering over the edge.

He could see Stacks Lodi just beneath. The man was holding a cigar in his hand. He raised it to his lips as Harry watched, and drew two long puffs. The cigar gleamed twice. The hand dropped with the cigar; then came up for another puff. Down again, it returned, and this time the smoker puffed five times.

The meaning of those short, bright glows suddenly dawned upon Harry. Stacks Lodi was flashing the number of his own room—a signal to hidden eyes in the outer darkness—across the street, where total blackness reigned!

After a brief pause, a second signal was given. Again, the cigar glowed twice. Down; then up; but this time, there was no increase of the light. On the third trip to the signaler's mouth, the tiny gleam occurred eight times—another slow procession of sustained puffs.

The first signal had been 2-1-5—the number of Stacks Lodi's room; the second had been 2-0-8—the number of Carter Boswick's room. Harry saw Stacks turn and walk back into the lobby. Waiting no longer, Harry crept into the hall and crouched there, expecting Stacks to come up the steps.

As minutes drifted by, Harry suddenly realized the man's plan. Stacks Lodi had given the number of his own room—indicating it as a spot of entrance for men from the dark. He had given Carter Boswick's room to tell them where to go. But he, himself, intended to remain in the lobby, establishing an alibi, no matter what might happen; and also being in a position to deal with the clerk, should such action be necessary!

HARRY returned to his own room. The light was still on. The moment that Harry entered, he stopped just within the door.

The side of the hotel was on a vacant field. If men were out there, they could easily see anyone within these rooms, while the lights were on. Harry recalled that he had been foolish enough to go over by the window when he had first entered. In fact, the window was slightly open now, as he had left it.

That must be corrected at once. Harry reached for the light switch; then his eyes spied an envelope that was lying beside the bed.

Stooping, Harry picked up the object. One corner of the envelope was smashed in. Harry realized that it had been scaled through the open window by someone standing in the outer darkness below. An accurate piece of swift marksmanship had sent this unexpected message here. Harry opened the envelope and drew out a folded note.

Clear blue ink greeted his eyes. The writing was in a code which Harry understood. A message from The Shadow! Harry translated it rapidly:

Bring Carter Boswick into your room. Explain that danger threatens. His place will be taken as soon as he is gone. Wait until after commotion has begun. It will convince him of danger. Drop from window. Your car has been moved to rear of hotel. Escape with Boswick.

As Harry watched, the writing began to disappear, as though an invisible hand were erasing every sentence. Word by word, the entire message faded.

That was the way with letters from The Shadow. If they fell into the wrong hands, the enemy could profit nothing. The ink which The Shadow used asserted its vanishing properties the moment that it came in contact with the air.

Harry turned out the light. He stole to the window; instead of closing it, he opened it wide. He could barely see the ground beneath. He recognized that the drop would be an easy one.

Now to call on Carter Boswick.

A tenseness had come over Harry, and under this influence he failed totally to calculate the time element. He did not realize that this message might have come into his room just after his departure, and that he had been away for many minutes during his observation from the porch outside the hall.

Nor did he know that almost immediately after Stacks Lodi had come back into the lobby, there had been a shadowy motion outside the door of the hotel.

Harry, by his dilatory action, was unwittingly holding back The Shadow's plan. In fact, as Harry crept along the hall, he was thinking too much of what The Shadow might intend to do—and not enough of his own part.

Carter Boswick out of Room 208—The Shadow there in his place! What a surprise that would be for those who might be coming up through the window of Lodi's room, to make an unexpected attack upon a sleeping victim!

This thought was uppermost in Harry Vincent's mind as he tapped at the door of Carter Boswick's room. The response that came gave Harry new assurance. The man within was still awake. His voice, though sleepy, showed that he would be ready to listen to what Harry had to say.

The time was here for Harry's first action in accordance with The Shadow's plan.

CHAPTER XII
THE ALLIANCE

"MR. BOSWICK?"

A prompt reply came to Harry's question.

"Yes," said a voice through the door. "What do you want?"

"I have an important message for you."

A key turned. The door opened. Carter Boswick faced Harry Vincent in the dim light of the hall. Carter was fully dressed, except for coat and vest. He had evidently been taking a short nap. Harry was pleased at this sign of vigilance.

"My name is Vincent," Harry explained. "I must talk with you. My room is down the hall— 222—and it would be wise to go there."

Suspicion showed in Carter Boswick's eyes. Suspicion faded. Harry's countenance was one that showed complete frankness. Carter realized that this unexpected visit must mean that trouble threatened. Harry looked like a friend.

Nodding his willingness to accompany the man who had come for him, Carter Boswick picked up his coat and vest from a chair beside the bed. Harry Vincent pointed to the other articles that could be seen from the hall—hat, overcoat, and two unpacked suitcases. He picked up the luggage while Carter took the hat and coat.

"Hurry along," whispered Harry tensely. For the first time, The Shadow's agent was beginning to realize the amount of time that had been consumed.

Harry preceded Carter along the hall. He noted the door of Room 215 as he passed. He turned to see if his companion was following him. Carter was some fifteen feet behind, just nearing the door of Stacks Lodi's room.

Instantly, Harry discovered an impending menace. During the moment that Harry had passed, the door had opened, unobserved by Carter, who was not watching it. The door had swung inward, and Harry could see the figure of a man crouching just within the darkness.

"Look out!" Harry blurted the warning as the crouching man leaped forward.

Swift action followed. Carter Boswick turned just in time to encounter the attacker. The man's uplifted arm was descending. The striking hand held a blackjack. With an instinctive defense, Carter struck the blow aside, and planted his fist against the side of the fellow's head.

Harry, dropping the suitcases, had simultaneously sprung to the rescue. He arrived just as the attacker tumbled to the floor. He grabbed Carter Boswick's arm, in a quick effort to draw his companion from the danger zone.

It was then that Carter blundered!

HUB ROWLEY and STACKS LODI
Two gangsters who act as the ruffians for the men behind this scheme
to take away rightful millions from
young Boswick.

Forgetting that Harry had given the warning, he thought that he had been led into a trap. He took Harry's present act as an indication of treachery. With an angry cry, he hurled himself upon the man who had befriended him.

AS the two young men struggled, the fellow with the blackjack came to his feet. It was Scully, Stacks Lodi's assistant.

There was no need for silence now. With snarling lips, Scully sounded the cry for a general attack.

Three men, armed with gleaming revolvers, pounced forth from Room 215. Scully, backed against the wall, clutched his blackjack and gave the order for murder.

"Get both of them!" was his snarl. "One is the guy we want. Bump the other one, too!"

These words came just as Harry Vincent managed to wrest himself free from Carter Boswick's grasp. In so doing, Harry had sent Carter spinning across the hall; Harry, in turn, was trying to catch himself against the wall. Both young men found themselves staring into the muzzles of revolvers.

Carter, in his staggering course, had stopped but two feet from where Scully stood. The gangster's hand came up with the blackjack. The beginning of its downward swing was the final signal for cold murder.

Fingers waited on triggers, ready to fire as that blow fell. Scully's action had brought a momentary lull, each villain ready to give their leader the opportunity for the first stroke.

As Scully's wrist poised viciously above his head, a shot sounded from the window at the end of the hall. A bullet skimmed Scully's unkempt hair, and struck the gangster's wrist.

A fiendish cry of rage came from Scully's bloated lips. The blackjack, as though plucked away by a hand from nowhere, snapped out of Scully's fingers, and made a long parabola toward the ceiling. The gangster collapsed, clutching his right wrist with his left hand.

Harry Vincent knew the source of that timely shot. The Shadow must have scaled the pillars at the front of the hotel. Lying on the porch, he had watched Harry's effort to lead Carter Boswick to safety.

Three armed gangsters! What did they matter now? The Shadow was there to pick them off. The cue was to drop out of danger, to give the hidden avenger a clear sweep.

A muffled shot sounded from the lobby below—a sign that Stacks Lodi had taken action there. But Harry Vincent scarcely heard it. He was dropping to the floor, away from the threatening guns, as he cried out to Carter Boswick to follow his example.

Harry's warning was too late. Carter had already sprung to action. He was leaping forward to mill with the armed gangsters.

Harry groaned as he reached in his pocket for his own gun. How could The Shadow save Carter Boswick now?

Carter was wrestling with one of the gunmen, and had the fellow's wrist in an iron clutch. The other gangsters swung to shoot. The grappling men were between them and the window, a protection against The Shadow's fire.

The wrestling pair swerved. Carter Boswick's stooping back caught the eye of the nearer gangster. The man stabbed the muzzle of his gun toward Carter's back, and snarled in elation. But the very situation that gave the would-be killer his opportunity to slay was also the break for which The Shadow had been watching.

A spurt of flame accompanied the roar that came from the window. The gangster sprawled forward, beside the struggling men, the triumphant leer fading from his writhing lips. The other free gunman shouted in rage. Raising his revolver, he blazed uselessly at the open window. There was no response. The Shadow, lying low, had stayed his fire.

With gun in hand, Harry Vincent leaped to his feet and attacked the firing man from behind. He struck a hard blow at the villain's head, but the man turned just in time to ward it off. He hurled Harry to the floor, and jabbed his revolver straight at Harry's forehead.

Harry saw the approaching muzzle. He could see the evil, merciless face behind it. Yellowed teeth were displayed in a loathsome grin.

Then a shot boomed, seemingly from faraway.

A shot sounded from the window … the blackjack snapped out of Scully's fingers …

The revolver flopped from the gangster's fingers. The man's eyes bulged; his lips closed; his body rolled sidewise to the floor.

As Harry's gaze turned, he saw the termination of the fight between Carter Boswick and the one remaining gunman. All through the struggle, Carter had held the advantage until now. But a turn in the fray had enabled the gangster to wrest away. At this instant, his gun hand was free, aiming to kill.

Harry's own revolver was in his hand. He swung it upward to prevent the kill. It was a belated gesture. Harry could never have beaten the gangster to the shot. But The Shadow's unfailing hand still remained in readiness.

The final bullet sped from the window. The gangster received it in the heart. When Harry fired, his shots reached the falling body of a dead man. The Shadow, hidden marksman of the night, had accounted for all the opposition.

HARRY and Carter reached their feet. There was no hesitation now. Carter followed Harry's lead. They hurried down the hall, carrying the suitcases with them. Scully, huddled and moaning on the floor, made no effort to stop them. His shattered wrist had ended his participation in the battle.

No explanations were necessary as Harry guided

Carter through Room 222 and threw a suitcase out the window. Within twenty seconds, Carter's two bags and Harry's single one were gone; Carter dropped out when he heard the order, and Harry followed.

Three minutes later, the two young men were rolling out of Junction City in Harry's coupé. Carter Boswick, tense and half bewildered, was staring at his companion. He realized now the importance of Harry's warning, and knew that he had found a man on whom he could rely.

"Say, old fellow"—Carter's voice was filled with gratitude—"you pulled me out of it tonight. I don't know where we're going, but—"

"We're going to stick together" was Harry's response.

"Right!" agreed Carter, with emphasis. "Say, old man, something tells me that this may just be the beginning. I've got a lot on my mind. I've kept it from everyone, because I didn't know whom I could trust. But you're one hundred percent. You're game enough to chance it with me."

Harry's right hand moved from the steering wheel. Carter caught it in a firm grasp. The two men held a prolonged clasp that betokened mutual confidence. No further words were necessary.

Harry Vincent, in the service of The Shadow, had formed an alliance with Carter Boswick, the man who sought the wealth that was his heritage. From now on, the quest would be theirs together!

CHAPTER XIII
THE MINING CABIN

THE next afternoon found Harry Vincent and Carter Boswick rolling along a narrow, rutted road in Harry's coupé. While Harry carefully guided the car, Carter studied a large map which was unfolded before him.

They were in a wild, unpopulated region. It was doubtful if a car could have been along this almost forgotten road since the beginning of the month. The road was curving upward toward the summit of a small hill. As they neared a clearing, Carter gave the signal to stop.

"This is as close as we can get," he declared. "Why not shove the car off in the clearing, and cut through the trees to that place up there?"

He pointed to a crag-like spot on the side of the hill. It was plain that the slight eminence would serve as an excellent lookout for the terrain below. Without a word, Harry turned the car from the road and stopped it at the fringe of the woods.

It was only a short tramp to the crag. Carter's supposition proved correct. Seated on the rock, he and Harry could observe a considerable extent of wooded ground. The country here was hilly; over

beyond a sloping valley, they saw another rise of ground that was rather low, but, nevertheless, mountainous in appearance.

"Down in there"—Carter was pointing to the valley—"is the probable location. I am sure that I have the latitude and longitude correct, but we may have to do considerable searching to find the exact place meant."

Harry nodded. Carter had explained the entire situation to him. In return, Harry had frankly told Carter that he was the agent of an unknown person who had gained knowledge of certain plans to rob Carter of his heritage.

"I feel positive," continued Carter, "that there must be some distinctive object to guide us—say a big tree—a small lake—a habitation."

"Look over there!" Harry pointed as he spoke. "That is a cabin of some sort, isn't it?"

Carter followed the direction of Harry's gaze. He, too, saw the object. The edge of a roof was barely visible in a large clearing that had been cut away at the base of the opposite hill. Carter turned to Harry with a triumphant smile.

"That's where we're going!" he stated. "Let's go back and get the supplies out of the coupé. Then we can investigate and stay, if it looks good."

AN hour later, the young men arrived at the clearing. They were carrying packs and boxes—items of provision and equipment that they had purchased in a small town that morning.

As they came out of the trees, they spied a fair-sized cabin that appeared to be in good condition, although it bore signs of desertion.

Finding the door unlocked, Harry and Carter entered. The cabin consisted of a single floor. In the center was a large room with a fireplace. There were three small bedrooms off at one side, and a dining room and kitchen at the other. The place was sparsely furnished, even to cots with springs.

In the kitchen, they discovered a stove and a complete array of pots and pans. A calendar was hanging on the wall. Harry pointed it out to Carter. The calendar was five years old.

"Do you think the place can have been deserted that long?" questioned Carter, in a tone of surprise.

"Very probably," said Harry. "The calendar looks like good evidence."

"But the furniture—the utensils?"

"No one touches anything in this country. If any people have been in here, they have taken it for granted that the owners intend to return."

The men went out the back door of the cabin. Across the clearing, they saw a square-shaped opening in the ground—something like the mouth of a large well. Investigating, they discovered a wooden ladder leading down into a deep pit, with stone interior that glimmered in spots.

"A vertical mining shaft," remarked Harry.

"Looks like galena," nodded Carter, pointing to one of the glittering patches.

"I think I've got it," declared Harry. "This is considerable of a mining region around here. The fellows that had this cabin sunk their shaft in hopes of a real strike."

"And then?"

"They probably got wind of a better location, where others were hitting it good. When a rush starts, the first people stand the best chance. Maybe they started out for the Nipigon region, in Canada. Anyway, they took along all that they could carry and never came back."

"It sounds logical."

"It's quite a usual occurrence," Harry stated. "This place has become absolutely useless. The custom of the forest is to use what comes your way, provided you do not injure it. This cabin is ours for the time being."

"There is no doubt in my mind," said Carter slowly, "concerning the importance of this spot. It appears to be the one place that could have been meant in my father's directions. Our search begins here."

"Right here," affirmed Harry, pointing to the shaft. "Who's going down, Carter? You or I?"

"I'll take the job," declared Carter promptly.

WHILE his companion made the descent into the shaft, Harry sat on the edge of the square wooden wall and kept careful watch. All seemed serene in this lonely clearing, but Harry could not avoid the suspicion of possible danger lurking nearby.

Harry, gazing downward at intervals, could see the occasional flash of Carter Boswick's electric torch. Fifteen minutes went by; a head and shoulders came over the side, and Carter rejoined Harry.

"Absolute blank," was Carter's comment. "I searched the shaft all the way down. About thirty feet, as I calculated it. Solid rock, every inch. Ends in a ragged bottom. Let's go back to the cabin."

When they reached the one-story building, Harry proposed a search within. The two men spent an hour going over the floor and walls. Here, as before, they could discover nothing. Harry entered the kitchen and cooked up some coffee. Seated at the old table, the two held council as they drank.

"Here is the whole situation," asserted Carter quietly. "My father was a most unusual man. He apparently had a contempt for wealth, despite the fact that the accumulation of it was his chief endeavor. He was also a stickler for perseverance.

"Somewhere in this locality, he has placed a sum that should be close to ten million dollars.

Naturally, he must have hidden it well—so effectively that chance visitors could find no clue to its location. But to a man in my position—one who knows the wealth is near—one who is willing to search every foot of the ground—the quest should certainly bring success."

"Good reliance on your perseverance," commented Harry.

"Exactly," responded Carter.

"How about your cousin?" questioned Harry. "You told me that the task would have gone to him had he been the heir. Could your father have relied upon his perseverance?"

"With ten million dollars involved?" came back Carter. "I should think anyone would persevere!"

"But if you fail—what of the money then?"

Carter Boswick shrugged his shoulders.

"It will lie where it is," he decided. "That's all. But I intend to find it."

Harry strolled to the window and stared out toward the woods. He studied the terrain of forest, with sloping hill beyond. He felt a sudden consciousness that eyes were watching from amid the trees. He had the same sensation when be crossed the kitchen and gazed from a second window. He said nothing of his suspicion to Carter. Instead, he expressed his willingness to begin the search.

"It's late now," declared Harry. "The time to get started is early in the morning. But be sure of this, Carter. We must stay together at all times. The episode back in the Junction House may be just the beginning."

"We'd better take shifts watching at night," observed Carter. "If other people are engaged in the hunt, they're liable to attack us then."

"Exactly," said Harry. "Well, we're each packing a pair of automatics. We can use them when we need them."

"How about"—Carter paused—"how about—your friend—whoever he is?"

"We're not to count on him," asserted Harry cryptically. "Our job is to work together. We were helped out plenty back at the hotel. We're likely to receive help in the future. But there may be a lot of angles to this that we don't know. Therefore, we have to take the attitude that we are on our own resources."

"You said something about gangsters," remarked Carter. "The fight at the Junction House bore that out. But what puzzles me is how they got into this at the start."

"I have no idea."

"YOU know," pondered Carter, "I made one mistake. I should have checked up on Drew Westling before I left New York. Farland Tracy warned me that my father was very suspicious; that he feared someone was trying to learn where the money was hidden. Prowlers entered the old mansion while father was away.

"Then there's that matter of the stolen message. When Tracy left the house, I may have shown, by my expression, that I had something on my mind. I covered up until after Tracy had gone. But as soon as Headley had closed the door, I was eager to start.

"Drew was in the dining room. He saw the direction that I took. I wanted him to think that I was going upstairs; but I went into the library instead."

"Post mortem won't help," decided Harry abruptly. "All we know is that someone is on your trail. There was a mob in back of it last night, but the crowd has thinned out considerably.

"One fellow—he's the bird who took Room 215—was on the train coming west from New York. He goes under the name of Antonio Lodi. He's still at large. But who he's working for or with is something that we may not know for a while."

"You're right," laughed Carter. "The best thing we can do is stick to our knitting. Maybe they'll leave us alone until after we've found the hiding place. Then—"

Harry nodded as he caught the inference. That might well be the enemy's plan, now that the goal had been neared.

Whatever might transpire, Harry Vincent was sure that a titanic struggle lay ahead. It would take more than himself and Carter Boswick to succeed. Harry realized fully that The Shadow's aid could be the only salvation.

Still by the window, Harry felt a prolonged sensation of uneasiness. Dusk was falling, and it added to the illusion of spying eyes watching from the woods. In an effort to curb his nervousness, Harry suggested dinner.

As Harry and Carter prepared their meal from canned goods, they returned to their original theme. The quest would begin tomorrow. By the next evening success might be theirs. If not, they would keep on.

For somewhere in this locality lay Carter Boswick's heritage. Time and trouble would be no barriers. The quest would not end until success had come.

CHAPTER XIV
FORCES OF CRIME

HARRY VINCENT'S intuitive sense was by no means a poor one. As darkness closed over the forest, a motion in the brush bore out his belief that a concealed observer had been watching the cabin. But Harry was not at hand to detect the presence of the prowler.

Pushing his way through the lower branches of the trees, a man hurried away from the vicinity of the clearing. After a mile of tramping, he struck a side road through the woods, and came to a spot where an old touring car was parked beside the road.

The man clambered into the automobile. He drove away and reached a better road that pointed toward the Wisconsin border. A lonely ride of a dozen miles brought him to an old roadhouse that was just beyond the outskirts of a small town.

The man alighted from this car and entered the building. His face was revealed in the lighted hall. It was Stacks Lodi.

The newcomer spied a man with a bandaged arm, lounging in a room off the hall. It was Scully. The crippled gangster grinned. He used his left hand to indicate a stairway.

"Room right at the top," he said. "He's in there, Stacks. Waiting for you."

Stacks Lodi ascended the stairs, knocked at the door, and opened the portal when he heard the gruff command to enter. He found Hub Rowley seated at a table, a bottle of liquor close at hand.

"Hello, Stacks," growled the big shot. "Have a drink. Tell me what you know."

"I've got Boswick located," said Stacks eagerly. "Him and another guy—"

"Start with the beginning," interrupted Hub impatiently. "I want to know all that happened."

"Didn't Scully tell you?"

"Yes. But I want your story."

"O.K., Hub. Well, when I landed in Junction City, trailing this bird Boswick, the boys were there like I expected. You certainly figured a way to beat Boswick's time, and they picked up the touring car like you suggested.

"I didn't fool around any. Just registered at the Junction House, and went outside to give the cigar signal. I hung around the lobby. Clerk sent the bellhops home. He and I were there alone, and I figured an easy fight upstairs.

"And then everything broke loose. Sounded like artillery fire. The clerk grabbed a gun and started up. So I plugged him. Then I yanked the sheet out of the hotel register, and threw it in the stove. Best thing to do, Hub. Alibis would have been a mess. I didn't know what the finish would be. I clipped the only bird who knew who I was— and who Boswick was, for that matter."

"All right," agreed Hub. "Go on."

"WHEN I got upstairs," continued Stacks, "I found Scully crawling along the hall. The rest of the mob was dead. I didn't lose any time. I dragged Scully along, and he told me where the car was.

"We ran into luck. Scully had stopped at this place on the way in. He knew it was a speakeasy, and a stop-off joint for bimbos running booze in from Canada. The boss took him to some hick sawbones. Said he got shot out hunting.

"That's when I wired you in Chicago—to come on here—like you said. Then, along about noon, I headed out to find the location. You had it picked mighty close. Boswick is there already. I don't know who the other bloke is."

"Are they camping on the ground?" queried Hub.

"No," grinned Stacks. "They're sitting pretty. Found a cabin there. That's why I'm sure they've got the place. I watched them from the woods. They were fooling around what looked like a big well."

"A mine shaft, probably. Did they find anything?"

"Don't think so. Boswick went down the shaft; if he'd been alone, I'd have nailed him then. But the other guy watched. I waited until after they went into the cabin. Then I cut over to the road, where I had parked my car."

"You're sure there's only two of them?"

"That's all."

Hub Rowley was thoughtful. Then, with an angry gesture, he gulped down a glass of liquor and stared coldly at his henchman.

"You know why I'm here?" he questioned.

Stacks shook his head.

"Because," said the big shot, "there's been too much foolishness. This is the third time, Stacks, that you have tried to get one man—Carter Boswick. In every instance, you had men capable of doing the job. They failed."

"I told you why, chief!" Stacks fairly blurted the words. "It wasn't Boswick that stopped them. I found it out on the boat. It was The Shadow!"

"So you say. But I've got to see the proof. First you claim your men tried to get Boswick at some joint in Havana. That may have been a story they cooked up. You can't prove that The Shadow was there. Your story about the boat sounds possible; but you admit that you had liquored up a bit during the card game. Then, last night—you didn't see The Shadow at the Junction House, did you?"

"I was downstairs. Ask Scully—he was up above."

"I questioned him. He said you talked about The Shadow. But he didn't see him. Scully says there was a fellow who helped Boswick out—but it wasn't The Shadow."

"Scully don't know all!" protested Stacks. "He was trying to blackjack Boswick, so he says, and the others were covering Boswick's friend. Then somebody plugs him in the wrist."

"The man with Boswick, probably."

"While he was covered by three rods? That don't sound right, Hub. I figure The Shadow was there, too."

"Maybe you're right," growled Hub Rowley. "Just the same, we're going to get that fellow Boswick. If he has another man with him, we'll pick him off, too. This time, I'll be there myself."

"Just you and me—with Scully?"

"Scully!" Hubs voice was contemptuous. "He's crippled. Say—you are a dumb one at times, Stacks. Do you think I've come here alone? I've got Twister downstairs, and a mob all ready. Brought along a gang from Chicago. They aren't here at this dump; but they're nearby."

"Say, Hub!" Stacks spoke in an admiring tone. "This will be soft. Those eggs are hanging out in that cabin. If you want to blot them out, it will be easy."

"We're blotting them out tonight!"

HUB ROWLEY arose and walked about the room. The big shot was planning. Finally, he turned to Stacks Lodi and delivered his final detail.

"We're starting out at midnight," declared the big shot. "You're going to lead us. Twister and you will boss the mob—under my direction. We'll get that cabin on all sides. I'm waiting now to hear from another man who's interested in this."

Hub paused and studied Stacks thoughtfully. The big shot was recalling the discussion on the night before Stacks left for Chicago. He was trying to remember just how much he had said to Stacks then. At last, Hub decided to go on, but he phrased his words cunningly.

"This is a big lay, Stacks," he said. "I got hold of a man who came out with it and offered to work with me on a split. He needed help on account of Carter Boswick being in the way. Savvy? Well, if we get rid of Boswick, it's clear, but we won't stop now.

"You remember that note that you found under the door of Boswick's house after you got the signal of the blinking light over the front door? That was what I was waiting for. It was swiped from Carter Boswick that night. Well, this fellow that's in the game arranged things so I got it. He's here now—and I'm going to see him tonight.

"He may not go along with us. Maybe he'll hang out at some town near here. At the same time, he may decide to come with me. That's why I'm going in my own car, following the rest of you. This fellow is working with me—on the ground floor. It's his only bet. I'm telling you this, so as you'll know to keep mum. Twister is on the q. t. The Chicago boys don't mean anything."

"All right, Hub," agreed Stacks. "I'm ready. I'll stick downstairs with Scully until I get the word."

Stacks Lodi left the big shot's room and joined

Twister and Scully on the floor below. Shortly afterward, Hub Rowley left the roadhouse. It was nearly midnight when a telephone call came for Stacks Lodi. Hub Rowley was on the wire.

"Tell Twister to get in touch with the mob" were Hub's instructions. "He can drive after them in your car. Line up and wait until I show up in the coupé. That will be the signal to start. Leave Scully there at the joint."

Stacks passed the message to Twister. The big shot's bodyguard sauntered forth. Stacks lounged around with Scully until he heard the noise of cars arriving on the road outside. He went out to find three automobiles in a row, his touring car at the head. Twister's hissing call summoned him.

"You lead the way," said the bodyguard. "Drive the first buggy. I'll run the second. Hold it until Hub gets here."

The lights of a coupé appeared while Twister was speaking. The car drew up in back of the procession. Stacks Lodi clambered into the driver's vacant seat of the touring car up front.

Hub Rowley had arrived; now was the time to start.

FOUR men were in Stacks Lodi's car. The ex-gambler listened to their muffled chatter as he drove ahead. Tough, uncouth mobsters recruited from the badlands of Chicago, these rowdies were a more vicious group than those who had served with Scully last night at the Junction House.

Two more cars—each with its quota of gunmen. These were following now. Stacks Lodi, glancing behind as he took the first curve in the dirt road, could see the other automobiles taking up the trail. Back at the very end, just starting, was Hub Rowley's coupé.

Stacks Lodi had only a momentary glance at the rearmost automobile. Its lights made it nothing more than a dim shape behind two beaming bulbs. Hence Stacks could not possibly have seen what was happening at the rear of that coupé.

Nor did Hub Rowley, at the wheel of his small car, know what was going on in back of him.

Just as the coupé was starting, a tall shape of blackness shot forward from the dark at the side of the road. The light from the road house dimly revealed a swiftly moving splotch upon the ground.

The red taillight of the coupé seemed to blink as a mass of darkness covered it; then the light shone crimson again as a lithe form stretched itself upon the closed rear of the car. Not a jolt—not a sound. Noiseless, a being from the night had come aboard the coupé.

As Hub's car shot forward, the phantom shape remained. A hidden rider, totally invisible upon the back of the last car in the row, was riding forth with the caravan that had set out to deliver a mass attack upon the cabin in the clearing.

Tonight, Hub Rowley had scoffed at the thought of The Shadow being concerned in the enterprise that centered about Carter Boswick's millions. Hub, perhaps, was of the same opinion now; but his derogatory belief did not alter the actual circumstances.

The Shadow, master of darkness, had joined the invaders. He, too, was traveling toward the scene of battle. When the attackers struck, The Shadow would be there!

CHAPTER XV
IN THE CLEARING

"HERE we are."

Stacks Lodi, close beside Hub Rowley, pointed out the cabin from the edge of the clearing. The little building was visible under the pale moonlight. Not a light showed in any of its windows.

Hub Rowley chuckled softly. Stacks Lodi was on one side of him; Twister Edmonds on the other. Behind them, like a ghostly crew, were the mobsters whom they had brought on this excursion.

"All right," growled Hub, in a low tone. "We'll spread here. You take half of the men, Stacks, and cut over to the right. You, with the other half, Twister, over to the left. Never mind the side toward the hill. If they try to get away up there, they'll be easy meat.

"Spread out and come in from two sides. If they make a break toward the center, we'll be able to cut in on them from two directions. Wait a minute"—Hub paused to survey the scene like a general in a campaign—"I'll follow up in back of your crew, Stacks. They're more likely to scoot out the rear door in a pinch, and that's where you're covering. Besides"—there was a touch of sarcasm in the big shot's tone—"I want to see how you handle things, Stacks. Maybe I'll have a chance to help you out this time."

Stacks Lodi made no reply. In a low, smooth voice, he called for half a dozen men, and these members of the mob separated themselves from the rest. Twister took the others.

Hub watched the two corps start out toward their respective posts. Then, with a final chuckle, the big shot glanced about to make sure that all his men had found a place. For a moment, he fancied that he saw a man still lurking in the darkness. His growl died on his lips when he realized that no one was there.

Nevertheless, as Hub trooped after Stacks Lodi's squad, the impression still persisted that he had actually sensed the presence of someone behind him. For a moment, he had a notion to return and investigate, but he decided that it would

As he saw the invaders toppling, Harry sensed the answer. The Shadow!

be useless. He came to the opinion that he must have been deceived by a darkened tree trunk.

HUB ROWLEY had a definite purpose in going with Stacks Lodi's outfit. The big shot intended to direct the advance; not to enter it himself, unless emergency required. He had discussed it briefly with Twister Edmonds, and he knew that his bodyguard would cue the actions of his squad according to those of Stacks Lodi's band.

Hub intended to attack swiftly and effectively. Hence it would be best to start Stacks first, and let Twister act accordingly.

"Ps-s-t!"

Harry's warning hiss awakened Carter in an instant. The young man groped his way toward The Shadow's agent. Harry gave another hiss for silence.

"Just thought I heard something," he whispered. "Listen! Maybe it will begin again."

Carter listened. He gripped Harry's arm.

"There's someone outside the cabin," he said, in a low tone. "I can't figure which side it is."

"Come on," replied Harry. "Crawl to the front door. Open it softly. We'll peek out there, and we can creep around the cabin in opposite directions Whoever it is, we'll find him."

"Maybe it's"—Carter hesitated—"maybe the one who sent you here."

Harry's grunt was negative. Well did Harry know that The Shadow, when he approached a place, moved with velvet silence. He was positive that some prowler had caused the sound, unless a roving animal of the woods might be responsible.

The door opened under Harry's touch. Both men peered out. Lying close to the floor, they had partially emerged, when Harry suddenly clutched Carter's arm with a desperate grip.

"Look there!"

Creeping in from the edge of the clearing were two lines of moving men. In the dim light, their numbers seemed weirdly formidable. Harry and Carter had gained the door just in time to witness the simultaneous advance of Hub Rowley's two squads of gangsters!

Two automatics were in Harry's hands. Carter Boswick was similarly equipped. Safety catches were unlocked. Here, in readiness, the young men held weapons that could repel the invaders. Yet the size of the attack was appalling.

Quick thoughts flashed through Harry's brain. If they fired now, most of their shots would go wide. If they waited, they would be at too close quarters. They would be able to do some damage; but could they resist a charge from those hordes?

HARRY'S hesitation ended. He suddenly saw merit in opening the attack. It was a desperate chance, but it seemed the only one.

"Give them everything we've got!" ordered Harry. "Plug away full speed. With four pistols going, we can make them think they're up against a gang. Catch them while they still have a chance to go back. Then they may scatter!"

"Good," agreed Carter. "I'll take the bunch on the right. Let's go!"

"Shoot!" ordered Harry.

The four automatics barked as the two defenders opened a vicious fire. The repeated flashes from the door of the cabin were followed by loud echoes from the trees.

The result was instantaneous. The rows of men dropped with one accord. Flat on the ground, they began to return the volley.

Stacks Lodi saw his men wavering. One gangster had been clipped, and was groaning on the ground. But Stacks showed a remarkable keenness in the face of this unexpected burst.

"There's only two of them!" he shouted, his voice audible above the barking revolvers of his men. "Give them the works!"

The encouragement rallied the gangsters. It passed to Twister Edmonds' crew. There, two men were down to stay; the others were almost on the point of flight. But the sight of Lodi's mob holding its ground was all that they needed.

The volley from the doorway had ended with the suddenness that had marked its beginning. Harry Vincent's plan had failed. Bullets were zimming against the sides of the cabin. With one accord, Harry and Carter flung themselves back in the big room.

"Reload!" was Harry's command.

Carter groaned as he started to obey. Through the crack of the door, he could see one row of invaders rising.

A mighty shout came from the edges of the clearing. Both Stacks and Twister had figured the trouble; two warriors within the cabin, ammunition spent. A rapid charge was starting from both sides!

Harry could see the attackers through the window. He understood Carter's groan. They were helpless, now that the ruse had failed. The attack seemed destined to end in massacre.

Then, above the shouts of the men rising for the charge, Harry heard the roaring booms of two cannon-like guns. Reload in hand, he stopped in momentary stupor. Those shots were coming from a bulging curve in the clearing, midway between the two advancing lines.

Gangsters began to sprawl upon the rough turf. Terrific bursts of flame, with roaring echoes, signaled the entry of a new contestant. As he saw the invaders toppling, first from one line, then from the other, Harry sensed the answer.

The Shadow!

FROM the projecting stretch of woods, the master of darkness was delivering an enfilade. His well-directed shots were speeding leaden messengers directly along the lines. He was not shooting at individuals; he was aiming into groups of men!

One fighter was succeeding where two had failed. The Shadow had withheld the power of his .45s until his enemies were completely at his mercy. With four automatics, two in hands and two beneath his cloak, he had reserve ammunition sufficient to wipe out the dastardly crew!

The proper type of fire proved Harry Vincent's theory. The advancing gangsters took to spreading flight. Half of them had fallen; the others were rushing away from the hidden menace. Men were sagging as they fled.

Only the mad break for safety saved the mobsters from annihilation. Some who had dropped were dead; others were wounded. But as the remainder became scattered targets, The Shadow's shots lessened in rapidity. A few pitiful enemies reached the woods and plunged into the underbrush.

Hub Rowley, alone, put up a stout effort to foil The Shadow. Back in the edge of the woods, he could see the flashes of The Shadow's guns. The big shot dropped behind a large rock and opened fire toward the bursts of flame. But although he prided himself as a marksman, he could not make a hit.

The Shadow, crouched in the darkness, swaying, moving, turning, was never in the same place twice. Hub was still firing as the few escaping mobsmen plunged to safety; and it was then that The Shadow proved his ability to do what Hub could not.

The flashes burst in Hub's direction. Picking a blind target, The Shadow aimed with amazing precision. Had it not been for the big rock, the first of the bullets would have found its mark.

Large slivers of rock chipped away as The Shadow's bullets smashed against Hub's natural barricade. These death messengers from nowhere clicked their threat of doom. Dropping to the ground, Hub crawled rapidly away through the brush, keeping constantly beyond the rock. He had no desire to wait until The Shadow had moved to deliver a fire from the side.

Seeing The Shadow's shots directed into the woods, Harry and Carter supposed that he was driving off reinforcements. With their reloading finished, they sallied forth across the clearing. A few wild shots came from wounded gangsters in the open area. Seeing this, they covered the men and approached to disarm them.

WITH this work finished, Harry and Carter again turned toward the woods. The Shadow's fire had ceased. They did not know what might have happened. By common decision, both defenders hurried toward the woods. They could hear plunging gangsters in the darkness, and they fired rapid shots to encourage the flight.

"Hold it!" ordered Harry suddenly. "We'd better get over to the side of the cabin by the hill. Maybe there are others up there!"

At the cabin, they separated. Harry swung around one side; Carter took the other. They met on the side toward the hill.

"All clear here," declared Harry. "Come on— we'll go back."

As Harry went around the side of the cabin, Carter turned to follow. Out of the corner of his eye, he caught sight of a man springing suddenly to his feet. He had been close to the cabin wall.

Before Carter could raise his revolver the man was a dozen yards away, dashing toward the hillside. As Carter aimed, the fugitive threw a hunted glance over his shoulder. Carter's finger trembled on his trigger. A wild exclamation came from his lips as his hand dropped to his side.

The cry brought Harry Vincent from the corner of the house. It was a second before Harry caught sight of the running man whom Carter had failed to stop. Impulsively, Harry fired three shots at the fugitive; but the range was too great. The runner kept on like a frightened deer, and gained the upward-sloping woods.

"Why didn't you get him?" demanded Harry.

"I—I couldn't," blurted Carter.

"Where did he come from?" questioned Harry angrily. "When did you see him?"

"He popped up right here," answered Carter. "He had gone a dozen yards before I had a chance to fire."

"But you didn't shoot."

"I—I couldn't. I was going to—then he turned his head, and I saw his face in the moonlight."

"His face? How did that matter? This is no time to worry when you see a face—"

Harry stopped short. Carter Boswick, pale in countenance, was slumped against the wall of the cabin. His gun was almost falling from his hand.

"What's the matter, old top?" asked Harry, in a tone of anxiety. "He didn't get you, did he?"

"No," murmured Carter, in a weak voice. "But I—I nearly got him. I couldn't do it, though, when I saw him. Harry, when I recognized him, I forgot all about enmities. I couldn't—couldn't think of him as being one of the crowd that came to murder us."

"You recognized him?" exclaimed Harry. "Who was he?"

"A man whom I had hoped was on the square," said Carter solemnly. "Harry, that fellow was my cousin, Drew Westling!"

CHAPTER XVI
THE SHADOW ORDERS

IT was several minutes before Carter Boswick had recovered from the shock that had gripped him. The sight of his cousin, here by the cabin, after all others had fled, was something that he could hardly believe. Even though Harry Vincent was anxious to get back to the front of the cabin, he waited for Carter to regain his nerve.

"Brace up, old fellow," pleaded Harry. "I know how you feel. You wouldn't mind shooting down a pack of gunmen face to face—but your cousin, on the run—"

"It's not that alone," responded Carter. "It's bad enough for him to have been in the mess; but to find him lurking, like a snake, ready to strike."

"Maybe he didn't have a chance to get away," smoothed Harry. "He didn't attack you when you came around the cabin."

"Lost his nerve," said Carter gruffly. "That's about the size of it, Harry. I feel steady now. Let's go."

Events had happened during the interim while Carter and Harry had been behind the house. Bodies of dead gangsters remained in view; but the wounded ones had managed to crawl to the cover of the woods.

This perturbed Harry for the moment; then he realized that potshots from that distance would be futile. The mobsmen had been so completely routed that there was no danger of their return.

The two defenders went into the cabin. Carter turned on an oil lamp in the main room. He stopped and pointed to an old table. An object lying upon it had caught his immediate attention.

"Look!" he exclaimed. "Who left that there?"

The object was a large envelope, propped on end against a tin of tobacco. Harry picked it up and opened it. He recognized the clear blue ink and coded writing of The Shadow. Carter stared over Harry's shoulder and gasped as he saw the words begin to disappear.

"What is it?" he questioned.

"A message from my chief," responded Harry quietly. "It tells us what to do."

"You mean from—from whomever it was who opened fire from the woods? Say! Has he been here, too?"

"Apparently. Come on, Carter, let's get going! We'll talk about it on the way to my car."

Packing some of their belongings, Harry and Carter strode out into the clearing. Harry maintained silence while they looked over the field of battle. Five mobsmen lay dead—among them was Twister Edmonds, whom neither knew.

"There must have been more than a dozen of them," remarked Carter. "If we figure five dead, and at least the same number wounded, they were pretty well mopped up."

THE two men reached the woods and advanced cautiously, using a flashlight as a guide. They had brought only essential luggage, so were not heavily burdened. Both were on the alert for hidden enemies.

"Where are we bound?" questioned Carter.

"To Summit Lake," answered Harry. "Town just over the Wisconsin line. Hotel there—that's where we'll stop."

"In these outfits?"

Carter was referring to khaki knickers and leather puttees which both were wearing.

"Why not?" asked Harry. "This is primitive country. They won't refuse to admit us at the Summit Lake Hotel. If we—" He stopped abruptly and skimmed his flashlight in wide circles, revealing a myriad of clustered tree trunks.

"Hear anything?" questioned Carter.

"I thought so," responded Harry. "Move along easy."

He extinguished the light, and the pair went silently forward. The night had clouded, and it was quite dark. After twenty or thirty yards, Harry stopped Carter with a grip, and waited before he again turned on the light.

"Keep listening," said Harry grimly. "Some of that mob may still be around. I thought I heard something moving off in the dark among the trees. I think we're clear now."

"Over the Wisconsin line," mused Carter softly. "That's not far south of here, is it? Say—I didn't think this northern peninsula of Michigan was so far up."

"It's a strip between Wisconsin and Lake Superior," reminded Harry. Then, with a laugh: "We've both been doing a good bit of map reading lately."

Carter's thoughts reverted to Harry's plans. He knew that this trip to Summit Lake must be in response to instructions left by The Shadow. The idea of abandoning the cabin was now becoming distasteful to him. He had a feeling of mistrust, awakened by his chance discovery of Drew Westling. Harry sensed Carter's uneasiness.

"We'll be back," said Harry, in a confidential tone. "It's best to be away. Now that Th—that my chief is here, we'll begin to get results. Leave it to him for the time being, Carter."

"All right," agreed Carter. "We need a change for a day, anyway. That was a tough ordeal tonight."

They reached the spot where they had left the coupé and found the car untouched. Harry took the wheel, and the journey began. Both riders felt an immediate fatigue; but Carter Boswick retained enough initiative to begin a cautious questioning regarding Harry's mysterious chief.

Under the present circumstances, and in accordance with a notation that he had read in The Shadow's message, Harry replied with a more detailed explanation. It was essential that he should retain Carter Boswick's confidence; and with millions at stake, it was natural that Carter should have qualms.

IN brief phrases Harry mentioned the strange part that The Shadow played in the affairs of the underworld. A man who moved by night, a lone wolf arrayed on the side of justice, this weird being could strike terror into the evil hearts of the most hardened crime masters.

The Shadow, Harry stated, was a man of many capabilities. Even as his agent, Harry did not know The Shadow's abode. He had been rescued from hopeless predicaments by The Shadow's intervention. In fact, his acquaintance with The Shadow had begun when he had been snatched from the brink of death by the being whose will he now obeyed.

Harry's words might have sounded fanciful to any but Carter Boswick. But with the recent demonstration still vivid in Carter's mind, there was no doubt of The Shadow's power.

Carter was still mulling over the amazing events and linking them with his remarkable escapes in Havana and aboard the *Southern Star,* when the coupé rolled into the outskirts of Summit Lake.

Harry and Carter not only found the Summit Lake Hotel to be an excellent one; but they also discovered that their garb was an accepted form of attire. Harry and Carter obtained adjoining rooms.

It was after three o'clock, but all-night card sessions were in progress. The two arrivals decided to stroll about a bit before retiring. Their nerves needed quieting after the excitement of this night.

On the veranda of the hotel, they finished a belated pipe smoke, and finally went inside. The period of vigilance had ended, and the change was a welcome relief. This was the very thought that Harry expressed to Carter, who had agreed.

Both were wrong. While they were going up to their rooms, another car was stopping outside the door of the Summit Lake Hotel. A new guest cautiously ascended to the veranda, and peered inside before entering. This newcomer grinned as he inscribed his name upon the register, and noted the signature of Carter Boswick.

For the new guest was none other than Stacks Lodi. He was one of the few who had scurried to safety in time to escape The Shadow's fire. He had been hiding among the trees when Harry Vincent and Carter Boswick had passed. He had heard the reference to the Summit Lake Hotel.

In the woods, Stacks had been afraid to attack two men alone. Here, in a crowded hotel, he was also unable to act. But he had brought himself upon the definite mission of trailing these men whose lives Hub Rowley wanted.

The big shot's mob had been defeated; but strategy might succeed where massed strength had failed. Even with The Shadow as an enemy, Stacks Lodi was willing to play the spy. The man was grinning his evil leer when he went up to the room assigned to him by the clerk.

His part was passive now, Stacks knew; but sooner or later, the men whom he was watching would return to the zone of danger. Tomorrow, he would communicate with Hub at the Michigan roadhouse. From then on, any move by Harry and Carter would be reported to the big shot.

The Shadow's agent and the man whom he protected were still under surveillance by the cunning underling who served as Hub Rowley's spy!

CHAPTER XVII
OUT OF THE SKY

LATE the next afternoon a strange ship of the sky appeared above the forested area north of the Wisconsin-Michigan border. Its flight was leisurely, due to the spinning blades that whirled horizontally above it.

The Shadow's autogiro was flying above the wilderness!

To the sharp eyes that stared downward from the ship, every feature of the terrain was clearly visible. The autogiro settled slowly. Less than a thousand feet from earth, it hovered above one spot.

Directly below was the clearing with the miner's cabin in the center. No bodies were there now. They had been removed at dawn, through a cautious foray directed by Hub Rowley. The big shot had found his men at the cars, and had lain there throughout the night.

All gangsters were gone, however. The Shadow had ascertained that fact. All seemed deserted below. The cabin was silent; the vertical mine shaft yawned, a square hole in the ground. These, however, were not the only objects that The Shadow sought.

In one brief flight, The Shadow was accomplishing something that had not occurred to Carter Boswick—a complete survey of all the territory about the cabin. The autogiro, after a slow hesitation that seemed a halt, turned toward the rising hillside. Beneath it was a structure that Harry Vincent and Carter Boswick had not discovered in their short survey on the ground.

This was a shack, halfway up the hillside. The building was sheltered amid the trees. Another unusual landmark was visible from the air. This was a path, so long forgotten that it could not have been noticed by a person on the ground, but which was slightly apparent from above.

The path began at the edge of the clearing by the hill. It ascended, past the shack, to fade upon the hillside. With strange precision, the autogiro seemed to follow that path until it reached a new angle of vision.

This brought another discovery—one that could not possibly have been made upon the ground. A cracked rock revealed itself in the midst of a thick cluster of trees and dried underbrush. As the autogiro circled, slowly nearing the ground, the meaning of that concealed ledge became apparent.

So artfully hidden that only a thorough and prolonged ground search could have uncovered it, was an opening between the rocks—the entrance to a hidden mine shaft on the hillside!

The tones of a weird laugh mingled with the throbbing of the autogiro's motor. The ship poised, seeking a landing spot.

An ordinary plane would have taken to the clearing, and landed there with difficulty. But this windmill of the air was scornful. It descended with the easy motion of a parachute, and came to rest upon a flat ledge a few hundred yards away from the spot where the rocky opening was located.

The landing was rough. The giro's wheels bumped as they struck irregular stone; but the hand that guided the plane used the utmost skill. The wheel made scarcely more than a single turn. The tilting ship righted itself, and rested in the barren spot like a huge bird come to earth.

THE SHADOW'S aerial inspection had been wisely planned. The conflict that had been waged in the clearing had caused a temporary withdrawal of the opposing forces. With a short interim at hand, the mysterious investigator had utilized air navigation as a method of observation.

Had an ordinary plane been used, its swift flight would have required more circling and interrupted study of the scene. With the hovering autogiro, The Shadow had gained quick results.

The darkening ground made excellent cover for the new progress of The Shadow. A black-clad figure appeared beside the plane. It glided stealthily along the ground, and reached a wooded area.

Feeling his way through the dusk, The Shadow, like a floating phantom, reached the clump of trees that his keen eyes had observed from an altitude of a thousand feet.

A flashlight flickered, and its rays showed the clustered barrier of wooden trunks. The position of the trees; the formation of the rocks; both conspired to completely conceal the opening which The Shadow sought. Even in the brightest light of day, a procession of men could have passed by this spot with no chance of detecting the hidden opening. Only The Shadow's positive knowledge sufficed him now.

The probing light picked a course around jutted points of tree-protected rock. It found a twisting, natural path of stony base. The Shadow's form poised momentarily above an overhanging rock; then sidled to the right, and glided to the ground below. Twisting into a short crevice, The Shadow halted directly in front of a cavernous opening.

The flashlight gleamed distinctly now. It showed a narrow, rock-jutted course that extended at an angle into the hill. The figure in black seemed to hide the light, except for brilliant flickers which occasionally glowed beyond it. Then both light and form were gone, into the recess of the earth!

Silence pervaded the place where The Shadow had disappeared. The moon, rising above the horizon, threw an eerie glow over this hidden scene as the gathering night increased. A motion occurred beyond the clump of trees that guarded the entrance of the cave.

That sound might have been the plunging of some wild animal. At first, there was nothing to indicate the positive presence of a human being. But the constant effort to work a way through the barrier soon betokened the action of a person. Then came pauses while a man breathed heavily.

Had someone, spying from the ground, noted the arrival of The Shadow's autogiro? Had that person, heading toward the spot where the ship had landed, seen tokens of The Shadow's presence through the glow of the probing flashlight?

This seemed the probable case yet the searcher was blind in his efforts. He could not make further discovery. His plowing in the brush became a clamber over jagged rocks.

It was then that his form became momentarily visible in the fringe of moonlight. The second investigator reached one of the overhanging portions of rock that hid the cave.

Here, all search would have ended fruitlessly. Perhaps, by day, the second man might have readily guessed that some important spot was below; but in the moonlight, his cautious, creeping form was heading toward the other side of the rock, away from the important spot.

It was chance that aided this new searcher. As he reached a cluster of saplings, he paused and stretched beneath the trees, listening between heavy breaths.

A glimmer of light had caught the searcher's attention. This glow had come almost from beneath the rock that he had just abandoned. It was like distant lightning, obscured by a heavy cloud—a chance flash that revealed nothing, yet which gave positive evidence of activity.

AS the spying man watched, the light was repeated. Then the flicker came for a third time, and its glow gave the momentary sign of a blackened shape that was emerging from the rock.

That, however, was the last betraying signal. Had the spying man tried, he could not have gained an advantage over The Shadow. For the moment that the outside had been reached, the master of darkness extinguished his light completely, and became a being of seeming nothingness.

The watcher waited. He listened for something to indicate where the arrival from the cavern had gone. No clue came. The Shadow, creeping through the blackness of the half-buried rock, was returning over his corkscrew course with the utmost skill. That being of blackness could feel his way over ground once established. The Shadow's caution was supreme.

Long, tense minutes passed. The man who watched was breathing heavily. Lying still, he gave sounds that could reveal him to listening ears; but The Shadow, with silent motion, had faded into nothingness.

At last, after twenty minutes, the spy became impatient. He had seen no new trace of the light; he inferred that the person below had gone away through the darkness.

It was then that the watcher moved. He emerged from trees into moonlight, and cautiously urged his way toward the side of the rock. His own flashlight glimmered, focused on the ground. Step by step, it revealed a rocky path; and after short difficulties, the new searcher found himself before the opening in the ground.

A muffled gasp of elation came from the man's lips. Probing cautiously into the gap, he used his light as a guide, and entered. Sure that the stranger of the night had departed, he could not resist the desire to conduct an investigation of his own.

After the second searcher had disappeared a new phenomenon took place. Silent motion occurred among the saplings where the spy had lain.

A soft laugh came from hidden lips as the form of The Shadow rose into the fringe of moonlight. Keen eyes glistened from beneath the brim of a slouch hat. The folds of a black cloak hung shroudlike from The Shadow's shoulders.

Coming softly through the blackness, The Shadow had sensed the presence of the spy. He had waited, a creature of invisibility. It had become his turn to watch.

More minutes elapsed. The Shadow, aware of every action that the spy had taken, was waiting for the man's return. The patience was rewarded. A glimmering ray of light announced that the second prober was returning.

At last his figure became plain as he emerged from the cavern and picked his way, by lighted steps, back up the rock. When the man reached the saplings, The Shadow was no longer there. Flat upon a ledge of overhanging rock, the being of darkness lay invisible.

The second searcher nervously made his course off through the trees. Intermittent flashes showed the route that he was taking. All during that passage a figure stalked close behind his heels. The Shadow was following him to his destination.

This proved to be the shack which The Shadow had observed from the air. Not far from the cavern, it formed a hidden abode among the trees.

The man's business there was brief but active. In the dim glow of an oil lamp, he gathered together various articles of food, blankets, tools. Bundling these, he extinguished the lamp and took it also. Then he emerged from the shack, and went back toward the hidden cavern, using his intermittent flashlight to guide the way.

Through the window of the shack, The Shadow's probing eyes had seen all. Now, once again, The Shadow was following the unwitting man who believed that he had gone. Observed had become observer. That was The Shadow's way.

WHILE the man laboriously lowered his burden from a ledge of rock, The Shadow's eyes still watched. When the man had finally reached the entrance to the cavern, the one who peered from darkness still remained unseen. At last, the flickering of a flashlight proved that the man from the shack had entered the cavern to stay.

The Shadow had learned the man's purpose. The cave which he had discovered and probed would be his abode.

A low, sinister laugh sounded through the moonlit night. The Shadow, too, had probed that cavern. He knew and understood the purpose which had guided the man there.

For The Shadow, keenly watchful, had seen the face of the man who had entered the cave. He had divined the fellow's purpose. Well had The Shadow studied the motives and cross-purposes that were rampant in this vicinity, where crime and death had come.

New action lay ahead. The Shadow's weird laugh betokened the activity of his mighty brain. The way to wealth had been discovered. It could be laid open to Carter Boswick now.

The Shadow's aerial visit had been made with the purpose of nullifying crime. Its successful result had proven to The Shadow's liking. The presence of the watching man from the shack had proven an unexpected factor. But The Shadow included even this in his calculations.

A moving form of obscure proportions flitted through the trees. The figure stopped beside the autogiro, and noiselessly stepped aboard. The motor purred with rhythm. No ears could hear it now. The one man in this locality had buried himself beneath the earth.

The blades above the ship were whirling. The autogiro moved forward. Its wheel lumbered across a smooth extent of rock, headed directly for dangerous, jagged points beyond the flat ledge. Before the wheels reached those menacing barriers of stone, the autogiro was in the air. Its flight was tending upward. It cleared the fringe of trees, and rose perfectly into the moonlight.

The ascent reached the vertical. The Shadow's ship hovered over the moon-bathed scene. The opening of the cavern was almost invisible now. The little shack, however, showed plainly among the trees. The cabin and the gaping hole of the vertical mine shaft were evident in the clearing.

Out of the air had The Shadow come. Into the air he had gone. He had learned the secret guarded by Houston Boswick; he had also witnessed another make the same discovery.

The plane headed rapidly southward. The Shadow had another brief mission on this night.

The loud eerie laugh that mingled with the whirring of the autogiro was the only sound that betokened The Shadow's purpose. That mockery, somehow, seemed to indicate that The Shadow's departure was only temporary. Soon he would return to this spot in the wilderness.

What then? What would be the outcome?

Would Carter Boswick and Harry Vincent find the long-sought wealth awaiting them? How did the man who had entered the cavern figure in the plot? What action would come from Hub Rowley and the unknown man who was working with him?

All depended upon circumstance; yet the guiding forces were the purposes of those who figured in this strange drama. The unraveling of twisted threads was necessary to view the future in an understanding way.

The Shadow, alone, had made such progress. Whether the future would result in complications, one positive result must be forthcoming; and could be, after The Shadow made his return.

The Shadow knew!

CHAPTER XVIII
THE SHADOW'S CHART

HARRY VINCENT awoke with a start. The dim light of dawn was hazy through the window of his hotel room. Everything seemed dim and obscure. Sitting up in bed, Harry stared about the room. Had he been dreaming? Or had he heard his name whispered weirdly in his ear?

There was no sign of anyone in the room. It would have been quite possible for a person to have entered, whispered that name, and then left while Harry was coming to consciousness. The door was closed, however, and Harry had not heard the slightest sound from that direction.

Two factors made Harry positive that he had been awakened by someone from outside. The first was that Harry seldom dreamed; the second, that he was constantly expecting some token from The Shadow. Under the circumstances, he decided to investigate.

He turned on a lamp that rested on the table beside his bed. The light revealed an envelope lying beneath it. Harry knew then that he had not been the victim of imagination. The Shadow had come into this room at the Summit Lake Hotel, and had left a message for him.

The envelope contained a note, brief and explicit in its directions. The coded writing faded.

But the envelope also held another sheet of paper—one inscribed in black ink, which did not disappear. Harry found himself staring at the detail of a well-formed chart—an exact map of the vicinity where he and Carter Boswick had found the abandoned mining cabin.

Without further ado, Harry carried the chart into Carter's room, and awakened his friend. They turned on another light, and examined the map together. A cry of elation came from Carter as he noted two cross lines, labeled, each in turn:

Lat. 46° 18' N.
Long. 88° 12' W.

The mining cabin was located a short distance from where the lines crossed. From the cabin, a lightly dotted course extended up the hillside. It showed the exact location of the cavern which The Shadow had discovered.

Harry found another portion of the map, and traced his own course, leading from the distant road where they had parked the coupé, directly to the indicated spot upon the hill.

"My directions," said Harry, in a low voice, "are to the spot on the hillside, avoiding the cabin if possible. We can do that without difficulty. If our enemies decide to return and watch the cabin, they will be guarding an empty bag."

"Great!" agreed Carter. "But what about this place on the hill?"

"The message stated that we will find a trail blazed for us. Tiny marks hewed in the trees and on the rocks, beginning from the barrier of woods marked near the entrance."

"Good," commented Carter. "Say, Harry, it looks as though we are getting somewhere."

"Sh-h!" Harry raised his hand in sudden warning. He arose and started toward his own room, Carter following. Harry crept to the door that led to the hall, and listened.

"What's up?" questioned Carter.

"Thought I heard someone in the hall," answered Harry.

THE two listened tensely. Whatever sound Harry had heard was ended now. But Harry's suspicion was not groundless. Someone had actually tried the door of the room, and had inadvertently made a noise. The same man was trying the door of Carter Boswick's room at present—this time with success.

While Harry and Carter were at the door of the one room, the door of the other opened softly, and

Stacks Lodi entered. Stationed across the hall from Harry's room, he had seen, through his own transom, the sudden gleam of light from Harry's.

In Carter Boswick's room, Stacks Lodi spied an object lying on the table. It was The Shadow's chart. The man stepped softly forward and reached to take it; then paused and studied the map. His eyes saw the dotted line running from the cabin to the spot on the hillside.

Stacks Lodi grinned. Hearing a sound from the adjoining room, he hastened softly to the hall. The door closed behind him just as Harry and Carter entered.

"Guess there's no one there," observed Carter. "You say the marks will lead us from the trees—"

"Sh-h!" warned Harry.

He closed the transom over Carter's door. He picked up the chart and folded it.

"We will start this afternoon," explained Harry. "We can reach the place at dusk. There will be enough light to guide us; but the darkness will enable us to work unseen."

After a final study of the chart, in which Carter, as well as Harry, memorized the details, Harry tore up the paper and burned it with a match flame. He crumpled the ashes in a little tray, and threw them from the window.

"We've got all day to wait," mused Carter. "Just the same, it's best. We might as well drive out at noon, Harry, and circle around until we get where we're going. You can't tell—someone may be spying on us here."

Harry nodded thoughtfully. The noise that he had fancied at his door might mean the presence of a hidden foe. He resolved that it would be wise to head south in the coupé, and then turn back; but he decided that it would not be necessary to leave as early as noon.

THE morning developed drearily, and Harry and Carter lounged about in the hotel. They could sense no menace, and they were mentally at ease.

They had no suspicion that this very hotel was harboring a dangerous villain from the enemy's camp. They did not know that Stacks Lodi had already called Hub Rowley at the Michigan roadhouse, to give the big shot an inkling of their plans.

Hence, at two o'clock in the afternoon, when the two companions took to Harry's coupé they had no knowledge that they were being watched by shrewd eyes that stared from an upstairs window of a hotel room. Stacks Lodi, an evil chuckle on his lips, saw the coupé start along the road that led southward into Wisconsin.

"Trying to fool anyone that's watching, eh?" thought Stacks. "Well, they've missed their guess this time!"

Fifteen minutes later, the ex-gambler who served as Hub Rowley's underling was driving away in his own car, heading toward the border of Michigan.

Meanwhile, Harry and Carter continued their routine ruse, which they had adopted merely as a precaution. They changed their course, drove back into Michigan, and found a roundabout way that led them to the hilly dirt road.

It was late afternoon when they parked the coupe at its former spot. They went to the rocky eminence, and viewed the land below. Harry pointed out a course that missed the cabin by several hundred yards.

"That's our layout," he declared. "It's getting gloomy now, Carter. What do you say we start?"

"Approved," responded Carter.

Five minutes later, the two men were pushing their way through the darkening forest. Away from all clearings, they had nothing to fear. Both felt elated, sure that their progress would be uninterrupted.

A half hour of tramping brought them to the hillside. Harry's first object was to locate the shack that had been marked on The Shadow's chart. It was nearly dark when they found the place.

"Pretty well hidden, isn't it?" questioned Harry, peering into the door of the empty building.

"Yes." agreed Carter. "Too bad we didn't have a day to look around up here. This would have been a better place to stay than the cabin."

"Yes," admitted Harry, "it would have been—if we had been on our own. But with The Shadow watching—well, we have considerably less enemies to deal with now if we encounter them!"

From the shack, they found the cluster of trees. On the base of one, Harry, with the aid of a flashlight, found a round mark, evidently of recent cut. The trail led to the right. Blackened spots upon the rock conducted them farther.

"We're getting there now." remarked Harry.

Carter Boswick smiled. He felt that he was nearing the end of his quest. He knew that Harry Vincent shared his enthusiasm. Neither man thought of any danger that might lie ahead. Even less, did they consider a menace from behind.

They did not know that Stacks Lodi, too, had found The Shadow's chart. Little did they realize that a crew of desperate foemen was approaching near at hand, and that soon their trails would meet!

CHAPTER XIX
MEN OF CRIME

DOWN in the woods beyond the mining-cabin clearing, a crew of evil ruffians was lurking in readiness. Grim faces were hidden in the gloom as Stacks Lodi, at Hub Rowley's request, explained the situation that lay ahead.

"We don't have to go across the clearing," declared Stacks, in a cautious tone. "We can slide around it, and I'll pick up the trail on the other side. There's a shack up the hill, and when we get to it, I can find the trees we want.

"I got that map straight, Hub. It was nice and plain—all fixed easy to remember. There's a place that was marked 'cave' just beyond the trees. Maybe it would be tough to find; but I heard this boob Boswick say something about marks that would lead them to the entrance. If they can find them—so can we."

As Stacks Lodi paused, Hub Rowley held a muffled conference with a man who stood beside him. Stacks had not seen Hub's companion. It had been Lodi's duty to bring a squad of new gangsters in one touring car. Hub had come with two other men in his coupé.

Stacks had inferred that reinforcements had been brought from Chicago. All told, there were nearly fifteen men here tonight. It was as large a crew as on the previous incursion; but then, the fight had been in the open. Tonight, it would be a question of trapping unsuspecting victims at close quarters.

"All right," growled Hub. "You lead the way, Stacks. Keep together, gang. There was a snooper in with us the other night. Nothing like that's going to happen again. I'll give the orders as we go along."

The men moved quietly among the trees. With the moonlit clearing as a guide, Stacks led the way around the fringe of woods. After the process of circumnavigation, he stopped as he neared the sloping hillside. Turning away from the clearing, Stacks led the way upward.

It was quite dark under the trees, and Stacks was forced to conduct the crowd by a zigzag course in order to make sure of finding the cabin. The contour of the hill was helpful. Stacks knew that he was keeping close to the dotted line that had showed upon The Shadow's chart.

TONIGHT'S plans had been made immediately after Stacks had reached Hub Rowley at the roadhouse. The big shot had decided to wait long enough for Carter Boswick and Harry Vincent to reach their destination. Furthermore, he had found it necessary to attend to important details before setting forth.

At present, Stacks Lodi had only one apprehension—namely, that he might fail to discover the end of the trail as quickly as Hub Rowley had expected.

Stacks worried as he trudged along until the glare of his flashlight suddenly revealed the side of the old cabin. At Hub's growled bidding, a pair of gangsters leaped forward and entered the building. They reported that it was deserted.

Changing his direction, Stacks Lodi soon located the clump of trees. Here, running his flashlight low, he discovered the same mark that Harry Vincent had found. It was the beginning of The Shadow's guiding trail.

Stacks pointed out the mark to Hub Rowley. He found other marks farther on. Soon the entire band was following the circuitous course over the rocks.

Clambering down the corkscrew twists, they neared that strange spot which The Shadow had seen from the air—where The Shadow had come and left, only to have his presence noted by a man in the darkness, whom, in turn, The Shadow had tracked.

First The Shadow had found this place. Then a second man. After that, Harry Vincent and Carter Boswick. Now, as a final touch, Hub Rowley, accompanied by strangers whom Stacks Lodi had not seen in the light, was here with his evil crew!

There was no indication that anyone had passed this way within the last half hour. Hub Rowley growled for silence.

"We've given those bozos time to get here," declared the big shot, as he viewed the crack between the rocks, which Stacks Lodi's flashlight showed. "Maybe they're here—maybe they aren't. So we'll find out—and be ready for them either way.

"When we get inside, I want two men to stay at the first good spot to lay. If our birds come in, close on them and give them the works. Meanwhile, the rest of us will go ahead—and if those bozos are already in, we'll have them trapped like rats."

Having finished these instructions, Hub turned to the man beside him and asked a question. After the response, Hub ordered Stacks to extinguish the flashlight. The mobsters, spread out among the rocks, waited in silence and darkness while Hub Rowley conferred with his companion.

It was evident that the big shot respected this man's advice. Stacks Lodi remembered the talk of another person involved in Hub's scheme of crime.

Stacks grinned to himself as he realized that much must be at stake tonight. He realized that only he and Twister Edmonds had possessed a considerable insight of the work that was brewing.

As favored underlings, Stacks had figured that he and Twister would come in for a good share of the proceeds from this enterprise. Twister was dead, slain in the battle at the cabin. Stacks Lodi had no regrets. Twister's death made him the only favored henchman.

Stacks could figure a very definite reason for the present delay. Now that they had reached the entrance to the cavern, there was no need for haste.

If the men whom they sought had already entered, they were trapped for now. If they had not arrived, they would reveal themselves when they came, because of the difficult corkscrew path that they would have to follow.

At last the break arrived. Hub Rowley had finished his conference with his companion. Stacks noted that the second of Hub's unknown friends was silent, merely serving as a henchman to the mystery man whose advice had been sought by the big shot.

Two had come with Hub; five with Stacks. That made a total of nine men altogether—a powerful squad to deal with two victims. Yet Stacks Lodi could not repress a momentary shudder. Here, in the dark, his mind was reverting to The Shadow.

In Havana—aboard the *Southern Star*—at the Junction House—by the cabin in the clearing. Each time, a mysterious being had come from nothingness to break down the plans of those who had sought Carter Boswick's life.

Would such intervention occur again tonight? Stacks hoped not. He felt that he could rely on Hub Rowley to deal with The Shadow, should the menace appear.

Then came the command for action. Hub Rowley's growl ordered Stacks to enter the break between the rocks; and to save his flashlight until he had moved well in from the opening. Stacks responded without delay.

Probing his way, he moved into the crevice. After twenty feet, he turned on his torch. The light revealed a twisting, natural course through broken rock.

Stacks Lodi was leading the murderous squad along the path that Harry Vincent and Carter Boswick had so recently taken. The trap was closing. Men of crime were here to deliver death!

CHAPTER XX
THE HIDDEN MINE

WHILE Stacks Lodi was conducting Hub Rowley and the mobsters along the wooded hillside, Harry Vincent and Carter Boswick had been making progress through the strange cavern which they had entered. A narrow, winding course through broken, rocky walls had led them on a tortuous descent of more than a hundred yards.

Progress had been slow. The roughness of the passage had delayed them; moreover, The Shadow's instructions had named nothing beyond the entrance. Therefore, both were alert, watching for any sign that might indicate the purpose of this odd corridor beneath the hill.

Harry's flashlight suddenly revealed an opening ahead. The beams glittered against the rocky wall of a man-hewn passage into which this natural channel entered. They stopped to find themselves coming into the side of a sloping mine shaft that ran at right angles to the course which they had followed to this point.

Side by side, the two men paused. Harry let his flashlight swing back and forth. The shaft which they had encountered was nearly eight feet in height, and almost the same in width. It sloped slightly downward to the left.

Harry's light glittered upon rusty rails that had been installed for the running of ore cars.

"Look what we've struck!" exclaimed Harry. "This shaft must be a couple of hundred yards in length!"

"No wonder they gave up the vertical shaft down by the cabin," asserted Carter. "It must have been more or less of an experiment."

"Certainly," responded Harry. "This rocky hill was a better bet. They sure gave it a trial after they abandoned the pit in the clearing."

"Looks like they may have been getting results," observed Carter. "See the sparkle on the wall over there? It's mineral ore, all right—"

"Nothing more than a promise," interposed Harry, with a shake of his head. "They were carving right into the center of the hill, looking for a worthwhile strike. They probably failed to get the results they wanted. Otherwise they wouldn't have abandoned this shaft."

"Say"—Carter Boswick's tone was puzzled—"where does this shaft begin? There wasn't any sign of it on the hill."

"We can find that out later," laughed Harry. "But it isn't any mystery to me, Carter. The excavators—or some who came here later—must have blocked the entrance, probably with a big lot of rocks and plenty of turf."

"Why?"

"One reason might be to keep the shaft for themselves. But I hardly think that is it. They still had the claim, I suppose. No, Carter, I can see a better reason—particularly for this shaft, with the natural entrance through which we have come."

"What is it?"

"Someone—in all probability your father—may have obtained possession of this old mine, and realized its possibilities as a hiding place for one who might choose to use it as such."

"You've hit it, Harry! With the entrance of the shaft blocked, no one could discover it unless they had some clew to this narrow side passage which we have just used. Remember how I said I'd search every foot of land before I'd give up? We'd have found this place eventually."

"I think we would. But now that we're in the main alley, it would be a good idea to go on."

Carter Boswick chuckled. He was positive that the end of the quest was within immediate reach. This sloping shaft could not be of any great length. He was more eager than Harry. Without further delay, he pushed into the shaft and urged his companion on.

THE downward course was the natural way to go. Harry and Carter trudged along the narrow-gauge track, the beam of the flashlight showing the way ahead. They had not traveled more than fifty feet before the presence of a blocking wall became detectable ahead. Either the shaft ended there or turned, Harry remarked.

As the men approached more closely, they saw that the wall marked the division of the shaft into two separate corridors: one to the left, the other to the right. The tracks ended at that point.

"Hold up a minute, Carter," said Harry. "We've got to pick our way, from here on. Evidently these fellows tried to turn, hoping to strike a good supply of ore. When their first effort failed, they went the other way."

They were at the end of the main shaft. The side corridors were like the bar on a letter T. Both ways were practically level; there appeared no choice.

Harry, in his deliberation, first turned the flash back up the main shaft. Its rays faded amid the long corridor. Then he illuminated the path to the left, to reveal a blocking wall about thirty feet distant.

Harry noted what appeared to be an opening in the floor of the side passage, at the barring wall.

"Try the other direction," suggested Carter.

Harry responded.

The same situation revealed itself. Thirty feet of passage; then a wall with glittering streaks. Beneath it, the edge of a gaping hole.

"When the turns didn't work, they must have excavated straight down," remarked Harry. "This mine must have been a heartbreaker. No wonder the others called it quits."

"Come on," urged Carter eagerly. "We're not calling quits. I'll bet there's something in this place besides galena or whatever that glittering stuff is. Strike out to the left, Harry."

They made their way along the passage which Carter had indicated. Here, the floor was rough, in contrast to the finished surface along which the track had been laid.

The investigators stopped when they came to the hole. Harry's conjecture proved correct. It was a vertical shaft, round and jagged, some thirty feet in depth.

"Nothing down there," observed Harry, as he turned the flashlight toward the bottom.

"Doesn't look that way," responded Carter, peering over the edge. "Let's try the other corridor. We can come back here later."

They turned and made their way to the dividing point. Both were tense. Harry began to feel an impending sense of danger within these depths. There was a sinister, spectral atmosphere in this forgotten mine. Carter Boswick sensed it, also.

"Creepy, isn't it?" he questioned, with a slight laugh.

"Come on," returned Harry. "We've got to take a look down this other corridor. It may be the finish."

"The finish?" repeated Carter solemnly. "That doesn't sound so good, Harry. Let's say it may be the beginning. If—"

He did not end the sentence. At that precise moment, the unexpected occurred. The investigators were almost at the end of the right passage—the hole which they were seeking was no more than a dozen feet away.

But as Carter Boswick spoke, there was a click from the hole beyond. The brilliant rays of an electric lantern filled the corridor, outshining Harry's light.

Caught in this sudden illumination, Harry and Carter stopped flat-footed, as a voice called out an order. The echoes of its threatening tone were hollow within that rocky vault.

"Stop where you are!" came the cry. "One step more, and you die! I've got you covered. Up with your hands!"

CARTER and Harry obeyed instinctively. The flashlight fell from Harry's grasp. Caught totally unaware, with their automatics in their pockets, instead of in their hands, both men were at the mercy of the one who had challenged them.

A nervous, frenzied laugh sounded from the hole ahead. Then, from the pit, emerged the head and shoulders of a man, a revolver sparkling in the light as it pointed forward from the extended hand that held it.

Into the illumination came the challenger; a white-faced individual who half raised himself from the hole. The man's revolver wavered, as though in an inexperienced hand; yet its muzzle formed a constant covering that was too dangerous to resist.

Harry Vincent clenched his upraised fists. He was angry to realize that he had led Carter Boswick into such a trap as this. He threw a sidelong glance at his companion. He was amazed to note that Carter's face was twitching with a sudden fury.

The reason came an instant later. Carter

Boswick had recognized the man whose hand had balked them. His voice, low and harsh, poured forth its imprecations.

"Drew Westling!" Carter was contemptuous as he pronounced his cousin's name. "Drew Westling! You double-crosser! I knew you were in this dirty game!"

CHAPTER XXI
THE ENEMY REVEALED

DREW WESTLING'S hand trembled as Carter Boswick spoke. The heir's cousin was resting on the brink of the pit from which he had come, blinking nervously at the men whom he had balked. His face was pale at the edge of the light; his eyes seemed bewildered.

"Go ahead!" growled Carter. "Shoot us, you snake! That's what you're here for!"

For the first time, Drew Westling seemed to recognize the voice that he heard. He still held the gun in his shaking hand but when he spoke, his tone was no longer one of menace.

"Carter!" he exclaimed. "Carter! It can't be you!"

Carter Boswick's gruff laugh and words of growled animosity left no doubt as to his identity. Drew Westling rubbed his free hand across a perspiring forehead.

"Carter!" Drew's voice was nervous. "Carter! I—I thought—you had gone!"

With that, the challenger sank exhausted at the edge of the pit. The revolver clattered from his hand. Carter Boswick, with an exultant cry of triumph, began to leap forward. Harry Vincent gripped him by the arm.

"Easy, old man!" Harry exclaimed. "Hold back! He's all right. Can't you see he's not your enemy? He's ready to drop from sheer exhaustion!"

Harry's words were restraining. Their truth was evident. Drew Wresting had stretched on the rough floor of the corridor. His breath was coming in long gasps. Carter Boswick's attitude changed instantly.

"Drew!" he exclaimed, in a kindly tone. "What's the matter, old man? Tell me—how did you get here?"

Carter was at his cousin's side. He was clasping the hand that Drew weakly proffered. Harry Vincent arrived beside the pair. Both he and Carter could see that Westling's face was deathly pale. They propped the frail young man against the side of the corridor. Drew Westling smiled weakly.

"Guess it's all"—he paused to draw a breath—"it's all—been—too much of a strain for me. Thinking—you had gone. Trying to do it—all alone—"

"Tell us about it," suggested Carter.

Drew pointed to the pit. Harry turned his own flashlight downward. The glow revealed a large flat slab at the bottom of a five-foot pit.

THE edges of the slab had been mortared to the rock. Tools lay upon it. Drew Westling had been working to pry the slab loose.

"It's yours, Carter!" gasped Drew. "Whatever is under there belongs to you. I came here—not to get it for myself—I came to get it—for you."

"I thought you were with the gang," said Carter, in a tone of remorse. "Steady, Drew. There's a lot I've got to know. Why didn't you tell me before?"

"I've got to explain, Carter," declared Drew, becoming suddenly calm. "Maybe I should have told you before; but I was afraid you wouldn't understand. I came here to help you, Carter, because I knew there was danger."

"Go on."

"You found the note, didn't you?"

"You mean the directions—latitude and longitude? Yes, I found it—but it was stolen. What do you know about it?"

"Stolen?"

"Yes. Right after I found it. I went to the library when Farland Tracy left the house, my first night home. I thought maybe you had taken it, Drew."

The pale young man shook his head. He moistened his lips and stared squarely into Carter's eyes.

"Let me tell you the beginning," he said. "I'll be brief. There's work to do. But we had better understand."

Carter nodded.

"Uncle Houston did not trust me," declared Drew Westling. "I knew it for a long while. He did not approve of my way of living. Sometimes he became so enraged at me that I wondered if he might be losing his mind.

"He talked about his estate—that it would go to you, if alive; otherwise to me. But he minimized his wealth—so outrageously that I could not believe him.

"One night, some months ago, he went into the library. He slammed the door behind him, and came out a short while later. He went upstairs, and I went into the library myself. I was a trifle apprehensive, Carter. I wondered what he had been doing.

"He had been talking about you as his heir; and the thoughts of old times impelled me to take down that old copy of Dumas. Running through its pages, I came across an envelope. I fingered the flap, and it opened. It had just been sealed. The glue was not quite dry.

"I knew that Uncle Houston had left it there. That must have been his purpose in the library. I opened the envelope and found the message. Latitude and longitude. I wondered what queer quirk had made him put the message there."

Drew paused reflectively; then, noting Carter's intense interest, proceeded.

"I came here for a few days last summer" continued Drew. "I couldn't understand why Uncle Houston had left a message naming this locality. I couldn't find a clue here. But later, when Farland Tracy called at the house, I heard Uncle Houston say something about money that no one could find.

"That was just before he took his trip to Florida. When he returned, he claimed that someone must have entered the house during his absence. He was very angry. He summoned Tracy.

"That night, I listened outside the door of the study. It was then that I heard him speak of hidden wealth; in a place that only his heir could find, because he would leave a clue for either you or me.

"Then I understood. The message in the Dumas book! How easy it would be for him to leave some word that would guide either of us to it! The night you came home, I was afraid you might not learn. That was why I brought up the subject at the dinner table.

"But as soon as Tracy left—I figured he had brought you a letter of some sort—I saw you start for the stairs, and I imagined that you were going to the library instead. You seemed worried that night. I felt sure that you had found the message. The next morning, you announced a trip to Europe. I was positive that you would come here instead."

"Why didn't you tell me so?" demanded Carter.

"Because I feared that you would not understand," answered Drew. "I owed money for gambling debts—my own fault—and Tracy knew about it. I was afraid that he had mentioned the matter to you. I couldn't forget that I would have been the heir if you had not returned. I didn't want your money, Carter.

"But to admit that I had pried into your father's secret; to try to get in on a search for wealth that might perhaps have come to me; to bring up a matter concerning which you had preserved absolute silence—"

"I understand now," nodded Carter thoughtfully. "I understand now, because I know I would not have understood then."

"Besides that," added Drew, "I feared for you. I knew that someone—somehow—had learned of this hidden wealth. It might have looked as though I had squealed—if you came here and ran into trouble—"

"So you came here alone?" interrupted Carter.

"Yes," admitted Drew. "I knew of the shack on the hill. I came here, to watch—to try to protect you. I saw you and your companion come to the cabin. That night, I crawled down to investigate. I was just outside the cabin—"

"That's what I heard," interposed Harry, nodding as he turned to Carter Boswick.

"—outside the cabin," went on Drew, in a monotone, "when the firing began. I laid low. When you two came around, I didn't know who you were at first. I didn't know until I ran, Carter. I saw you were ready to shoot. I kept on, hoping that you would not recognize me. I was afraid you would not understand my motive, my being there at that time."

"I didn't," said Carter grimly.

"So I stayed in the shack," explained Drew. "I waited there, hoping you were safe, afraid that the others would come to search if you did not return. Last night, an autogiro landed near this spot. I saw a light flickering among the trees. It came out of the cave on the hill.

"After the person with the light was gone, I discovered the cave—the spot for which I had searched last summer! I was sure, then, that the enemy had found the place. So I came in here immediately.

"I have been working, trying to uncover what is under the slab—to get it out before they came. I wanted to save it for you, Carter, and there was no time to lose. When you two came in here tonight, I thought you were the others. That's why I came up with the gun."

Carter Boswick thumped his cousin on the back. Harry Vincent sat in silence. He knew the significance of the autogiro. He thought of that corkscrew entrance to the cave. Invisible to eyes on the ground—visible to the eyes of The Shadow from the air!

A SLIGHT sound interrupted Harry's reverie. The noise seemed to come from back in the main shaft. Harry reached forward, and extinguished the lantern. He spoke softly in the darkness.

"I think we're safe enough," he said. "I know who it was who found this place for us, Carter. The enemy can't know about it. Just the same, it would be wise to go back to the shaft and look about a bit. Come on. I'll turn on the light when we reach the main shaft."

Cautiously, Harry led the way. They reached the junction of the main shaft and the side corridor. With Harry whispering for silence, the three moved on through the darkness. They had not gone a dozen feet before Drew Westling stumbled over one rail of the track. He blurted an exclamation as he fell.

Harry delivered a warning hiss. It came too late. The sound of the fall had traveled along the shaft. As if by a signal, a battery of flashlights turned on, toward the spot where the passage from the rocks entered the shaft.

Harry and his companions fell back. Gloating cries sounded loudly in their ears as those shouts echoed down the shaft. The three young men were covered by five revolvers. It was too late!

The enemy had come. They were trapped by a squad of murderers who had somehow found this place. Harsh commands sounded along the shaft. The cornered men raised their hands and let their guns fall. It was the only hope that their lives might be spared.

Harry Vincent, knowing the brutality of the men with whom they had fought before, expected instant death. He was sorry the moment that he dropped his automatic. It would have been better to have died fighting, he decided, now that it was too late.

But the death shots did not come. Instead, a man stepped into the light, assuming a position in which his face could be seen. Harry Vincent did not recognize the cold, leering countenance; but the cries of surprise which Carter and Drew uttered showed that the cousins knew their adversary.

The man who had withheld gunfire that he might ridicule the victims was Farland Tracy, the attorney!

CHAPTER XXII
SHOTS OF DEATH

FARLAND TRACY indulged in an evil laugh as he showed himself to the trio at the end of the shaft. Backed by glimmering revolvers, the lawyer had nothing to fear from the men whom he and Hub Rowley had trapped.

There was no kindliness in the attorney's features. His face, usually feigning sympathy and understanding, had become the gloating countenance of a fiend. The accustomed mask had lifted.

"So the cousins have joined forces," sneered the lawyer, in a low, sarcastic tone. "They've talked things over, maybe? Wondered why they didn't understand each other fully? Well, they've found out, now.

"Easy money for Carter Boswick, eh? Letting Cousin Drew in on the wealth, perhaps. Well, it's all off now, my boys. You and your helper made a lot of trouble; but we've got you where we want you—and we'll leave you here!"

Another face appeared beside the lawyer's. Hub Rowley was stepping forward to add his malicious approval. Drew Westling was the only one who recognized the big shot.

"Don't blame Cousin Drew," jeered Tracy, addressing Carter Boswick. "It was your father's folly that brought you here—although Drew was

partly responsible. I knew all about you father's clever secret—all except where the hiding place could be found. It looked like you were never coming back; and Drew was kind enough to get himself into trouble—with this gentleman who stands beside me.

"A gambling debt. Money owed to Mr. Rowley. So I called on Mr. Rowley—with kindly intentions at first. But when I learned that Mr. Rowley deliberately intended to bleed Drew Westling, I decided it would be a good idea. I made a deal with Mr. Rowley, involving Houston Boswick's hidden wealth.

"We decided to find it for ourselves. We knew that we could take care of little Drew Westling. When we couldn't find it at the old mansion, we decided we would pump Drew after the legacy became his. The old man didn't have so long to live.

"But when you popped up, Carter Boswick, we decided to put you nicely out of the way. I learned that you were coming from Montevideo. I called Mr. Rowley, and he sent a man to meet you. Somehow, you were fortunate enough to get home."

Carter Boswick clenched his teeth. He thought of Havana—of the *Southern Star.* Then, again, he was listening to the sarcastic tones of Farland Tracy's voice.

"We didn't get you," announced the lawyer, "but we did get the message that you found. We had a very able agent planted in your house. Step forward, Headley."

Houston Boswick's former servant stepped into the light. The malicious grin upon his face betrayed his treacherous nature. He, like Farland Tracy, had worn a mask in the past.

"You see," purred the lawyer, "I had long had dealings with Mr. Rowley. He is a gentleman who delights in evading the law; hence he frequently calls on capable legal counsel. He has a way of dealing with peopl   e—and our friend Headley chanced to be one with whom he had dealt in the past.

"Headley was very useful. He took the message. He was watching when it was discovered. He signaled for a messenger, who was waiting patiently outside. Mr. Rowley and I went into conference that very evening."

The lawyer's cold tones ended.

HE needed to say no more. All was plain to Carter Boswick and Drew Westling. Harry Vincent understood also.

Big brains had formed an alliance. A crooked lawyer, thinking more of millions than the trust that was his to keep, had called in a supermind of crime to aid him in the purloining of vast wealth.

Now came a new statement—one that showed

a reason for Farland Tracy's restraining action. The lawyer had more than a merely malicious purpose in withholding death.

"It would be most unfortunate," declared Tracy, "if you had managed, somehow, to remove the fortune that Houston Boswick deposited in this place. There is that possibility, however, since we have discovered you at the probable spot.

"So to mollify your previous endeavors, we shall investigate before we pay our final respects to you. Mr. Rowley and myself have agreed that such should be the best procedure. We may find it necessary to question you before you die. Previously, your instant death would have been preferable. Now we can afford to grant you a brief respite."

With that, Farland Tracy advanced along the side of the shaft. Hub Rowley and Headley followed him. All three were armed, but their revolvers were lowered. The mobsmen in the shaft, Stacks Lodi in command, were the ones who covered Harry Vincent and his comrades.

The advance merely increased the hopelessness of the situation. It was bringing three deadly enemies to closer range. Harry Vincent was longing for a break. He and his companions were only a few yards from the corridor that ended in the treasure vault.

With a loaded automatic still in his pocket, with Carter Boswick similarly equipped, Harry knew that they could put up a short struggle if they could gain the pit. It would be better to die fighting in the face of odds, than be mercilessly butchered. But the threatening revolvers up ahead were held by men whose aim would surely be fatal, unless some unexpected surprise might intervene.

Somehow, these villains had kept watch. Harry realized that he and Carter had failed to use the proper precaution. The Shadow had given them their opportunity. The meeting with Drew Westling had added to their strength.

But in the meanwhile, the enemy had gained by strategy. Where mass attacks had failed, cunning had succeeded.

The position now was one that would tax The Shadow, even should he appear upon the scene.

Harry groaned inwardly as he realized his own stupidity had brought this finish. Had he and his companions remained at the end of the side corridor, they would have been in a stronghold. His foolish desire to investigate had brought himself and two others face to face with an overpowering force.

THESE thoughts swept through Harry's brain with the rapidity of lightning. A man who faces grim death thinks of all neglected possibilities.

Harry was no exception. His mind turned over the entire situation during the interval of a scant few seconds.

A break! If it would only come!

Anything—a stumble on the part of one of the three approaching men—an argument among the covering mobsters—anything that would grant the opportunity for a dive into the corridor where Harry and Carter had found Drew Westling!

Harry's fists tightened.

Shots of death! Let them come! He would make the break himself and take the consequences. He felt no qualms at sacrificing his companions. They were surely doomed—the sooner the end came, the better.

Harry spoke; but his lips did not move in the effort. The undertone was heard only by Carter Boswick and Drew Westling, for Farland Tracy and Hub Rowley were still twenty feet away.

"When I say, 'Go!'"—these were Harry's words—"jump for the corridor. It's our only chance. Ready—"

Before Harry could pronounce the next word, a terrific roar came through the sloping shaft. Someone had opened fire from the section beyond the spot where the side entrance converged within the mine. The heavy booming of automatics sounded like a cannonade.

One of the covering gangsters staggered. The others, with one, accord, dropped to the ground, and turned in the direction of the fire. Farland Tracy and Hub Rowley turned in alarm.

Amid the thundering echoes came Harry's hoarse command:

"Go!"

The break had come—and the word was timed with it! With Carter Boswick and Drew Westling, Harry scrambled for the side corridor. Only one man sought to stop them.

Headley, alone, had not yielded to the momentary surprise that had gripped the others of the invading crew. He saw the doomed men escaping. He fired quick shots in their direction. Fortunately, his aim was hasty.

A bullet skimmed Drew Westling's shoulder. Drew staggered headforemost into the side corridor. Harry and Carter caught him as he fell and dragged him with them. A few moments later they were in the pit.

Suddenly a terrific tumult sounded through the mine shaft. Mobsters were firing up the slope toward their hidden foe. The roar of automatics was responding.

Harry Vincent knew the answer, as he grimly drew forth his automatic. The Shadow, alone, had brought this timely rescue. The master of darkness had opened fire upon the mob, to save the three whose doom had seemed so certain.

Bullets of death! The Shadow had loosed them. But The Shadow, like Harry Vincent and his comrades, was trapped by a merciless mob!

CHAPTER XXIII
THE LAST FIGHT

VOLLEYS thundered through the sloping shaft of the forgotten mine. Gangsters, prone upon the rusted track, were blazing furiously at an unseen target. Bullets ricocheted from jagged walls. Answering shots responded from above.

Flashlights, glimmering intermittently so that they would not reveal the men who held them, were the advantage which the mobsmen possessed. Those flashes of light showed a wavering form in black, retreating up the shaft.

The Shadow was retiring in the face of formidable odds. The cover of darkness was his no longer. The walls of the shaft afforded no spot from which he could thrust a pistoled hand while his form remained in safety.

Those shots with which The Shadow had begun the fray had been distant ones. For The Shadow had realized the danger of close approach. Even now he was in the utmost danger; for although the range was long, the gunmen had a veritable shooting gallery along which to aim.

Bullets that ricocheted could prove as deadly as those which were discharged with perfect aim. Had The Shadow not taken all factors into consideration, he would have fallen with the first volley sent in his direction.

Retreat was the only game; and in that retreat, The Shadow gave high encouragement to the men who opposed him. Stacks Lodi had shouted out the identity of the antagonist.

The Shadow was on the run!

Evil mobsters spat oaths as they fired. All the venom of the underworld was loosed tonight. The Shadow trapped! Death to The Shadow! He would never escape this trap alive!

Two of the mobsmen had fallen. Two others had received wounds, but were still in action.

As Stacks Lodi urged his men forward, they passed the spot where the secret entrance joined the shaft and there they were reinforced by the two gunmen who had been left to guard the outer opening.

The Shadow's retreat had increased in speed. His form was hidden by the increasing slope of the shaft. Stacks Lodi shouted for prompt pursuit.

Why not? The range was long. The advantage was equal for every shooter. The horde outnumbered The Shadow more than eight to one. If they could catch a glimpse of that retreating form within the glare of their flickering lights, death would

stalk The Shadow.

Into Stacks Lodi's cunning brain came the realization that the opening of this shaft must be blocked. There, The Shadow would be at bay. When he was backed against the final wall, lights would no longer glimmer. A barrage sweeping through the darkness would surely spell The Shadow's doom!

Below, Farland Tracy and Hub Rowley were keeping the three trapped men from escaping. Headley was with them. Stacks could hear the echoing sound of shots. He surmised what was going on.

Peering from the edge of the wall, into the short corridor that led to the right, the lawyer and the big shot were sniping at Harry Vincent and Carter Boswick. Harry and Carter were wisely withholding their fire as they lay within the shelter of the pit. Every shot counted now. They waited for the enemy to appear in the corridor itself.

Stacks Lodi still urged his men up the shaft. The slope was one which increased as they proceeded. This accounted for The Shadow's disappearance. The ceiling formed a curve that covered his retreat.

Suddenly, as a flashlight illuminated the rising cavern, a gangster emitted a cry of exultation.

"There he is! There he is!"

As the light went out, Stacks Lodi caught sight of a stooping figure up ahead.

The Shadow!

Stacks had seen the flowing cloak and the lowered head, buried beneath the slouch hat.

BEFORE the gangsters could fire, four quick shots came down the shaft. Bullets glanced from the ground, and one gangster coughed out his life amid the darkness.

What was one man now? Stacks aimed and fired into the blackness. The range was closer than before. They had neared the end of the shaft.

The mobsters followed the example. The darkness showed repeated spurts of flame; the air reeked with powder fumes.

"Hold it! Hold it!"

Stacks Lodi's command was heard. Echoes of the final shots rolled dimly down the shaft. Silence followed. A hiss of exultation came from Stacks Lodi's evil lips.

The Shadow was no longer returning the fire. Perhaps he lay wounded or dead!

On the contrary, he might be resting for the final moment, seeking to trap his enemies by some ruse. If so, it would be futile. One more revelation of that black-garbed form, and The Shadow's end would be at hand!

"Ready!" growled Stacks. "Get set, and we'll give him all the light he wants. Keep it on this time. Bust loose when I shoot the big light."

As Stacks pressed the switch of a bull's-eye lantern, a strange sound manifested itself from above. A low rumble occurred in the darkness. The light came on. A snarl burst from Stacks an instant before the gangsters opened fire.

From a hundred feet up the shaft, a mining car was slowly starting down the slope. Its sides of metal, its interior brimming with a huge load of glistening rock, this carrier was the first car of an entire train!

Gangster bullets spattered against the steel front of the car. They did no harm. The Shadow was behind—beyond—in safety.

Stacks Lodi cried out in terror. He understood now why The Shadow had been stooping when they last had seen him. The lone fighter had released a mighty Juggernaut upon his enemies!

The ore train of the abandoned mine! Still loaded with its last burden of rock that had never been taken away. Rusted wheels were responding under the impetus of the great weight. Cars with bulging sides were about to sweep cleanly through the deserted shaft!

Before Stacks Lodi could cry an order to his men, the terrorized gangsters were on their feet, turning to dash along the shaft. Only one remained with Stacks. He, like the leader, had seen the only chance for safety; to leap upon the foremost car before it gathered dangerous speed.

That moment was approaching now. The rumble had become a roar. The cars were coming steadily down the slope. Stacks Lodi and his single companion rose grimly to meet them. Then came loud, bursting shots from the stack of ore atop the foremost car.

THE SHADOW was clearing the way! He wanted no riders upon his train of destruction. With the cars in motion, he had sprung aboard and come to the mound that topped the leading carrier.

Stacks Lodi staggered and fell against the side of the shaft. His companion collapsed at his feet. The crushing cars came on; when they arrived, the head of the train threw the two bodies between the tracks and the wall, crushing them to mangled forms.

Neither Stacks nor the gangster was alive to feel that fate. The Shadow's clearing bullets had silenced them forever. Even as the train gained speed along the slope, the black-garbed figure was following another purpose. It was crawling rapidly back along the cars.

Fleeing gangsters had gained a precious lead in their dash down the slope. But the uneven footing of the trackage stayed their progress. The descending train was gathering impetus. Faster by thrice than a man could run, it hurtled down upon these maddened underlings of crime.

As the heavy cars surged toward the midpoint of the shaft, The Shadow dropped from the rear car. The only token of his presence was the sinister laugh that now echoed through the man-made cavern. The Shadow had reserved that mockery for the moment when his terrible avalanche of death would strike.

The plunging cars brooked no interference. A screaming gangster was thrown forward a dozen feet when the head of the train overtook him. He was crushed to death while the cars swept on.

Another victim came a second later—then a third. Still the train roared on, as it passed the only spot of safety between the top and the bottom of the shaft—the entrance to the natural passage that led from the mine.

A pair of mobsters cowered there—the last of Stacks Lodi's pursuing crew. They had reached the safety point just in time. They, alone of those who had cried death to The Shadow, remained to see the death that he had delivered to his trappers.

As the train thundered onward, a gleam of light appeared from up the shaft. It signified the presence of a living being—one who had escaped the grinding death. Behind that light was The Shadow, the avenger who had loosed the train of destruction.

The light spotted the gangsters. They knew who held it. With vengeful snarls, they raised their revolvers to fire at the unseen being.

As the revolvers spoke, quick bursts of flame came from below the gleaming light. The Shadow, crouching, had drawn the mobsmen's aim upward.

The gangsters fell while firing. They sprawled forward into the shaft, across the rails, as dead as their mangled fellows.

Quick had been that action. As The Shadow rose to stride down the slope, the roar of the hurtling cars was still in progress. The Juggernaut of doom had not yet come to its stopping place.

BELOW, other men of crime now knew the menace. Hub Rowley had been the first to hear the rumble of the cars. He had spoken tensely to his companions. They had stayed their fire to await the outcome.

Now, in the light that Headley shot up along the shaft, they could see the terrible approach. The train, surging on at terrific speed, was an irresistible menace that they could not stop.

With one accord, the three invaders turned to safety. They did not seek the corridor where Harry Vincent and Carter Boswick were located. Instead, they sprang for the cover of the opposite passage.

A flashlight glared as they leaped. With one accord, Harry and Carter fired at the fleeing men. Headley went down in the passage. The following shots would have found their marks, but for the intervention of the train, which suddenly arrived to protect the men whom it had threatened.

A mighty crash shattered the end wall of the slope. The heavy cars piled up amid a deluge of flying ore that spread in all directions. The burden of broken rock alone prevented the train from telescoping.

Twisted, battered, the cars sagged back on the rebound, and lay, a mass of wreckage, along the bottom of the mine slope.

As the continued echoes died away, Harry and Carter sprang from their pit. They had fired futilely as the cars arrived; then they had ducked to escape chunks of hurtling ore. They still had enemies with whom to deal; and they knew where the others had gone.

Grimly, they climbed over piles of rocks and reached the nearest car. Harry reached forward to fire. The burst of a revolver drove him back. Hub Rowley and Farland Tracy had chosen the same purpose.

New shots sounded amid the wreckage. Faces appeared above the car. Harry and Carter scrambled back to the pit, the only place from which they could return the fire. High up, near the ceiling of the shaft, the enemy had the protection of the upturned car that had headed the death train.

THE advantage was with the plotting villains. Their angle enabled them to fire down into the edge of the pit. Harry and Carter crouched low, unable to return the shots. Hub Rowley, snarling, had crawled to one side, to gain a better shot.

A light shone from beside the battered train. Hub turned, and his gold teeth glimmered in an evil grin. He raised his revolver to fire at the menace which he knew was there. An automatic roared its greeting.

Hub Rowley swayed crazily. His loathsome smile became a sickly grimace. His revolver twirled as it fell from his fingers. His body lost its balance and plunged to the ground.

Farland Tracy saw the approaching light. With a fiendish cry, the lawyer backed from the upturned car and sought the refuge of the corridor, where Headley's body lay half-covered with broken ore.

Firing intermittent shots, the crooked lawyer sought to prevent the approach of the dreaded being who had deprived him of his allies. His effort failed. He could not thwart The Shadow.

Backing toward the wall of the short passage, Tracy half-raised his arms as a token of surrender.

He held the revolver pointing upward. The Shadow did not fire when he saw the gesture.

But Farland Tracy's action was a ruse. He suddenly lowered his hand to fire a quick shot. His treacherous deed received a prompt penalty. The Shadow's automatic spoke before Tracy could shoot. The bullet struck the lowering arm, as token of The Shadow's power. The offending hand dropped the gun.

Farland Tracy, justly crippled for his foul attempt, blurted a cry of pain and staggered backward. He was ignorant of the fact that the short corridor ended in a precipitous shaft. His back never reached the wall that it sought.

The lawyer lost his footing on the brink of the pit. With a wild, screaming snarl, he threw his good arm outward, but in vain. His body toppled backward, and plunged to the jagged bottom of the hole, more than thirty feet below.

No further cry came from the blackened shaft. Farland Tracy, like the others, had gone to a deserved doom. The last fight was ended. The Shadow was the conqueror.

A long, weird laugh shivered through the gloomy corridors. It returned, a cry of ghoulish echoes. That laugh was mirthless. The Shadow's triumph was given as a solemn knell to crime. Justice had won in the last fight!

CHAPTER XXIV
THE SETTLEMENT

MORNING had dawned. A trio of solemn men were beside the cabin in the clearing. The sunlight of another day made this place seem strangely far from the gloomy shaft of the forgotten mine.

"Ready?"

Harry Vincent, standing, put the question to Carter Boswick, who was beside him. Carter nodded. Both turned to Drew Westling, who was seated on a metal box, his face pale, and his shoulder bulging from bandages that had been packed beneath his coat.

"Come on," said Harry, with a grin. "Time to be moving, young fellow. Remove yourself from those millions. We have to take them with us."

Drew Westling complied. Harry and Carter lifted the heavy box and carried it between them, while Drew followed unsteadily.

It was a long trudge, with frequent stops, before they reached the coupé. Drew was more tired than the others. They helped him into the car, and packed the chest in the back.

"All I can say," remarked Harry, as he mopped his brow, "is that I appreciate your father's foresight in packing away paper currency and securities in preference to gold."

Hub Rowley swayed crazily … his revolver fell from his fingers …

"It helped out a lot," responded Carter, as they entered the car. "The big job was cracking open the slab. It wasn't so much for the two of us—Drew had gotten along pretty far when we arrived."

They discussed the subject as they rolled along. There had been two hours work at the pit in the mine after The Shadow's fight had ended. There, continuing sturdily despite the ordeal they had undergone, Harry and Carter had unearthed the coffer, while Drew Westling had lain asleep from complete exhaustion.

They had taken Drew to the cabin first; then they had returned to the shaft of death to bring the box of millions. Both Harry and Carter had been pleased because Drew was groggy when they took him from the mine. The scenes where the secret entrance joined the shaft were not pleasant to remember.

The metal box had proven, indeed, to be a treasure chest. There was no clue to its placement in the mine. Whether Houston Boswick had taken it there himself—old though he was—or had relied upon trusted helpers, was a matter of speculation.

It was also impossible to determine how long the wealth had been hidden. Two years seemed the limit, judging by some of the documents. Long-term bonds had view with government certificates of high denomination.

Among the mass of wealth, Harry and Carter had discovered a few stocks that were apparently worthless. In their thorough inspection at the cabin, they had found stock certificates showing complete ownership of the Golden Glow Mine—and this had proven to be the mine in which the treasure had been hidden.

AS they rode along toward the Wisconsin border, Drew Westling explained his dealings with Hub Rowley. Harry and Carter laughed when Drew spoke of the I O Us which the dead big shot had held.

"Let someone try to collect now," declared Carter grimly. "Those are out now, Drew."

"But if someone does—"

"I'll take care of them," laughed Carter. "Don't worry, Drew. You can put that income of yours away in the bank. You're due to your share of this harvest."

A moment of silence; then Carter spoke to Harry.

"And for you, old fellow—"

Harry stopped him with a gesture.

"Forget it, Carter," he said. "I was working under orders. I'm out of the division."

"But the—the person who sent you to help me. Perhaps you can arrange with him."

"Whatever he wishes, he can call for. But you may not hear from him. He does not expect return for what he gives."

There was a cryptic meaning in Harry's statement. Carter Boswick smiled seriously as he recalled last night's events. Then, The Shadow had given—but had avoided all return. He had delivered messengers of lead, and had loosed a thunderbolt of steel. The results had been dire to fiends of crime.

What had become of The Shadow?

Carter Boswick did not know, and he realized that Harry Vincent shared his ignorance. They had both heard the final cry of triumph. But after its sinister echoes, no further sound had come.

Carter had expressed a fear for their mysterious protector. Harry had answered it with a knowing smile. The Shadow triumphant was a living Shadow!

The old mine was again forgotten. Within its sordid corridors, deep silence lay. The bodies of dead men, if ever found, would be taken as the reason for the closing of the mine—years before last night's event. The shattered wreckage of the death train would appear as evidence of an accident that had been buried to avoid an inquest.

As they reached the Michigan border, Carter Boswick reached into his pocket and drew forth the only documents that he had removed from the chest of wealth. These were the stock certificates of the Golden Glow Mine.

Methodically, Carter tore the papers into tiny fragments. He let them trickle in batches from the window, where a rising breeze swirled and scattered them far apart.

Harry Vincent, smiling, approved the action. Let the forgotten mine remain forgotten. The only records of its existence would appear in those secret books which none would ever find—the hidden archives of The Shadow.

For to The Shadow belonged the triumph. His hidden presence, haunting the innermost recesses of the discovered shaft, had distributed rescue and destruction simultaneously—each apportioned to the ones who rightfully deserved it.

The menace that had threatened Carter Boswick's heritage was gone forever. Vile schemes had ended—and the schemers had gone with them.

The Shadow had prevailed, and justice ruled!

THE END

INTERLUDE by Will Murray

The theme for this Nostalgia Ventures *Shadow* volume is exemplified by our feature novel. *The Shadow's Justice* showcases Walter Gibson's classic early incarnation of the Master of Darkness: sinister, enigmatic, yet a relentless and lethal punisher of criminals. Here, he's pitted against a traditional menace rather than a typical supercriminal operating on a grandiose scale. And since he operates outside the law, The Shadow takes upon himself the role of judge, jury and executioner.

This was only one of the many types of Shadow stories which allowed Street & Smith to publish *The Shadow Magazine* every two weeks without readers becoming jaded by repetitive plots.

Walter Gibson once observed, "Keen analysts have classified The Shadow novels in three patterns—the 'classic,' the 'thriller,' and the 'hardboiled'—and these frequently could be used in combination, producing a diversity of types which kept up the tempo and sustained reader interest through a constant expectancy that usually resulted in the unexpected.

"This gave The Shadow a marked advantage over mystery characters who were forced to maintain fixed patterns; and that, in turn, made it easy to write about him. There was never need for lengthy debate regarding what The Shadow should do next, or what course of action he should follow to keep in character. He could meet any exigency on the spur of the moment, and if he suddenly acted in a manner totally opposed to his usual custom, it could always be explained later by The Shadow himself, through the facile pen of Maxwell Grant."

The Broken Napoleons introduces a new wrinkle in The Shadow's war on crime which on the surface contradicts his merciless methods. Fearing that readers would grow bored with scene after blood-spattered scene of the Dark Avenger gunning down felons in a bullet-pocked climax, Gibson and his editors revealed yet another side of their cloaked hero. Shadow fans in 1936 were probably stunned to learn of their hero's secret efforts to save some criminals from themselves. But he had been doing so all along in change-of-pace stories like *Road of Crime* and *Crooks Go Straight.*

Without question, this story was inspired by Doc Savage's humane approach to criminal rehabilitation. Doc maintained a "Crime College" in upstate New York where crooks he captured were retrained and returned to society as normal citizens. (Unlike The Shadow, Doc Savage refused to kill.) The methods Doc employed were as extreme as The Shadow's in their way, but at least they were considered scientific by the standards of the day.

Gibson and Dent's amazing output were spotlighted in typewriter ads.

The Broken Napoleons is also an excellent example of one of Gibson's favorite type of Shadow novels. We'll let him explain:

"Many stories involved a 'proxy hero,' whose fate was a bone of contention between The Shadow and the villains with whom he was currently concerned, therefore, no fixed style of writing was required, since the 'proxy' rather than The Shadow was temporarily the central character."

And for those who think of The Shadow as exclusively a creature of Manhattan, both of our novels take readers to the high seas as the Master Avenger prosecutes his peculiar brands of justice far from his usual haunts. While *The Shadow's Justice* veers into Cuban waters, much of *The Broken Napoleons* takes place in the Bahamas. The latter locale author Walter Gibson visited in 1931 while writing one of the earliest stories in the Shadow canon, working with Blackstone the Magician's traveling troupe. He made mental notes for the day he could unleash The Shadow on this locale, and this exciting story is the result.

The Broken Napoleons also illustrates the sometimes strange synchronicities that flowed back and forth between *The Shadow* and *Doc Savage* magazines like an electrical current.

It's not giving away anything to mention that the villain of this 1936 novel goes by a name that translates as "The Vulture." In fact, "The Vulture" was the story's working title. Gibson penned this tale unaware that three years previously Doc Savage's Lester Dent had concocted a Shadow villain known as The Golden Vulture for a tale of the same title. That story sat in a Street & Smith manuscript safe until Gibson was asked to rewrite it in 1938.

When Dent outlined *The Golden Vulture*, he planned a scene in which The Shadow was trapped in an old Chinese junk in San Francisco harbor, from which he must escape *a la* Houdini. An identical scene, also set in that city, was included in Gibson's *Green Eyes*, which had just been accepted by Street & Smith. Original *Shadow* editor Frank Blackwell asked Dent to abandon that particular climax and the locale before writing his tale. Without having any contact with Walter Gibson, Lester Dent had apparently read his mind!

It did not stop there. Many parallels haunted both series. The Golden Vulture and his minions, whom Dent called "feathers," became the model for future Shadow foes like The Cobra, The Python and The Hydra, and their various "fangs," "coils" and "heads." Possibly Street & Smith fed this conceit to Gibson as a way of getting some return on their investment in a manuscript they thought might never see print.

In February 1933, The Shadow discovered a lost tribe of Aztecs in Mexico just weeks before Doc Savage found the Mayan metropolis that was the focus of his first adventure. Gibson's novel was written months earlier, but whether by accident or by Street & Smith editorial design, they broke into print at virtually the same time.

After The Shadow confronted evil imposters in *The Third Shadow,* the Man of Bronze tangled with devilish duplicates in *Mad Eyes* and *The Land of Fear.* The villain in Gibson's *Bells of Doom* apparently read the September, 1933 issue of *Doc Savage Magazine.* He copied The Czar of Fear's use of tolling bells to announce the demise of his latest victim.

Being a physician and bound by the Hippocratic Oath, Doc Savage evolved specific strategies for dealing with criminals in nonlethal ways. One was much copied. The Vulcan neck pinch made famous by *Star Trek*'s Mr. Spock was nothing but a steal of Doc's preferred method of rendering his foes unconscious. It was no coincidence that after a few years, The Shadow also took up the practice, or that Doc once appropriated his stealthy tactic of blending into the shadows.

Lester Dent freely adopted the use of the proxy hero—although in *Doc Savage* this device often manifested as a proxy heroine. Gibson's masterful technique of having his hero operate in a clever disguise, unsuspected by reader and characters alike, shows up in *Doc Savage Magazine* as well.

THE *Shadow*

TWICE A MONTH

THE GOLDEN VULTURE
COMPLETE MYSTERY NOVEL
and other stories

The Shadow Knows

BIGGEST and BEST
128 Pages
OF THRILLS and ACTION

Doc Savage and The Shadow both encountered dinosaurs early in 1943.

Not long after The Shadow's secret Sanctum is invaded by criminals in 1937, Doc's equivalent, his *Fortress of Solitude,* suffers a similar fate. The success of The Shadow's first recurring foe, the Voodoo Master, opened the way for Doc's own returning arch nemesis, John Sunlight. It was probably no coincidence that just as Dent was working on the first story of that modern Napoleon, John Sunlight, Gibson was finishing *Shadow over Alcatraz,* in which his hero challenged the Napoleon of Crime known only as Zanigew.

Although Gibson claimed he never read *Doc Savage,* Dent sometimes dipped into *The Shadow.* He acknowledged that his 1941 novel *The Golden Man* was inspired by Gibson's 1940 Shadow mystery, *The Veiled Prophet.* There were many such examples of pulp cross-pollination.

Early in 1942, both writers produced stories derived from the vampire theme. Their treatment was very different, with Gibson delving into traditional undead lore in *The Vampire Murders,* while Dent took a more imaginative approach in the tale he called "The Lost Vampire" and his editor rechristened *The Fiery Menace.*

A few months later, they again attacked a parallel theme: dinosaurs. Doc Savage was an old hand at prehistoric reptiles, having battled herds of them going back to his second adventure, but for The Shadow, *The Devil Monsters* represented a weird departure from his usual activities.

The explanation for many of these coincidences was that they were *not* coincidences. All Doc Savage and Shadow stories were plotted in conference with Street & Smith executive Henry W. Ralston, editor John L. Nanovic and the writer. From time to time, they suggested similar springboards to both writers, confident that Gibson and Dent would go in completely different directions.

A striking coincidence took place in 1945, after Nanovic had moved on and Ralston was no longer involved in plotting sessions. Therefore it was truly uncanny.

At roughly the same time, Gibson and Dent submitted novels in which their heroes were drawn into adventures revolving around a mysterious package containing a Satan costume with matching devil mask. When his editor discovered this accidental duplication, Dent was asked to change the Satanic outfit in *Terror Takes 7* to something less sinister. Gibson's *Mask of Mephisto* was published as he wrote it. It was only fair. "Maxwell Grant" had submitted his manuscript first. To further the coincidence, Dent had originally entitled his story "Satan Slew Seven."

The Shadow and Doc Savage never met one another in the pages of any Street & Smith pulp magazine, but their paths certainly crossed in strange and unusual ways.

*Each one
a broken life,
a ruined fortune!
Who was the Vulture
who served as cashier?*

The Broken Napoleons

A Complete Book-length Novel from the Private Annals of The Shadow,
as told to

Maxwell Grant

CHAPTER I
ABOVE THE HUDSON

ALTHOUGH there were more than a dozen cars on the heights near Peekskill, looking over the shimmering expanse of the Hudson River, few knew what was being unfolded beneath them. Some might have seen one of these events, but none—not even those who were enacting the scene—realized the other.

And no one ever imagined that these two events would prove to be a joint venture.

The first event, which everyone could see, took place on the river. Beating its way down the stream was an old, rust-covered boat, the *Reciprocity.* It had been built fifteen years ago, and its hopeful title indicated it would succeed in foreign trade. Unfortunately, the owners did not realize that hope, and it had found a haven in the "ghost fleet" of the upper Hudson—the graveyard of ships too good to scrap, but not worth operating.

Someone had picked it out of the group and intended to make different use of it. From its life of uselessness, it was entering into a new era of usefulness.

High on the bank above the river, another scene was taking place. Two men sat in a coupé, watching the boat sail down the stream as they talked.

Few noticed this second scene in the gathering dusk. No one realized that here a man who had gone straight was being tempted to again enter into crime. A useless boat was entering a useful life; a good citizen was being tempted with crime!

The one man in the coupé was square-jawed, and almost straight in profile. He looked like a fighter; but with it, he had the air of a man who could hold his place in the better realms of society.

The other man was pasty-faced, sharp-eyed.

"Butch is counting on you, Curt," he said. "Butch is a good guy to be with."

"That's news," remarked Curt Sturley, his gaze

fixed upon the river. "By that, I suppose he needs me."

"You guessed it, Curt. Say, Butch is sitting pretty. I'm not stringing you. There's nobody bigger than Butch."

Sturley pulled a pipe from his pocket and began to stuff it with tobacco. Eagerly, the other repeated the claim that he had just made.

"There's nobody bigger than Butch Drongo—"

"Probably not," interrupted Sturley, with a gruff laugh. "I've been reading the newspapers, Shim, up in Toronto. If Butch Drongo is a big shot, I know why."

"You mean because other guys have been taking it on the lam?"

"Absolutely. Those that are bigger than Butch have left New York. He ought to be big."

"Shim" shrugged his shoulders. Sturley made a new comment.

"There must be some reason why they don't want to stay," he remarked, steadily. "Maybe they have had sense enough to get out. Perhaps Butch hasn't."

"That's not it," insisted Shim. "Things were crowded, that was all. Some of them have probably headed out to Chi. There's others gone down to Miami. Butch had the brains to stick. That's why he's ready to step out on top."

"And why he needs me, I suppose."

"Sure. Butch hasn't forgotten the way you helped him once. He's set to pull some big jobs; but he wants to work them smart. Here's his proposition, Curt. Join up and you're his right bower, ahead of all the rest of us. I'm stepping out of where I stand, on your account."

"Nice of you, Shim."

"No kidding. You got as good a bean as Butch. We'll all be sitting pretty if you work with him."

CURT STURLEY leaned back behind the wheel. He puffed his pipe, stared toward the dwindling steamship and declared:

"Tell Butch that I hold only one regret. That is the fact that I ever had any dealings with him in the past. That is also why I kept this appointment. I wanted to tell Butch—or whoever he sent to meet me—that he can expect no favors from me in the future."

"But, Curt—"

"No moral reform is responsible for my decision. I am simply employing the brains which I possess—the intelligence that you and Butch seem to admire so highly. Tell Butch that whatever his game is, he will not have me with it."

"But Butch is due for something big; you'll be the guy closest to him—"

"You mean that Butch would like me to be his chief lieutenant? His wishes, however, will not be respected."

Sturley pressed the starter pedal. He began to back the coupé from the wall, swinging it so he could turn into the highway and take a northward course. Shim gulped another protest.

"You've got to join up with Butch," he affirmed. "He's counting on you, Curt. Butch said—"

"Nothing that Butch said is of consequence."

"But he said you wouldn't turn down the offer—"

"I have already refused it."

"But Butch said you wouldn't, not if I handed you this."

Shim had dug one hand into a vest pocket. The car was almost in the highway when the rat-faced man pulled out his paw and thrust a gleaming object into view. Gold glittered from between Shim's thumb and forefinger.

Curt Sturley jammed on the brakes. His eyes shone; his lips tightened. With his right hand he plucked the bit of gold from Shim's fingers. The object was the broken half of a gold coin, the size of a five-dollar gold piece.

Sturley's lips spoke aloud as they read letters that were stamped upon the coin:

"N—A—P—O—" He stopped, turned over the half coin and spoke the last two figures of a number, the coin's date: "One—five—"

"That's it, Curt," expressed Shim. "Butch told me what the coin was. It's called a napoleon; that's the half of a broken one. An old coin the Frenchies used to use. A gold napoleon, dated 1815."

STURLEY'S gaze was as fixed as if he had been hypnotized. His fingers, mechanical in their motion, kept turning the coin over. He eyed the profile of the Emperor Napoleon, which was stamped on this half of the broken coin. He read the letters—the date—both out loud. Shim could see the flash of Sturley's eyes, the increased compression of his lips.

"Butch said for me to tell you, Curt, that—"

"What Butch said does not count," interrupted Sturley. "What he has sent me does. This is what I wanted."

"Then you're coming into New York, to join up with Butch?"

"Whatever game Butch plans, he can count me in on it."

There was a firm decisiveness in Sturley's tone. Shim saw Sturley placing the broken napoleon carefully within a wallet. After pocketing his prize, Sturley tugged at the gear shift.

The coupé swung forward, southward bound, took the sweeping curve of the highway to New

York. Wheeling beyond a curve it roared along the heights. It passed the plodding steamship *Reciprocity*; Curt Sturley's eyes did not move in the direction of the river. His interest in navigation was ended.

The coupé was powerful. Its speedometer registered seventy miles an hour as it straightened along a level road beside the Hudson. Sturley had turned on the headlamps. His eyes fixed upon their glowing path, he maintained the speed that he had set.

The coupé drew up beside a speeding limited that was roaring toward New York, along the track that lined the Hudson River. Shim saw Sturley press the accelerator farther down. The speeding train was left behind, its whistle blaring wildly in the dusk.

Curt Sturley had become a man with but one present ambition: to reach New York within the shortest possible time space. "Butch" Drongo had won his point; he had gained the man he wanted.

Planning for crime, the big shot had seen use for the services of Curt Sturley. Butch Drongo had obtained those services through the inspiration of a broken napoleon.

CHAPTER II
A FOLLOWED TRAIL

MILES from New York, Curt Sturley and Shim Torson had discussed crime as it existed in Manhattan. Their conversation had definitely indicated that unusual conditions were present in New York.

Shim had told Curt that certain crooks had left the metropolis. Curt had mentioned reading that fact in a Toronto newspaper. The news had spread everywhere; and in its wake was mystery. The underworld itself had no answer.

The law had made no sudden drive against crime. There had been no huge feuds among the lawless. No sudden opportunities elsewhere had caused an exodus of criminals. Yet the fact stood: crime was latent in New York; and that state existed because notorious men of crime were nowhere about.

Scumland, itself, looked the same. Slouchy, suspicious characters were in evidence. Hopheads, panhandlers, stool pigeons were in abundance. There were even a great many thuggish strollers who looked like potential gun-toters. But the important links were absent.

Crooks who formed the backbone of notorious mobs; killers and the lieutenants who commanded them; even certain rogues of higher aspirations who claimed to be "big shots"—none of these was in sight.

The word was piped along the grapevine that racketeers were fuming, idle. They depended upon strong-arm crews to back their schemes of extortion. They could not find the gorillas whom they wanted. It had been noised that a squad of torpedoes or pineapple handlers could command its own price. But no such crew was available.

Of all the places where rumor was rife, the Black Ship predominated. It was a dive where the toughest thugs congregated. The Black Ship produced rumors simply because it had lost the greatest percentage of patrons.

SOON after dusk on this particular night, a rugged, poker-faced customer entered the Black Ship. He was well-attired; his chiseled visage commanded immediate recognition. This arrival

The tramp steamer *Reciprocity*

produced a buzzed conversation in a secluded corner of the dive.

"Say!" whispered a squinty-eyed lounger. "Dat's Cliff Marsland. Lamp de guy, Koke. He's one bozo dat ain't took it on de lam."

"Koke," a bleary-eyed, pock-faced thug, looked up from a glass of grog and snorted.

"Maybe he ain't, Knuckler. But there ain't nothing in Cliff still being here."

"Why not? Cliff's a killer, ain't he?"

"Sure. But he don't travel with no outfit."

"I get it, Koke. Dere's been nobody tipping him off to what's doing out of town, him not being wid a mob."

Koke nodded.

"Cliff's a smart gazebo, anyway," decided "Knuckler," after a brief consideration. "He ought to be wise to something—at least dat's de way I figure it."

"Maybe he is," scoffed Koke. "Why don't you ankle over and ask him?"

Knuckler grinned.

"Think I ain't got de nerve?" he queried. "Keep your lamps open, wise guy, while I go and chin wid Cliff."

Knuckler left the table; he crossed the stone-walled room and planked himself at a table, where Cliff was seated alone. Cliff nodded in recognition.

"Hello, Knuckler," he remarked. "Want to talk to me?"

"Sure," replied Knuckler. "Say, Cliff, maybe you got de lowdown on all dis hooey dat's been handed around. Where's all dese gorillas dat's moved out?"

"Why ask me, Knuckler? I don't deal with them."

"I know dat. But you rate better den any of dem."

"Glad to hear that. Maybe that explains why I'm still around."

Knuckler guffawed.

"Dat's good dope, Cliff," he agreed. "You don't need to hook up with no outfit to stick, or to go places, neither. All de guys has been mugs dat work togedder."

"I've heard that there's been new faces showing up in Chicago."

"I heard dat, too, Cliff. And dere's some saying de same about Miami. Only nobody's heard from any pals. Anybody dat's gone West or South ain't talked about it."

"Would you, Knuckler?"

The rowdy scratched his head, then delivered a shake.

"Guess I wouldn't, Cliff. I hadn't thought about it just dat way. All I been thinking is it's a good idea to stick here. Koke feels de same way about it."

"Sure. When some big shot gets enough gorillas to start a squad, he may sign you birds up."

"Dat's just it, only nobody's been starting no outfits. Dat's de tough part about it. Nobody, except—well, I don't know who's de guy; but he's busy."

CLIFF'S gaze was steadied. Knuckler felt uneasy. He had spoken the truth when he had stated that he could not name the big shot in question. But his wording had indicated otherwise. Knuckler was too squeamish to risk the antagonism of so noted a gun handler as Cliff Marsland.

"Lemme explain it, Cliff," insisted Knuckler. "Dere's two guys, see? And it's a cinch dey's wid an outfit. But dey ain't working at it. Ain't been seen much, neider. Dem guys is Sneak Losbach and Weed Hessel."

"I haven't seen them."

"Nobody has much." Knuckler leaned forward and lowered his voice to a whisper. "If it wasn't for me knowing Deek Calligan, I wouldn't know nothing about dem. Savvy?"

"What's Deek got to do with Sneak and Weed?"

"Nothing—so far as Deek knows Sneak and Weed is on de lookout for him, see? I gotta hunch Deek's due for a ride when dey get him."

"And you're a friend of Deek's?"

Knuckler shook his head in violent protest.

"Not a chance," he declared. "I just knowed dat Deek has two joints where he stays. One's de Hotel Santiago. De other's a fancy apartment house called de Ladronne.

"You know de kind of lug Deek is. A wise guy dat don't talk to nobody much. Handles his jobs on his own, or works for somebody widout spilling nothing to nobody else. Deek ain't around. But Sneak and Weed is. One's at de Santiago; de other's at de Ladronne. Dat makes it simple, don't it?"

Cliff shrugged his shoulders. His gaze, however, belied his gesture of indifference. Narrow-eyed, Cliff's orbs were fixed on Knuckler's squinty face in a close scrutiny. Knuckler shifted.

"I wasn't meaning nothing, Cliff," he remarked. "Just figuring dat some big shot had an outfit, but wasn't using his mob. On account of Sneak an' Weed being busy right now—"

"I've got the idea, Knuckler," interrupted Cliff. "It sounded pat enough, like you'd spilled it before."

"Not a chance, Cliff. You're the first guy I've spoke to."

"And maybe the last."

Knuckler winced. His voice turned whiny.

"Say, Cliff—you ain't meaning—"

"I'm meaning nothing. Forget it, and forget what else you've remembered. Guesswork isn't healthy sometimes."

Cliff arose and walked from the Black Ship. Knuckler sidled back to join Koke.

"What'd you ask him?" queried Koke.

"Nothing at all," returned Knuckler. "Nothing, Koke. He's a tough bird to talk to, Cliff is."

OUTSIDE the Black Ship, Cliff Marsland was indulging in a smile. Cliff had learned facts that he had wanted. He was interested in the whereabouts of any hoodlums who were dangerous enough to form the nucleus of a thuggish mob.

Knuckler had named such men: "Sneak" Losbach and "Weed" Hessel. Knuckler's guess was logical; by their activities, the two crooks appeared to be on the lookout for "Deek" Calligan. Cliff had silenced Knuckler after the news had been spilled.

By his manner, Cliff had left Knuckler puzzled. The squeamish crook could not decide whether Cliff was working with Sneak and Weed or whether he was a pal of the absent Deek Calligan. In either case, Knuckler would be wise enough to keep his future guesses to himself.

Through his bluff, Cliff had kept his actual business covered. Cliff's status in the underworld was a blind. He was interested in crime for one reason only. Cliff was an agent of The Shadow.

Serving a mysterious master whose very name brought terror to crookdom, Cliff had visited the Black Ship in search of news like that which he had gained.

The Shadow was watching the badlands. He knew the situation there; he wanted to learn of any groups of thugs who were about to form new bands. The Shadow wanted information regarding the big shots who might be backing such outfits.

Cliff had gained a lead. He lost no time in relaying it to headquarters. Reaching the outskirts of this disreputable district, he entered an old drugstore. From a telephone booth, The Shadow's agent put in a call. A quiet voice responded. It was Burbank, The Shadow's contact man.

Cliff reported. He hung up the receiver and awaited a return call. It came, five minutes later. Burbank supplied instructions. Faring forth, Cliff strolled toward the Bowery; he was on his way to the Hotel Santiago.

Soon afterward, a taxicab stopped somewhere in the Sixties. A huddled, quick-shifting man sidled from the cab. He hugged the walls of buildings, until he neared an old-fashioned apartment house. This was the Ladronne. There the hunch-shouldered man paused.

Another of The Shadow's agents had taken his post. This was "Hawkeye," one of the cleverest spotters in the business. Hawkeye had frequently teamed with Cliff. Like Cliff, Hawkeye knew both Sneak Losbach and Weed Hessel by sight.

ELSEWHERE in Manhattan was a dark-walled room, wherein a bluish light glowed upon a table in the corner. Beneath that glow were long, white hands, moving as they handled stacks of newspaper clippings and typewritten report cards. A brilliant gem—a magnificent fire opal—glimmered from the finger of one hand. Its depths reflected ever-changing hues.

These were the hands of The Shadow. The jewel, a rare girasol, was The Shadow's emblem. The Shadow was in his sanctum, that hidden abode wherein he planned his forays against men of crime.

A tiny white bulb glowed from the wall. The Shadow reached for the earphones. He raised them above the shaded light. He spoke in a sinister whisper; a quiet voice responded:

"Burbank speaking."

"Report," ordered The Shadow.

"Report from Marsland," stated the quiet-toned contact man. "Stationed near the Hotel Santiago. Weed Hessel made a telephone call five minutes ago. Marsland did not learn the number, but he thinks it was a routine call."

"Report received."

"Report from Hawkeye. Stationed near the Ladronne Apartments. Sneak Losbach made two calls, both to the same number. The first apparently brought a busy signal. Presumably routine calls."

A whispered laugh from The Shadow. Sneak's first call had probably conflicted with Weed's. That would explain the busy signal.

"The number," continued Burbank, "was Freeland 6-3824. Hawkeye saw the dial through the door of the telephone booth. Check on special directory listings gives the name J. L. Drongo; residence, 42 Northley Place."

"Report received."

The Shadow hung up the earphones. The tiny light went out. The Shadow's hands disappeared; when they returned to the glow of the bluish lamp, they carried a cardboard folder brought from a file cabinet.

Within the folder were photographs and documents, all bearing reference to the racketeer called Butch Drongo, whose initials, J. L., were used only for such purposes as directory listings.

Minutes passed, while The Shadow studied his complete notations. Then a hand clicked the bluish light. The sanctum was plunged into absolute darkness. A whispered laugh crept through the gloom; when it faded, only stillness remained.

The Shadow had left his sanctum. An invisible prowler of the night, he had fared forth to investigate the affairs of Butch Drongo. Circumstances indicated that Butch was the big shot whom Sneak Losbach and Weed Hessel served.

SOON afterward, the drowsy chauffeur of a big limousine came suddenly to life as he heard a quiet voice speak through the tube to the front seat.

"Wake up, Stanley," came the words. "Drive to 42 Northley Place."

"Yes, Mr. Cranston."

Stanley chewed his lips as he started the car. As chauffeur for Lamont Cranston, to whom this car belonged, Stanley encountered many puzzling experiences. One baffling point was the ease with which Cranston entered the car and left it—unseen and unheard.

Perhaps Stanley's bewilderment would have lessened had he known more facts. Actually, the chauffeur served two masters. One, the real Cranston, was at present absent from New York. The other was a mysterious personage who passed himself as Cranston whenever the millionaire was away.

The occupant of the rear seat was The Shadow. Garbed in black, shrouded in darkness, he had simply used an imitation of Cranston's voice to give the order to Stanley. When they reached their destination, The Shadow would tell Stanley to wait. Again unseen, he would leave the big car.

After that—still unseen—The Shadow intended a secret visit to the domicile of Butch Drongo.

CHAPTER III
THE CLOSED DEAL

WHILE The Shadow was planning his trip to 42 Northley Place, other visitors had already arrived there. Curt Sturley and Shim Torson had reached New York. They had alighted in front of a squatty apartment building and Shim was ordering a tall, ugly-faced doorman to send Curt's coupé to the garage.

Curt was studying his surroundings. Northley Place was a dead-end street where several apartment buildings sprouted from among old, decrepit houses. Shim chuckled as he walked Curt into the lobby of No. 42.

"These joints was supposed to be spiffy," explained Shim, "but they went sour. The guys that built the apartment houses left too many dumpy places along the street. This one here—

No. 42—was sold off cheap. Butch Drongo bought it."

"And that's why he lives here?"

"Sure. It's a good address, and Butch always likes to put on the dog. Some of the rest of us have got apartments here. Butch will fix you up with one."

"The doorman works for Butch?"

"Yeah. And Butch owns the garage where your car is going."

Curt noticed a gloomy stairway leading up from the lobby. They passed it; Shim rang the bell of an elevator. A car arrived, manned by an operator as tough-faced as the doorman. Curt and Shim rode up to the sixth floor. There they stepped into a narrow hall. Shim nudged his thumb frontward.

"That door," he explained, "blocks off the stairs. Butch don't want no guys sneaking up. Out there"—he pointed to the rear of the hall, where a door stood open—"is nothing but a balcony. Kind of an upstairs porch, like they have on all the floors; but nobody can get to it.

"This is where we're going." Shim was facing straight across the hall, where Curt saw a single door. "It's Butch's apartment. Takes up the whole of this floor."

As Shim spoke, the door opened. A sad-faced, glinty-eyed man looked out at them. Shim waved a greeting.

"Hello, Jigger."

"Hello, Shim. Butch is expecting you. Come on in."

Curt entered with Shim. They walked to the rear of the apartment and found a comfortable living room. Looking from the window, Curt saw a continuation of the balcony that lined the rear of the building. Off beyond, distant in the night, were the myriad lights of Manhattan.

"Here's Butch—"

Curt turned about at Shim's words. A bulky man had stepped into the living room from another door. He was attired in tuxedo shirt and smoking jacket; above his stiff collar, he displayed a face that wore a pleased leer. Curt recognized Butch Drongo.

"BUTCH" DRONGO —leader of a band of crooks.

THE racketeer had a proper nickname. His face was wide-jawed, ruddy of complexion. His long, solid chin formed a contrast to his broad, stubby nose. His forehead was straight; prominent brows hung high above his sharp, narrow-slitted eyes.

When Butch grinned, he showed large, blunt teeth, well adorned with gold mountings. His hand was the size of a small ham. It carried a crunching grip when Butch received Curt's clasp.

"Hello, Curt," greeted Butch, in a pleased voice. Then, to Shim: "Outside."

Shim departed by the door which Jigger had previously taken. Butch waved Curt to a chair, pulled fat cigars from his pocket and offered one to the arrival. They lighted the cigars and Butch's grin hardened as he put a remark.

"I thought I'd fetch you, Curt."

Curt nodded. His straight features registered no expression. Curt simply placed his hand into his vest pocket and produced the half of the gold napoleon.

"Where did you get this, Butch?"

Butch laughed.

"It's the McCoy, ain't it?" he quizzed. "The thing you told me you'd been looking for?"

Curt nodded.

"It came off a dead man," stated Butch. "A guy that looked like a sailor. Nobody knows who he was."

"Do you know who killed him?"

"I've got an idea, but there's no way to be sure until we find the guy."

"Who is he—the one that you suspect?"

Butch shook his head. He eyed Curt and puffed his cigar. When he spoke, his words carried growled emphasis.

"Look here, Curt," announced Butch. "You and me are friends. You worked with me once, and you were useful. We cracked some nifty cribs, and you were the guy that figured the ways to get into them."

"Then we washed up, Butch. I was through with that business."

"So was I, Curt." Butch grunted a harsh laugh. "The rackets looked better. I had dough. I got into them. I didn't need you, but I didn't forget you. I need you now."

Curt gave no response.

"The rackets have slipped," continued Butch. "I've been looking for something else. Right now's the time to spring it. Plenty of smart guys have been moving out of town. There's chance for some big jobs.

"That's why I need you. I knew there was a way to get you. Once you told me what you were after. You said you'd gone crooked because you were sore about something, and because you figured it was the best way to find something you wanted. I thought you were screwy when you talked about a half a coin—a thing you called a broken napoleon.

"Then I came across one. You've got it right there, in your mitt. It's yours to keep, but I'm wise enough to know that you need more dope on it. All right—I'll help you. But you've got to be in with me."

CURT was meditative. Without speaking, he reached into another pocket, twisted something from the lining. Gold gleamed between his fingers. Butch gaped as he saw another half of a broken napoleon.

"You've got one already!"

Curt nodded his head.

"I had this one all along, Butch," he replied. "But I had no way of finding the man it came from."

"It's the other half of the one I handed you through Shim?"

"No. Look at them, Butch. Each one is the same half, each from a different coin."

Butch examined the broken napoleon and nodded, puzzled.

"I've got to find the man they came from," insisted Curt. "That's part of the deal, Butch."

Butch displayed a hard grin that looked unpleasant.

"That wasn't the way you put it, Curt. You were coming in with me, anytime I picked up a broken napoleon."

"I'm in, Butch. That's why I want to know who bumped the sailor."

The ugliness departed from Butch's grin. The big shot leaned back in his chair.

"We'll get the guy," he promised. "You'll know who he is afterward."

"You don't trust me, Butch?"

"Sure, I trust you. But I want to see you work. The first thing is to pull the job that I'm thinking about. That will rate you ace high with the outfit. Then I'll tell you who's the mug you want. Don't worry—he'll keep. I've got two torpedoes watching for him."

Butch returned the broken napoleons. Curt pocketed them, then put a question:

"Tell me just one thing, Butch. Does the man call himself Levautour?"

Butch shook his head.

"Never heard that moniker," he declared, emphatically. "No. The bird we're after never called himself Levautour. He's not a Frenchman, either."

Curt was speculative.

"I'm not sure that Levautour is a Frenchman," he declared. "All I know is that he is the brains behind his business. His subordinates called him Levautour, but it's probably not his real name."

"Why not?"

"Because it has a significant meaning. Levautour is the French for *le vautour*. Translated, that means 'the vulture.'"

BUTCH showed interest. It was Curt's turn to change the subject.

"The man you're watching," he declared, "is probably a subordinate. Nevertheless, he may lead me to the man higher up. All I ask is that you keep watching him, that you tell me when you've trapped him."

"That's a deal, Curt."

"All right. Then we can talk our own business. What's this job you want my advice about?"

Butch broadened his smile. He leaned forward in his chair.

"It began with a hot tip, Curt," he explained. "There's an old bank—the East Side Trust Co.— that don't ordinarily have much dough in the vault. But it's got a fund there, right now. Plenty of mazuma—cash and securities not to be moved out for a couple of days yet.

"We've dug a tunnel, right up to the vault room. All set to soup it. When that blows, we move through. But there's a catch to it."

"The wall is too weak?"

"You guessed it, Curt. If we let it ride, we may knock out the underpinnings. That would queer the job. So much junk would drop that the hole wouldn't do us any good. We've got to have a way to keep the wall from ruining us."

Curt smiled.

"Not difficult," he decided. "Simply a matter of engineering. I can arrange supports that will off-set any structural weakness."

"Great!"

Leering in pleased fashion, Butch produced a folded paper. Curt studied a penciled diagram. He nodded approvingly, for he saw that the measurements had been carefully recorded.

"I'll figure this in a couple of hours, Butch," declared the engineer. "You can put men to work tomorrow; I'll supervise the job."

"We can get to the tunnel easy. But how long will it take to put in the braces, after you've figured where they belong?"

"Several hours at the most."

Curt pocketed the diagram for future reference. Butch thwacked a big fist against an opened palm.

"Great!" he asserted. "Then we can set the job for tomorrow midnight. Listen, Curt. I've got a room here in the apartment for you. Stay here tonight and dope things out the way you want them."

Rising, Butch crossed the room and opened the door. He called; Shim appeared with "Jigger"; then came two others: the thugs who had accompanied them in the ride up along the Hudson. They had arrived back in the touring car. Butch motioned all the men to chairs. In satisfied fashion, the big shot was ready to deliver a proclamation.

ALL were watching Butch, as he stood at one end of the room. None had their eyes toward the window; hence they did not observe the slight motion that occurred upon the balcony. Outside, the rail showed dingy white. It darkened as a blackish shape moved over it, obliterating the stone posts.

The window was open, for the night was mild. Advancing blackness blocked the city lights. A shape was close against the window. Muffled in a sable-hued cloak, that form produced inkiness alone.

The floor inside the window caught a portion of the blackness and showed it as an encroaching blot. Motionless, that patch formed a grotesque silhouette that made a hawkish profile. No one within the room observed it.

The Shadow had arrived upon the balcony. He, like Butch's henchmen, was present to hear the big shot's announcement.

"We've got a new setup," growled Butch. "You guys are to pass it along to the rest. Curt Sturley here rates ahead of everybody but me. He's my partner. Get it?"

Nods from the seated listeners.

"What Curt says goes," added Butch. "It goes, the same as if it came from me. There won't be any question of us giving different orders. We know how to work together. This partnership sticks—unless one or the other of us is knocked off, which won't be likely. But if either of us goes, the other owns the outfit."

More nods.

"Tomorrow night," concluded Butch, "we pull that East Side Trust Co. job. Curt is going to be in charge of it until I get there. You'll know more about it tomorrow. Pipe the news about Curt in the meantime."

Butch waved toward the door. His henchmen made their departure. Butch closed the door. Standing there, he motioned to Curt. His new partner approached.

"That shows I'm on the level, Curt," declared the big shot. "You don't want anything more, do you?"

"I didn't want that much, Butch."

"I know, Curt. That's one reason why I set you up so big. But there's something you've got to remember. In case anything hits me, the outfit is yours. So you can keep on working for what you're after."

"Thanks, Butch."

"And there's only one way to keep it going right," added Butch. "That's to use rods. You used to lay off of guns. That don't get you anywhere. These mugs like a guy who handles a gat and lets them do the same."

Curt's smile hardened.

"I understand, Butch," he declared. "Don't worry about that. I've been plenty of places where guns were in order. I can handle a six-shooter better than any of these fellows that work for you."

"You can?" Butch's eyes gleamed their approval. "Say—I never knew that, Curt. You always said you didn't want a gat."

"Just as a matter of policy. I didn't rate as a big shot in the old days."

"You can handle a smoke-wagon?"

"Certainly. When I was out West, I carried a .45 and used it out in that country."

"Then it's all jake. I've got a rod for you, Curt. When these gorillas see you carting a big Roscoe, they'll be all for you."

Butch opened the door and beckoned. He and Curt went out to join the others. The door closed.

DARKNESS moved by the window. There was no need for further motionless vigil by The Shadow. Outside, a stretching figure became visible on the balcony. Gloved hands gripped the stone rail; a soft laugh came from unseen, whispering lips.

The Shadow swung out into darkness, hanging batlike above a courtyard more than fifty feet below. His hands moved downward, alternately, until he was clinging to the very bottom of a stout stone post.

From this precarious position, The Shadow swung outward, then inward. His feet aimed for the space of the balcony on the lower floor. His hands released their hold. With a swish, The Shadow cleared the rail below; his inward course landed him upon the fifth-floor balcony.

The Shadow entered a darkened apartment. He emerged later, into a deserted hall. He reached the stairway and descended to the ground floor. The lobby was empty; The Shadow glided to an obscure corner.

Soon the hard-faced doorman entered and went to the elevator to ring for the operator. The Shadow's shape emerged from gloom. A tall, cloaked figure, it moved ghostlike to the street. Burning eyes peered from beneath the brim of a slouch hat. The way was clear to the limousine, parked a hundred feet away.

Soon, Stanley heard an order through the speaking tube. The chauffeur responded; the big car pulled away. But what Stanley did not hear was the whispered laugh that sounded later. It was audible only in the rear of the car.

The Shadow had cause for mirth. Silently, secretly, he had penetrated to Butch Drongo's headquarters. There, he had learned of crime that was to come. He had seen Curt Sturley, Butch's new partner in the game. The Shadow would be ready to meet crime.

But The Shadow, although he knew the result of the deal between Butch and Curt, had heard nothing of the earlier details. He knew where crime was due to strike; he had no facts concerning the preliminary preparations.

Nor had The Shadow gained the reason why Curt Sturley had joined up with Butch Drongo. To The Shadow, Curt was merely a newcomer in a vicious game, one who looked competent and could conceivably have closed a deal with the big shot.

Butch had spoken of the past. The Shadow knew, therefore, that the partnership was a renewal of something that had gone before. But the vital fact of the new setup was still lacking.

The Shadow had heard no mention of those mysterious objects that were responsible for the ultimate arrangement, nor had The Shadow spied those bits of gold that Curt Sturley had replaced in his pocket.

The Shadow had gained no inkling of the broken napoleons.

CHAPTER IV
THE KING IS DEAD

THE next night brought a deluge to Manhattan. The rain began at noon; it increased after sunset. Before midnight, the downpour was terrific. Traffic was halted by stalled taxicabs. The streets were clear of pedestrians. All this was to the liking of a leering man who was riding in the rear of a sedan.

That man was Butch Drongo. The big shot saw stormy weather as an aid to his schemes. He was divulging that fact to Shim, seated beside him, while they listened to Terry mutter at the wheel.

"Curt has fixed things right," declared Butch. "He's waiting for me to pass the word. Then we're going through. A quick job with a getaway."

"And plenty of guys to cover," added Shim. "We put four cars near the bank."

"If the bulls see those busses," chuckled Butch, "they'll think they're stalled on account of the rain. It's a cinch, Shim, this job."

"That's what Jigger says. There weren't many people going into the bank when he was watching it this afternoon."

"Which means there's been no leak, no chance for coppers to be posted inside."

The sedan skidded; Terry righted it and cursed through the half-opened window. His remarks were directed toward the square-faced driver of a coupé that had swung across the sedan's path. Half a minute later, Terry swung wide of a stalled taxicab.

Taking a side street, the sedan slowed and rolled into the door of an obscure garage. A tough-faced attendant was waiting there. He closed the door as soon as the car had entered. Butch and his companions alighted. They went into a little room at the rear of the garage.

Shim raised a trapdoor to reveal a flight of stone steps. The men descended. Butch led the way along a stone-walled corridor. They met two guards. Butch growled orders.

"Stick here, Shim," commanded the big shot. "Keep posted on what's doing in the garage. I don't want any trouble up there."

BUTCH continued along the passage. Its lighted sector ended. Terry produced a flashlight. Butch proceeded amid a glare that showed rough-hewn walls. This was a cramped portion of the tunnel that had been burrowed to the East Side Trust Co.

A turn in the tunnel. Bull's-eye lanterns showed a group of men stationed in a hollowed room. Beyond was a wall, braced with heavy beams. Curt Sturley, grimy-looking, delivered a grin when he saw Butch.

"All set?" queried the big shot.

"Right," replied the engineer. "Look it over, Butch. What do you think of it?"

"Looks like a jigsaw puzzle to me."

Curt Sturley smiled. Grins showed on the faces of the thuggish workers who had placed the bracings under Curt's direction.

"But if you say it will work," added Butch, "I'll know it's the McCoy."

"It will fill the bill, Butch."

"Then give it the soup."

Curt ordered the blast. Fuses were lighted. The entire band withdrew beyond the turn in the tunnel. Soon came a boom that quivered the thick air of the passage. Stone trembled. A clatter sounded from the chamber beyond, then died.

Butch Drongo was the first to reach the shattered wall. The big shot delivered a cry of satisfaction.

The wall had been shattered by the explosive. Huge cracks showed in the remaining masonry, but the blasted passage stood open. Ladderlike timbers, properly placed, had dropped apart into a new position. Like buttresses, they were supporting the cracked sections of the wall.

"Great!" ejaculated Butch, turning to Curt. "We'd have wrecked the works if it hadn't been for you, Curt! You know your stuff!"

"Get the swag," suggested Curt. "I'll stay here with two men. We'll fix it so as we can blow the timbers as soon as you're out."

Butch and three followers surged through the gap. They reached a broken wall. On one side lay the vault, on the other, a flight of steps that led to the main floor of the bank. The vault door still stood; but it was useless. The blast had shattered the side of the vault.

Bull's-eye lanterns revealed stacked boxes in the vault. Butch pointed; before he could give an order a sharp cry came from a man beside him. The fellow had chanced to turn his lantern toward the stairs. The light had revealed a singular sight.

Rigid on the steps, black against the whitened stone, stood a cloaked figure. Above shrouded shoulders were blazing eyes. Peering from beneath a hat brim, they caught the glare of the electric lantern and burned back their challenge. Gloved fists projected from the cloak; each gripped a heavy automatic.

"The Shadow!" snarled Butch. "Get him!"

SWAG forgotten, the big shot whipped forth a revolver. His henchmen jerked guns into play. They saw but one present mission: to down this being who had placed himself at a vantage point close by their long-sought goal.

As revolvers aimed, automatics tongued flame. With the first roar of gunfire came a weird, amazing laugh—the cry of an incredible battler who had sought the strife that was to be. It was the laugh of The Shadow; eerie mirth that spelled dismay to Butch Drongo's henchmen.

The roar of The Shadow's big guns was accompanied by the sharp staccato of revolvers. Bullets chipped the stone steps as crooks delivered their hasty outburst. Butch and his fighters were wide in their fire. But The Shadow's aim was true and efficient.

Crooks sprawled beside the big shot. Butch, half covered by the bodies of his crippled minions, was unready to own defeat. Rising with a venomous cry, Butch steadied, finger on trigger. He had a bead on The Shadow.

The black-clad battler faded with an elusive twist, forward down the steps. Butch pressed the trigger. A crackle sounded as his bullet clipped stone. Still snarling, Butch lowered his aim toward a moving form of blackness. Before he could fire, a spurt of flame arrowed straight in his direction.

Butch sagged. His revolver dropped from his hand. Staggering backward, Butch stumbled through the wall into the outside chamber. He slipped past the clutch of the two thugs who were there with Curt. Reaching the engineer, Butch slumped his heavy bulk upon Curt's shoulders.

"The Shadow!" he gulped. "Get him!"

The thugs heard the order. Guns came from their pockets. They sprang forward through the gap, with flashlights to show the way. Curt heard guns roar as he supported Butch.

"I'm—I'm done," gasped Butch. "The Shadow got me. The mob's yours, Curt. Shim—Shim knows—"

"About the broken napoleon?"

"Ask him—ask Shim—about Deek Calligan—"

Butch rolled from Curt's grasp. The big shot was dead. His successor wheeled toward the gaping wall. Gunfire had ended; the two reserves were sprawling from the hole. They had fared badly with The Shadow.

CURT sprang forward. He pressed the button of a flashlight that was attached to a fuse. That done, he dived for the turn in the tunnel. Reaching it, he dashed in the direction of the garage, expecting to hear a shuddering blast from behind him.

No explosion came. Curt did not realize why until he had reached Shim Torson, standing with two henchmen, by the steps up to the garage. Then the answer dawned. The Shadow had come through the opening from the bank. He had extinguished the short fuse that Curt had started with the electric current.

Instead of being felled beneath a mass of exploded debris, The Shadow was still prepared for battle. Realizing that he was in sole command, Curt barked an order to the men beside him.

"Butch is through," he cried. "I'm the big shot. We're dealing with The Shadow. He's here, I tell you. Coming through—"

Cries from the men beside Shim. They had flicked flashlights along the passage. The blaze showed a blackened shape that had made the turn. A laugh came quivering through the tunnel. It was a ghoulish burst of merriment—a new challenge to men of crime.

Revolvers blazed. With their flash came the stabs of automatics. Bullets sizzled through the tunnel. Walls crackled as the shots ricocheted. The two crooks dropped, groaning. Their flashlights bounced upon the rough floor of the passage.

Curt made a grab for one. Shim stopped him.

"Upstairs!" croaked the lieutenant, in the darkness. "Don't let him see a light! We'll get him when he comes after us!"

They reached the steps. There, Curt wrested savagely away from Shim. Aiming along the darkened tunnel, he fired rapid shots in the direction of The Shadow. Shim had previously extinguished the lights near the stairs. Curt thought that his strategy would work.

Instead, a mocking laugh came from the blackness. The Shadow had expected the fire. Flattened somewhere, he had remained unscathed by the barrage.

"Hurry, Curt!"

The new big shot heeded Shim's cry. Together, Curt and his lieutenant reached the garage above. Shim sprang to the wheel of the sedan, which was headed outward. Curt reached the seat beside him, then aimed toward the stairs, through the door to the room that housed the trapdoor.

INSTANTLY, a figure appeared there. Like a being from a tomb, The Shadow emerged. Curt saw the outline of the cloaked avenger. Savagely, he pressed the trigger of his revolver. The hammer clicked.

For the first time, Curt realized that he had used every cartridge in that wild fire through the darkened passage. He had gained the aim he wanted; it proved futile since his revolver was empty.

Again The Shadow laughed. His left hand swung its automatic into play. Curt was saved by Shim's sudden action. The attendant had opened the garage door. Shim shot the sedan forward.

The Shadow's bullets found space alone. The sedan had whisked away before he could loose quick shots. Ending his fire, The Shadow sprang out into the garage, just as the sedan swung to the safety of the street.

The garage attendant—a hoodlum like the others—was jumping to the wheel of an old roadster. He swung about as The Shadow reached him; but he had no time to aim a gun that he was tugging from his pocket.

The Shadow had thrust one .45 beneath his cloak. With his free hand, he gripped the thug by the neck and hoisted him bodily from the car.

The crook's gun clattered off to a corner. The man himself lay half dazed while The Shadow boarded the roadster and drove off in pursuit.

Sirens were wailing from the street. The police had received the alarm. Cars were everywhere; scattering crooks were firing vainly as they sped through the rain.

As The Shadow's car roared to the chase, a coupé drove a touring car upon the sidewalk. Crooks, leaping from the touring car, ran squarely into the hands of two patrolmen. The coupé sped away.

The Shadow's laugh sounded within the roadster. Cliff Marsland was the driver of the coupé.

The scene was repeated at another corner, where a taxicab suddenly blocked the path of a crook-manned automobile. Swinging about, the crooks encountered a radio-patrol car. The thugs surrendered amid a hail of bullets.

That cab belonged to The Shadow. Its driver, a

hackie named Moe Shrevnitz, had been posted to stop the getaway of crooks.

The Shadow, himself, was after greater game. He wanted to bag the coupé that contained Curt Sturley and Shim Torson. But the new big shot and his lieutenant had managed a lucky getaway. Scouring the rain-swept streets, The Shadow could gain no trail amid the deluge.

The Shadow had thwarted crooks. Butch Drongo had fallen in fair combat. Underlings were scattered—wounded, dead and prisoners, they had reached the hands of the law. Curt, Shim and a few others were all who had escaped of a score or more who had been on the job, either inside or outside.

BLOCKS away from the scene of thwarted crime, Shim Torson swung the sedan into a dead-end street. Jumping from the car, he motioned Curt Sturley to follow him.

Together, they cut through two blocks and entered a small apartment house. They went to the second floor; there, Shim unlocked a door and turned on a light to show a poorly furnished room.

"Not much of a joint," declaimed the lieutenant, shakily, "but it ought to do us. Butch had it ready for a hideout."

"We can use it then," decided Curt, gruffly. "The king is dead."

"Who do you mean? Butch?"

"Yes." Curt doffed a water-soaked raincoat and tossed his flabby hat upon a table. "The king is dead. You know what comes next. Long live the king."

"I don't get it. Butch was rubbed out, so how can he—"

"I'm the king right now."

Shim grinned in pleased manner as he heard the announcement. He shoved forward a congratulating hand.

"Sure," he agreed. "That's right. That's the way Butch wanted it. You're the big shot, Curt."

Shim stood by, as if expecting an immediate order.

"Butch told me something," declared Curt. "He said to ask you about Deek Calligan."

"When did Butch tell you that? Just before he croaked?"

"Yes. Down in the tunnel."

Shim nodded slowly.

"I sort of figured it was on your account," he declared. "Yeah, on your account that Butch was watching for Deek. He's got two guys on the job. Sneak Losbach and Weed Hessel."

"Whereabouts?"

"Watching the places where Deek is likely to show up."

"And what about the dead sailor? Who was he?"

"Some bird that Deek bumped, down on the waterfront. It was on him that we found that half of a coin. Butch didn't want me to tell you all I knew."

"What else do you know?"

"That's all. Some guy saw Deek Calligan one night. Then he found the dead sailor. The busted coin was lying alongside the sailor. So this guy—it was a pal of Jigger's—brought it to Butch. We figured Deek bumped the sailor right enough, because Deek took it on the lam. But the bulls aren't wise, so it's likely Deek will be back."

SHIM paused while Curt pondered. After an interval, Shim added:

"There's some of the guys got clear tonight. There's other gorillas, too, that Butch didn't need on the job. They're all for you, Curt. I can get them together—and there's some good jobs waiting when you're ready."

"Good," decided Curt. "I'm in this game, Shim, and I'm going to stick in it. But there are two jobs that will come first. One is to get Deek Calligan."

Shim nodded. The fact that Butch had intended to get Deek was sufficient to win his approval.

"And the second," added Curt, grimly, "is to get The Shadow."

Shim gaped. His expression changed, however, when he eyed Curt's face. The new king was grim. His features were set; his eyes shone with a dangerous glint.

Shim Torson was impressed. If ever he had seen a man who looked capable of his boast, it was Curt Sturley. Whatever his past inclinations had been, Curt had definitely changed them. He had turned to crime. He was prepared to stay.

Two motives inspired him; both of vengeance. One was to follow the trail of his own, that of the broken napoleons. It could be reached through Deek Calligan.

Curt's other motive, to deal with The Shadow, had gained its inspiration tonight. The Shadow had balked Curt's intended path. The Shadow would suffer.

Deek Calligan came first, purely because the capture of that man would mark a step along a much-sought trail. Curt was ready to let The Shadow rest until afterward. But when he considered his two motives, Curt did not realize that they already held a definite connection.

The chances were that when the newly-crowned big shot sought Deek Calligan, he might find The Shadow also.

CHAPTER V
MEN IN THE DARK

IT was two nights later. The stir of thwarted crime had died. The law had taken credit for the bagging of Butch Drongo. It was believed that the big shot's power had been so thoroughly shattered that no one could restore it.

One fact, however, belied that opinion. It was a situation that the law did not observe. Two rowdies—former henchmen of Butch Drongo—were still at their appointed posts. Weed Hessel was watching the Hotel Santiago. Sneak Losbach was lookout at the Ladronne Apartments.

On this second night that followed crime, a tall, peak-faced man arrived at the Hotel Santiago. He entered the lobby, nodded to the clerk and put the nervous question:

"Anybody been asking for me?"

"Nobody, Mr. Calligan," replied the clerk. "No messages either. Staying here overnight, are you?"

"Maybe. I'll be back."

Deek Calligan stalked from the lobby. Outside, he paused and strolled about, looking toward the Bowery; at times, peering back into the hotel.

He did not notice a man who was standing in the doorway of a cigar store, chatting with the proprietor. That man, squatty and dark-visaged, was Weed Hessel.

Nor did Deek observe a furtive, hunch-shouldered man who sidled away soon after his arrival. Neither did Weed spy this observer. It was Hawkeye, departing to make a call to Burbank.

Deek went back into the hotel and lounged there for a dozen minutes. All the while, he watched passersby outside the window. Satisfied at last that no one was on his trail, Deek left the Santiago. Instead of taking a taxi, he began a stroll.

Weed Hessel followed.

A BLOCK away from the Santiago, Deek stopped in a drugstore and made a few purchases. When he came out, Weed again took up the trail. He met a thuggish-faced lounger near the corner and tipped him to stay closer to Deek. This man was one of the survivors of the fray at the East Side Trust Co.

Weed, himself, stayed farther back, so that Deek would not see him. This system of changing the trailer was a good one. Weed liked it so well that he paused as he crossed a darkened street and struck a match to light a cigar.

As he stood there on the curb, Weed heard a voice deliver a raspy whisper:

"Psst! Weed!"

"Yeah?"

"Slide down here a minute. Got a tip for you."

Weed stepped into the darkness beside the wall. There was a brief sound of a scuffle, then silence. Weed did not emerge.

Two blocks ahead, Deek had quickened his pace; but only for a short interval. He began to loiter in a lighted area; the man who was trailing him lingered by a gloomy corner. There, the follower was joined by two others. They formed a plan among them, interrupted only when a truck lumbered along the side street and parked a short distance away.

Deek had started forward, briskly. One of the three men took up the trail. The others of Curt's minions remained to give him a head start. As they lingered by the corner, they heard footsteps close beside them. Both men wheeled.

Instantly, attackers closed with them. The two crooks never had a chance. They sagged beneath the power of competent foemen. Their companion, up ahead, did not know what had happened to the pair that he had left.

Blocks farther on, the trail was passed to another of Curt's henchmen. The one who dropped it was immediately decoyed by a cautious whisper. Like the others, he did not return from the darkened spot where he advanced.

WHEN Deek finished a long walk that brought him close to the Ladronne Apartments, the last of many relayed followers took up his trail. This was Jigger, erstwhile bodyguard of Butch Drongo, deceased.

Jigger was only two dozen paces in back when Deek entered the apartment house. About to follow, Jigger heard a whisper from a darkened spot against the grimy wall.

"Psst! Jigger!"

"Yeah? That you, Sneak?"

"Sure. Listen, Jigger. Slide into the drugstore. Stick in the second phone booth."

"What for?"

"So's you can tip me off to what's what. You'll find a number written right under the pay box. It's an apartment up in the Ladronne."

"Near Deek Calligan's?"

"Sure. That's where I'll be posted."

Jigger headed into the drugstore, only thirty feet beyond the apartment house. He found the telephone number, noted it, then came outside. He lounged about; but saw no sign of Sneak Losbach. He decided that the watcher had gone into the apartment house.

Jigger went back into the drugstore, put in a telephone call and came out again. He had communicated with Curt and Shim. He was to await their prompt arrival.

MEANWHILE, Deek Calligan had reached the eighth floor of the apartment house. He had unlocked the door of an apartment; inside, he had turned on the lights of a living room. Deek pulled an envelope from his pocket.

It was an opened letter; one that bore a Bermuda stamp. It was addressed to D. B. Calligan. General Delivery, Jersey City. Deek drew the letter from the envelope, read its contents and managed a wry smile.

He then proceeded to a task which he had apparently not found opportunity to perform before. He lighted a match and carefully applied the flame to the corner of the envelope.

At that instant, a click made Deek turn rapidly about. The match dropped from his fingers; the flame had no more than scorched the envelope's corner. Deek listened; he had thought the sound came from the door. He decided that it might have originated in the courtyard. Thrusting the letter into his pocket, he opened a window and peered downward.

All was silent. Deek heard the click again. This time he was sure it came from the door. Spinning about, he shoved a nervous hand to his coat pocket. He was too late. The door had opened; it was swinging shut. But it had admitted a visitor.

Deek saw The Shadow.

Formidable upon the threshold, the cloaked fighter stood as a figure of vengeance. A gloved fist held an automatic; the gun loomed forward as The Shadow advanced. Deek stood still, numbed with fear.

Burning eyes bore accusation. Deek failed in a snarl; trembling, he jumped to a denial before it was demanded.

"It—it wasn't me!" he gasped. "I didn't bump Eddie Moroy. Honest—it was some sailors off the ship he came in on! I didn't—"

The Shadow had noted Deek's left hand. The crook's right had given up its endeavor to draw a gun; but the left had moved. It was covering the pocket wherein Deek had thrust the telltale letter. The Shadow's eyes bored in that direction.

Slowly, Deek pulled the singed envelope into view. He wavered as he thrust it forward. The Shadow received it, a mirthless laugh coming from his lips.

Frenzy seized Deek. He had turned coward at sight of The Shadow. But at heart, Deek was vicious; he was a killer. A sudden realization that he could expect no mercy brought Deek to an unexpected action.

JABBING forward, he grabbed The Shadow's arm and thrust it aside. As his left hand acted in that fashion, Deek found his gun with his right.

The Shadow swung forward. Like a blackened avalanche, he sent Deek against the wall beside the window. The very power of the attack should have overwhelmed the murderer. But Deek's head struck a window drapery; the thud was lessened.

With the combined drive of rage and terror, Deek grappled with his foe. Neither he nor The Shadow could bring a gun hand into play. They swung back and forth in front of the window, locked in a powerful struggle.

Suddenly, The Shadow sagged. With a triumphant snarl, Deek swung his gun arm and leaped forward to deliver a stroke upon The Shadow's head. In his effort, he forgot his grip upon The Shadow's gun arm.

An automatic jabbed upward, its report muffled by Deek's descending arm. The bullet clipped the crook's wrist. As The Shadow twisted aside, Deek went headlong, howling, straight upon the low-sided window. Swinging up, The Shadow heard a shriek and saw his enemy toppling outward.

Deek's hurtle had thrown him off balance. The Shadow was too faraway to save him unless Deek could manage temporarily to stay his own fall. Deek tried to save himself.

His effort was mistaken. Wildly, the killer thrust his right arm toward the window frame. His fingers, numbed by the bullet, were useless. They slid scrappily from the woodwork. Deek launched headlong into the blackness of the courtyard.

The Shadow reached the window just as the murderer disappeared upon his plunge. Staring downward, The Shadow glimpsed a flicker against lighted windows. Then a crackly thud sounded from below. Stillness followed.

Deek Calligan had gone to his doom. Murderer of Eddie Moroy, he had deserved the death that his own viciousness had brought him. No one in the apartment building had heard the muffled shot of The Shadow's gun; nor had the finish of Deek's fall attracted attention. Courtyard windows remained closed.

STOOPING, The Shadow picked up the envelope. He had thrown it to the floor at the beginning of the fray. His gun beneath his cloak, The Shadow used both hands to extract the letter. He read terse lines.

Softly, The Shadow laughed. His tone was chilling; it bespoke a knell for Deek Calligan. It carried a prophetic note, as if The Shadow had learned news that belonged with the future. Whispered echoes tongued back their answer from the wall, as if in corroboration of The Shadow's thoughts.

Slowly, The Shadow moved from this room that Deek Calligan would no longer occupy. Outside the apartment, he crossed the hall and delivered a series of muffled taps upon an opposite door. The door opened; The Shadow stepped into darkness. The door closed.

All was silent in the lighted hall. Closed doors gave no token of the action that had occurred. No one would have known that Deek Calligan had plunged to death from one apartment, that The Shadow had joined the darkness of another room.

Curt Sturley, the recognized big shot, had mapped a plan to trap Deek Calligan. He had wanted to make the murderer talk. Curt Sturley would never gain his long-awaited chance.

The Shadow had visited Deek Calligan before him.

CHAPTER VI

VANISHED FOEMEN

SOON after The Shadow had met with stern adventure in the Ladronne Apartments, a taxicab wheeled up in front of the building. Two men alighted. One paid the driver and the cab rolled away. The other began to look warily about.

The arrivals were Curt Sturley and Shim Torson. Curt had dismissed the cab; Shim was looking for Jigger.

The pair was visible in front of the building. Jigger saw them and approached from a spot near the drugstore.

"Anything from Sneak?" queried Shim.

Jigger shook his head.

"He's waiting to hear from me," he replied. "I can give him a buzz, now that you're here."

Shim turned to Curt:

"How about it, boss?"

Curt gave the nod, but when Jigger started away, the new chief stopped him. Curt passed an order to Shim.

"You talk to Sneak instead of having Jigger do it. Jigger has been in that drugstore before."

Shim nodded and entered the drugstore. Curt made query of Jigger.

"Seen any of the outfit, Jigger?"

"Only one guy," replied Jigger, with a wise grin. "The rest are laying low, like they're supposed to."

"Good. We'll wait here for Shim."

THE lieutenant appeared a few minutes later. He spoke to Curt in an excited whisper.

"Sneak wised me to something," explained Shim. "He's in an apartment a good ways off from Deek Calligan's. A couple of minutes ago, he slid over by Deek's door. It didn't sound like Deek was in there."

"What did Sneak hear?"

"Nothing. That's why he's worried. His apartment is at the back of the building. Looking out the window, he saw a truck pulled up in the next street. It's sitting there, with the motor going."

"And what does that mean?"

"Sneak thinks that Deek's got it posted there, ready for a getaway."

"There's a rear exit?"

"Sure. Down through the fire tower."

Curt pondered, then snapped his fingers.

"Here's the gag we'll work," decided the big shot. "Leave Sneak where he is. Jigger, you go up and check. Get into Deek's apartment, if it seems that he has gone.

"Shim, you and I will go around to the back. Pass the signals all along, so the boys will be ready when we need them. We can stop by the truck and wait for Jigger to join us."

Plans made, the trio parted. Curt took one route, Shim the other. Each as he walked along, paused at intervals in darkness, to light a cigarette. Each made a bobbing signal with the match flame. It was a call for all gorillas to assemble.

Jigger entered the apartment house. He took the automatic elevator and rode up to Deek Calligan's floor. He found the murderer's apartment and listened by the door. The report that Shim had brought appeared to be correct. Jigger heard no sounds from the interior.

Trying the door, Jigger found that it was unlocked. Elated, the rowdy entered. He looked about the living room and noticed the opened window. Approaching it, Jigger peered down into the courtyard. He did not observe the outline of Deek's crushed form.

Jigger had left the door open. He went out into the hall, closing the door behind him. He looked about for signs of Sneak Losbach. Gaining none, Jigger took a stealthy course past a turn in the hall. He was making for the fire tower.

Half a minute later, a door opened. The Shadow appeared from the apartment where he had taken temporary abode. Gleaming eyes had watched Jigger's departure. Those same optics blazed keenly as The Shadow traveled toward the fire tower.

DOWN below, Curt and Shim had reached the back of the apartment house. They had spotted the truck; it was a small storage van, with big doors in the back. The front seat was encased in glass; there, a driver was crouched sleepily over the wheel. The motor was throbbing; apparently the truck driver expected to leave very soon.

Curt and Shim held a confab on the sidewalk behind the truck. The lieutenant vouchsafed information.

"Them windows is bulletproof," determined Shim. "That gives us a tip to what's up. Deek Calligan's taking no chances. He knows somebody's looking for him. He's got things fixed for a getaway."

"That's obvious," agreed Curt. "What's more, there's only one way Deek can work it smoothly. When he shows up, he'll pile into the back of this van. Then the driver will pull away from here—"

"And there'll be no chance of bagging Deek, unless we lay for him right here, Curt."

"There's a better way than that, Shim."

Curt was eyeing the closed van. Shim caught the idea.

"I get it!" popped the lieutenant. "If we get inside, we'll grab Deek when he gets here."

"That's it," chuckled the big shot. "We won't be taking chances, either. We have a dozen men all around here." He swept his arm to indicate the street. "They'll be wise to what we want done. They'll stop the van if they have to blockade it."

"Sure," agreed Shim. "What's more, Curt, it's a bet that there's a way from the inside up to the front seat, so Deek can crawl up with the driver. We'll land both of them, and then—"

"Shh! There's somebody coming from the fire tower!"

The speakers paused and edged back into the darkness. A cautious form appeared. Shim whispered to Curt:

"It's Jigger."

"Good," returned the big shot. "Find out what he knows—"

SHIM approached Jigger. The underling gave the news of his visit to Deek's apartment. Curt, joining the speakers, made a prompt decision.

"Deek's waiting somewhere in the building. He wants to be sure the coast is clear. We're ready for our stunt, Shim. Signal the outfit—"

"What about Jigger, Curt?"

"He'll get into the van with us."

Shim stepped to a lighted spot near the closed rear of the van. He made gesticulations, pointing to the van, then spreading his arms and bringing them together, a sign that hidden thugs were to close in when the vehicle attempted a getaway.

Curt was opening the doors of the van. They were unlocked; the interior showed nothing but blackness. The big shot motioned to his two companions. The trio crept into the van. Curt drew the doors almost shut. In total blackness, he whispered:

"Crawl up, Jigger, and find the way into the driver's seat. You stick here, Shim, along with me. One on each side of the door. Ready with your gat. I have a smoke-wagon all set."

"If we both jab Deek, he'll shove his dukes up in a hurry."

"That's the ticket, Shim. Be ready."

A whisper came from Jigger. The searcher was crawling back from the front of the van.

"There's no way through to the front seat—"

There came an interruption. A sharp click came from the rear of the van. Like hungry jaws, the big doors snapped shut; the clash of a lock told that Curt Sturley and his subordinates were trapped.

"THE driver!" exclaimed the big shot. "He's got the van wired. He heard us talking; he must have yanked a lever to close those doors."

"Maybe we can smash them," gulped Shim. "We gotta get out of here, Curt."

"We can't make it that way. If we can get at the driver—"

It was Jigger who interrupted, reiterating his former statement.

"We can't get through to the driver, Curt—"

A rumble came from the front of the van. The machine was in motion. Jolting off at an angle, it was swinging along the street, carrying the prisoners.

Curt delivered a savage outburst.

"Levautour!" he roared. "This is his work! Deek Calligan was his man! Deek murdered the sailor who had the broken napoleon!"

The lumbering van was increasing its speed. Shim, who knew nothing of Levautour, shouted more pressing news.

"The outfit ain't on the job! Nobody's stopping this bus! We gotta shoot our way out of it, Curt!"

Jigger had produced a flashlight. He clicked it. The rays showed the blank interior of the van, its floor carpeted; its walls steel-lined. As they rolled around a corner, Curt pounded the floor with the butt of his revolver. The sound proved that metal lay beneath the carpet.

Wildly, the big shot looked back and forth, within the range of Jigger's flashlight. The van was a veritable black Maria. It gave no chance for an exit. The only openings were tiny holes near the roof, that looked like ventilators.

"We'll make things hop, though!" rasped Curt, defiantly. "Plug away at those holes up there. Maybe some of the gorillas will hear the shots."

Before the big shot took aim, a response came from the holes themselves. A hissing sound filled the jouncing van. A soporific odor reached the nostrils of the prisoners.

"Gas!" ejaculated Curt. "Those aren't ventilators—they're gas jets. We're through—"

Curt had dropped his big revolver. He was burying his nose beneath the upturned collar of his coat, to gain pure air. Shim flung his gun aside; Jigger threw away his flashlight. They copied the big shot's example.

It was useless. Gasping in the darkness, the trio

subsided, overwhelmed by the flow of hissing vapor that had been loosed upon them.

BACK at the rear of the Ladronne Apartments, a figure had arrived near the lighted patch of sidewalk where the van had been stationed. It was The Shadow. Shrouded in fringing darkness, the master sleuth turned his keen gaze upon the deserted street.

There was no sign of the departed van; there were no skulking figures in the darkness. The gorillas upon whom Curt Sturley had counted had been absent all along. They had been bagged beforehand. Like Weed Hessel, they had been taken all along the line.

Curt Sturley, the new big shot, was gone. With him, the members of his organized band were departing for places unknown. A Manhattan mystery had been repeated. As other riffraff had been removed in the past weeks, so had hoodlums gone the same route tonight.

Crooks had met with the unexpected. Where they had been trapped, The Shadow now stood alone. A specter in the darkness, he surveyed desolation.

A grim laugh issued from The Shadow's lips. That mirth was difficult to interpret except for one pronounced feature. It bore a prophetic tone, as though The Shadow were contemplating a task that lay ahead.

Paper crinkled in a black-gloved fist. It was the letter that The Shadow had taken as trophy of his fray with Deek Calligan. From The Shadow's lips came a whispered name, one which he had read as the signature of the letter which Deek had received.

"Levautour—"

The Shadow had gained a clue to a master crook—one whom Curt Sturley had hoped to combat. The quest for Levautour had become The Shadow's own.

Already, The Shadow was formulating plans that would carry him along the path that Curt Sturley had sought. Through his intervention in schemes of crime, The Shadow had gained the trail that involved the broken napoleons.

CHAPTER VII
NEW MYSTERY

IT was daylight when Curt Sturley fully awakened. Clouded daylight that carried the gloomy tint of approaching dusk. Amid intermittent slumber, Curt had sensed many sounds: scrapings, clankings, and with them, swaying motion.

But he had never expected to find himself in his present surroundings. Lifting himself from a crinkly mattress, Curt blinked. His eyes saw bluishness that rose and disappeared. His nostrils sniffed the tang of sea air. Blinking again, Curt saw steel bars; beyond them a rail.

The blue expanse came into view below the clouded sky. A hoisting roll followed. The blue was gone. Curt turned to see the grimy white of cabins. He was seated upon a mattress that rested on the deck of a ship. But he could not leave his present location. He was surrounded by the steel bars of a cage.

There was a door to the cage, but it was padlocked. All along the line were other cages. In them, appropriately, Curt saw the thugs whom Shim had termed "gorillas." Every remaining member of Butch Drongo's band had been taken in a roundup.

A face peered toward Curt. It was Shim's. Like the others, the ratty-faced lieutenant had been assigned to an individual cage. Shim's pasty features showed a sickly look. His grin was sour.

"Where are we?" queried Curt, hoarsely. "How did we get here, Shim?"

"We got loaded aboard," returned Shim. "Last night. Out of the van."

"You were awake then?"

Shim shook his head.

"I just guessed it," he replied, sourly. "When I came to, it was morning. You must have sniffed the gas heavier than I did."

"You were in this cage when you woke up?"

"Yeah. And at noon, a guy brought me some chow. We all had grub; we'll be getting more pretty soon."

Rising, crouched, Shim gripped the bars of his cage. He spoke in a wise, confiding tone.

"Say, Curt—I found out one thing. I've got the name of this packet we're aboard. The guy that brought the grub told me when I asked him. You know what this tub is?"

Curt shook his head.

"It's the old ghost ship," declared Shim. "The one we saw floating down the Hudson. It's the *Reciprocity*."

Curt gaped. Shim managed a grin at the big shot's surprise. Then, huskily, Curt put another question.

"Where are they taking us?"

Shim shook his head. He looked troubled.

"Who else have you seen?" demanded Curt. "Have you gotten a look at the skipper?"

Another headshake.

Curt arose. Unsteadily, he paced the small area of his cage, muttering to himself. Shim, listening, overheard the grumbles of the man who could no longer claim to be a big shot.

"It's Levautour," mumbled Curt. "Levautour— the vulture. He's aboard this tub. Levautour—if I could get at him—if only—"

"Here's the mug with the chow," interrupted Shim, cautiously. "Don't let him hear you talking, Curt."

A MAN was approaching, wheeling a table ahead of him. He was attired in a simple uniform, and wore a visored cap. He was evidently serving as a steward. From the table, he took bowls of food and cups of water, to pass them through the bars of cages.

"Look at those monkeys," scoffed Curt to Shim. "Yellow, the lot of them. Once they've been trapped, they lose their fight."

Shim, himself, was reaching eagerly through the bars of his cage, to receive a bowl of food. Curt watched contemptuously. The steward arrived at his cage. Curt made no effort to reach for the bowl that the man proffered. He saw the steward grin.

"Sorehead, eh?" queried the steward. "Or maybe you're starting a hunger strike?"

"Neither," retorted Curt. "I'm no monkey— that's all. Shove that bowl through the bars—and add an extra cup of water. If you're the soup disher on this packet, I want service."

The steward nodded. He looked pleased. Politely, he placed the food within Curt's reach. The unthroned big shot surveyed an excellent stew and nodded his commendation.

"It looks good," declared Curt. "I'll give you my opinion after I've eaten it. If it comes up to expectations, I'll forward my approval to the cook."

"I guess he'd like to get it," returned the steward, pleasantly. "You look like the only judge of good food among the passengers."

With this reference to the prisoners, the steward followed his route. Curt watched the rest of the captives snatch at the bowls that he gave them. Nodding slowly, Curt smiled. He had made a good start with the steward. He felt that he could gain further results.

Darkness had settled before the prisoners had finished their meal. The *Reciprocity* was ploughing steadily southward. Lights were glimmering along the cabins. The roll of the ship, though considerable, had not bothered the captured landlubbers.

"Guess they'll put us into cabins soon," remarked Shim to Curt. "There's bars on the doors."

The prediction proved correct. An hour after dinner, the steward appeared with a pair of husky sailors, who wore holsters with revolvers. The steward unlocked a cage; its prisoner was marched sheepishly into a cabin. The cabin door was locked; the steward ordered the transfer of another prisoner.

When the trio reached Curt's cage, the former big shot made a polite request.

"Mind if I stay out here?" he asked. "I like sea air. I've slept on decks before."

"Stay here if you want to," replied the steward. "The same goes for the rest of you." He moved on to Shim's cage. "How about it, fellow? Want to go inside?"

"Yeah," decided Shim. "I don't want to sleep out here."

The rest of the prisoners made the same decision as Shim. After they had all been transferred, Curt sprawled out upon his mattress. Alone, he stared up toward the darkened sky.

A CLICK of bowls roused him from his reverie. The steward was collecting the dinner dishes. When he arrived at Curt's cage, the man passed in a pack of cigarettes.

"These were in your cabin," he stated. "They're supplied to all on board. I thought you'd want them out here."

"Thanks."

"And how did you like your dinner?" The deck lights showed a friendly smile on the steward's face. "Shall I compliment the cook for you?"

"Sure. Say, by the way"—Curt pointed to the lights—"when do you douse the glims?"

"Pretty soon. Why?"

"I'm likely to get lonely when it's dark," Curt smiled as he opened the pack of cigarettes. "Drop around and say hello. Maybe I can tell you a few ghost stories."

The steward's smile ended. A sober expression showed instead. Curt pretended not to notice it. He was lighting a cigarette. Without another word, the steward proceeded on his way.

Half an hour later, the lights were extinguished. Curt had finished four cigarettes; he started another in the darkness. While he was smoking, he heard a whisper outside the cage. It was the steward's voice—a cautious hello.

"Hello," returned Curt. "I thought you'd be back. You're a regular guy."

A pleased chuckle from the steward.

"Something I wanted to ask you," proceeded Curt, "but I didn't want those lugs to listen in. Who's the skipper of this packet?"

"The skipper?" queried the steward. Then, after a pause: "His name is Captain Trayvor."

"He owns the ship?"

"No. He is in command, that's all."

"Who's the owner?"

"I don't know."

Curt grunted. The steward's own words had shown puzzlement.

"Is he aboard?" demanded Curt. "The owner, I mean?"

"Yes," returned the steward. "But he keeps to his cabin."

"Tell me. Did you ever hear the name Levautour? A mention of a man by that name?"

"No. Who is he?"

Curt responded with a cautious, impressive whisper.

"Levautour is the owner we're talking about," he confided. "He's a crook—and a dangerous one. He's smooth, Levautour is."

"You've met him?"

THE steward's tone betokened worriment. Curt pressed home his answer.

"No. But I've heard about him and his methods. You know what he'll do with this ship? He'll scuttle it—with all on board."

"Including the crew?"

"Of course. He wants to sink me and the other prisoners. You don't think he'll leave Captain Trayvor and the rest of you alive to talk about it, do you?"

No comment from the steward.

"I want a showdown!" insisted Curt. "One that will work for both of us. That's fair enough, isn't it? You've locked up the prisoners for the night. I'm willing to work alone—with you to call in the captain as a judge."

"What's your plan?" asked the steward. His voice was tense in the darkness. "You can't start a mutiny."

"I don't want to. Let me out of this coop. Slip me a gun and show me the way to the owner's cabin. I'll walk in on Levautour and make him talk turkey. You'll be outside, ready to call the captain when I give the order."

"But I'll be blamed for any trouble."

"Not at all. You can say that I grabbed you through the bars, snatched your keys and unlocked the gate, that I left you groggy. When you finally found me, I was in the owner's cabin and that I'd picked up a gun somewhere."

"I have a gun with me now."

"Good. They'll think I took yours from you. Naturally, you'd call the captain. When he shows up, I'll make him listen."

Curt's scheme must have impressed the steward. The prisoner heard a clatter of the lock. The steward was opening it with a key. The door swung wide; in the darkness, Curt felt metal press his hand. It was the steward's gun.

"Come along," whispered Curt. "Show me the cabin."

They moved into the ship. Under a light, Curt cracked open the revolver. It was a .32, fully loaded. Closing the weapon, Curt took the passage that the steward indicated. At a turn, he heard the man whisper:

"The second door on the right. Be cautious when you enter. I'll wait here. Leave the door open so I can listen."

"Good," decided Curt. "Then you can hear me talk to Levautour. Your testimony may help when the captain arrives."

Leaving the steward, Curt stalked to the door. He listened outside; then, slowly, he turned the knob with his left hand. With the barrier free, Curt pressed it inward. Edging into a lighted room, he half closed the door behind him. Curt gripped his gun in his right hand.

IN the center of the cabin was a desk. Behind it sat a middle-aged man with grayish hair. His features had a dignity; yet they possessed a hardness. The man was studying a stack of documents. The slight nods that accompanied the perusal appeared to be a habit with the man.

While the *Reciprocity* rolled onward, the pound of its old engines thrummed the passing moments. Steady, ready with his gun, Curt Sturley scowled as he eyed the man before him. He moved a few paces toward the desk. Under his stare, the seated man became suddenly conscious of the intrusion.

The man looked up. His features showed new hardness. His eyes glinted, unblinking, at the sight of the revolver. He must have recognized Curt as one of the prisoners, but he gave no token of surprise.

Tense moments; then the man at the desk delivered a harsh question:

"Why have you come here?"

Curt took another pace forward.

"To have a showdown!" he rasped. "To make you come clean, Levautour!"

No change of expression showed upon the solid visage of the man behind the desk. His lips spoke a puzzled query:

"Levautour? That is not my name."

"You are Levautour," challenged Curt. "That's the alias you have used. Death is better than you deserve, but it's all I'm going to give you."

"You intend to kill me?"

"Yes."

"Ah!" The man nodded. "My conjecture is correct. I supposed that I was faced by a murderer."

"You were wrong. I have never killed before. I am the one who is dealing with a murderer. It is you, Levautour—"

A hand raised in interruption.

"Before you make your decision," announced the man at the desk, "I advise you to notice the mirror which is in back of me. It affords an excellent view of the door, that you just entered."

The door swung wide; in the darkness, Curt felt metal press his hand. It was the steward's gun.

CURT'S gaze raised instinctively. He saw the mirror; but it did not reflect the door. Blackness had banished sight of the barrier. From blackness peered two eyes, that were mirrored like living coals. A harsh oath escaped Curt's lips.

Curt wheeled to face the doorway. He stopped, his gun half aimed. A quivering laugh came mockingly to his ears. Realizing his dilemma, Curt began to slowly inch his revolver toward the figure that had challenged him.

Then, from behind him, came a pounce. It was the man at the desk, the one whom Curt had denounced as Levautour. Hard-gripping fingers caught Curt's gun wrist. A powerful twist sent Curt wheeling to the right. His hand lost its clutch; his revolver thudded the floor. The man from the desk dropped back to his chair.

Disarmed, Curt Sturley could only stare at the being who blocked the door. Hands raised, Curt looked squarely into the looming muzzle of an automatic. Lifting his gaze, he saw burning eyes above cloaked shoulders. Those eyes shone from beneath the brim of a slouch hat.

Curt Sturley had come here to seek a man whom he regarded as a foe. He had come in quest of Levautour; he had thought that he had found him. The tables had been turned by another entrant. Curt was faced by the personage who had intervened.

Thereby, Curt had met another whom he swore to encounter—one whom he had never connected with Levautour; a foeman whom he had not expected to find upon this ship. He was faced by one from whom he could seek no mercy; for Curt—only a few nights ago—had deliberately tried to kill the person who now held him helpless.

Curt Sturley's path of freedom had been short-lived. Weaponless, he stood face to face with The Shadow!

CHAPTER VIII
THE MUTUAL QUEST

THE SHADOW stepped in from the doorway. He closed the door behind him. His cloaked figure plain in the light, The Shadow calmly put away his automatic and moved closer to Curt Sturley. With a sweeping gesture, The Shadow indicated a chair in front of the desk. Wondering, Curt seated himself.

Enlightenment had come upon the prisoner. The *Reciprocity* was The Shadow's ship. Curt had been mistaken in his surmise that the man behind the desk was Levautour.

That man was speaking. Curt saw The Shadow deliver another gesture. Understanding, Curt turned to face the man at the desk. He saw a cold smile upon strong lips. The man spoke.

"My name," he announced, "is Slade Farrow.* You were mistaken when you called me Levautour."

Curt nodded. He looked uneasily to his left, where The Shadow had taken a position beside the desk. It seemed that The Shadow was to pass judgment upon what was to come. New realization struck Curt. That steward, on deck, had been The Shadow!

"I am a criminologist," declared Farrow, regaining Curt's attention. "I have devoted my life to reclaiming men who have chosen crooked paths. I learned, long ago, that environment was an element which all men could not conquer.

"Statistics show that crime is far more prevalent in localities where opportunities for crime exist. There is one way, therefore, to deal with the chronic criminal. That is to place him in an environment where he will find crime useless."

The atmosphere had changed. Curt had been taken into conference. The Shadow's threat was ended. Bewildered, Curt could only nod in agreement with Farrow's words.

"It is true," continued the criminologist, "that certain men have criminal instincts. They differ, therefore, from those who have simply chosen crime because it seems profitable, or because associations compel them.

"The law, however, does not differentiate, except in cases of the criminally insane. A term in prison is as much a punishment as a cure. Frequently it fails in both requirements. Our penitentiaries accomplish one thing, definitely: They remove men who are a menace to society and keep them away from persons upon whom they could prey."

FARROW paused. Curt, staring, could hardly believe his present surroundings. The motion of the *Reciprocity* kept telling him that he was on shipboard; but the setting was more like that of an office, wherein a conference was under way.

"Two obstacles confront the penitentiary system," proceeded Farrow. "One is the difficulty of placing minor offenders there. The other is the premature release of men who should remain longer. Besides these, we have cases of persons who scarcely belong in prison at all; those who have realized the folly of crime, even before they have been ordered to pay the penalty for misdeeds.

"Basically, society should be considered. Men who seize opportunities for crime should be immediately removed. That accomplished, we can consider the welfare of the men who have been weeded from society. There is no reason why they should not be given opportunities of their own.

---

*Note: See *The Chinese Disks,* Volume 2

"Some months ago, I was enabled to put this plan into practice. I obtained the finances necessary, through a friend who saw the merit of my purpose. I established an environment wherein crime would be useless."

Farrow smiled slightly. Curt saw him glance toward The Shadow. Curt guessed promptly that The Shadow was the friend to whom Farrow had referred.

"Picture a cluster of tropical isles," declared Farrow, "where necessities have been provided, where there is work for men to do; leisure to enjoy. Where money is absent; where fight for possession is not needed.

"Such is the colony which was established, to which this ship is bound, carrying a new cargo of men to join those who have gone before. Segregated from the world, they will gain an opportunity to live as they should; to develop, under suggestion, a self-government of their own.

"True, there are problems. That is why the colony is subdivided. After preliminary sojourn upon one island, where supervision exists, the colonists move to another where fuller privileges are allowed, unless they prove incorrigible. Then they are placed upon an island with others of their kind.

"All have the option of being returned to the place from which they came; there, to be given over to the law, with full evidence of crime that they have committed. None—even among the incorrigible—have exercised that privilege.

"The best community of our group is at present ready to receive relatives and friends of those who live there. We have arranged to extend invitations to those who will come. They will find it a most enjoyable environment. Even those who qualify to return to New York have preferred to remain in their new surroundings."

Farrow stopped, apparently awaiting Curt's comment. The glint of Farrow's eyes was kindly. Curt smiled.

"I understand," he said. "I'm ready for the treatment. I like the sound of it, Mr. Farrow. My own experience has been unusual; my reasons for turning crooked are somewhat unique. Nevertheless, I'm no better than anyone else."

RISING, Curt turned to The Shadow. "I'm ready to go back to my cage," he declared, frankly, "or perhaps the cabin would be better. I have no further scheme. I made a wrong guess; that's why I took a chance. I wanted to find Levautour."

The Shadow's eyes gleamed their approval. His lips spoke a command to Farrow. The criminologist nodded and addressed Curt.

"Sit down again, Mr. Sturley," suggested Farrow. "We would like to discuss a different matter with you—one that concerns this."

Curt turned as he heard a clinking sound upon the desk. Farrow had tossed a metal object there. Curt stared at sight of a broken napoleon.

"One of mine!" he exclaimed. "I had two—"

"Yours are here," interposed Farrow, producing a small envelope. "They were taken from your pocket. This is a third—one that was already in our possession."

There was emphasis on the word "our"; Curt realized that it meant The Shadow.

"You knew about Levautour?" Curt turned to The Shadow, then back to Farrow. "About the half napoleons?"

"Suppose," suggested Farrow, "that we hear your full story?"

Curt nodded. He was anxious to begin.

"A few years ago," he stated, "my father, Jonathan Sturley, owned timber properties in the Northwest. He became involved in a series of transactions. He kept them to himself; but they involved a man who called himself Levautour.

"How deeply my father was concerned, I do not know. He showed worriment; I gained the opinion that he had found Levautour to be a swindler. Apparently, my father made some deal with the man, in hope of self-preservation, for he falsified accounts that were not his own.

"I had gone into engineering. I saw my father only at intervals. I knew, however, that his entire fortune was at stake. If he lost the timberlands, he would be deprived of property worth considerably over a million dollars.

"One day, when I was home, my father received a letter. When he opened it, he turned pale. I saw him remove an object of gold. He went immediately to the library. He forgot to take the letter with him. I read it; it stated simply that the token was inclosed. The letter was signed 'Levautour.'

"My father came back and picked up the letter. He went again to the library. A few minutes later, I heard a muffled shot. I hurried to the library; I found my father dead. The letter was burning in the fireplace. But beside the gun which had dropped from my father's hand was the broken napoleon."

CURT paused. His face showed the ordeal that he had undergone in telling his story. While the *Reciprocity* pounded onward, Curt steadied. The thrum of the engines seemingly drew him from the sadness that memory had produced.

"My father was blamed for steps that he had taken," declared Curt. "My story of Levautour was ridiculed. It was classed as a fable which I had concocted to clear my father's name. Because the law would not believe me, I became contemptuous of the law.

"I knew that Levautour was an existing criminal. I believed that through a career of crime I could learn his real identity. I met Butch Drongo; I devoted my engineering talents to helping him with robbery. I came to my senses and gave up that practice.

"But I had told Butch of the broken napoleon. I promised to join him again, if he could provide a clue to Levautour. A week ago, Butch gained a half coin of his own. It was found on a dead sailor—some poor devil who had probably incurred Levautour's wrath. As with my father, the delivery of that token must have meant doom.

"I had guessed why my father had committed suicide. He had known that death was coming. The sailor had probably tried to escape it. He was murdered by a rascal named Deek Calligan. Butch promised results, if I became his partner. That was why I returned to crime."

Curt paused, then added, soberly:

"When Butch died, I became the big shot. I took on two tasks. The first to trap Deek Calligan, through the measures that Butch had already provided. The second"—the young man turned to The Shadow—"was to meet you again, to deliver the death that I had failed to give, that night in the tunnel."

Curt was ready to receive the wrath of The Shadow. It did not come. Instead, The Shadow delivered a low-toned laugh—a sinister mockery that made the young man realize the futility of his wild desire for vengeance. The Shadow spoke.

"You were marked," came his whisper. "Marked for capture. Your henchmen were taken, one by one. Sneak Losbach was also captured. I spoke with Jigger, in his stead.

"Your career of crime has ended. Your thoughts of evil purpose are forgotten. You have been called upon to make amends. You are willing?"

"I am willing," acknowledged Curt, sincerely, "even though I do not deserve your friendship."

"You deserve it. You have spoken the truth. You chose one commendable cause. You sought Levautour. Your errors can be attributed to that fact."

The Shadow reached toward the desk and plucked up the broken napoleon that Farrow had placed there.

"This token," declared The Shadow, in an awesome tone, "has long been in my possession. You are right; it stands for death. It came from the body of an unknown victim.

"Last night, I found the broken napoleons that you carried. You were seeking Deek Calligan. I had already found him. Upon his person was this letter."

FARROW produced the letter from the stack of papers. He handed it to Curt. The young man gave an excited cry.

"From Levautour!" he exclaimed. "It bears his signature!"

"From Levautour," added The Shadow. "The rogue whose pseudonym means 'the vulture.' It was Levautour who ordered Calligan to murder a sailor named Moroy. It was Levautour, at present in Bermuda, who mailed this letter telling of his new plans."

Aloud, Curt read the brief note, in mechanical fashion:

" 'Will sail on the sixteenth. Deal will be completed during voyage. Trip ends at Boston. Be ready there.' "

"Signed by Levautour," added Farrow, taking the letter. "Do you recognize the signature?"

"Yes," nodded Curt, emphatically. "It is identical with the one that appeared upon my father's letter."

A whispered laugh chilled the room. It was one that promised doom for a man of crime. Curt swung, amazed; The Shadow, though, was no longer beside the desk. Turning about, Curt saw the door of the cabin close. The Shadow had departed.

It was Farrow who brought Curt back from his startlement.

"Plans have been made," declared the criminologist, quietly. "They were dependent upon a test of your nerve. You showed your strength tonight. Crime was not your field. Yet you were ready to strike for what you considered right."

"I wanted to steel myself—"

"For a meeting with Levautour. That was one reason why you tried crime as a forerunner. Very well; you shall have your chance to meet Levautour."

"You know his identity?"

"No. But there is only one boat scheduled to sail from Bermuda on the sixteenth. That is the yacht *Nepenthe*. It is owned by a millionaire named Hubert Craylon. There are several guests on board."

Farrow produced a large sealed envelope, well wadded with documents. He handed the packet to Curt.

"Tomorrow," he stated, "you will be placed aboard a sailing cruiser that will meet us at sea. We are near Bermuda; you will go there as a passenger on the sailing ship. When you land, you will visit the person to whom you have a letter of introduction—which you will find in the envelope.

"Steps will be taken to make you a guest aboard the *Nepenthe*. There you will do your utmost to identify the person who is Levautour. He will certainly be aboard the yacht. Measures have been taken to conceal the fact of Deek Calligan's death."

Curt nodded, then questioned:

"And when I discover Levautour?"

"You will be instructed," replied Farrow. "You may rely upon that."

Rising, the criminologist extended his hand across the desk. Curt received Farrow's clasp.

"You will have a cabin of your own tonight," smiled Farrow. "One without bars. The number is fifteen. You will find it in the next passage. You will need sleep. We meet the cruiser early tomorrow."

THRUSTING the packet into his pocket, Curt left Farrow and went to the cabin that the criminologist had designated. There, he found two suitcases; they contained new apparel for his coming journey.

Curt was about to open his envelope; he decided to wait until the morning. He would not need the information until after he was aboard the cruiser.

Turning in, Curt felt the urge for sleep. The long rolls of the steamship were lulling. But there were thoughts that filled the young man's mind and held him awake for minutes longer.

Mystery was explained. The exodus of crooks from Manhattan had not been voluntary. The Shadow had removed lawbreakers, wholesale, until only one dangerous mob remained: Butch Drongo's.

Those ranks had been thinned by conflict. Then, aided by agents, The Shadow had gathered up the remnants. Curt—with Shim and Jigger— had been the last to fall into the mesh.

Curt Sturley was through with crime. With his relinquishment of evil, he had gained a new purpose, an opportunity to show his real desire for justice.

Curt Sturley, deposed from the big-shot glory that he had not sought, was again a man of honor. He was in the service of The Shadow.

CHAPTER IX
IN BERMUDA

IT was two days after Curt Sturley's meeting with The Shadow and Slade Farrow. A long, slim sailing cruiser was keeling through a rising swell, heading between two promontories where tropical trees showed upon the shore.

Curt, perched by the bow, was studying the brilliant blue of the water. He was gaining his first view of Bermuda.

A broad-faced man approached and clapped Curt on the back. Curt looked about to see a friendly smile. The man removed a pipe from his mouth and commented:

"Well, old bean, here we are. Over to the right"—he gestured with his pipe—"is the dockyard. Something of a naval base, you know. That craft"—he indicated a long, rakish ship that was steaming toward the harbor—"is a cutter. All engines, with a cockpit barely large enough for a dozen passengers."

Curt was pulling his own pipe from his pocket. The broad-faced man produced a pouch and offered him tobacco.

"Thanks, Mr. Lemuel," said Curt. "Not only for the tobacco, but for the trip. I appreciate your meeting the *Reciprocity*."

"Why mention it, old chap?" queried Lemuel. "Jove! When Lord Jenley notified me that a friend of his had taken a tramp steamer from New York, expecting to call at Bermuda, only to find that he was mistaken, I was more than gratified with the privilege of bringing that friend ashore. Quite a lark for both of us. Fancy you boarding a tramp steamer. Fancy me, meeting the vessel at sea."

"Yes. It was a lot of fun."

Lemuel strolled away, chuckling.

CURT, again staring at the water, pondered.

The letter of introduction that he carried was addressed to Lord Basil Jenley. Two facts were apparent: Lord Jenley was a visitor of great consequence in Bermuda; he was also a friend of The Shadow.

Probably he knew The Shadow by some other identity. Whatever the case, Lord Jenley's presence in Bermuda had been fortunate. The Shadow, in planning a campaign against Levautour, had cabled or radioed Lord Jenley. Matters had been arranged. Lemuel, a Bermudian who enjoyed sailing cruises, had been dispatched to meet the *Reciprocity*.

The cruiser had swung within a headland. They were approaching a landlocked harbor. Lemuel came forward and pointed again with his pipe.

"Cute navigation for you," he remarked. "Watch us negotiate this passage. Those are the Two Rocks, one on either side."

"Just about space enough to scrape through."

"No, Mr. Sturley. More than that. Large steamships travel through Two Rock Passage. But it is scarcely a biscuit toss to either rock."

"Too bad we don't have the biscuits."

"My word! That would be admirable. We could test the bally claim, couldn't we?"

Lemuel chuckled continuously until they had glided through the passage. Then, in a changed tone, he spoke words of caution.

"Nothing is to be said regarding our new passengers," stated Lemuel. "Such were Lord Jenley's orders. You came in from New York on a steamship; you understand that, Mr. Sturley. No passports are necessary in Bermuda."

"I understand."

"You merely chanced to go with me on a short cruise off the islands. Nothing's to be said about the Steamship *Reciprocity*."

"Of course not."

Lemuel pointed to the waterfront. They were passing hotels that faced Hamilton Harbor. Docks lay beyond. While Curt studied the interesting scene, Lemuel walked away. But he left Curt puzzled. Lemuel had mentioned "passengers" from the *Reciprocity*. Until now, Curt thought that he had been the only one to come aboard the sailboat.

THE boat docked. Curt saw a tall, sharp-visaged man upon the shore. Erect of carriage, bronzed of features, this person had an appearance of importance. He wore a dark mustache, which contrasted with his white attire. Curt studied the face beneath the pith helmet. He saw the man glance in his direction.

Close beside Curt, Lemuel whispered:

"Lord Jenley."

His lordship must have recognized Curt as the passenger; for the moment the young man stepped ashore, he was welcomed. Lord Jenley delivered a hearty handclasp, then spoke to Lemuel. After a short chat, Lord Jenley invited Curt to ride with him in a waiting victoria.

They entered the carriage and rode through the town of Hamilton. Listening to the click-click of the horse's hoofs, Curt studied the scenes that they passed. All traffic was on the left. Carriages were numerous; so were bicycles. Automobiles were conspicuously absent.

The atmosphere reminded Curt of a hothouse; yet it was pleasant. Quaint old buildings intrigued him. As they ascended a hill on the outskirts of Hamilton, Curt noted houses, all of blinding white. The carriage was approaching one of these residences.

"My cottage," remarked Lord Jenley. Then, in an undertone, which the driver could not hear: "You have the letter?"

Curt produced it. His lordship read the message, then nodded.

"From my friend Lamont Cranston," he remarked. "Very well, Mr. Sturley. We can soon discuss matters. I have arranged everything."

THE carriage stopped; they alighted and entered the cottage which proved to be of ample proportions. A servant brought cooling drinks. Alone, in a huge living room, the two men were ready for their conference.

"Concerning your proposed voyage," asserted Lord Jenley, "I have made full arrangements for you to go aboard the yacht *Nepenthe*."

"Tomorrow?" queried Curt. "The sixteenth?"

"Yes. The *Nepenthe* is to sail shortly before sunset. It is fitting that I should advise you regarding certain circumstances."

Curt nodded. Lord Jenley meditatively tilted his drinking glass. Ice tinkled; his lordship took a swallow, then proceeded:

"The *Nepenthe* flies the British flag. It is commanded by Captain Petterton, an officer of high recognition. The yacht, you understand, is owned by Hubert Craylon, an American. He spends his winters in Bermuda; hence the yacht, which he purchased here, is of British registry."

Curt expressed his understanding.

"Mention was made to me," stated Lord Jenley, "of a man called Levautour. I have heard of him. He is a scoundrel. His hand has reached to many lands. He has been responsible for cunning swindles in various portions of the British Empire.

"I understand that he may be aboard the *Nepenthe*. Therefore, I quite willingly acceded to the request that you be introduced to Mr. Craylon. I have cabled London, asking the C. I. D. men be dispatched hither from Scotland Yard. While we await their arrival, it is advisable that none aboard the *Nepenthe* know of our suspicions.

"You have been recommended to me as an investigator. You shall have *carte blanche* while you are on the *Nepenthe*. Whatever may occur, your testimony will be given first consideration."

Curt smiled. The possibilities pleased him.

"I have arranged matters subtly," declared Lord Jenley. "It is known that the *Nepenthe* intends to call at Boston. I communicated with Mr. Craylon and requested that he take a friend of mine as passenger. You will be that friend."

"When will you introduce me to Craylon?"

"Presently. He is to visit me this afternoon. Jove!" Lord Jenley set down his glass and stared through the window. "This must be his carriage. We are in luck, Sturley. Craylon is not alone. One of his guests is with him. You will have opportunity to size the man beforehand."

CURT was looking through the window. Two men were stepping from a victoria. One was tall, elderly and dignified. His gray hair contrasted with the briskness of his manner; for he was quick of footing as he stepped from the carriage.

The other man was huge. He was of middle age, bulky in build, beefy of countenance.

Powerful, but overweight, he used a stout cane as he stepped to the ground.

"The gray-haired man is Craylon?"

Lord Jenley nodded as he heard Curt's question. "And the other?"

"An American. His name is Gregg Lownden. A Westerner, I understand. Reputedly a magnate, a mine owner. He completed one short cruise aboard the *Nepenthe,* and has evidently managed an invitation for the coming one."

Lord Jenley met the arrivals at the door. Curt was beside him; the Englishman made immediate introductions. Hubert Craylon delivered a dry but friendly smile, with a warm handclasp.

"We shall be pleased to have you with us, Mr. Sturley," announced the yacht owner. "When my friend, Lord Jenley, asked that I carry a passenger to Boston, I assured him that whomever he recommended would be welcome."

Gregg Lownden had extended a massive hand. Curt received it. He was impressed by the strength of the beefy man's grip. Lownden rumbled a basso greeting, that seemed thunderous in contrast to Craylon's milder, higher tone.

"You'll enjoy the cruise, Mr. Sturley," he assured. "Our last excursion was excellent. The *Nepenthe* is a dandy ship. We'll show you a good time on board."

"Step inside," suggested Lord Jenley. "We can chat a while."

"Sorry, sir," returned Craylon. "We have to ride into Hamilton. The captain has taken on two new crew members. I must interview them. You know we lost a man overboard during the last cruise."

Lord Jenley raised his eyebrows in surprise. Lownden rumbled a comment.

"The man was morbid," he announced. "He had brought some grog aboard. He must have been drunk. He was missing one morning. Such things happen on any ship."

"They should not occur on the *Nepenthe,*" rebuked Craylon. "As owner of the yacht, I felt responsible. My opinion was that we might have been undermanned. I discussed the matter with Captain Petterton. He agreed that we should take on two new crew members to replace the one."

"You never lost a member of the crew before," put in Lownden. "Don't forget that, Craylon. That, in itself, is proof that the man himself was to blame."

"Perhaps," conceded Craylon. "Nevertheless, Lownden, we shall be prepared for a future emergency. Moreover, we are taking on another man, an English butler who claims that he can serve as steward."

"Unusual," remarked Lord Jenley.

"So I thought," chuckled Craylon. "I heard of the fellow some time ago, when he applied for a berth on the *Nepenthe.* His name is Leigh; and he bobbed up here in Bermuda. Apparently, he came here some time ago, on the chance that I would hire him."

"So you intend to do so?"

"Yes. The man has excellent recommendations. I intend to interview him this evening."

CRAYLON bowed his departure. Lownden gave a clumsy wave. The two reentered the victoria. With Lord Jenley, Curt watched the carriage roll away.

"You knew about the sailor going overboard?" queried Curt. "The fellow that they mentioned?"

"Yes," replied Lord Jenley. "His name was Dyson. But I doubt that the incident has any significance. Lownden was right on that point. Every so often, a roustabout manages to ship aboard a vessel. One can never tell what will happen to such unreliable beggars."

Curt was thinking of a sailor named Moroy— the one who had been murdered in New York. He wondered if Moroy had once been with the crew of the *Nepenthe.* Before he could question Lord Jenley, the Britisher gripped his arm.

"More luck!" he exclaimed. "See this carriage, Sturley? It contains two others who will be with you on the *Nepenthe.*"

Another single victoria had drawn up before the cottage. A dapper young man had alighted. Of medium build, he had a foreign air. His face was sallow; his hair, like his pointed mustache, was dark and shiny.

"Count Louis Surronne," remarked Lord Jenley, in an undertone. "Presumably of the old French nobility, but something of an adventurer."

The count was helping a girl from the carriage. Curt noted that she was stylishly attired, attractive of face. The girl was a pronounced blonde; her hair shone golden in the sunlight.

"Hubert Craylon's daughter," informed Lord Jenley. "Her name is Diana Craylon. Come—we shall meet them."

Advancing, Jenley and Curt met the arrivals on the walk. He welcomed them and made introductions. Curt noticed the manner in which the pair received the news that he was to be a guest aboard the *Nepenthe.* Count Louis showed a tightening of his sallow lips; his eyes held an unpleasant glare.

Diana Craylon, on the contrary, seemed quite pleased at the prospect of a new passenger. That fact could have accounted for Surronne's displeasure; for it was apparent that the count was interested in the girl and probably wished no rivals.

The two had come to inquire for Hubert Craylon. Diana said that her father had left word

COUNT LOUIS SURRONNE—guest aboard the *Nepenthe*.

that he intended to visit Lord Jenley. Learning that Craylon and Lownden had gone, Surronne and Diana made their prompt departure.

"Was Surronne on the previous cruise?" queried Curt, as he and Lord Jenley walked back into the cottage.

"Yes," replied The Shadow's friend. "Count Louis has been on several cruises. Well, Sturley, you have met them all. That is, everyone of consequence, with the exception of Captain Petterton, for whom I can vouch."

"You mean," returned Curt, "that one of those persons may be Levautour?"

"Yes. It is quite possible."

"What about the butler from London?"

LORD JENLEY looked surprised, then delivered a brief laugh. As he noticed the serious expression on Curt's face, his lordship sobered.

"I had quite forgotten the new steward," he declared. "What did Craylon say the chap's name was?"

"Leigh. And he added that the man had arrived in Bermuda a while ago."

"Yes." Lord Jenley nodded. "I recall that Craylon did make that statement. You have raised an excellent point, Sturley. I advise you to watch this man Leigh. He is a factor to be considered."

"And the new crew members?"

"Ah, yes. They should also be observed. Along with the others. But come, my friend! You are crossing the bridge too early. At present you are my guest—not a passenger aboard the *Nepenthe*. Let us summon the carriage and take a short drive to the provinces. You must see Bermuda while you are here. The scenery is delightful."

Twilight showed Curt Sturley and Lord Jenley, in the latter's victoria, approaching the outskirts of Hamilton. The air was glorious; the fragrance of the isle was conducive of lulling thoughts. But Curt's mind remained upon the coming task.

With tomorrow, he would begin a game of wits. It would be his duty to learn the identity of Levautour, the master rogue whose tokens of doom were broken napoleons.

Curt Sturley was more than anxious to repay his obligation to The Shadow.

CHAPTER X
BEYOND THE HARBOR

IT was after sunset, on the sixteenth.

The yacht *Nepenthe* had cleared Hamilton Harbor. Steaming past the dockyard, the ship had passed the last vessel in view, a long gray cutter, inward bound.

The *Nepenthe* had been navigated beyond the coral reefs that surrounded the Bermuda Isles. Long, sleek and seaworthy, its white sides flecked with foam, the yacht was dipping into rising waves.

They were due for heavy weather. Hubert Craylon had made dry mention of that fact while they were seated at the dinner table. He had added that the *Nepenthe* could outride any tropical storm. Craylon apparently had confidence in the size and construction of the yacht.

Curt had shared the confidence. The *Nepenthe* was a much larger boat than he had anticipated. His own knowledge of ships told him that the owner's opinion was correct.

Curt had made a brief study of the yacht itself, to learn the plan of the vessel. Forward was a large salon that served as combination dining room and lounge. It was the social portion of the yacht.

The front of the large lounge formed a half oval, well supplied with windows. The rear wall was straight and had a large doorway with sliding doors. Stepping through these, one came to a cross passage that had end doors to the opposite decks. The decks themselves began with a large space forward, circled the large lounge and continued to the stern.

From the cross corridor behind the lounge, one had two choices. He could either take an obscure stairway that led below, to the galley and the engine room, or he could head directly along a central passage that went sternward.

This terminated in a flight of steps. Descending, the corridor continued. On each side were the doors of staterooms. Beyond the long rows of cabins was another cross passage that consisted merely of two alcoves.

From each of these, steps went upward; at right angles to the ship, joining at the top to form an exit on the stern deck. The stairway had banisters; they were placed crosswise, so as to occupy less longitudinal space. The only reason for two flights of steps at the stern was to produce a symmetry whereby a balanced appearance was obtained.

DURING dinner, Curt met Captain Petterton, a grizzled old sea dog who looked solemn when Craylon prophesied that the yacht might encounter a heavy blow. He also gained his first view of the new steward, Leigh. Because of his ability as a butler, Leigh had been ordered to serve dinner.

The man was an excellent butler; and he looked the part. He was tall, solemn-faced and silent. Though deliberate of motion, he was prompt with every duty. His face was high-checked and ruddy; his lips had a droop that did not change throughout the meal.

There was another steward on board, who took up duty after dinner. His name was Trenge; he seemed slipshod in comparison to Leigh. In fact, Trenge looked like a former crew member who had finally rated a steward's job.

Curt took Trenge for an Englishman who had acquired some American mannerisms. The fellow looked like one who had had cockney antecedents, but had glossed over those traits. His attitude toward Leigh was paradoxical.

Trenge showed resentment because another steward was on board; at the same time, he seemed pleased to be relieved of the duties for which he was not fitted. Trenge, though he supplied drinks and cigars as called for, was not suited to the capacity of butler.

As for the crew members, Curt had made no progress in his preliminary investigation. There were more than two dozen on the yacht; but there was no way to pick the two new men from the others. Curt did not intend to make inquiry.

One thought, however, gripped him. Someone besides himself had come from the *Reciprocity*. Two new men had joined the crew of the *Nepenthe*. It was possible, therefore, that The Shadow might be aboard, passing as a member of the crew.

Curt hoped that such might be the case. He could foresee difficulties; not only in identifying Levautour, but in handling matters afterward.

Curt realized his own limitations. He would prefer to aid The Shadow, rather than attempt tasks lone-handed.

DUSK had deepened. The *Nepenthe* was wallowing in the rising sea. Slight pitches; long rolls—these told that the yacht was due for heavy weather. Curt was stretched in an easy chair, reading a magazine. He lighted a cigar and gained an opportunity to survey the room.

Hubert Craylon and Gregg Lownden were engaged in an unimportant discussion across a card table. Trenge had gone down to the galley; Leigh was on duty in his stead. Apparently the two stewards were sharing the work during these evening hours.

Curt remembered that Diana Craylon had gone from the lounge some time before. His present survey showed him that Count Louis Surronne was also absent.

Without a word, Curt placed his magazine aside. He strolled to the doorway, steadied himself as the ship pitched, then continued across the cross passage and along the corridor that led in the direction of the cabins.

He descended the stairway, passed the long rows of closed doors and stopped when he reached the double stairway at the stern. After a short pause, he went up to the stern deck. Gloom greeted him; only a few feeble lights showed a portion of the deck.

There was a sweep of wind; the splash of spray. The deck was not inviting. But with a lull, there came the sound of voices. Crouched in the gloomy doorway, Curt peered in the direction of the sound.

He saw two persons, near to the wall beside the opening. He had recognized the speakers: Count

The yacht *Nepenthe*

Louis Surronne and Diana Craylon. The yacht rolled; water surged across the rail. The two drew closer to the doorway. It brought them close enough for Curt to hear the conversation.

"I tell you, Diana!" Surronne's exclamation was a sharp one. "The opportunity is immense. It would interest your father."

"I hardly believe so, Louis," returned the girl. "He has so many investments already."

"Of course!" Surronne's English, though colloquial, had a French accent. "That is why he would be interested in ones that are better."

"Then why don't you tell him about the Algerian properties?"

"Bah! Your father does not take stock in what I say. He thinks that I am an adventurer."

"Perhaps he is right, Louis."

"Suppose he may be? What difference? I have friends in Paris, important men who give me information. It is on their word—not mine—that I say these Algerian properties are valuable."

The count paused, then spoke in a purring tone.

"The French government is to buy them," he emphasized. "Within two years—three—the properties will be worth millions of francs. I have heard this from important deputies."

"Yet they have not bought the land?"

"Of course not. They dare not. There would be scandals. Such things happen often in France. Those deputies must keep their hands away. Not even their friends can venture."

"You are one of their friends?"

"Not a real friend to any deputy. Only a chance person who overheard statements that were indiscreet. Should your father purchase lands, none would suspect."

"But you would ask a share?"

"A portion of the gain. That would be fair, Diana."

"Then you want me to tell my father about the properties—"

"So that he will be better impressed. I would choose to have him make inquiry of me."

THERE was a pause. Diana was apparently considering Surronne's request. So was Curt. He suspected a game behind it.

If the Algerian properties were a genuine investment, the proposition would be a fair one. But there was a chance—a strong one—that Surronne was peddling worthless holdings. That would make the Frenchman a swindler.

Could Surronne be Levautour?

It was possible. The name "Levautour" was French; and the count was a Frenchman. Curt felt that he had made an important beginning. A sudden change of the conversation forced him to a doubt.

It was Diana who spoke. The girl asked:

"Why not talk to Gregg Lownden? He has as much money as my father. He might buy the Algerian properties."

"Lownden?" snapped Surronne. "Paugh! He has no money!"

"He is immensely wealthy."

"These properties would cost a million of your dollars."

"Lownden has millions."

"In holdings, yes."

"That is the case with father."

"True, Diana. But your father's wealth is solid. His securities would be acceptable for transfer. Lownden's would not."

The girl gave a startled exclamation.

"I mean it, Diana!" insisted Surronne. "Your father is unwise to treat with Lownden. I do not like to see them talk business together."

"Lownden owns gold mines," remarked Diana, soberly. "My father is negotiating for them. Do you mean, Louis, that the gold mines are worthless?"

"Worthless," returned Surronne, "or nearly so."

"But Mr. Lownden has insisted that he does not want to part with them."

"Only because that impresses your father. It is what they call a 'come-on' in your American parlance."

"Then Lownden is a swindler!"

The girl stepped toward the doorway. Curt was about to duck below when he heard Surronne stay Diana with a purred remark.

"I cannot say that he is a swindler," declared the Frenchman. "That remains to be discovered. I say only that I believe his mines to be worthless."

"Then I must tell my father so."

"No, no. You must be more subtle. Mention my Algerian proposition. Turn your father's thoughts away from Lownden's mines."

Diana made a comment that Curt could not hear. Surronne's reply was audible, however.

"*Certainement,*" purred the Frenchman. "Most certainly. I give you time to consider what I have said. *Parbleu!* It is a matter that can wait until tomorrow."

Diana was moving toward the doorway. Curt took to the stairs. Reaching the bottom, he guessed that he would not have time to gain his cabin. Diana, however, was coming down the steps opposite the ones that he had taken.

Curt slipped back to the vacant stairs. The girl's back was toward him; he saw her disappear, then heard her take the long corridor and open her cabin.

Surronne had remained upon deck. Probably he was going to the lounge by the outside route. That would cover the fact that he had been talking with Diana.

CURT made the lounge his own destination. He took the inside corridor, moving stealthily past Diana's door. When he reached the lounge, he heard a discussion. Craylon's dry voice was joining with Lownden's rumble.

"You have changed your mind then, Lownden? You are ready to part with your gold mines?"

"Of course. You want them, Craylon. I'll take your securities instead."

"Very well. I shall think it over—"

"Think it over? What nonsense, Craylon! You have wanted the mining stock; I am ready to deliver it. Now you want time to think it over!"

"Only for a day or two, Lownden. I have more than enough securities to meet your terms. I wish to choose the ones that are to be yours."

"All right. That goes."

Curt stepped into the lounge. At the same moment, Surronne appeared from the deck and came through the cross corridor. Craylon and Lownden heard Curt's entry. Their conversation ended. They invited Curt to sit with them; when Surronne appeared, they extended him the same invitation.

Lownden called for drinks. Leigh appeared, bowed, and went to get them. During the butler's absence, Diana appeared.

"Here are my jewels, father," said the girl, to Craylon. "Will you place them in the safe, in your stateroom?"

"Certainly, my dear," Craylon glanced at a clock above the lounge door. It was one with two faces, that could be seen from the corridor also. "Nine o'clock. I believe that I shall retire early."

"I shall do the same," decided Diana.

Taking the jewels, Craylon paused for a few words with Lownden.

"We can talk later," said Craylon, "about the subject that we discussed."

"It was interesting," boomed Lownden. "Remind me about it tomorrow, Craylon."

SURRONNE had risen and was standing beside Diana. He spoke, scarcely moving his lips, under cover of the conversation between Craylon and Lownden. But Curt was close enough to catch Surronne's words, without the count's knowledge.

"Remember," reminded Surronne, "Lownden is a great talker. Too great a talker, Diana. He has nothing. His mines are fakes. If he sells them to your father, money will be lost."

Diana nodded. She looked troubled.

Craylon departed, bidding all good night. Diana sat down and indulged in an extra drink that Leigh had brought for her father. Then the girl made her departure. Curt was alone with Lownden and Surronne.

One thought gripped Curt Sturley. He must watch the pair who formed his present companions. Of the two—Lownden and Surronne—one could be the master rogue who styled himself Levautour.

CHAPTER XI
THE SHADOW'S SIGN

"ANOTHER drink?"

Count Louis Surronne put the suave request. He had finished his glass; his words were intended to open conversation with Lownden. The big mine owner swung about.

"Leigh!" he bassoed. "Hi, steward!"

Leigh was gone. He had left shortly after Craylon and Diana. Lownden boomed a louder summons. A man appeared in the doorway. It was Trenge.

"Isn't Leigh here, sir?" queried Trenge. "He's not in the galley."

"You'll do," returned Lownden. "The count wants another drink. Bring me one while you're about it. How about you, Sturley?"

Curt shook his head. Lownden waved Trenge to a departure. Curt eyed the doorway. He wondered what had become of Leigh. At that moment, the butler appeared; he came from the direction of the corridor that led to the cabins.

Leigh's face was as changeless as ever. Nevertheless, Curt gained a suspicion. Leigh had been here when Diana had given her jewels to her father. Craylon was to have placed them in his cabin safe. It was possible that Leigh had gone below to spy on that procedure.

Perhaps Leigh was Levautour!

The thought brought Curt to a new consideration of Lownden and Surronne. He decided to let this pair prove themselves. If both passed suspicion, Leigh would be the next bet.

Count Louis had placed his glass on the table. He caught it as the ship rolled. Liquid splattered from the glass and poured upon loose playing cards that were at a corner of the table.

"Bah!" ejaculated Surronne. "The cards are spoiled. Look, three of them are soaked. The pack is useless. Throw it away, Leigh."

Lownden intervened as the butler stepped forward. The big man picked up the cards himself, neglecting the few that had been sopped. He finished his drink; then, in rumbling tone remarked:

"Here's how we get rid of cards where I come from."

CLAMPING the bulk of the deck between his heavy fists, Lownden delivered a slow, rotary twist. The action tore the pack of cards. With the pasteboards completely torn in half, Lownden laughed and threw the portions on the table. Leigh gathered them solemnly.

"Finished with them, sir?"

"Not yet," returned Lownden. "Here—watch this."

He clamped the halves together, making a pack of a hundred half cards. Gripping them heavily, he repeated his twisting motion. Lownden's effort was apparent. His face purpled with his muscular strain. The cards yielded. Triumphantly, Lownden threw the quarters to the table.

"Take them away, Leigh."

Lownden's rumble was a satisfied one. Surronne followed with a compliment.

"Bravo!" exclaimed the count. "I have seen one pack torn; but never a double one."

"You've seen it now," laughed Lownden. "You can talk about it, Count, when you get back to Paris."

"I shall do so. Yet there are men there also, who boast of their strength."

"You won't see a better trick than mine."

"Ah, no. I suppose not. But I have seen a different one. Look."

Surronne drew a silver coin from his pocket. It was about the size of a half dollar. He tossed it on the table.

"What's this?" queried Lownden. "Some of that funny-looking money from Bermuda? A florin—no, it's big enough for a half crown—"

"It is neither," interposed Surronne. "It is a French coin; a ten-franc piece. Of silver, but quite thin."

Lownden examined the coin and nodded.

"Not as thick as a half dollar," he commented. "What about it, count?"

"I have seen a man," declared Surronne, "who could twist a ten-franc piece between his thumbs and fingers. Who could bend it—break it—as you have done with that pack of cards."

Curt became tense. He thought instantly of the broken napoleons. Gold coins, snapped in half. Fingers that could accomplish such a deed could also break this silver piece!

Surronne had made a motion with his fingers, as though indicating how the action should be done. The count's eyes were gleaming as they watched Lownden's expression.

"You want me to try it?" demanded Lownden. "All right. Here goes. You'll be out ten francs, count."

THE big man gripped the coin. His face reddened; veins stood out upon his forehead. Curt could see the straining of Lownden's biceps. He was throwing his shoulders into the effort.

The coin did not yield. Lownden gained another grip and began again. His teeth gritted in a fierce smile. With the pressure that he saw exerted, Curt was sure that the silver piece would snap.

Count Louis was leaning forward across the table, watching Lownden's effort. Suddenly, a change came over the big man's face. He relaxed.

Perhaps some sudden stroke of judgment had stopped Lownden's effort. That, however, was not the explanation that the mine owner gave. He flung the coin upon the table.

"Too slippery," he announced. "I can't get the right grip on it. I'll try it some other time, count."

Surronne made no effort to capitalize on Lownden's failure. He merely picked up the silver coin and pocketed it, with the commendation:

"Trés bon. An excellent endeavor, M'sieu' Lownden."

There had been a spectator other than Curt. For the first time, Curt realized it. The onlooker was Leigh, who was holding the torn playing cards. Curt glanced toward the butler. Leigh had changed neither his position nor his demeanor. He had remained fixed in one spot, despite the motion of the yacht.

Conversation lagged. Lownden and Surronne respectively avoided all mention of mining stocks and Algerian lands. It was not long before Lownden suggested that they turn in for the night. Surronne agreed. They dismissed Leigh; Curt followed the others to the cabins.

Each man entered his respective door. In his own cabin, Curt leaned against the wall beside the porthole. The *Nepenthe* had increased its pitch; at intervals water was deluged across the deck, to strike furiously upon the rounded window.

Curt was finishing a cigar. A chance thought prompted him to step out into the corridor. He went to the door, opened it and peered cautiously. Turning toward the rear of the corridor, he saw a figure move quickly from view, into an alcove by the rear stairs.

Instant suspicion gripped Curt. He had recognized the person who had slipped from sight. It was Leigh.

Curt stepped nonchalantly into the corridor. Balanced in the center of the ship, he stood smoking, idly watching the rear of the corridor. He was deciding upon a way whereby he could surprise Leigh without arousing the butler's suspicion.

The idle watching was the first part of Curt's plan. It kept Leigh in the alcove; for if the fellow tried to ascend the rear stairs, he would be visible through the stretch of banister.

SOMEONE spoke suddenly from the front of the corridor. Curt swung about instinctively. He saw Trenge.

Curt, as watcher, had been surprised by the steward's arrival. For the moment, Curt forgot Leigh.

"Anything wrong, sir?" queried Trenge in a whisper. "Is there anything you want?"

Trenge's undertone was explainable. Persons had gone to sleep in the cabins along the corridor.

"Nothing at all," replied Curt, quietly. "I was finishing a cigar; I didn't want to open a port- hole to toss it overboard. So I decided to step up on deck. Come along, Trenge."

He saw a whitened hand in the darkness. From the hand ... came a sparkling glimmer.

Curt led the way to the stern. He wanted to trap Leigh with Trenge along. It would be inter- esting to observe any rivalry between the steward and the new man who had taken over part of Trenge's duties.

When they reached the alcove, Curt was disappointed. Leigh had gone up the stairs when Trenge had encountered Curt. Turning to talk to the steward, Curt had ended his lookout. Leigh had probably guessed the situation.

Curt went up the stairs and flicked the cigar through the open doorway. The deck was almost awash. Water was spattering into the double stair- way.

"I'd better close that door, sir," announced

Trenge. "It shouldn't have been left open. By the way, sir, I'll be on duty until four o'clock, in the lounge."

"How does that happen?" queried Curt.

"Mr. Craylon's orders, sir," replied Trenge. "Since Leigh has joined ship, there is one of us for night duty. Frequently, a passenger finds it difficult to sleep and goes to the lounge instead."

"Hence your services may be necessary."

"That's it, sir."

Curt nodded and went to his stateroom, while Trenge remained to close the door to the stern deck. Once in his cabin, Curt opened a suitcase. From an inner pocket, he produced an automatic. He listened by the door. There were no footsteps indicating Trenge. Curt decided that the steward had gone around by the deck.

Tense, Curt wanted to investigate. Two men puzzled him: Surronne and Lownden. One was a Frenchman; the other had the strength to break coins, even though he had suddenly desisted. Both had deals that involved transfers of wealth. Either could be Levautour.

There was a third man who baffled Curt. That was Leigh. The butler looked innocuous; yet twice, tonight, Curt had gained evidence that Leigh was in the game. Curt wanted more facts. He chose to be armed when he sought them.

With his hand on the doorknob, Curt heard the roaring splash of water against the porthole. The Nepenthe rolled, then steadied. There was a lull that followed the one huge wave.

BEFORE he could open the door, Curt heard another sound. It came mysteriously, a click-click that sounded like metal against glass. Curt swung toward the porthole.

He saw a whitened hand in the darkness. From the hand, pressed against the outside glass, came a sparkling glimmer. Curt approached; even with the glass intervening, he could see the lustre of a fiery gem.

To Curt's mind came recollection of instructions that he had read in the orders given him by Slade Farrow. He was to recognize a token should it be revealed to him. That token was a fire opal, a sparkling girasol. The sign of The Shadow!

The hand moved from sight. A sweep of water bashed the porthole. As the spray ceased, Curt unfastened the circular window. The Shadow, he knew, must be above, leaning from the long roof that covered the cabins.

The Shadow had peered into the cabin. He had seen Curt ready for a move. That was why The Shadow had tapped. Moreover, The Shadow was hearing Curt's attempt to open the porthole. The hand reappeared, palm open. A signal for Curt to stop.

Only the mysterious hand showed against the darkness of the sea. The Shadow knew that his hand was observed. Without lowering himself to the porthole, he signaled with his hand alone.

Curt saw fingers make a motion as if bolting a door. Then came a downward stroke, to indicate the pressing of a light switch. Next a forefinger pointed in the direction of the berth. The hand doubled; twice it clicked the girasol against the glass. Pulling a coin from his pocket, Curt answered with a double click, to indicate that he understood.

Instantly, the hand joined darkness. The yacht had rolled; the sea again beat against the window. A trickle of water came through the edges of the loosened porthole. Curt clamped the fastening tight. He crossed the cabin, bolted the door, then turned out the light.

Pursuant to The Shadow's instructions, Curt went to his bunk. He removed coat, vest, and necktie. He kicked off his shoes and sprawled upon the berth. He grinned while the roll of the Nepenthe swayed him back and forth across his bed.

Though ready for any call, Curt was remaining in his cabin. There was no need for him to prowl the yacht. His task had become that of a subordinate. Another, more capable, would show the way.

Curt's hope had been realized.

The Shadow was aboard the Nepenthe.

CHAPTER XII
DOOM DECREED

HOURS had passed when Curt Sturley awoke.

His first impression was that of engulfing blackness; of motion that tossed him relentlessly; of a roaring beat that surged and subsided, only to repeat its fury.

Curt realized suddenly that he was aboard the Nepenthe.

Night had not ended. The storm had increased. The yacht was in the grip of a fierce gale. Yet Curt realized that something—something apart from all this tumult, had awakened him.

It came again, a scratching sound. Curt recalled it, as if from a dream. The noise was at the door of the cabin.

Edging from the berth Curt found his coat. He pulled his automatic from the pocket. Creeping to the door he drew the bolt. He opened the door, ready to jab the pistol through the crack.

A man was crouched in the corridor. It was Trenge. The steward's face was pitiful. Curt opened the door wider.

"I must see you, sir!" whispered Trenge, hoarsely. "It's life or death, sir—"

"What's the trouble?" asked Curt, quickly.

"Come upstairs, sir," returned the steward, "like you were going to the lounge. You'll find me there, sir—"

Curt nodded. Whatever Trenge's purpose, his fear was genuine. Curt motioned Trenge away and closed the door.

Donning his shoes and coat, Curt left the cabin. Trenge was gone from the corridor. Timing his passage to the roll of the yacht, Curt went toward the front stairway. He ascended and gained the cross passage. He noted that the clock showed five minutes of four. The lounge was lighted but deserted.

Trenge popped into view from the stairway to the galley. Motioning, he pointed toward the deck.

"Outside, sir," he whispered. "In front of the salon windows, Mr. Sturley. It's important."

CURT followed the man. The roar of wind swept them as they reached the deck. Combers lashed across the rail and left the two men dripping. Clutching every available hold, Curt and Trenge arrived at a quieter spot, the space in front of the large salon, where the bridge above them, broke the sweep of the gale.

Trenge's face showed pale in the glow from the lighted lounge room. The steward clutched Curt's arm.

"It's much I 'ave to tell you, sir," insisted Trenge. His cockney accent was coming through its gloss. "You've got to 'elp me. It's life or death."

"Let's have it."

"There's trouble aboard this ship," proceeded Trenge, "on account of the fiend that's with us. A murderer, the same that 'as done murder afore."

"Levautour?"

Trenge's eyes popped at Curt's mention of the name. Gasping, the steward clutched Curt tight and nodded.

"You can 'elp me!" exclaimed Trenge. "I'd 'oped you knowed the trouble, sir!"

"Which man is Levautour?"

Trenge shook his head. He steadied.

"I can't say, sir. If I knew, I'd speak. Levautour may 'ave been aboard before; that, I can't say. There was a man lost overboard—Kit Dyson—but that means nothin'. Eddie Moroy was on this yacht once. He was murdered after he'd shipped to New York."

Curt nodded. Trenge continued.

"I'll make a clean breast, sir." The steward's manner had changed. "I'm one of Levautour's men, like others that 'ave been long aboard this yacht. We've been waitin' for somethin'; and all the while there's been spies among us.

"Let a man talk unwise—that's the end of him. It was that with Eddie Moroy; the same with Kit Dyson. I'd minded my business; but maybe there was something I said that got to Levautour. Eddie Moroy had been a pal of mine."

The yacht's prow dipped. The cap of a huge wave came surging over the bow. Ghostlike, the water broke and foamed; its spray deluged the men below the bridge. Perhaps the threat of the waves broke Trenge's morale. The steward reverted to his fearful, unsteady jargon.

"I drank to the 'ealth of Moroy," gulped Trenge. "There, while we was ashore in 'Amilton. Blimey! I drank to the 'ealth of an old matey. It was Levautour that must 'ave 'eard. But there was nothin' said, sir—not then.

"There was somethin' we knowed about—me and Moroy. A full year ago, in London, when a toff was found dead in Limehouse. On a 'orrid night, sir, when the pea-souper was thicker than the water in them waves that's been sweepin' us.

"It was footpads did it, so they said at the Yard. But Moroy and me—we seen it 'appen in the fog. It was Levautour killed the toff. Killed 'im for 'is blinkin' fortune. Hafter 'avin' swindled 'im. 'E 'ad to be put so 'e'd be quiet."

CURT stopped Trenge's story.

"You saw Levautour that night?" he queried. "Couldn't you recognize him again?"

"'E was 'azy in the fog," returned Trenge. Then, steadying: "It was Levautour, though, sir. We were 'is men; we kept quiet, until Eddie Moroy talked. He didn't say much; but he was murdered for it. And me—don't you see it, sir— me, being friend to Eddie—drinking to 'is 'ealth? It made it look like I might talk."

"I get it, Trenge."

"There's one way I know Levautour's on board, sir. There's one deed he does—for his own self— one that he trusts to nobody else. Let me tell you how it come about. I was in the lounge, right inside these windows, intendin' to stay until four o'clock."

"As you told me."

"Yes, sir. But about 'alf past three, it was a nip I wanted. Some grog from my own cabin, forward. It was there I went, Mr. Sturley. Nobody was about, you understand.

"Leigh must 'ave been long since in bed, sir. There was only the sea roarin'—the waves beatin'—when I went into my cabin. In a tin box, I found the corkscrew. But that wasn't all I found, sir. I found this!"

Trenge pulled his hand from his pocket. He opened it. There in the steward's palm was an object that Curt had seen before. It was the half of a broken napoleon!

"You know its meanin', sir?" queried Trenge,

in tremolo. His dialect returned: "The 'alf napoleon? With old Bony's face showin' on it? Them numbers—fifteen?"

"Levautour's token," declared Curt solemnly. "Death to the man who receives it."

"That's it, sir," quavered Trenge, "and there's no mistakin' it. I'll tell you why, Mr. Sturley. The only coins like these are the ones that Levautour 'as.

"Not a blarsted other one like them, nowhere. Never used, they wasn't. That's why Levautour sends them. So's people will know they're from 'im."

"And the other halves?"

"'E keeps them, like they was notches on a gun. To remember 'ow many 'e 'as killed. There was one on the toff in Limehouse. Eddie and me took it off 'im with 'is wallet."

"And kept it?"

Trenge trembled as he shook his head.

"Never!" he exclaimed. "It would 'ave been death for us, sir. It was in the Thames that we throwed it. Deep into the river, that 'alf napoleon. But it was each of us as 'ad ours given us since, sir."

WILDLY, Trenge flung the broken napoleon before Curt could stop him. The bit of gold vanished toward the starboard rail, as the ship rolled to that side and water foamed upon the deck. Cowering, dropping below the range of the lounge-room lights, Trenge raised a pleading tone above a sudden howl of the storm.

"You've got to save me!" cried the steward. "I've done my crimes—I've murdered, like the rest of Levautour's lot! I'll tell all I know! I'll 'elp to find the fiend 'imself! But it's save me you must, Mr. Sturley!

"It was to you I came because I thought you'd 'elp, sir." Steadying, Trenge was again showing his ability to control his speech. "You've told me enough to let me know I was right. It's Levautour who's your enemy, too. Eddie Moroy tried to run away. He was murdered. Kit Dyson jumped overboard, with the broken napoleon in his pocket.

"It's meant for me to do the same as Kit. If I don't, I'll fare the way of Eddie. A score of men have had Levautour's token. Not one of them lives to tell it. Only myself—and it's not long that I'll live, unless you help me."

Curt clapped the cowering man upon the shoulder.

"I'll help you, Trenge," he told the steward. "First, I've got to put you somewhere that no one will suspect. Otherwise one of Levautour's cutthroats will be looking for you, to see if you've taken the hint."

"That's the way it's figured, sir."

"The best place is my cabin. You came there before. It's unlocked. Get inside there and wait until I come."

"But I'll be alone, sir—"

"Not long. You'll be safe. When I arrive, your worry will be ended."

Trenge came to his feet. The confidence of Curt's tone had restored the steward's nerve. Curt had a reason to feel confident. His plan was simply. He intended to walk the decks and stop finally in the lounge room. Somewhere, he was sure, The Shadow would observe him.

That would bring new contact. Word to The Shadow. That gained, Trenge would be protected. The man would deliver new clues. Through them, a meeting would be had with Levautour. Doom would be turned against the fiend.

So Curt reasoned in this tense moment when he faced the wailing gale. But he had forgotten one important factor. Time had passed; it was after four o'clock, the hour at which Trenge was to have found the broken napoleon.

When Levautour was close; when henchmen were at the master murderer's beck, doom could come swiftly to a man who had received a broken napoleon.

Curt was to learn that in the case of Trenge.

CHAPTER XIII
DEATH BRINGS RESCUE

TRENGE had started toward the starboard rail. The steward paused while the Nepenthe ploughed deep into a mammoth wave. Tons of water threatened, then broke upon the deck as the bow bobbed upward. Curt urged the steward on his way.

Gripping bars below the salon windows, Trenge made the turn to the starboard deck. Clutching his automatic, Curt followed. Since he was moving to the right, he was forced to travel slowly and clumsily. For Curt was gripping his automatic in his right hand; he was forced to reach across with his left in order to hold the bars by the windows.

Curt realized that he should have sent Trenge to port, instead of starboard. It was too late to rectify that error.

The yacht rolled; its starboard side took an immense dip. Curt saw Trenge come flinging outward, on the side deck. The man had lost his hold by the windows; he stopped when he struck the rail. The light from the lounge showed fright upon Trenge's face as the man turned about. Trenge had experienced a narrow escape.

As the starboard rail lifted, Trenge was about to dive back toward the windows. It was then that

Curt saw terror seize the man. Trenge behaved unaccountably. He let go of the rail entirely; he made a move as if to dash toward the bow.

A toss staggered Trenge. With the ship's pitch, Curt sprang toward the steward, inspired by the realization that Trenge had encountered danger. Leaping from the opposite direction came a blocking figure, a huge crew member, whom Curt had heard called by name.

He was Rodlick, a murderous-looking ruffian, one of the few whom Curt had been ready to class as members of Levautour's band.

CURT yanked out his automatic from his coat pocket. He stabbed a shot at the huge man who had leaped toward Trenge. The effort was useless. Curt's shot went wide as the ship's roll sent him sprawling. Flattened upon the deck, he saw Rodlick reach his quarry.

A sweeping knife blade glimmered in the light from the windows. Rodlick swayed as he delivered a fierce stroke. So did Trenge; the two shifted in the same direction. The blade found its mark. Curt saw its glimmer vanish into Trenge's chest. The steward sank to the deck and slid against the rail. Only the knife hilt projected from his wobbling body.

The sea's roar had drowned Curt's shot. Rodlick had not noted the attempt at rescue. The big murderer was hoisting Trenge's body. As Curt steadied on one elbow, Rodlick swung to toss his burden into the sea.

Curt fired two quick shots. Again, the yacht's sway ruined his usually perfect marksmanship. The bullets battered the rail; Rodlick, unmolested, completed his mighty swing. Like a straw-stuffed effigy, Trenge's body went sprawling out into the sea.

The knife had burrowed the steward's heart. Rodlick had simply thrown the body overboard to get rid of it. Levautour's threat had been carried through by the assassin. Only a dozen minutes before, Trenge had flung his broken napoleon into the deep. The victim, his life ended, had been consigned to the same abode.

Levautour's token had been delivered. So had the doom that the split coin signified.

Pounding sea swept furiously inward, as if enraged by its forced reception of Trenge's corpse. The helmsman on the bridge, without knowing what had occurred below, had altered the yacht's course.

The roaring wave that found the deck came sweeping in at an angle across the starboard rail. It picked up the two men that it found there: Curt and Rodlick. It threw the two inward, against the windows of the lounge room.

Foiled rescuer and successful murderer landed almost together. Sprawled, they came to their hands and knees as the deck tilted upward. Sliding on the slippery surface, they swung face to face. Curt had lost Rodlick, only to again locate him. For the first time, Rodlick saw Curt.

Curt was holding the automatic, clamped against the deck. Coming upward, he aimed the weapon for Rodlick. The huge murderer snarled; his vicious oath was lost amid the gale. But his action served as he intended.

Rodlick launched himself in a mighty spring. The ship's pitch added impetus. A furious Goliath, he came grappling upon Curt before the latter could manage to press the automatic's trigger.

The *Nepenthe* finished its lurch the instant that Rodlick landed. Its return jolt acted as a recoil. The giant had smothered Curt against the deck. Hurled back upon his haunches, Rodlick hauled Curt with him. The two locked in a reckless battle.

Totally disregarding the yacht's pitches and wallows, the fighters warred for one object: Curt's automatic. Rodlick had jammed Curt's arm backward.

Curt had no opportunity to use his gun. He could have dropped it, to fight bare-handed against his huge antagonist. That would have been folly. Rodlick outweighed Curt by nearly forty pounds. Curt needed every possible advantage.

One chance to bring his gun into play would enable him to offset Rodlick's greater physical power. Curt clung to the weapon. He tried to twist his arm from Rodlick's hold. Meanwhile, he clinched with his other arm.

IT was a grotesque fight. Two stalwarts staggering haphazard with every toss of the yacht. From windows to rail; from light to darkness, they wrestled zigzag on the slippery deck. Either the waves gave precedence to the struggle, or the yacht's new course was favorable, for the grapplers were not stopped by any insurge of the sea.

Sometimes one lost his footing, usually because of the roll. The slipping fighter held on; the return motion of the yacht invariably brought him back to equality with his foeman.

Levautour had designated one lone killer to do away with Trenge. There had been no expectation of a second encounter after the steward's murder. Hence, Rodlick, like Curt, was forced to battle alone. The fight had become a deadlock; but if either would need aid, Curt would eventually be the one.

He was fighting more gamely than Rodlick. The giant was reserving strength. Endurance—

which Rodlick had—would prove the winning element if the battle continued unimpaired.

While the gale howled, a momentary clatter sounded from the entrance to the cross passage behind the lounge. With the noise came a brief spasm of light. The door of the passage had opened; then closed.

A few moments later, the window lights revealed an arrival. The struggle on the deck was no longer unwitnessed. A newcomer was present to observe it.

The arrival was The Shadow.

TALL, sinister, a weird shape in the darkness, the master fighter had somehow reached the scene. Though uninformed of Curt's meeting with Trenge, The Shadow had divined that trouble was afoot.

Though present, The Shadow was hampered like the fighters. The *Nepenthe* was cavorting through the tempest. Its tosses were capricious, irregular, impossible to gauge.

Wisely, The Shadow had clutched a brace with his left hand, while he gripped an automatic with his right. The fighters were forward. He was in a position to take aim.

The Shadow was cloaked in black, the guise that suited an approach in darkness. His cloak was flowing with the whistling wind. His form was swaying madly; but all the while it kept its place beside the window, where mellow light outlined The Shadow's spectral shape.

The light was sufficient for The Shadow to identify both fighters. There were reasons, though, why he could not be prompt with aid in Curt's behalf.

The fighters were writhing, twisting in such confusion that instants only were afforded for aim at Rodlick. The roll of the yacht made sure aim impossible, even for The Shadow, except at those intervals when the *Nepenthe* ended one jolting tilt to begin another. Opportunity did not arrive at any of those moments.

The battling pair had rolled away from the windows. They were against the rail, hanging there as the *Nepenthe* dipped. A wave slithered over the rail; still grappling, the two hurtled up against the windows, at the curve by the bridge. They were carried by the water, plus the returning heave that quivered the *Nepenthe*.

Again, they went sliding headlong, bound straight for the foam. This time the pitch jolted them before they struck the rail. They faltered, held ground through combined efforts, though neither Curt nor Rodlick were seeking other than to become master of the fray.

Slipping to the rail, the fighters seemed to cling there, held by the yacht's irregular bobs. The course was changing slightly; the fighters were at a standstill, though each was struggling with a bullish fury. Curt was giving his last pounds of strength. Rodlick was powerful enough to allow no yield.

Curt's back was toward The Shadow. With opportunity to use his automatic, thanks to the ship's changed motion, The Shadow could not fire. The slightest waver would have ruined his effort to clip the fringe of Rodlick's form that showed beyond Curt's body.

The two were hanging onto the rail itself. Their instinctive shifts were all that kept them from heaving overboard. Even a bullet that would wound Rodlick might prove to Curt's undoing. If Rodlick should grip Curt frantically, then lose his balance, both would go over the yacht's side.

Yet The Shadow sensed a coming opportunity. One that might arrive through Curt's own failing stamina.

Once, as the two men staggered inward, The Shadow was about to press his action. A twist of the yacht reversed the situation and flung the pair against the rail again. The Shadow waited. His opportunity came.

RODLICK gained a grasp on Curt's automatic. The murderer accomplished it when Curt weakened. By clutching the gun, Rodlick still held his advantage. It gave Curt no free use of his arm.

Curt twisted. Rodlick pounded him against the rail; then they swung back again. In that momentary spell, The Shadow was again handicapped by the yacht's motion. The situation was the same as before: Curt between The Shadow and Rodlick. But Curt was almost through. His form was a swaying, groggy one.

Rodlick deliberately plucked the automatic by its barrel. He wrested it from Curt's last grasp. Lifting a huge arm, the giant prepared to deliver a crushing stroke that Curt sought to ward away by a shaky maneuver of his free arm.

Rodlick paused. He wanted to swing when the roll of the vessel brought him full force toward Curt. The Shadow waited also. He saw advantage in the same opportunity. His gun was steady; his eyes ablaze.

The *Nepenthe* jounced upward, then thwacked the waves, rolling hard to starboard. As the ship keeled, Rodlick's long stroke began. The Shadow delayed for a split-second—the nearest instant that he could allow to the moment when the yacht would be at the lowest point of its tilt.

The automatic spoke. It flashed like a gun in an old-fashioned, soundless movie; for the noise of the report was drowned by massed foam that swept the starboard bow.

Rodlick's arm jolted crazily. The Shadow's bullet had cracked it in midswing. Rodlick's fingers opened as his arm swept downward. The gun which served the murderer as bludgeon went slithering past Curt's head. Thrown off balance by the stinging slug that had struck him from the dark, Rodlick followed the changed direction of his own arm.

Spinning about, the murderer came back toward The Shadow. Sidewise, he pitched halfway across the rail, carrying Curt in the grip of his powerful left arm. Helpless, Curt rolled forward. Both men were balanced on the brink. The Shadow's automatic spat, once more; this time at the very instant when the yacht seemed motionless.

Rodlick's left shoulder quivered. The murderer joined the teeming water that was level with the rail. For an instant, the waves were ready to pitch him bodily back upon the deck. Then the rail raised. Rodlick was gone.

Curt was grappling the darkness. He found the rail instead of Rodlick. The *Nepenthe* performed another intricate cavort. Its bow dipped, tilting. Curt's arms stretched toward the inviting coolness of the sea.

The Shadow was springing forward, with a long, reckless leap. He had tossed his automatic aside. His spring seemed suicidal, an effort to launch himself overboard.

His spring ended in a dive along the deck, just within the rail. As Curt's weight went outward, as his feet left the deck, The Shadow caught him with a wide-armed grasp.

CURT'S body wavered, then swung sidewise, inward. A long, furious sweep of sea came rolling from the bow, as if to claim both rescuer and saved. But with that surge, the *Nepenthe* leveled; the wave, itself, proved advantageous to The Shadow and Curt. It swept them clear across the deck, against the windows.

One arm gripping Curt, The Shadow used his free fist to engage a bar. The sweeping surf subsided, owning defeat. Dragging Curt's inert form toward the door of the passage, The Shadow gained his objective before the yacht took another prolonged roll.

Forcing the doorway open, The Shadow hauled Curt inside the passage, then barred the door against the gale. Curt was moving his lips, trying to mumble. No words came from his throat. Dimly, he seemed to see The Shadow. He sagged helplessly as his rescuer raised him from the floor.

Down the stairway, through the corridor, The Shadow carried his heavy burden. Balanced in the center of the wallowing yacht, The Shadow never lost his footing.

As the ship keeled ...

He reached Curt's cabin, opened the door and swung toward Curt's berth in the dark. He let Curt roll from his grasp; the rescued man delivered a gasped sigh as he settled on the mattress.

The Shadow closed the door. He stood close by, listening to Curt's heavy, tired breathing. Then came a whisper in the blackness. It was a solemn, low-toned laugh that spoke of a task accomplished.

Death had brought life. The Shadow, through his timely elimination of Rodlick, had saved Curt from doom in the deep. A murderer had been finished. The Shadow could learn Curt's story later.

Yet, without Curt's tale regarding Trenge, The Shadow knew that the trail was closing upon Levautour, the master rogue who paid his victims with broken napoleons.

The Shadow delayed for a split-second. Then the automatic spoke.

CHAPTER XIV
CROSS-PURPOSES

IT was ten o'clock when Curt again awakened. Daylight was streaming through the porthole. The dips of the yacht showed alternate sweeps of heaving blue ocean and white, cloud-scudded sky.

The *Nepenthe* had cleared the storm area. Waves were no longer lashing. The yacht, however, was still rolling under the impetus of long, gigantic swells.

From a blur of events, Curt recollected salient occurrences.

Trenge—the broken napoleon; Rodlick—the knife thrust; then, the battle on the heaving deck. After that, rescue by The Shadow.

The clock above the lounge-room door had impressed itself upon Curt's memory. It had registered five minutes of four when he had gone out with Trenge. It had shown twenty minutes past the hour when The Shadow had brought Curt in from the deck.

For Curt had hazy recollections of that passage. He remembered The Shadow's laugh, delivered in this cabin. He recalled, also, that he himself had mumbled forth his story while The Shadow listened.

Curt had managed later to don his pajamas. His spray-soaked clothes were strewn on a chair. Curt had other garments in his luggage. He dressed, then picked up the clothing that had been drenched. They were partly dry; Curt hung them on a chair, near the window, then opened the porthole so that the breeze would complete the drying process.

Curt was satisfied upon two counts: first, that he had told The Shadow all about Trenge. The other point—one which induced speculative thought—was how The Shadow had gained knowledge of the battle on the deck, in time to bring rescue. Curt was sure that he had gained the answer.

He had assumed The Shadow to be one of the new crew members. That would have made The Shadow an occupant of the forecastle, where Rodlick had quarters. The Shadow could have noticed the giant's sudden absence, shortly after four o'clock. That would account for The Shadow's own appearance on deck.

CURT went up to the lounge. There, he found the others assembled. Like himself, they had slept late; but they showed signs of weariness from the tossing of the storm. All were finishing breakfast. Curt received a cheery greeting from Craylon. The young man sat down at the table.

Leigh appeared. The solemn-faced butler was unruffled. He looked like one who had enjoyed sleep. Hubert Craylon commented on the fact.

"Look at Leigh," chuckled the yacht owner. Then, to the butler: "You must be an old sea dog, Leigh. The tempest did not disturb you."

"It was my former service, sir. It was mentioned among the references that I dispatched to you from London."

"Ah, yes. I recall that you had once served as steward aboard a British yacht."

"The *Sprightly,* sir, was the name of the vessel. It was owned by the Marquis of Duncannon. The *Sprightly* voyaged in Far Eastern waters, sir."

"And encountered typhoons?"

"Quite so, sir."

Craylon smiled.

"No wonder you have your sea legs, Leigh," he remarked. "Well, that is fortunate. We needed your services this morning. Since Trenge is on late duty, he will have to sleep until noon."

"I meant to speak to you concerning Trenge, sir."

Craylon looked sour when he heard Leigh's statement.

"Is Trenge intoxicated?" queried the yacht owner. "I reprimanded him on that score before our previous voyage. I thought that he had confined his drunkenness to shore."

"This morning, sir," stated Leigh, "I found the lights burning in this salon. On that account, I stopped at Trenge's cabin, on a chance that he might be awake."

"To inquire about the lights," nodded Craylon. "And you found Trenge in a drunken stupor?"

"Conversely, sir, I did not find Trenge at all."

Curt was watching the persons at the table. He marked every expression that he viewed.

HUBERT CRAYLON —owner of the yacht Nepenthe

HUBERT CRAYLON stared, his brow furrowed, showing puzzlement at Leigh's words. Gregg Lownden's mouth opened, as though to deliver an ejaculation, one which did not come. Count Louis Surronne glanced up with interest, apparently intrigued by a matter that promised mystery. Diana Craylon gasped.

It was Craylon who spoke, after a pause.

"Not in his cabin!" he exclaimed. "Do you mean, Leigh, that something has happened to Trenge?"

"Possibly, sir."

Lownden broke the next pause.

"The man's gone overboard," rumbled the mine owner. "Drunk, probably, as you suspected, Craylon."

"We have no proof that he was intoxicated," objected Craylon. "You are building an assumption, Lownden."

"Why shouldn't I?" demanded Lownden. "Trenge was on a long shift, up here alone. It was just the sort of occasion that he would choose for a fall from the water wagon."

"But the man had promised—"

"To stay off liquor while aboard ship? What of it? This was his first night out from shore. I saw him drunk in Hamilton only the night before. Last night overtaxed his restraint, that's all. You'll probably find a liquor bottle in his room."

Craylon looked questioningly toward Leigh.

"Yes, sir," acknowledged the butler. "There was a bottle there. But only a sip had been taken, sir."

"Trenge probably polished off one bottle," boomed Lownden, "and pitched it overboard. That shows he may have gone on deck, to sober up."

Craylon looked for other opinions. Count Louis gave a shrug of his shoulders. Curt made no comment. Craylon turned to Leigh, gave an order:

"Summon Captain Petterton."

Leigh turned toward the door. At that moment, the captain himself appeared. He was spick-and-span in his uniform, but his face was haggard. The skipper had spent long hours on the bridge.

"I am just off duty, Mr. Craylon," announced the captain. "I came here to report the loss of a man. The unfortunate fellow was probably swept overboard during the gale."

"That is our theory, captain," returned Craylon. "We have just been discussing the matter."

The captain looked perplexed.

"How did you learn about it, Mr. Craylon?"

"Leigh told us, captain."

"Leigh? What was he doing in the forecastle?"

"Trenge was not in the forecastle, captain."

"Trenge? The steward? What has he to do with the loss of a crew member?"

This query brought audible exclamations from all about the table. Craylon did not seem to understand; but both Lownden and Surronne did. Lownden, bluff when he had heard of Trenge's disappearance, was stumped on this occasion. Surronne, formerly indifferent, was gaping at the inference of a second tragedy.

THE captain stared. Faces told him what had happened. Hoarsely, he queried:

"Trenge is missing also?"

"Yes." Craylon was the one who replied. "Who was the crew member, captain?"

"The big fellow," replied Petterton, "Rodlick, a giant of a man. That is what astonishes me. He is the last one whom I would ever have expected to lose."

"Rodlick—" Craylon nodded as he recalled the man. "With us on two voyages, was he not?"

"Three," corrected Petterton. "A good sailor, too, despite his ugly face."

"I remember the one you mean," remarked Surronne. "He brought my trunk aboard. Ah, certainement, he looked to be a ruffian. He reminded me of a sansculotte."

"I never saw him," asserted Lownden, abruptly. "Maybe he was drunk, like Trenge."

Captain Petterton shook his head.

"Rodlick was always sober. His loss puzzles me."

"Perhaps Lownden has a theory," remarked Craylon, in a dryish, solemn tone. "He has explained how Trenge could have disappeared. He believes that Trenge drank an entire bottle of liquor and went on deck to sober."

"Possible enough," decided the captain. "But that does not account for Rodlick."

"Perhaps it does," rumbled Lownden, suddenly. "Suppose Rodlick happened to go on deck at the same time? He would have seen Trenge staggering by the rail."

"If so," declared the captain, "Rodlick would have aided Trenge."

"And gone overboard with him," finished Lownden, pounding the table with a brawny fist. "Last night was a ripsnorter, a bad time to attempt a rescue on a slippery deck."

Captain Petterton considered, then nodded. He turned to Craylon and stated, in agreement:

"That would account for it, Mr. Lownden."

Lownden's expression showed bluff triumph. Curt noted Surronne and thought that he saw a slight smile on the count's sallow lips. The captain was talking with Craylon, telling the yacht owner that he would make an entry in the log concerning the loss of the two men.

After Petterton had gone, Craylon spoke ruefully.

"These are tragedies," he declared. "Most unfortunate. Two men lost, while we are bound on a pleasure cruise."

"It was the storm's fault, father," put in Diana, speaking for the first time. "You must not take it so to heart."

"I suppose not. Nevertheless, I feel badly troubled. We lost a man on a previous cruise. It is fortunate that I had the foresight to take on extra crew members. We can replace Trenge with a man from the crew. A man to assist Leigh."

"Pardon, Mr. Craylon," remarked the butler. "I shall have to perform my duties unaided."

"That will overtax you, Leigh."

"Perhaps, sir. But you will have no man available."

"We took on an extra man in Hamilton."

"And you have lost one, sir."

Craylon was momentarily perplexed; then his face showed understanding.

"You are right, Leigh," he acknowledged. "I was still thinking that the crew had a one-man surplus. Rodlick's loss has overcome that. There is no one whom we could use in Trenge's place. Very well, Leigh, you shall be our only steward. You shall have ordinary hours."

"I thank you, Mr. Craylon."

GLOOM had fallen upon the passengers, despite the clearing weather. Hubert Craylon kept pondering upon the tragedies. Gregg Lownden sat silent in a corner. Count Louis decided to walk upon the deck. Diana complained of slight sea sickness and retired to her cabin.

Curt remained in the lounge for a while, then went below. He entered his own cabin, found the soggy clothes sufficiently dried to pack them. That accomplished, Curt stepped out into the corridor.

He overheard voices, as he had the night before. They were whispers from an alcove at the rear of the passage, by the double stairs. Curt recognized the tones of Surronne and Diana.

Creeping close, Curt listened.

"You have spoken to your father"—the query was from Surronne—"regarding the Algerian properties?"

"Not yet," replied Diana. "I asked him about the

mine options which Mr. Lownden has promised him."

"The deal is closed?"

"Lownden wants to complete it."

"Ah! So M'sieu' Lownden has changed policy?"

"Yes, but don't worry about father, Louis. He told me an important fact when I questioned him."

"Regarding M'sieu' Lownden?"

"In a way. Father has a package of report sheets which he received by mail in Hamilton. They contain confidential information of the matter regarding Lownden's mines."

"Ah! And this information?"

"Father has not studied it. He intends to do so today. If Lownden is attempting to deliver worthless holdings in return for sound securities, father will know it."

A pause; then a purred suggestion from Surronne.

"Learn all that you can, Diana," urged the count. "Then, *ma cherie,* tell me what you have learned. I can, perhaps, act with new wisdom."

"Regarding Lownden?"

"Yes. If his wealth should be real, *trés ben.* I can speak with him instead of your father. M'sieu' Lownden might show an interest in Algerian properties."

"Wait until the end of the cruise."

"Certainement. But you must learn much about—"

The whispers faded; Curt edged back as he saw Surronne and Diana go up the steps to the stern deck.

STEPPING slowly toward his cabin, Curt formed a quick summary. He saw two marked possibilities.

First: that Lownden could be Levautour. The mine owner's prompt theories regarding the lost men could have been good policy for a crook. If Lownden were Levautour, the proof was aboard the *Nepenthe,* in the form of the reports that Craylon had received in Bermuda.

Curt gained a sudden wish to see those documents, which were probably lodged in Craylon's safe. Should the reports show Lownden's holdings to be fake ones, the man would be a swindler, and, therefore, Levautour.

The second possibility involved Count Louis Surronne. His suave manner at the breakfast table could likewise have fitted Levautour. Proof regarding Surronne could also be found in the reports within Craylon's safe. Should the data show Lownden's options to be genuine, suspicion would no longer rest upon the mine owner.

Count Louis, then, could be Levautour. His interest in the information about Lownden could be the result of a secret motive. Assuming that

Surronne was out to swindle, his concentration upon Diana would indicate that he wanted to rob the girl's father and had chosen Hubert Craylon as a man of established wealth.

Under this circumstance, Surronne would naturally have disregarded Lownden as an uncertainty. But should he find Lownden to be bona fide, Surronne—as Levautour—would have two potential victims instead of one.

The papers in Craylon's safe appeared to be all-important. This was word that Curt must pass to The Shadow at the earliest opportunity.

These thoughts had flashed quickly. Curt still held them as he was locking the door of his cabin. He turned, hearing footsteps from the rear of the corridor. He saw Greg Lownden. The big man had descended by the same steps that Surronne and Diana had taken to the deck.

"Hello, Sturley," rumbled Lownden, cheerily. "Seems like I'm meeting everyone on board. Just saw Diana and the count while I was strolling on deck."

"I thought you were in the lounge."

"I was. I took a walk on deck, but there's too much roll for comfort. I'm going forward again, to the lounge. Coming that way?"

Curt nodded. He pocketed his key and walked along with Lownden. On the way, he held a hunch. Lownden could have been on the stern deck, listening to the conversation from the steps. There was a chance that Lownden, like Curt, had overheard the discussion between Surronne and Diana.

WHATEVER that possibility, there existed a certainty which Curt did not recognize. It was proven, less than a minute after Curt and Lownden had gone to the lounge. The corridor was empty; the door of a cabin opened. That door was close to the rear stairs; it had been ajar.

An eavesdropper stepped into the corridor. It was Leigh.

His features fixed in their solemn droopiness, the newly appointed steward followed the course that Curt and Lownden had taken. Leigh was returning to the lounge, to resume his duties there.

Like Curt, like Lownden, Leigh had been in a position to overhear the talk between Surronne and Diana. There was something foreboding in that fact. It proved what Curt had suspected; that Leigh was a factor in the game.

This day would pass serenely, but darkness would bring events as startling as those of the night before. New action was due aboard the *Nepenthe,* involving men on board.

That possibility might have troubled Curt, had he foreseen it. There was, however, an approaching factor that could offset the danger of dusk.

Night, the time when evil brewed, was also the period that would produce a being who could offset crime.

When plotters moved, so would The Shadow.

CHAPTER XV
WORD TO THE SHADOW

LEVAUTOUR.

The name was paramount in Curt Sturley's mind, as he sat silent during the conclusion of the dinner hour.

Dusk had arrived. Danger was close. Trouble could come from Levautour, the insidious crook whose translated title meant "the vulture."

A vulture. Such was Levautour. A criminal who preyed upon the spoils of dead men—one who murdered victims, as he had Curt's father. When dupes were ready for the plucking, Levautour ordered doom that he might plunder.

Other dead men were to Levautour's liking, because they could no longer tell of work that they had done. Work in the evil service of Levautour. Curt thought of Moroy, of Dyson, of Trenge.

Two had died besides those: Calligan and Rodlick. They had never incurred Levautour's wrath; hence they had never received broken napoleons. Instead of dooming gold, they had gained death-producing lead from one who could fight as capably as Levautour.

The Shadow had sealed the doom of those two murderers. The Shadow, Curt hoped, would soon meet Levautour.

Who was Levautour?

Curt's brain still throbbed with the question. The riddle remained unanswered. Yet Curt, as he looked about him, knew that Levautour was here in this very lounge room. The scene was peaceful; it seemed hard to believe that a master fiend was present.

HUBERT CRAYLON was at the head of the table, his face tired, but less troubled than it had been this morning. Gregg Lownden was leaning back heavily in his chair, puffing at a fat cigar. Count Louis Surronne was bowing politely to Diana. Leigh was standing solemnly beside the table.

"Levautour—Levautour—Levautour—"

Each throb of the yacht's motors pounded the name through Curt's brain. The *Nepenthe* was riding more evenly, for heavy swells had lessened. The storm area was far distant; and with good reason. It had passed the vicinity of Bermuda; and the yacht was heading back to the islands.

That course had been decided through a conference between Craylon and Petterton. The captain was back upon the bridge. The return trip had been deemed advisable for a double reason.

The yacht's wireless had been ruined from the storm. Hence it might be believed that the *Nepenthe* was in distress. A return to port would settle that question.

Then there was the matter of the men lost overboard. The *Nepenthe* hailed from Bermuda and flew the British flag. It was better that the tragedies be reported there than in Boston, or any other American port.

Tomorrow, the yacht would sight Bermuda. If swindles were to be completed, they might be attempted soon. Perhaps crime would be necessary; if so, Levautour might move.

Last night, the supercrook had certainly gone to Trenge's cabin to deposit the broken napoleon. That incident, however, could have occurred at anytime between ten o'clock and four. It gave no clue to Levautour's identity.

Curt could anticipate financial discussions. Talk of gold mines between Lownden and Craylon; chat regarding Algerian properties between Surronne and either of the other two.

Curt had gained no chance to report to The Shadow. He had no inkling whether or not Craylon had perused the information that concerned Lownden's mines. Nor did he know if Craylon had talked to Diana, or if the girl had transmitted facts to Surronne.

The sliding doors of the lounge room were closed. Leigh had shut them; whether by order or choice, Curt did not know. However, the fact afforded an ideal setting for a business conference. Curt was sure that one would come.

The clock above the doorway had stopped. Its works had been damaged by the storm; but it had not been broken until shortly before the breakfast hour. No attempt had been made to fix it. Craylon had told Leigh to let it alone. This applied to both dials: one facing the lounge; the other, the cross passage outside the double doors.

The clock, Curt had heard, was complicated in its mechanism. The dials were independent and could be set separately; but they were synchronized when the clock was in operation.

While others were engaged in conversation, Curt happened to look toward the front windows. There was reason why he should glance in that direction; out there, beneath the bridge, was where he had heard Trenge's plea the night before.

Two men were visible beyond the windows. They were seamen; though Curt could not see their faces he recognized that they must be members of the crew. Curt glimpsed a grim hand. It thrust an object into a receiving paw. The seamen moved away; one of the fellows who had received the object, was heading for the port deck.

There was opportunity to leave the lounge. Surronne and Diana had started for a stroll on deck. Leigh was about to close the sliding doors from the other side. Hurriedly, Curt arose and went through the doorway. As the butler slid the doors shut, Curt took the route to the port side.

A brisk breeze swept Curt's face. Looking about, Curt saw the sailor passing sternward. Curt had arrived too late to encounter the man. There were lights along the deck, but they failed to show the sailor's face, for his back was turned.

Something fluttered from the rail.

It was a slip of paper, crumpled, whisked by the breeze.

The note that the sailor had received!

The sailor was gone, past the outside of the cabins. Curt skidded to the rail, stopped himself by clutching the slippery metal and snatched the piece of paper as the wind wafted it outward. Moving back to the center wall, he examined his prize.

The piece of paper was a note, written in a hand that Curt recognized:

Be ready at your post. The time may come tonight. All others are prepared. LEVAUTOUR.

The sailor was one of the master crook's henchmen. Such was probably the case with a majority of the crew. There were honest men aboard: Captain Petterton and some of the seamen; but it was also certain that Levautour could command a considerable band.

Cruise by cruise, the supercrook had supplemented the personnel of the *Nepenthe* with rogues who served him; building always to the time when they would be needed.

The task had not been difficult; good seamen were none too plentiful in Bermuda. With applicants constantly on hand, Levautour had slowly, steadily made progress until he stood ready to seize control of the yacht.

That was why matters had not been rushed. Both Lownden and Surronne—independently—had cruised before with Craylon. As for Leigh, he could have wisely waited until this cruise before coming aboard. Matters remained the same; any one of the three might be Levautour.

The sailor who had received this message had tossed the billet overboard. Incoming wind had

plucked it; held it fluttering for Curt to find the paper. Curt crumpled the message and thrust it into his pocket. He stepped toward the doorway that led indoors.

A voice from darkness stayed him.

Unseen, unheard, a figure had approached from somewhere, to take its stand in a stretch of gloom between Curt and the door. The Shadow was making comment. Curt knew the whispered tone:

"Report."

QUICKLY, Curt responded to his invisible chief. He told of the day's doings. He repeated the contents of the note; as he did, he drew the paper from his pocket and thrust it into darkness. It was received by a gloved hand.

"Be in your cabin," whispered The Shadow. "Await the tapping signal. Go to the lounge; note the clock outside the door. Retire at the time it indicates."

A pause; then final instructions which filled Curt with elation:

"After that, be ready. There will be work tonight."

A whispered laugh; then silence. Curt waited; he realized suddenly that the blackness seemed empty. He pressed closer to the wall. The Shadow was gone.

Bewilderment gripped Curt for the next few minutes. At last, he came to his senses. The Shadow had ordered him below. Following instructions, Curt entered the cross passage. The doors of the lounge were closed. The clock above them had not been changed.

Count Louis Surronne appeared from the central corridor. He nodded to Curt and started to enter the lounge. The doors slid open at that moment. Curt and Surronne saw Leigh. They heard Craylon's voice, delivering an order to the steward.

"Mr. Lownden and I have business to discuss," Craylon was saying. "If anyone comes here, Leigh, tell them that we do not wish to be disturbed."

"Quite so, sir."

Neither Craylon nor Lownden had seen the men outside. Leigh saw them, however, as soon as he had closed the doors. Standing in the cross passage, the steward bowed and delivered polite words:

"Pardon, gentlemen. Mr. Craylon and Mr. Lownden are in conference. They do not wish to be disturbed. I shall open the doors after they summon me to say that they are finished."

Pompously, Leigh descended the steps to the galley. Curt laughed as he turned to Surronne.

"I guess that lets us out," he declared. "I'm going to my cabin."

Surronne hesitated, his lips twitching impatiently. Curt knew that the Frenchman would like to interrupt the conference. Surronne decided not to do so, because of Curt's presence. With a shrug of his shoulders, the count remarked:

"Ah, yes, m'sieu'. That is wise. I shall go to my cabin also."

THE two descended the stairway together. They separated, to enter their respective cabins. Alone again, Curt rested his hand upon his hip, where he carried a fresh automatic, replacing the one that had gone overboard with Rodlick.

Craylon and Lownden were in conference.

That meant a decision regarding the gold-mine options. Perhaps an agreement; perhaps a refusal—according to whatever Craylon might have learned concerning the value of the mines.

Later—soon, perhaps—Count Louis Surronne might crash the gate to inject himself into the discussion. Complications seemed inevitable.

How could they be avoided?

Curt did not know. Anxiously, he paced his cabin. He could only wait, counting upon some action by The Shadow. Such action must surely be approaching; The Shadow had indicated it by his words on deck.

Even while Curt pondered, action had begun. Curt would have been further puzzled had he opened the door and stared out into the corridor.

There, he would have seen The Shadow, cloaked in black. Like Curt and Surronne, the master of darkness had come below. Silent, sinister, The Shadow stood outside a door. He was ready to rap a request for admittance.

The Shadow had chosen the cabin of Count Louis Surronne!

CHAPTER XVI
BELOW AND ABOVE

TAP–TAP–TAP–TAP—

The Shadow's knock was quick, yet cautious. His gloved hand paused with each momentary stroke. A response came from within the count's cabin. Close against the door, The Shadow could hear motion.

Surronne had approached the door. There was an audible tone:

"Diana?"

Again, The Shadow tapped rapidly. He performed the action with his right hand. His left was ready beneath his cloak. A key turned in the lock.

"Diana!"

Surronne's word was a whisper. The door had opened a tiny space, to The Shadow's left. The gloved hand glided from beneath the cloak. The Shadow jabbed the muzzle of a .45 through the opening.

Count Louis, from within, saw only blackness beyond. But the muzzle of the automatic loomed squarely between his eyes. Surronne delivered a hissed gasp. Instinctively, he backed into the cabin.

The Shadow's cloaked arm slid clear through the door space; his right hand, on the knob, kept the barrier from opening too far. His left elbow shifted to the left, then pulled back and jolted downward. It clicked the light switch. The room went black.

The Shadow had known the location of that switch; he had also previously determined the direction in which it was to be pressed. Downward.

All that Surronne had seen was an automatic clutched in a black-gloved fist. He knew that the gun was still aimed in his direction. The door was moving inward; blackness, coming through, cut off the light of the corridor. Surronne saw nothing more than a shrouded shape.

NEVERTHELESS, the count displayed sudden nerve. He could not be seen in the dark. He doubted that the gun still covered him. He shifted; as the door clicked shut, Surronne sprang forward to deal with the intruder.

Where a solid form had been, the count struck blankness. The Shadow had faced sidewise, downward. Surronne's spring was carrying him headlong against the door. All that saved the unfortunate attacker were shoulders that snapped upward with the speed of trip hammers.

Arms caught the diving form of Surronne, spun him about and rolled him helpless to the floor. The count's head glanced the door; the blow was slight. Unstunned, Surronne tried to struggle. The battle was short-lived.

The *Nepenthe* was enjoying no rollicking pitches tonight. The yacht's roll was uniform. Surronne could gain no chance advantage to prolong the fray. The Shadow's viselike arms paralyzed him. The folds of the cloak stifled Surronne's outcries.

Hunching his prisoner on the floor, The Shadow twisted his wrists behind him and lashed them with a thonglike strip of leather.

Surronne attempted some footwork but it fluked. His knees were doubled. Pressing the man to the floor, The Shadow applied a tight gag. When Surronne suddenly managed to flay wildly with his feet, The Shadow threw his full weight upon the count's ankles. A minute later, Surronne's legs were bound.

The Shadow lifted the helpless man and dropped him upon the cabin berth. While Surronne chafed in futile fashion, the cloaked victor went from the cabin, closing the door behind him. His departure was as evasive as his entry.

In the corridor, The Shadow paused by Curt's door. Lightly, he gave a succession of quick taps, as he had done with the girasol against the window. Turning, The Shadow stalked rapidly to the steps at the rear of the corridor.

The cloaked sleuth was gone when Curt stepped out into the corridor.

To Curt, the signal meant one definite duty. A trip to the lounge, in accordance with The Shadow's instructions. Curt went to the front of the corridor and ascended the stairs.

He expected trouble if he met Leigh, for the steward had instructions to keep persons out. But Leigh had already informed Curt and Surronne that they were not to enter. Therefore, he had apparently seen no need to guard the doors.

Leigh was absent when Curt arrived. Deliberately, Curt pulled back a sliding door and stepped into the lounge. Craylon and Lownden were nodding as they talked across the card table. Both turned when Curt entered.

Curt saw a sudden tightening of Lownden's fists. Craylon's brow furrowed. The men sat back in their chairs; Craylon looked a bit indignant, while Lownden showed suppressed anger on his beefy face.

The men made no comment; Curt merely nodded in greeting, as if he did not know that he had intruded. Then came a clink of glasses. Leigh appeared in the doorway, carrying a tray.

"Where were you, Leigh?" inquired Craylon, tartly. "Why were you not outside the door?"

"You sent me for drinks, sir."

"So I did." Craylon bit his lips, then smiled. "Well, I suppose you cannot be in two places at once."

"Hardly, sir."

Curt had taken a seat in the corner. He was bringing out his pipe. Noting Leigh from the corner of his eye, he wondered if the steward would comment upon the fact that he had warned both Curt and Surronne not to enter the lounge.

Leigh looked as if he wished to speak; but to do so, he would have violated the rule of the well-trained butler.

Leigh merely placed the glasses on the card table, paused, as if hoping that Craylon would make other inquiry. Craylon asked no question. Leigh turned toward Curt. Almost coldly, the steward asked:

"Would you care for a drink, sir?"

"No, thanks, Leigh."

The servant walked away and closed the doors. He acted almost sullen; ruffled, apparently, because Craylon had not caught the hint that he had more to say if questioned.

CRAYLON spoke to Lownden. The latter nodded, then beckoned Curt to the card table. Craylon opened conversation while Lownden pocketed a slender sheaf of papers. Curt knew that they had been arranging the transfer of the gold-mine options.

"We shall be in Bermuda, tomorrow," remarked Craylon, cordially, to Curt. Then, to Lownden: "By the way, Gregg, those matters we mentioned. We can let them go until the morning."

"Of course," rumbled Lownden. "Unless we should decide to discuss them later this evening. As you wish, Hubert."

"I have some data in my cabin," reminded Craylon. "It will clear the points that puzzle us. I shall look it up later."

Curt wondered what the reference meant. Had Craylon satisfied himself that Lownden's mines were valuable? By "data" did he mean securities that he was to give the mine owner for the options?

Or was he actually referring to the reports of the investigators, intimating that they had shown Lownden's holdings to be worthless? If so, Craylon could be keeping them for a surprise, to show Lownden why he did not intend to conclude a deal.

Curt could not guess the riddle. Another matter perplexed him. Where was Count Louis?

Though his own stay below had been brief, Curt had certainly expected to find Surronne here ahead of him. He had not supposed that the count would remain long in his cabin. Curt did not guess that the suave Frenchman had been forcibly detained.

As conversation continued, Curt realized that he had made a blunder. He had forgotten to look at the clock outside the doors. He itched to go out and consult it; but he could find no reason to make a sudden departure and then return.

Lownden was glancing at his watch.

"Humph," grunted the big man. "Half past nine. I intended to retire before ten."

"There is no need to stay up later," remarked Craylon. "Have another drink, Lownden, then you can turn in. I won't stay up much later. I am merely waiting to talk to Diana, then to Captain Petterton. He will come in from the bridge at half past ten."

"Another drink, then," decided Lownden. "Hi, steward! Leigh!"

Leigh had turned to open the sliding doors. Someone was tugging at them from the other side.

A door slid back. Diana entered the lounge. The girl was breathless.

"Father!" she exclaimed. "Something—something has happened to Count Louis! I knocked at his door—I heard him choking, groaning—"

Craylon came to his feet.

"Was his door locked, Diana?"

"I—I don't know. I was frightened—"

Lownden was up.

"Come along!" roared the big man. "We'll find out what's the trouble!"

LOWNDEN led the dash down to the corridor. He yanked at the door of Surronne's cabin; it opened so easily that Lownden was almost precipitated within.

Craylon turned on the light. On the floor they saw the count, rolling in his bonds, trying desperately to release himself of the gag. He was making inarticulate attempts to call for aid.

Lownden produced a knife. He carved the thongs. Craylon relieved Surronne of his gag. Curt helped them get the man to his feet.

"What happened, Surronne?" demanded Craylon. "Who put you in this plight?"

"Are you hurt, Louis?" questioned Diana. The girl's tone showed huge anxiety. "Are you hurt?"

"No." Surronne steadied himself and panted. "Just—just some intruder who took me unexpectedly. Paugh! I should have overpowered the rogue!"

"Who was he?" queried Craylon. "Can you describe him?"

"No. It was dark. I saw a hand, with a pistol. Paugh! What could I do? Nothing, m'sieu, until the light was gone. It was then I struggled. The dark— it made things impossible. I became a prisoner."

"Let us go up to the lounge," decided Craylon. His tone carried indignation at Surronne's treatment. "Leigh, hurry ahead and bring some brandy for Count Louis."

They reached the lounge. This time, Curt noted the clock. Its hands indicated the hour of ten. A dozen minutes had passed since half past nine. Shortly, Curt would have to find an excuse to retire.

Inside the lounge, Surronne was sipping brandy, pausing at moments to repeat the story. His description of the fight was not illuminating. He had no idea who his adversary could have been.

"We must question the crew," decided Craylon. "I shall speak to Captain Petterton when he arrives."

"Is that wise?" demanded Lownden, abruptly. "Won't it make too much talk?"

"Talk does not matter. Who else can we question? You and I were here, Lownden. Leigh was serving us. Sturley entered."

Lownden looked glaringly toward Curt. Abruptly he demanded:

"Yet you entered here, Sturley. You came from your cabin, didn't you?"

"Of course," returned Curt. "Count Louis and I went down there together."

"Did you hear the struggle?"

"I would have mentioned it if I had."

"You heard no sounds—yet you were in your cabin—"

"Come, Lownden!" intervened Craylon. "You are assuming too much authority. Your tone sounds like an accusation against Sturley."

"I didn't mean it that way," growled Lownden. "I'm trying to get at the bottom of the mess."

"Mr. Sturley is my guest. He is a friend of Lord Jenley, whom I esteem."

"He was down in his cabin, wasn't he? He's the only man who could have—"

"Could have what?"

Lownden clenched his fists in challenge.

"The only person," he gritted, "who could have been in the business!"

Curt responded for himself:

"Then you accuse me, Mr. Lownden?"

"No," replied the mine owner. "I am leaving that to Count Louis."

CURT turned to Surronne; the count smiled and shook his head. He faced Lownden, not Curt.

"Ah, m'sieu'," said Surronne to Lownden.

"What can I say? It was not possible for me to see the man in the dark. But I could not say that it was M'sieu' Sturley.

"Ah, non." He turned to Curt. "You are my friend, M'sieu' Sturley. Why should you so suddenly have decided to strike me? We have been good friends since we have been on this fine yacht. I cannot say that it was you, m'sieu'."

"Let us talk later with Captain Petterton," declared Craylon. "You can make your accusation then, Lownden."

"I'll wait up to see the captain," grumbled the big man. "Meanwhile, don't say that I've made insinuations. I was too blunt, that's all."

His manner changed, Lownden thrust out a hand which Curt accepted. He noted, however, that Lownden did not appear entirely convinced. There was an awkward silence. Curt broke it.

"I'm going below," he declared, glancing at his watch. "It's only ten o'clock, but I'm tired. I'll wait in my own cabin. If anyone arrives, call out who you are. I don't want the same misfortune that struck Count Louis."

Nodding good night, Curt strode from the lounge. Outside the door, he smiled. Mystery had thickened; but a break seemed due. How close the time would be, Curt could not guess. He expected that The Shadow might be prepared to bring some quick development.

Oddly, Curt himself was faring forth to produce a startling result. His smile would not have been so broad had he realized the immediate developments that his own efforts would bring.

The Shadow had made plans. Only a blunder could alter them. Curt, through overwillingness to aid, was due to provide the blunder.

There would be consequences that even The Shadow had not foreseen.

CHAPTER XVII
MURDERER'S PROOF

CURT STURLEY lacked theories when he descended the broad stairway to the cabin corridor. The episode of Count Louis Surronne had left him baffled.

His thoughts harping upon Levautour, Curt could think only of the master crook where violence was involved. Therefore, the temporary elimination of Surronne had caused a void in Curt's processes of deduction.

Lownden had been in the lounge with Craylon. Leigh had come up from the galley. Surronne had been alone in his cabin. How could Levautour have been at large?

Impossible, unless Surronne was Levautour. But he could not have tied himself in those tight bonds. Curt thought suddenly of Diana. His theory came when he had reached the cabin corridor.

The girl could have tied Surronne!

That was it—a device to attract Craylon's attention! Diana, participating in a scheme of Surronne's design. But what particular purpose did it serve? Curt could not guess.

His theory had drawn him far from the truth. Without it, he might have suddenly connected The Shadow with the Surronne episode. But the theory that involved Diana seemed so logical that Curt accepted it in belief that the purpose could be guessed later.

Curt had received instructions from The Shadow. He had seen the clock, set at the hour of ten. He did not know when or how The Shadow had managed the signal; but there had probably been opportunities, since the closed doors of the lounge had cut off view of the cross passage.

FOLLOWING orders, Curt was on his way to his cabin, there to remain, prepared for eventualities. The Shadow's instructions were working well. Everyone except Curt was in the lounge; matters such as gold mines and Algerian investments would be deferred.

Curt's present duty was simple. Too simple, in fact. So simple that it could be altered by any event that promised active opportunity. Such an event occurred just as Curt neared his cabin door.

The *Nepenthe* rolled lazily in a long swell. There was a clatter. Curt turned about. He saw a cabin door swing inward, then sway back to a closed position. Its latch did not click.

The door was the one to Hubert Craylon's cabin.

Curt remembered that the yacht owner had stopped in his own stateroom for a moment before they took Surronne up to the lounge. Craylon had left the door unlatched.

Opportunity!

A chance, perhaps, to find those investigation documents that would prove Gregg Lownden's colors!

Curt was resentful since his encounter with Lownden. In his present mood, he was itching to learn the mine owner's status. Moreover, such a

LORD BASIL JENLEY—a friend of Lamont Cranston

step would settle the case of Levautour. A quick search for the papers—a lucky find—a brief examination; Curt could picture it all.

Either Lownden would be Levautour; or Surronne would be. Thus did Curt reason; for he was convinced in his theory that Surronne—through Diana's aid—had staged a fake game tonight. Lownden or Surronne.

Which?

Craylon's door swayed inward, paused, then wobbled crazily, ready to slam shut. Curt bounded across the corridor, caught the door and stepped into the cabin. He closed the door behind him and turned on the light.

Quickly, he looked for loose papers. He saw none. In the far wall, he spied Craylon's safe. Which was built into a bulkhead. The door of the safe was closed; but Curt decided to try it. All the coolness which had once made Curt useful to Butch Drongo was returned.

This was not crime. It was investigation. A duty to The Shadow. More important than idleness in his cabin. Thus did Curt reason. Then he became elated.

The door of the safe swung outward as Curt turned the knob!

The safe was small; but it was stuffed with papers. Curt saw securities galore, stacks of them, printed in banknote style. These were the good stocks that Craylon was ready to trade for Lownden's gold-mine options.

Pulling the stacks aside, Curt found sheaves of currency. There were crisp green bills of American money; stacks of British currency, besides, including a loose heap of red ten-shilling notes that fluttered to the floor when Curt disturbed them.

Small change for Hubert Craylon, those ten-shilling notes. For the stacks of currency were notes of high denomination. They represented thousands in American dollars; thousands, also, in British pounds.

Curt gritted his teeth at thought of all this wealth unwatched. Stocks, bonds and currency—the whole might represent more than a million dollars!

Wealth which Levautour wanted. Here, open to access, where Hubert Craylon, kindly, trustful, and forgetful, had left it without remembering to lock his safe!

Easy to steal; but not in Levautour's fashion.

The master rogue had other ways. He fleeced his victims, made them pay willingly. If they faltered, realizing themselves dupes, Levautour tricked them, as he had tricked Curt's father, forcing him to betray a trust. Then the payoff: death!

Such was Levautour's method.

THROBBING thoughts racked Curt's brain. He felt an urge for speed. He wanted the papers that concerned the gold mines. He found them, stretched neatly upon a pair of square boxes that were fashioned of ornamented silver.

Curt spread the papers. He read typewritten lines. He grunted, half disappointed. The reports of the investigators had been combined into a definite preliminary statement. The preamble left no question.

Gregg Lownden's mines were good.

The report classed them "to be as represented"; it referred to "attached affidavits"; it stated that the mines were "already paying dividends," and could be regarded as "a more than favorable investment." Curt needed no more evidence.

Gregg Lownden was not Levautour.

Therefore, Count Louis Surronne must be.

About to replace the papers and the currency, Curt noted the silver boxes. He opened one and nodded, as he saw Diana's jewels. He remembered that Craylon had placed his daughter's gems in the safe. Emeralds sparkled with sapphires. Intrigued by the glitter, Curt opened the other silver box.

A hoarse gulp came from his throat. He clutched the second box and trembled as he carried it from the safe. Shaking between Curt's hands, the box delivered a clatter.

Curt's eyes were frozen at the sight of gold within. Mechanically, he gripped the box with one hand and dipped the other hand downward.

His shaky fingers moved gold coins aside. They came out, bringing less than a coin. They carried half a coin; one fragment that was matched by others in the box, each a dread reminder.

Between his thumb and forefinger, Curt Sturley held a broken napoleon!

There were complete napoleons within that box, at least two dozen of them, all with the incriminating date of 1815. These were surrounded by the fragments of broken coins. Each half was like the piece which Curt held.

The broken napoleon did not show the facial portion of the emperor's profile. It displayed the back of the head. These broken halves were the ones that Levautour had kept!

Nearly twenty in number, each told a story of death. The broken napoleons were murderer's proof. They were tokens that Levautour had kept as souvenirs of delivered crime; recollections of victims who had died at his dread command.

Curt could not stop his flood of thoughts.

Gregg Lownden was innocent. His gold mines were good. So was Count Louis Surronne; the Algerian properties the Frenchman wanted were probably a sound investment. Leigh was not a criminal. Only one man could be Levautour.

Hubert Craylon!

CUNNINGLY, Craylon had played his game. He passed as a man of wealth and station; a lavish host who wintered in Bermuda and invited friends aboard his yacht.

That was not surprising, once the truth was known. Craylon was a man of millions, gained through his operations as Levautour. He had thirsted for more. The higher his station, the easier he found it to defraud his dupes.

Lownden had not been trying to palm off gold-mine options on Craylon. The reverse was the case. Craylon had been craftily fishing for Lownden's valuable options, intending to trade him bogus securities in their stead. False or worthless stocks, represented by the sheaves which Curt had bundled from the safe.

Surronne was merely a supercargo, probably invited aboard by Diana, who cared for him. The Frenchman's hope of selling Algerian properties had probably urged him further to accept the invitation, on the chance that Craylon would finance the scheme.

To Craylon, Surronne was merely a useful added guest. A French count added tone to the social qualifications of the *Nepenthe*.

Broken napoleons. Curt had raised a handful. The halved coins were trickling from his fingers, clattering as they fell into the silver box. The noise ended. Curt heard a dry chuckle. Tightening, he swung about.

The door had opened; later it had closed. Upon the threshold, one hand on the knob, stood Hubert Craylon. With his other fist, the yacht owner clutched a shining revolver.

Curt Sturley had gained the meeting that he wanted, only to find himself unprepared.

He was face to face with Levautour, revealed.

CHAPTER XVIII
THE THREAT REVERSED

"LET the box fall," remarked Craylon, coldly. "Its contents can be gathered later."

Curt obliged. He raised his hands as the silver box struck the floor, scattering the napoleons, whole and broken. Curt knew that he was helpless before Levautour's steady aim.

"It may surprise you, Mr. Sturley," sneered Craylon, his kindly pose forgotten. "Yes, it may surprise you to know that I seldom forget a name or a face.

"Your name is your father's. Your face resembles his. I could hardly have overlooked the coincidence. It is strange that you should have done so."

Curt was startled. The thought had never occurred to him before this instant. Then came wonderment. Why had The Shadow failed to foresee that logical connection?

"There was a chance, of course," continued Craylon, "that you were ignorant of matters. I rather relished that possibility. I almost believed that it existed. Until tonight. Then your error changed the situation.

"I knew that you were seeking Levautour because of your attack on Count Surronne. Naturally, you supposed that he was Levautour, since he was a Frenchman. You decided to make him a prisoner, trusting that he would not be missed for a while.

"Unfortunately for you, my daughter has lately been a party to my schemes. She was alert; she found the count soon after you had bound him. I took your side, Sturley, in the argument upstairs. I wanted to see you go below. I had left bait which I felt sure that you would find."

The open door; the unlocked safe! Both were explained. But with it, Curt had gained a thought that rendered him despondent. With Diana leagued with her father, Curt's theory concerning Surronne was ended. In his stress Curt guessed the truth.

The Shadow had bound Surronne.

The Shadow, too, had blundered. With that thought, Curt felt his hopes subside.

"Tonight," promised Craylon, "you may choose a broken napoleon. You know my methods; you are entitled to my courtesies. Others found the sea inviting; those who did not choose that death were slain in less pleasant fashion. Therefore, Sturley, I—"

Craylon stopped. Someone was tapping at the door. Curt's heart gave a hopeful bound. Craylon's evil smile ended Curt's mental rally. The leer was ugly enough to belong to Levautour.

"It is my daughter," remarked Craylon. Revolver still leveled, he drew the door toward him: "Come in, Diana."

THE girl entered quickly. Curt saw her tremble. She tapped Craylon's arm; the man understood. He let Diana close the door.

"Leigh is coming. I saw him on the stairway."

Diana's whisper was breathless. Craylon merely smiled.

"Speak to Leigh," ordered Craylon, quietly, "through the crack of the door."

Glaring toward Curt, Levautour delivered a silent command for silence. Curt saw the uselessness of outcry. It would mean his own prompt death, followed probably by the sacrifice of Leigh.

The steward was rapping at the door. Diana

opened the barrier a few inches and peered through the chink.

"What is it, Leigh?"

"A message, Miss Diana, from Mr. Lownden."

"Wait for a reply."

Diana closed the door. She opened an envelope and pulled out a slip of paper. She spoke to her father:

"Lownden wants to transfer the options. He asks if you want him to come down here to the cabin."

Craylon shook his head.

"Speak to Leigh," he said. "Have him tell Lownden that I shall come to the lounge within the next fifteen minutes."

Diana opened the door a trifle and gave the order to Leigh. Curt heard the steward's stolid footsteps. Again, Diana closed the door.

"Lownden and I shall conclude our business in the lounge," chuckled Craylon, harshly. "He will sign over his options when he sees the securities that I bring him. Lownden will lose a million dollars. All that he possesses.

"Your part, Diana, will be to talk with Count Louis. Walk with him on the deck while I conclude my transaction with Lownden. You may tell Count Louis that I am interested in Algerian properties. It sounds like an excellent beginning for our next trip abroad. I can use such holdings as a wedge to interest wealthy Frenchmen in other investments."

The girl waited; Craylon motioned his free hand toward the door.

"Go at once," he ordered. "Give the flashlight signal on the starboard deck. I need men here to take charge of our prisoner. The ones appointed will understand the signal."

DIANA made a quick exit. The girl had been pitifully anxious to depart. Curt realized that fear alone had impelled her to take part in Levautour's villainy.

Craylon was not through with Curt. The fiend's smugness vanished with Diana's departure. Leering, snarling, his face a mass of rage, the supercrook drew closer, ready with his gun.

"Folly put you here!" he spat. "Who inspired that folly? How did you manage to trace this yacht as my headquarters? Who spoke? Who ordered you? Answer!"

Curt remained silent; his face had hardened.

"How did you meet Lord Jenley?" added Craylon. "How much does he know? Who else has aided you?"

Curt clenched his upraised fists. He was determined not to speak. His life depended upon Levautour's hope of learning facts. Craylon saw Curt's game. He stopped short, fuming.

"Torture can precede death," he reminded, savagely. "Moreover, there are slow ways to deliver death itself. My tortures do not end when a prisoner talks. They continue, so that the victim may repent the fact that he failed to speak when ordered.

"My tortures are quick. There is a place upon this yacht where they can be applied. Your chance to speak is now. This minute is one that you will regret if you maintain your stubborn silence. Speak!"

Craylon's face was livid in its glare; a fiendish countenance that only a demonish villain could have possessed. It befitted Levautour. Despite his rage, Craylon was motionless with his revolver. But he was oblivious to all about him, with the exception of the man who stood before him.

Curt, too, was strained. He knew that Levautour could carry through his threats. He felt that none could save him—not even The Shadow. Nevertheless, Curt was inspired by a trust in the being who had given him opportunity.

Whether or not The Shadow failed, Curt had received The Shadow's confidence. Like others who had served The Shadow, he could feel a thrill that came with set endurance. Curt was loyal to The Shadow. He could claim that he had imbibed strength from that master fighter's trust.

Levautour's tortures were no threat. They could be fierce, prolonged; throughout them, Curt would glory in the fact that he had not betrayed The Shadow.

FIRM, unyielding, Curt met Levautour's challenge. His fixed expression told with finality that he would never speak. Craylon, snarling, gave his verdict.

"Your minute has ended," he mouthed. "I have no time to waste with you. Torture? Bah! Let them carry a dead body from this room! My decree is death!"

A clawlike finger rested on the revolver trigger as Craylon stepped back. A venomous hiss escaped his writhed lips, then died with startling suddenness. It had been drowned by another tone.

Weird, impelling, a whispered laugh rose within the cabin. Instinctively, Craylon turned his head to the left. Over his shoulder he saw the door. Again, it had been opened and closed in silence, to admit an arrival, stealthier than Levautour in approach.

Curt gulped a thankful welcome.

Within the door, clutching an automatic that was leveled straight for Craylon, was the cloaked rescuer whose arrival Curt had not expected.

The Shadow had come to Levautour's lair!

CHAPTER XIX
THE LAST THRUST

ASTONISHMENT riveted Hubert Craylon.

In his career as Levautour the gray-haired rogue had heard of The Shadow. Craylon had always prided himself upon his uncanny power to elude the master sleuth. He had never supposed that The Shadow could find clues sufficient to gain a steady trail.

Craylon had erred. He had learned who had backed Curt Sturley. Faced by The Shadow, Craylon lost the supernerve that he would have kept against any other adversary.

It was incredible: The Shadow aboard the *Nepenthe*!

Craylon's fingers opened. His revolver struck the floor. Viciously, he clawed the air. A spasm gripped his erect frame. His emotion ended suddenly. Though weaponless, helpless, Craylon delivered a sneer of challenge.

The Shadow spoke. His tone was sibilant.

"You sought facts," came the sinister whisper. "You failed to receive them. You shall have them, Levautour."

Craylon tightened as The Shadow uttered the alias. Savagely, he delivered a retort.

"Who are you?" he demanded, huskily. "How did you come here?"

"I?" queried The Shadow, his tone a mocking inflection. "I was Leigh. An excellent part"—his tone was a gibing imitation of the one which he had used while acting as steward—"with which to deceive Levautour."

Craylon had no snarl. He was stupefied.

CURT gained a flood of facts. As Leigh, The Shadow had learned much. Tonight, he had changed the clock. He had found opportunity to overpower Surronne; to rap for Curt; then to return to the galley. Curt remembered that he had lingered a few moments after The Shadow's summons.

In and out of the lounge; always with his cloak and hat available, The Shadow had shifted tactics whenever he chose. More than that, Curt had the real explanation of The Shadow's arrival in time to handle Rodlick. The Shadow had expected Trenge to come to his bunk at four o'clock. Quartered near Trenge, The Shadow had heard him arrive and then depart; but Trenge had not returned.

Craylon realized something else. He snarled a question:

"You saw?"

"Yes," returned The Shadow. "I witnessed your visit when you placed the broken napoleon in Trenge's room. The man's own mistakes prevented me from saving his life. But that was not needed for your recognition, Levautour."

The Shadow paused, then added, emphatically:

"Your note to Calligan." Slowly, The Shadow drove each point. "You, alone, could have assured departure on the sixteenth. Your hiring of two crew members instead of one, with an extra steward. It showed that you intended to murder Trenge, then replace him.

"Surronne could not be Levautour. That title was chosen to deceive; hence no Frenchman would have adopted it. Nor could Lownden have been Levautour. You did not witness his attempt to break a coin. I did. Levautour would not have begun such a move. It would have been folly for him to show a connection with broken napoleons."

The facts rang home to Curt. He realized that those which he had valued as positive were actually negative.

"No fingers broke those napoleons," snarled Craylon, suddenly. "I twisted them, with padded pliers. My rare napoleons!" He emitted a harsh laugh. "No others in existence like them. Each one that I destroyed increased the value of the others.

"Someday, all shall be gone but one. I shall sell it for a fortune as great as a hundred would produce, for it will be unique. Remember, I am speaking of my future actions. You cannot dare to kill me. My men would overwhelm you. They are everywhere upon this yacht.

"You have shown cleverness. You have also shown stupidity. You let Sturley use his own name when he came aboard. The attack upon Surronne—whether made by you or Sturley—worked badly. It made me know that Sturley was an enemy."

The Shadow's taunting laugh followed Craylon's final outburst. The whisper was eerie. It told the supercrook that he was wrong.

"I see your motive!" cried Craylon, suddenly, while Curt stood puzzled. "You let me watch Sturley, so that I would forget Leigh! You bound Surronne, so that I would come to get Sturley! He should have been in his cabin, prepared. I could not have encountered him before you arrived.

"That was why you came here as Leigh; you delayed only because Lownden happened to write a note. You thought that Sturley would be safe. You knew that I had laid a trap; but you had confidence that he would avoid it."

A pause; steadying in cunning fashion, Craylon spoke with evil composure.

"I take it," he remarked, "that you found opportunity to prowl here. That you managed to open my safe and study its contents. That you knew of

Levantour's band; they had come as their chief had declared.

the broken napoleons that lay with the false securities that I kept for dupes like Lownden.

"There is one fact, however, that you do not know. The mission upon which I sent Diana. The emergency measure that I provided for such a pass as this."

Craylon leered, then raised his voice to a wild, shrill pitch:

"Look to the door! There you will find death! Aid! Aid to Levautour!"

THE SHADOW had already begun a swing. He had heard sounds outside the door. Levautour's band; they had come, as their chief had declared. Both of The Shadow's hands were in action; each had a massive automatic. Blackness streaked forward as the door ripped inward. The Shadow's guns tongued the first blast.

Two rough-faced crew members had aimed from the doorway. They never fired. The Shadow's shots, loud-echoed in the close-walled room, were as withering as lightning with its thunderous accompaniment.

Bullets sprawled the two attackers. A pair of slugs for each. As bodies sagged, The Shadow sprang across them. Revolvers were flashing in the corridor. A dozen foemen were surging to attack.

Stopped in the doorway, arms braced on either frame, The Shadow volleyed with both guns. He was meeting a massed attack; the odds were strong against him. But The Shadow had counted upon aid that came.

Shouts sounded from stairways. New revolvers barked. Surging ruffians spun about; harried by The Shadow's fire, they dashed in both directions, squarely into fighters who covered both ends of the corridor.

Captain Petterton was there. Loyal crew members were with him. Lownden and Surronne had joined the ranks. The Shadow had dropped villains dead and wounded. The remnants, some crippled, were less numerous than those who blocked their two-way flight.

In swinging to the door, The Shadow had abandoned Hubert Craylon. He had left Levautour to Curt Sturley. The Shadow had seen the bulge of the gun on Curt's hip. Craylon's weapon was lying on the floor. Curt had the edge. The Shadow knew that he would use it. Curt did.

He had drawn his revolver while Craylon was grasping the gun from the floor. Whipping to quick aim, Curt fired. With a snarl, Craylon staggered. Curt fired again as Craylon aimed wide and snapped his trigger.

CURT had the edge; but Craylon seemed invulnerable. Bullets wavered him, destroyed his fire; yet the rogue would not fall. He was Levautour,

the invincible, fighting to live that he might kill. Curt's drilling shots ended. Stupefied, Curt realized that he was holding an emptied gun.

Craylon sagged. Almost flattened to the floor, he rallied. Snarling, he raised his gun. His glassy eyes were fixed upon Curt; his leer was forced, but it remained.

Firing had ended at the doorway. The Shadow turned. He had reserved a final bullet. He saw Curt's danger; steadily, The Shadow aimed for Craylon. The last shot was unnecessary.

Craylon had not strength to press his trigger. His clawish hand opened; his revolver hit the floor. Craylon thumped beside it. He rolled, writhing in a last energetic spasm. Clutching hopelessly, blindly, he tried to regain his gun.

While The Shadow watched, Craylon's fingers encountered metal. They grasped it, tightened in a death clutch. A tremor; Craylon's form collapsed. Motionless, he lay with one hand opened; the other, the one that had found metal, still formed a fist. Then the knuckles thumped the floor. The hand opened and lay flattened, palm upward.

Hubert Craylon, master fiend, was dead. There, in his hand, lay the object which he had gained in his last effort to play the role of murderer. Levautour had been paid in his own chosen coin.

In Craylon's palm was the token of death.

He held a broken napoleon.

CHAPTER XX
LIFE ANEW

THE *Nepenthe* had reached Bermuda. Cutters had welcomed the yacht, but had asked for no news until the ship docked. Its wireless out of commission, the *Nepenthe* had been unable to radio the story of Levautour's end.

The word was told immediately at the pier. Lord Jenley, anxious-eyed, was on hand. He had suspected trouble, but had waited to hear from those on board.

Curt Sturley told his story. He gave the salient details. Proof of Hubert Craylon's villainy was full. It was supported by ample testimony. Diana Craylon knew the details of her father's latest crimes; she was believed when she told how he had threatened her with death should she refuse to aid him.

Crew members, captured at the end of battle, confessed that they were Levautour's men. They were taken into prompt custody, to pay the penalty of various crimes.

Yet in all the testimony, there was no mention of The Shadow. Only Curt could vouch for The Shadow's presence on the *Nepenthe*. In his brief, sufficient story, Curt found no need to mention the deeds performed by his chief.

Rogues had reached the stern during their fight

in the corridor. They had fled there, scattering, wildly trying to beat off surrounding captors who held loaded guns. That had happened at almost the exact time of Craylon's death. The Shadow had departed by the rear corridor.

He had appeared soon after, as Leigh. That was not surprising, since he had stopped long enough to fling his black garb in Curt's cabin. As Leigh, The Shadow had been foremost in rounding up a last pair of desperadoes who tried to deliver death to those who sought their capture.

As Leigh, The Shadow had snapped two quick volleys, three rounds each, from a handy revolver. His marksmanship had accounted for the last pair of ruffians. The two had been picked up, wounded.

CAPTAIN PETTERTON provided a mystery. Shortly before ten o'clock, he had found a folded message under the door of the bridge. He had read it carefully; amazed, he had thrust the note into his pocket. That message had told him what might be due.

The skipper had not credited it at first. It told that Hubert Craylon was a murderer; that more than half the crew would rally when he gave the call for massacre.

Petterton, however, had not forgotten that men had gone overboard from the *Nepenthe*. He watched for any movement from the forecastle. He had seen stealthy men assemble on deck.

Then Petterton had acted. He had called the mates; quietly, they had quickly armed the remaining sailors. One mate had called Lownden and Surronne. Thus had reserves been ready to aid The Shadow when the gunfire began. Levautour's crew had not suspected. The only person who could have told was Diana. She had remained in the lounge.

Captain Petterton would have liked to learn from whom the note had come. He stated that he no longer had the message. Thoughtlessly, he had tossed the paper overboard. That statement was true; but Petterton did not add another detail.

When he had examined the note, after the battle, he had found it blank. That was why he had thoughtfully become thoughtless and tossed the note away. Captain Petterton wanted to be truthful; he also wished to be believed. A lost message was better than a blank one.

Lord Jenley had received word from Scotland Yard. Facts concerning Levautour, though meager, fitted with Hubert Craylon, once the man's identity was known.

Since the *Nepenthe* flew the British flag, the Bermuda authorities were prompt to clear up the case. One day later, Curt Sturley stood on board a steamship that was ready to sail for New York.

Two others were with him: Gregg Lownden and Count Louis Surronne.

"Come along to New York," Lownden was insisting. "I'm going West, Sturley. You'll like the country. I can use an excellent engineer like yourself. There is opportunity at my mines."

"Sorry," replied Curt, ruefully. "I'm waiting for a message here."

Curt had come to like Lownden immensely; he had wanted to accept the offer. But Curt knew that he had another duty. His crimes of the past, though unknown to the law, had been discovered by The Shadow. Curt had been set ashore from the Steamship *Reciprocity* in order to perform a service. He was awaiting new orders that would send him to Slade Farrow's colony.

"You're staying here?"

Lownden put the question to Surronne. Count Louis smiled.

"Yes," he replied. "Diana and I are to be married. Our love was sincere. Her father's death has made our future possible."

LOWNDEN and Curt were prompt with their congratulations. Count Louis had proven his worth. Diana, all agreed, had been a victim, not an accomplice in her father's scheme of crime.

"Good," asserted Lownden, in his hearty basso. "Communicate with me, Surronne. If Algerian property is for sale, any purchase will be honest. I shall gladly finance it for you."

The call came for all ashore. Lownden looked toward the pier, where boys were stretching to catch broad English pennies that the ship's passengers tossed from the upper deck.

"By the way," he remarked. "Where is Lord Jenley?"

"Aboard the *Nepenthe*," replied Count Louis, "with an American who arrived today. A wealthy New Yorker, named Lamont Cranston."

"They have gone to make an inventory of Craylon's loot?"

"Yes. Lord Jenley believes that it will exceed the five millions estimated. New York and London have already cabled statements of his money. Ah, M'sieu' Lownden, this man Levautour was as greedy as any vulture."

Already, Curt knew, much had been discovered concerning Levautour's spoils. As Hubert Craylon, the super-swindler had passed suspicion. With his actual ways known, Craylon's estate was recognized as a mass of pilfered pelf.

Bogus stocks; valueless bonds—Craylon had carried them to bestow upon his dupes. With these, he had also kept half a million dollars' worth of gilt-edged securities. They were the "come-on" stocks that he could flash in order to build up interest in the worthless stuff.

It was such display that had bluffed Lownden, who was ordinarily wary. Craylon's actual wealth was unquestionably stolen. In addition to the hoard aboard the *Nepenthe*, huge amounts of currency had been found with negotiable securities in safe deposit vaults at Hamilton.

Banks in New York and London were disgorging huge accounts kept in the name of Hubert Craylon. But the Bermuda safe-deposits had revealed another feature: a list that named many of Levautour's victims and the amounts that they had lost to the murderous swindler.

Craylon had gloried in his evil strength. He had never expected that his lists would be discovered. Restitution would be made to living victims; to the relatives or heirs of those who had been slain.

"One matter more," requested Lownden. "Whereabouts is that fellow Leigh? I'll never forget his sharp work with the revolver."

"He sailed for Canada, I suppose," replied Count Louis. "A steamer left this morning."

Surronne went toward the gangplank, with Curt following. At the top, a ship's officer stopped Curt.

"Mr. Sturley?"

Curt nodded.

"Your luggage is aboard, sir."

"My luggage?"

"Yes, sir. Here is your passage and a message."

CURT tore open the envelope. He saw the steamship ticket; he spied a folded note. He opened the message. Blue-inked lines carried a simple order. Curt was to accept Lownden's offer.

The gangplank had rumbled. The steamer was moving from the dock. Curt dashed back to find Lownden. He started to thrust the message into his friend's hand. Suddenly, he saw that the note was blank. He put the piece of paper into a coat pocket.

Curt, like Petterton, had received a message from The Shadow. Words inscribed in an ink that faded, once its story had been told.

"I'm coming with you, Lownden," declared Curt. "It worked out as I wanted, right at the last minute."

"Fine!" exclaimed Lownden, heartily. Then: "Look—there is the *Nepenthe*, anchored. We're passing close to her."

Curt gazed from the steamship's rail. The sun was setting; by the dulling light he could see two figures standing on the yacht. One was Lord Jenley, near the bow; the other was a tall personage who had paused momentarily on the starboard deck.

Something about that figure reminded Lownden of Leigh, an opinion which Lownden expressed. But Curt could visualize a different shape; that of a weird being garbed in inky cloak.

The steamship had passed the yacht. The figure on the deck could be seen no more. But Curt was sure he heard a sound upon the waters; a strange, weird echo of a triumphant, trailing mirth.

Lownden did not hear it. Curt guessed that it must be a living memory of the past. Yet he would have sworn that he had heard the audible token.

The laugh of The Shadow lived.

THE END

SPOTLIGHT on THE SHADOW
Tom Lovell: Studies in Light and Darkness
by Anthony Tollin and Tom Roberts

The Shadow Magazine was graced with some of the finest cover and interior art of any pulp magazine. Through much of the 1930s, George Rozen's dynamic cover paintings were supported by superb interior illustrations by Tom Lovell. Lovell began visualizing The Dark Avenger's adventures with the sixteenth issue *(The Ghost Makers,* October 15, 1932), and his work graced every issue of *The Shadow Magazine* through mid-1936 when he began alternating with Edd Cartier. Lovell ended his *Shadow* tenure with the October 1, 1937 issue (featuring Theodore Tinsley's *The Pooltex Tangle),* though a few holdover illustrations appeared in later issues.

Tom Lovell was born in New York City in 1909, and spent his childhood in Nutley, New Jersey. After graduating from high school in 1926, he worked as a deckhand on the *U.S.S. Leviathan* and later as a timekeeper for the W.J.D. Lynch Construction Company. In 1927, Lovell entered the College of Fine Arts at Syracuse University, where he studied art with Dr. Irene Sargent and was inspired to pursue a career in illustration by instructor Hibbard V. B. Kline.

During his junior year, Lovell assembled a portfolio and began seeking professional assignments from New York publishers, making his first sale to Hersey Publications. Tom's initial assignment was so well received that he was given an entire issue to do, receiving the assignment for the color cover painting and all the interior black and white illustrations. He received six dollars per illustration and sixty dollars for the cover. The young artist continued to sell pulp illustrations during his final year at Syracuse University.

After earning his Bachelor of Fine Arts degree, Lovell relocated to New York City where he shared studio space with his Syracuse classmates, Harry Anderson and Al "Nick" Carter. Street & Smith's art director Will James gave him interior assignments for *Wild West Weekly* and other magazines, and Lovell was soon assigned to *The Shadow*

Tom Lovell in 1935

Lovell art for *The Blue Sphinx* (1935)

Magazine, the first of the hero pulps. "That was the time of deep depression," he later recalled. *"The Shadow* [initially] brought me, I think, forty dollars a month. At the beginning that was practically my only bread and butter. So I was happy to have the work. Keep in mind there were well dressed men on the street corner selling apples for ten cents. It was a horrible time."

The *Shadow* assignment was fortuitous, since the magazine had just been promoted to twice-monthly status. "My wife, who also posed for all the imperiled girls, would read all the manuscripts and mark action spots for me, incidently [sic] picking up a very unladylike vocabulary of gangster slang," Lovell later recalled. "Obviously each picture was based on some action. There was a lot of padding in between so she would save me time by giving me something on page thirty and something on page sixty-five and so on.

"I faked everything in the interior illustrations. That is, I drew from the mirror or [out of] my head, which was great training. I did a dozen or so illustrations for *The Shadow* each month at $12 per.

"I remember I did *The Shadow* things in three days. That would have been about eight drawings."

Lovell was a grand master of the "dry brush" technique favored by pulp magazine art directors because it simulated expensive halftones within the limitations of cheaper line engraving. "The dry brush technique is achieved by dipping the brush into a bottle of India ink," he explained, "then brushing out most of the ink on a scratch pad, thereby spreading the hairs of the brush. Then, when applied to the drawing surface, it creates a stroke of many, fine parallel lines, yielding a grey tone instead of solid black."

After marrying Gloyd "Pink" Simmons, Lovell relocated to Montclair, New Jersey and later to New Rochelle, New York, a thriving illustrators' colony whose residents included such legends as Norman Rockwell and J. C. Leyendecker and a number of young pulp artists including Graves Gladney and future *Doc Savage* cover artists Robert G. Harris and Emery Clarke.

In 1936, after illustrating nearly a hundred issues of *The Shadow Magazine,* Lovell cut back his interior assignments to pursue cover work for Popular Publications and other pulp houses, while Edd Cartier began alternating on the art chores.

Lovell's pulp covers featured many of the same dynamic lighting techniques favored by *The Shadow*'s premier cover artist, George Rozen. "Pulp covers sometimes pictured figures in dramatic (lurid) lighting conditions," Lovell explained. "To cope with this, my model was posed in a cubicle of black cloth and bathed in a 'Baby Anderson' spotlight, generally red or green. With a model

Top: *The London Crimes* (1935)

Facing page: *The Crime Crypt* (1934), reproduced from the original art

Bottom: *Partners of Peril* (1936)

Lovell covers for *Dime Mystery* (May 1937) and *Star Western* (November 1935)

lighted on one side with a startling red glow, the effect of complementary green shadows was hard to overlook on the newsstand.

"I continued to do the dry-brush drawings for *The Shadow* right up until 1937 and then when I got other work, well, that was the end of the pulps."

When Lovell announced in 1937 that he was leaving the pulp field to seek more lucrative commissions from slick magazines, future *Shadow* artist Graves Gladney volunteered to play the role of assistant and carry Lovell's portfolio. "You shouldn't go in to see an art director dripping with sweat," Gladney insisted. "I'll be your packhorse."

Though past draft age, Lovell and his friend John Clymer enlisted in the Marines in 1944, where they produced illustrations for *Leatherneck Magazine* and *The Marine Corps Gazette* as well as a series of large paintings on the Corps' history.

Returning to civilian life after the war, Lovell relaunched his career with an advertising assignment depicting the cannons of Fort Ticonderoga for the Dixon Crucible Company. He also began a long association with *True* magazine, producing images of Civil War battles, whaling operations and the war in Africa. His illustrations for *True* proved a stepping stone to his next assignment, creating historical artwork for *National Geographic Magazine*. His superbly researched paintings chronicled the history of the Olympic Games, the

Crusades, the Norman Conquest and General Lee's surrender at Appomattox. He also produced art for *Life* and *The Saturday Evening Post*.

Tom Lovell considered himself a "storyteller with a brush," and was the first artist to win the National Academy of Western Art's highest honor, the Prix de West. He was elected to the Society of Illustrators' Hall of Fame in 1974, and in 1992 received Lifetime Achievement awards and exhibitions from the National Cowboy Hall of Fame and the National Academy of Western Art. Lovell was still producing new works when his brush was stilled by a fatal car crash in 1997.

"Tom Lovell was the last *great* illustrator in the classic American tradition that started with Howard Pyle and continued with such giants as Harvey Dunn, N. C. Wyeth and Norman Rockwell," observed his longtime friend, Everett Raymond Kinstler. "That glorious era of American illustration ended with Tom."

Tom Lovell's paintings are housed in many major collections including the National Cowboy Hall of Fame, the U.S. Marine Headquarters, the National Geographic Society and the New Britain Museum. His Western, Native American and Civil War paintings are also showcased in The Art of Tom Lovell: An Invitation to History, *published in 1993 by The Greenwich Workshop.*

THE MAN WHO CAST THE SHADOW

Walter B. Gibson (1897-1985) was born in Germantown, Pennsylvania. His first published feature, a puzzle titled "Enigma," appeared in *St. Nicholas Magazine* when Walter was only eight years old. In 1912, Gibson's second published piece won a literary prize, presented by former President Howard Taft who expressed the hope that this would be the beginning of a great literary career. Building upon a lifelong fascination with magic and sleight of hand, Gibson later became a frequent contributor to magic magazines and worked briefly as a carnival magician. He joined the reporting staff of the *Philadelphia North American* after graduating from Colgate University in 1920, moved over to the *Philadelphia Public Ledger* the following year and was soon producing a huge volume of syndicated features for NEA and the Ledger Syndicate, while also ghosting books for magicians Houdini, Thurston, Blackstone and Dunninger.

A 1930 visit to Street & Smith's offices led to his being hired to write novels featuring The Shadow, the mysterious host of CBS' *Detective Story Program*. Originally intended as a quarterly, *The Shadow Magazine* was promoted to monthly publication when the first two issues sold out and, a year later, began the amazing twice-a-month frequency it would enjoy for the next decade. "This was during the Depression, so this was a good thing to be doing. I just dropped everything else and did *The Shadow* for 15 years. I was pretty much Depression-proof." Working on a battery of three typewriters, Gibson often wrote his Shadow novels in four or five days, averaging a million and a half words a year. He pounded out 24 Shadow novels during the final ten months of 1932; he

Walter B. Gibson in 1941, celebrating ten years of *The Shadow Magazine* and more than 200 novels.

Litzka and Walter Gibson with their pet Chinese Cochin rooster, China Boy

eventually wrote 283 Shadow novels totalling some 15 million words.

Gibson also scripted the lead features for *Shadow Comics* and *Super-Magician Comics,* and organized a Philadelphia-based comic art shop utilizing former *Evening Ledger* artists. He also found time for radio, plotting and co-scripting *The Return of Nick Carter, Chick Carter, The Avenger, Frank Merriwell* and *Blackstone, the Magic Detective.* He wrote hundreds of true crime articles for magazines and scripted numerous commercial, industrial and political comic books, pioneering the use of comics as an educational tool. In his book *Man of Magic and Mystery: a Guide to the Work of Walter B. Gibson,* bibliographer J. Randolph Cox documents more than 30 million words published in 150 books, some 500 magazine stories and articles, more than 3000 syndicated newspaper features and hundreds of radio and comic scripts.

Walter also hosted ABC's *Strange* and wrote scores of books on magic and psychic phenomena, many co-authored with his wife, Litzka Raymond Gibson. Walter also wrote five *Biff Brewster* juvenile adventure novels for Grosset and Dunlap (as "Andy Adams"), a *Vicki Barr, Air Stewardess* book and a *Cherry Ames, Nurse* story (as "Helen Wells"), *The Twilight Zone* and such publishing staples as *Hoyle's Simplified Guide to the Popular Card Games* and *Fell's Official Guide to Knots and How to Tie Them.*

No one was happier than Gibson when The

Shadow staged a revival in the sixties and seventies. Walter wrote *Return of The Shadow* in 1963 and three years later selected three vintage stories to appear in a hardcover anthology entitled *The Weird Adventures of The Shadow.* Several series of paperback and hardcover reprints followed and Walter wrote two new Shadow short stories, "The Riddle of the Rangoon Ruby" and "Blackmail Bay." A frequent guest at nostalgia, mystery, and comic conventions, Gibson attended the annual Pulpcon and Friends of Old-Time Radio conventions on a regular basis, always delighted to perform a few magic tricks and sign autographs as both Gibson and Grant, using his distinctive double-X signature. His last completed work of fiction, "The Batman Encounters—Gray Face," appeared as a text feature in the 500th issue of *Detective Comics.*

Walter Gibson died on December 6, 1985, a recently-begun Shadow novel sitting unfinished in his typewriter. "I always enjoyed writing the Shadow stories," he remarked to me a few years earlier. "There was never a time when I wasn't enjoying the story I was writing or looking forward to beginning the next one." Walter paused and then added, a touch of sadness in his voice, "I wish I was still writing the Shadow stories."

So do I, old friend. So do I.

—Anthony Tollin

Photo by Geoffrey Wynkoop

Anthony Tollin and Walter Gibson with *The Shadow Scrapbook* in 1979